EVALUATING HARRY

"Oh?" Harry came around the edge of the desk and pulled back a chair for her. Two apples, a number of crumpled neckcloths, and a small brown and black salamander tumbled from the mass of papers that sat upon the chair. "What—just ignore the salamander, it's one of McTavish's pets, it's harmless, I'm quite sure. Temple's story about it biting off one of the footman's fingertips is nothing but the grossest sort of fiction—what did you find lacking?"

Plum took a deep breath, and reminded herself that she was neither a shy virgin, nor a woman inexperienced with men and the intimate acts they did with their wives. She knew thirteen different standing positions alone for said intimate acts, and women who knew such things did not blush when they were mentioned in casual conversation. She was a mature, rational woman. Harry was her husband. She very much looked forward to investigating his person in a thorough and lengthy manner.

Harry's eyes narrowed as he peered into her face. "Are you well? You look flushed, as if you have a fever."

"I'm quite fine," she answered, ignoring the fact that her cheeks were so hot she could probably fry an egg or two on them. "What I found lacking in my bedchamber last night was you."

KATIE MACALISTER

THE TROUBLE WITH HARRY

LEISURE BOOKS NEW YORK CITY

A LEISURE BOOK®

January 2006

Published by

Dorchester Publishing Co., Inc.
200 Madison Avenue
New York, NY 10016

ISBN 0-8439-5144-3

Visit us on the web at www.dorchesterpub.com.

*As someone who spends her days
typing away at her computer, I've come to
cherish the friendships I have wih women who
share my love of romances, drool with me over dishy
men with green eyes, and understand my wacky sense of
humor. DeborahAnne MacGillivray is one such friend.
Many thanks for all the support and help, LadyA!*

MORE PRAISE FOR KATIE MACALISTER!

SEX, LIES, AND VAMPIRES

"Another wonderfully original, practically perfect para-normal treat."

—Booklist

"MacAlister's offbeat humor and sexy situations make these Moravian books truly irresistible."

—RT BOOKclub (Top Pick)

"No one combines humor and vampires better than Katie MacAlister.... A surreal tale in which the story line is fun, amusing, and biting, typical of Ms. MacAlister, who always entertains." *—The Midwest Book Review*

SEX AND THE SINGLE VAMPIRE

"Pull up a chair and settle in for a truly hilarious and exhilarating read.... This outrageously funny book is a genuine delight. Witty and wacky, this is one book you won't want to put down!"

—Romantic Times

A GIRL'S GUIDE TO VAMPIRES

A Girl's Guide to Vampires has "wickedly sharp bite. With...writing that manages to be both sexy and humor-ous, this contemporary paranormal love story is an abso-lute delight."

—Booklist

"Katie MacAlister knows how to write fun romances! *A Girl's Guide to Vampires* is just oozing with charm; I couldn't put it down!"

—RomanceReviews.com

IMPROPER ENGLISH

"Funny, quirky, and enjoyable. Don't miss this one!"

—Millie Criswell, *USA Today* Bestselling Author

"Charming and irresistible! A tale to make you smile and pursue your own dreams."

—Patricia Potter, *USA Today* Bestselling Author

The TROUBLE WITH HARRY

Dear Reader:

I'm sure some die-hard Regency-era fans are looking at the cover of this book and muttering to themselves, "I know what the trouble with Harry is—someone has sent a rubber ducky back in time to him."

I don't think anyone would dispute the fact that bright yellow rubber duckies were not around in the period this book was set. Because I'm sure historical purists will object to the duck's presence on the cover, I feel it best to explain that, yes, we all know that the ducky on the cover is an anachronism. It was placed there not to slap historical inaccuracy in the face, but to reflect the humorous, fun tone of this tale.

Besides, a time-traveling rubber ducky is definitely not the worst trouble to plague Harry. . . .

Katie MacAlister

Chapter One

Harry wished he was dead. Well, perhaps death was an exaggeration, although St. Peter alone knew how long he'd be able to stand up to this sort of continued torture.

"And then what happens?" His tormentor stared at him with eyes that were very familiar to him, eyes that he saw every morning in his shaving mirror, a mixture of brown, grey, and green that was pleasant enough on him, but when surrounded by the lush brown eyelashes of his inquisitor looked particularly charming. And innocent. And innocuous . . . something the possessor of the eyes was most decidedly not. "Well? Then what happens? Aren't you going to tell me?"

Harry ran his finger between his neckcloth and his neck, tugging on the cloth to loosen its constricting grasp on his windpipe, wishing for the fifteenth time in the last ten minutes that he had been able to escape capture.

"I want to know!"

Or found another victim to throw to the one who held him prisoner.

"You have to tell me!"

Perhaps death wasn't such a wild thought after all. Surely if he were to die at that exact moment, he would be admitted into heaven. Surely St. Peter would look upon the deeds he had done for the benefit of others, deeds such as spending fifteen years working as a spy for the Home Office, and grant him asylum. Surely he wouldn't be turned away from his rightful reward, damned to eternal torment, left to an eternity of hell such as he was in now, a hell dominated by—

"Papa! Then . . . what . . . happened?"

Harry sighed and pushed his spectacles high onto the bridge of his nose, bowing his head in acknowledgment of defeat. "After the hen and the rooster are . . . er . . . married, they will naturally wish to produce chicks."

"You already said that," his thirteen-year-old inquisitor said with the narrowed eyes and impatient tone of one who is through being reasonable. "What happens after that? And what do chickens have to do with my unpleasantness?"

"It's the process of producing offspring that is related to your unpleasantness. When a mother hen wishes to have chicks, she and the rooster must . . . er . . . perhaps chickens aren't the best example to explain the situation."

Lady India Haversham, eldest daughter of the Marquis Rosse, tapped her fingers on the table at her side, and glared at her father. "You said you were going to explain the unpleasantness! George says I'm not going to die despite the fact that I'm bleeding, and that it's a very special time for girls, although I do not see what's special about having pains in my stomach, and *you* said you'd tell me and now you're talking about bees and flowers, and chickens, and fish in the river. What do they have to do with *me*?"

No, Harry decided as he looked at the earnest, if stormy, eyes of his oldest child, death was distinctly preferable to having to explain the whys and hows of reproduction—particularly the female's role in reproduction, with a specific emphasis on their monthly indispositions—to India. He decided that although he had been three times commended by the prime minister for bravery, he was at heart a coward, because he simply could not stand the torture any longer.

"Ask Gertie. She'll explain it all to you," he said hastily as he jumped up from a narrow pink chair and fled the sunny room given over to his children, shamelessly ignoring the cries of "Papa! You *said* you'd tell me!"

"You haven't seen me," Harry said as he raced through a small, windowless room that served as an antechamber to his estate office. "You haven't seen me, you don't know where I am, in fact, you might just decry knowledge of me altogether. It's safer that way. Throw the bolt on the door, would you, Temple? And perhaps you should put a chair in front of it. Or the desk. I wouldn't put it past the little devils to find a way in with only the door bolted."

Templeton Harris, secretary and man of affairs,

pursed his lips as his noble employer raced into the adjacent room.

"What was it this time, sir?" Temple asked as he followed Harry. Weak sunlight filtered through the dingy windows, lighting motes of dust sent dancing in the air by Harry's rush through the room. "Did McTavish present you with another of his finds? Has Lord Marston decided he wishes to become a blacksmith rather than inherit your title? Are the twins trying to fly from the stable roof again?"

Harry shuddered visibly as he gulped down a healthy swig of brandy. "Nothing so benign. India wished to know certain facts. *Woman things.*"

Temple's pale blue eyes widened considerably. "But . . . but Lady India is only a child. Surely such concepts are beyond her?"

Harry took a deep, shaky breath and leaned toward a window thick with grime. Using his elbow he cleaned a small patch, just enough to peer out into the wilderness that once was a garden. "She might be a child to our minds, Temple, but according to nature, she's trembling on the brink of womanhood."

"Oh, *those* sorts of woman things."

Harry held out the empty brandy snifter silently, and just as silently Temple poured a judicious amount of smoky amber liquid into it. "Have one yourself. It's not every day a man can say his daughter has . . . er . . . trembled."

Temple poured himself a small amount and silently toasted his employer.

"I can remember when she was born," Harry said, as he stared out through the clean patch of glass, enjoying the burn of the brandy as it warmed its way down his throat. "Beatrice was disappointed that she was a girl, but I thought she was perfect with her tiny little nose, and a mop of brown curls, and eyes that used to watch me so seriously. It was like she was an angel, sent down to grace our lives, a ray of light, a beam of sunshine, a joy to behold." He took another deep breath as three quicksilver shadows flickered across the dirty window, the high, carefree laughter of children up to some devilment trailing after them. Harry flung himself backward, against the wall, clutching his glass with fingers gone white with strain. "And then she grew up and had her woman's time, and demanded that I explain everything to her. What's next, Temple, I ask you, what's next?"

Temple set his glass down in the same spot it had previously occupied, and wiped his fingers on his handkerchief, trying not to grimace at the dust and decay rampant in the room. It disturbed his tidy nature immensely to know that the room had not seen a maid's hand since they had arrived some three weeks before. "I assume, my lord, that as Lady Anne is now eight years old, in some five years' time she will be demanding the very same information. Would you not allow a maid to just clean around your books? I can promise you that none of your important papers or items will be touched during the cleaning process. Indeed, I would be happy to tend to the cleaning myself if you would just give me leave—"

Harry, caught up in the hellish thought of having to repeat with his youngest daughter the scene he'd just—barely—escaped, shook his head. "No. This is my room, the one room in the whole house that is my sanctuary. No one but you is permitted in it, not the children, not the maids, no one. I must have someplace that is wholly mine, Temple, somewhere sacred, somewhere that I can just be myself."

Temple glanced around the room. He knew the contents well enough, he'd had to carry in the boxes of Harry's books, his estate papers, the small bureau of curios, the horribly muddied watercolors that graced the walls. "Perhaps if I had the curtains washed—"

"No," Harry repeated, sliding a quick glance toward the window before daring to cross the room to a large rosewood desk covered in papers, scattered quills, stands of ink, books, a large statue of Pan, and other assorted items too numerous to catalog. "I have something else for you to do than wash my curtains."

Temple, about to admit that he hadn't intended on washing the drapery himself, decided that information wasn't relevant to his employer's happiness, and settled with a sigh into the comfortable leather chair to one side of the desk. He withdrew a memorandum notepad and pencil from his inner pocket. "Sir?"

Harry paced from the desk to the unlit fireplace. "How long have you been with me, Temple?"

"Fourteen years on Midsummer Day," that worthy replied promptly.

"That's just a fortnight away."

Temple allowed that was so.

"I had married Beatrice the summer before," Harry continued, staring into the dark emptiness of the fireplace as if his life were laid out there amid the heap of coal waiting to be lit should the warm weather turn cold.

"I believe when I came into your service that Lady Rosse was . . . er . . . in expectation of Lady India's arrival."

"Hmm. It's been almost five years since Bea died."

Temple murmured an agreement.

"Five years is a long time," Harry said, his hazel eyes dark behind the lenses of his spectacles. "The children are running wild. God knows they don't listen to me, and Gertie and George are hard put to keep up with the twins and McTavish, let alone Digger and India."

Temple's eyebrows rose a fraction of an inch. He had a suspicion of just where the conversation was going, but was clueless to envision what role the marquis felt he could serve in such a delicate matter.

Harry took a deep breath, rubbed his nose, then turned and stalked back to the deep green leather chair behind the desk. He sat and waved his hand toward the paper in Temple's hand. "I've decided the children need the attention of a woman. I want you to help me find one."

"A governess?"

Harry's lips thinned. "No. After Miss Reynauld died in the fire . . . no. The children must have time to recover from that horror. The woman I speak of"—he glanced over at the miniature that sat in prominence on the corner of his desk—"will be my marchioness. The children need a mother, and I . . ."

"Need a wife?" Temple said gently as Harry's voice trailed off. Despite his best intentions not to allow himself to become emotionally involved in his employer's life—emotions so often made one uncomfortable and untidy—he had, over the years, developed quite a fondness for Harry and his brood of five hellions. He was well aware that Harry had an affection for his wife that might not have been an all-consuming love, but was strong enough to keep him bound in grief for several years after her death in childbirth.

"Yes," Harry said with a sigh, slouching back into the comfortable embrace of the chair. "I came late to the married state, but must admit that I found it an enjoyable one, Temple. You might not think it possible for someone who is hounded night and day by his rampaging herd of children, but I find myself lonely of late. For a woman. A wife," he corrected quickly, a faint frown creasing his brow. "I have determined that the answer to this natural desire for a companion, and the need for someone to take the children in hand, is a wife. With that thought in mind, I would like you to take down an advertisement I wish you to run in the nearest local newspaper. What is the name of it? The *Dolphin's Derriere Daily*?"

"The *Ram's Bottom Gazette*, sir, so named because the journal originates in the town of Ram's Bottom, which is, I believe, located some eight miles to the west. I must confess, however, as to being a bit confused by your determination to place an advertisement for a woman to claim the position of marchioness. I had always assumed that a gentleman of your consequence looked to other members of your society for such a candidate, rather than placing an advertisement in an organ given over to discussions that are primarily agricultural in nature."

Harry waved away that suggestion. "I've thought

about that, but I have no wish to go into town until I have to."

"But surely you must have friends, acquaintances who know of eligible women of your own class—"

"No." Harry leaned back in his chair, propping his feet up on the corner of his desk. "I've looked over all my friends' relatives, none of them will suit. Most of them are too young, and the ones who aren't just want me for the title."

Temple was at a loss. "But, sir, the woman will be your marchioness, the mother of your yet unborn children—"

Harry's feet came down with a thump as he sat up and glared at his secretary. "No more children! I'm not going through that again. I won't sacrifice another woman on *that* altar." He rubbed his nose once more and re-propped his feet. "I don't have time to hunt for a wife through conventional means. I mean to acquire one before anyone in the neighborhood knows who I am, before the grasping title-seekers get me in their sights. Cousin Gerard dying suddenly and leaving me this place offers me the perfect opportunity to find a woman who will need a husband as much as I need a wife. I want an honest woman, one gently born and educated, but not necessarily of great family—a solid country gentlewoman, that's what's needed. She must like children, and wish to . . . er . . . participate in a physical relationship with me."

"But," Temple said, his hands spreading wide in confusion. "But . . . ladies who participate in a physical relationship often bear children."

"I shall see to it that my wife will not be stretched upon the rack of childbirth," Harry said carelessly, then visibly flinched when somewhere nearby a door slammed, and what sounded like a hundred elephants thundered down the hallway outside his office. "Take this down, Temple. *Wanted: an honest, educated woman between the ages of thirty-five and fifty, who desires to be joined in the wedded state to a man, forty-five years of age, in good health and with sufficient means to ensure her comfort. Must desire children. Applicants may forward their particulars and references to Mr. T. Harris, Raving-by-the-Sea. Interviews will be scheduled the week following.* That should do it, don't you think? You may screen the applicants for the position, and bring me the ones who you think are suitable. I shall interview them and weed out those who won't suit."

"Sir . . ." Temple said, even more at a loss as to how to counsel his employer from such a ramshackle method of finding a wife. "I . . . what if . . . how will I know who you will find suitable?"

Harry frowned over the top of an estate ledger. "I've already told you what I want, man! Someone honest, intelligent, and she must like children. I would prefer it if she possessed a certain charm to her appearance, but that's not absolutely necessary."

Temple swallowed his objections, and asked meekly, "Where do you wish to interview the candidates for your hand? Surely not here, at Ashleigh Court?"

Harry ran his finger down a column of figures, his eyes narrowing at the proof of abuse by his late cousin's steward. "The man should be hung, draining the estate dry like that. What did you say? Oh, no, any woman of sense would take one look at this monstrosity and run screaming in horror. Find somewhere in town, somewhere I can meet with the ladies and have a quiet conversation with them. Individually, of course. Group appointments will not do at all."

"Of course," Temple agreed, and staggered from the room, his mind awhirl. The only thing that cheered him up was the thought that Harry's wife, whoever she would turn out to be, would no doubt insist on the house being cleaned from attic to cellars.

Harry was just settling down to make notes about what needed attention first on the estate, when a sudden high-pitched shriek had him out of the chair, and almost to the door before Temple appeared in the open doorway to the hall.

Harry hesitated at the sight of Temple's weak smile. "The children . . . is someone hurt?"

"Peacocks," Temple said concisely.

Harry blinked, then relaxed. "Peacocks? Oh, peacocks. Yes, they do have an ungodly scream. I thought one of the children—"

Another bloodcurdling screech cut across his words. Before Harry could draw a breath, a huge green-and-blue bird raced passed him down the hall, its once magnificent tail feathers now ragged and muddy. Hoots, yells, and assorted shouts followed the peacock as the three younger children pounded after the poor bird. Anne stopped next to the great curved staircase, threw her head back, and let forth the most hair-raising sound Harry had ever heard.

"As I was about to say, sir, it is not the peacock making the noise, it is the children."

Harry closed the door quietly, leaning back

against it as the sounds of one agitated peacock being pursued by three noisy children around and around the hall filtered through the solid door. "Write the advertisement, Temple."

A loud avian squawk followed by the sound of something large and ceramic shattering upon the hall's marble floor sent Harry running back into his sanctuary. "Now! For God's sake, man, write it now!"

Chapter Two

Plum nuzzled the soft, downy head lying against her breastbone, and breathed deeply of the milky, soapy smell, ignoring the less pleasing odor that wafted upward.

"There you are, I thought you would be in the vicarage. How has Baby been for you—oh, heaven, he's rank!"

Mrs. Bapwhistle bustled into the tiny garden and before Plum could object, plucked the youngest Bapwhistle from her arms and handed the sweet baby over to a waiting nurse. "Clean him up, Withers. He smells as if he'd been dunked in the cesspit."

"I would be happy to bathe—" Plum started to say, halfway rising from the shaded bench. The nurse wrinkled up her nose, and hurried off with her charge before Plum could finish her sentence.

"No, no, that won't be at all necessary. That's

what I engage a nurse for, to do all the many unpleasant chores connected with children. Now sit down, do, and allow me to speak to you for a moment. I have something of great importance to discuss with you."

"But . . . I was hoping I would be able to feed the baby—" Plum felt as if her heart had been ripped from her arms with the babe. He was so sweet, so adorable, so small and needy.

"You can feed him another time, Plum. This is important."

Plum leaned back against the carved back of the bench, and idly plucked a leaf from the hydrangea that grew alongside, trying hard to keep the peevish tone from her voice. "You promised me I could take care of Colin while you were out paying calls, Cordelia. I think it's unkind of you to hand him over to Nurse when you promised *me* I could care for him."

"Honestly, Plum, you don't want to be present when he's filled his napkin. The mess that baby can make—it's positively horrifying." Cordelia Bapwhistle, wife of the vicar and Plum's closest friend, raised her hand and cut off Plum's objection. "I know, I know, you don't find anything about dear little Colin objectionable, no more than you found anything objectionable about Constance, Connor, or Columbine, but my dear, dear friend, you must take it from one who knows—babies aren't all sweet little bundles of delight."

Plum's gaze dropped from her friend's eyes to the faded blue material over her knees. She smoothed her gown and tried not to look as if Cordelia's words—kindly meant, to be sure—had caused her pain. "I know they aren't perfect, Del. I'm not stupid. I *have* raised a child."

Cordelia set aside the newspaper she'd been clutching and gave her friend's hand a sympathetic pat. "I never in a million years imagined you were stupid, Plum. You're the smartest, most giving woman I know, and you've done a marvelous job with Thomasine, although she wasn't really a child when she came to you. How old was she when her uncle died?"

"Fifteen," Plum admitted.

"You've done wonderfully raising her these past five years, and you know you'll always be welcome here. The children adore you. . . ."

The unvoiced objection pierced Plum's heart with an arrow's quickness. She looked up at her friend, the black eyebrows that refused all her attempts to make them arch settled into a thick slash across her brow. "But?"

Cordelia squeezed her hand. "But it's time you had a family of your own."

Plum raised her eyes heavenward for a moment. "Do you think I haven't been trying to find a man who would take me? Good heavens, Del, you yourself have introduced me to every eligible bachelor in the county, and I've examined all of the ineligible ones. There's not a man in all of Dorset who hasn't heard of the scandal, and thus won't sully his reputation by marrying me. The rest of them are either drunkards or wife-beaters or too poor to support Thom and me. And before you tell me I'm being too finicky, I assure you I'm not looking for a man of fortune—just one who has the means to support a wife and one small niece."

Cordelia laughed. "I would never call you finicky, Plum. Some of the men you even *thought* about marrying . . ." She gave a little shudder. "But that's neither here nor there. Look, see what old Mrs. Tavernosh heard was posted in yesterday's paper." She held out the newspaper for Plum to examine the small advertisement that had been circled by a blue pencil.

Plum read the paragraph, her eyebrows lifting as she looked up to meet her friend's bright, dancing eyes. "You cannot be serious!"

"Why not? This man needs a wife, wants someone who likes children, and says he has comfortable means."

Plum allowed her mouth to gape open, just a little, just enough for her friend to see how shocked she was. "Why not? Why not? Cordelia Bapwhistle, have you or have you not been lecturing me these last two years I've been husband hunting about the folly of accepting just any man?"

"Well, yes, but—"

"And are you not the very person who weekly lectures me about how women can be perfectly happy and productive without bearing a child or being a wife?"

"Yes, and I stand behind that statement. Children are not for everyone, Plum. Some women—"

"And yet you, you who regularly tells me that I should be grateful to be unencumbered and free to live my life the way I want—although I'd like to point out that poor as a church mouse and unloved by anyone but a niece who prefers the company of animals to people is *not* the life I wish to live—*you*

are suggesting that I answer this ridiculous advertisement inserted by a man I know nothing about?"

"Well, of course you'd have to find out something
about him, I'm not suggesting you take him sight
unseen. He might not be suitable at all. The advert
says you should send particulars, and you will be
contacted if the man wishes to interview you."

"Interview me!" Plum said, indignation rising at
just the thought of being *interviewed.* She gave a
ladylike snort. "As if I were a servant? I think not!"

Cordelia watched her with an eye lit from within
by warmth, affection, and a good deal of humor.
"There's nothing to stop you from interviewing him,
as well, you know. And really, what is an interview
but time to get to know someone? You've done as
much with the men you've pursued."

A faint blush the color of a nearby rose colored
Plum's cheek as she looked away from her friend.
"You make it sound as if I was desperate, hunting
men the way a fox hunts its prey."

"Plum, you know I want you to be happy. If your
experience with Charles has not put you off men for
life and you are sure that you want to be married
and have a family, then I will do everything I can to
help you."

"My marriage with Charles did nothing to put me
off all men, Del. I assume that he was the exception
to the norm, and that most men would hesitate to
marry a woman when they already have a wife living. And as for the family, I fear it's too late for that.
I'm forty years old. Surely most women my age have
finished having children by now."

"Ah, but you're not most women," Cordelia said,

her smile warming Plum's heart. "You're Frederica Pelham, daughter of Sir Frederick Pelham, the woman of breeding if not fortune, who just so happens to also be the author of the most popular, most scandalous book of the century."

Plum glanced around the small garden worriedly. The last thing she needed was for anyone in Ram's Bottom to find out she was the notorious Vyvyan La Blue, author of the famed *Guide to Connubial Calisthenics*, a book so shocking it was banned as obscene by the government—and subsequently went into three separate printings to fulfill the demands by members of the *ton*.

"I did have Old Mab Shayne examine me," Plum named the local midwife hesitantly, unwilling to get her hopes up about something that meant so much to her. "She said there was nothing wrong with my womanly parts, and she knew of several women who had children well into their mid-forties."

"There, you see? If you really want to have a family despite me telling you just how appallingly horrible childbirth can be, then you owe it to yourself to investigate this advertisement."

Plum nibbled on her lower lip, her gaze slipping to the paper. Although the method the man had used to state his desire for a wife off-put her almost as much as the word *interview* rankled, Cordelia did have a point. There was nothing to stop her from examining the man to see if he would make a suitable partner for her. She'd more or less done as much with the other men of the area she had considered. "There is the problem of my past," she said slowly. "I have lost more than one potential suitor upon his finding out that I was Charles's mistress."

"You weren't his mistress—you married him in good faith. He is the one who wronged you, he is the one who used you and threw you away without any regard or concern for your future."

"We both know that, but gentlemen, alas, do not care that Charles lied to me when he wed me. They only see a woman who gave herself to a man who was not lawfully her husband, one who caused a scandal so great that it resulted in Charles being sent abroad, Papa disowning me, and poor Susanna ostracized and reviled by society for the mere fact that she was my sister. She went into a decline because of the scandal, Del. It's my fault she died and left baby Thom to be brought up by her uncle Beauclerc."

"It's not your fault in the least, so stop martyring yourself. Besides, there is a simple solution to the problem: Don't tell this man who you are. *Were*."

Plum stared in surprise at her friend. "You want me to lie?"

"No, of course not, that would be sinful and wrong. I simply suggest that you not tell the man everything—until you're wed. Then, after such time has passed as is needed for him to fall in love with you, you tell him the truth. By then it will be too late for him to do anything about it."

"That's rather callous," Plum said, her fingers fretting the material of her gown. "After the experience with Charles, honesty is at the top of the list of qualities I seek in a husband. I will not again marry a man who has secrets from me."

"Mmm, well I'm afraid that lets out every man in the British Isles who can still draw breath." Cordelia paused for a moment, then asked, "You have a *list* of qualities you desire in a husband?"

"Yes, of course I do. Lists are excellent ways to become organized. I keep them for many things. Husbandly attributes are just one of the many lists I maintain—"

"What is on it?"

"On the husband list?" Cordelia nodded. Plum thought for a moment, then ticked items off on her fingers. "Honesty is the most important, as I mentioned. And a good nature is also necessary."

"I should think so."

"A sense of humor is a definite plus."

"I agree completely."

"Of course, he must want children."

"Of course," Cordelia said somberly. Plum slid a glance toward her to see whether or not she was being mocked. Cordelia's face was all seriousness, although there was a glint in her dark gray eyes that made Plum suspect otherwise.

"Financial security is also necessary, although I will not be demanding regarding the amount, so long as he is able to provide a secure home for me, and for Thom as long as she is with us."

"Mmm. More is better when it comes to items of a fiduciary nature."

"And last of all, the man I wed must be very, very limber. Double-jointedness is preferred, although I would settle for a normally jointed man so long as he was fit and limber."

Cordelia blinked. "Limber? Why ever should he be limb . . . oh! You mean for . . . in . . . when he and you . . ."

"Yes, exactly. I may not have much experience being a wife, but even I know that one must indulge in connubial calisthenics in order to get with child.

And you must admit that when it comes to such things, it's much easier to have a limber husband than one who is unable to perform even the simplest of calisthenics like *Bull Elephant at Hadrian's Wall*."

Cordelia opened her mouth as if she was going to speak, then evidently thought better of it, and shook her head instead.

"Although I have a number of qualities my prospective mate must meet, the first and foremost items are honesty and forthrightness in all things. After Charles, I just couldn't tolerate anything less, and if I demand that in a spouse, I must provide the same. I will have to tell him about my past."

"Yes, but Plum, you don't really have that luxury, do you?"

The words, although softly spoken, carried a sting with them. Plum's heart sank as she once again shouldered the burden she had cast off for a few hours of enjoyment of young Colin. "No, I don't. To be truthful, my situation is worse than you know. The money from the last of my jewels ran out earlier this year. The lease on our cottage expires at the end of this month, and Sir Jasper·has warned me that he cannot be as accommodating on the rates as he has been. Mrs. Feeny has told Mr. Feeny he is not to extend me any more credit until I pay what I owe them, and all other shops in town are following suit."

"I will be happy to ask Mark for a sum to tide you over until the next draft arrives from your publisher—"

Plum shook her head before her friend could finish her sentence. "There won't be any more drafts.

The last one was for such a miniscule amount, I wrote to Mr. Belltoad. He informed me that the *Guide*, although extremely popular with members of the *ton*, had limited appeal to those of a lower class, who evidently feel the book to be more pornographic than a celebration of physical affection between spouses."

"But surely there must be something you can do! Some employment you can find. . . ."

Plum blinked back tears of self-pity. One of the first things she had learned was that tears never helped. "I'm a gentleman's daughter, Del. My education has been limited to those things suitable to running a household and bearing children."

"You could be a governess or a teacher."

"With my reputation?"

Cordelia's gaze dropped. "Oh, yes, I had forgotten that."

"I can assure you that you are the only one who has." Plum sighed. Sighing, like tears, did not do much good, but at least it made one feel better without leaving red eyes and a drippy nose.

"What about another book?" Cordelia looked up, her eyes bright. "You could write another *Guide*!"

"No, I couldn't. Even if I had enough material for another *Guide*—which I don't, my time with Charles having been limited to just six weeks—I've asked the publisher, and he says the lawsuits and attention from the government are not worth the profit. I'm afraid Vyvyan La Blue has no further literary career."

"Oh."

Plum's shoulders drooped as she looked out over

the small, but well-tended lawn of the vicarage. Bees buzzed happily in the roses and hyacinth, the air filled with the sounds and scents that Plum had come to love so much. If only she could stay tucked away in her safe little cottage until she had time to find a husband, the man who would seamlessly blend his life with hers. "I'm afraid all that stands between me and the poorhouse is the five shillings I have tucked away in an old glove, and the meager amount that Thom receives quarterly. I have been obliged to borrow from her, but even that is not enough to support us."

"I had no idea things were as bad as that," Cordelia said, her eyes full of sympathy. Plum turned away, unable to bear the look for long. "Well, then, you really do have no choice, you must marry, and marry immediately."

"That is easier said than done."

"Nonsense, you've had several suitors."

"All of whom withdrew their suit once they knew of my history."

Cordelia smiled. "Then the answer to your problem is clear: If you insist on telling the truth about your past, you must do so—but wait until after you are wed."

Plum nibbled on her lip again. "It seems wrong—"

"Being married to a bounder who was already wed is wrong, Plum. You were innocent of any wrongdoing. Why punish yourself further for something that was not your fault? You must seize opportunity if it is presented to you, and worry about such minor things later. Besides, Charles is dead, God rest his soul even if he deserves to rot in whatever Italian ocean he drowned in. He can't hurt you any more, so as long as you keep quiet about your past, no one else will bring it up."

"It was the Mediterranean, somewhere off Greece, I believe." It was tempting to do as Cordelia suggested, Plum admitted that much to herself. She had been so close to marrying before, but each time she had bared her past, the man in question had fled, not wanting her stain of shame to taint him. Perhaps if she could find a man who would be so obliging as to fall in love with her, perhaps he wouldn't mind her past too much. Perhaps he would understand that she had been young and foolish, and had no experience with men to judge Charles for the heartless rake he was. Perhaps she could find a man who simply wanted a wife, a mother for his children, a companion, someone with whom to share the joys and sorrows of life. Plum thought of what her life held for her—poverty, loneliness, and the responsibility of seeing Thom happily settled—and decided that for once, she'd take the less honorable road. Her heart lightened at the decision, as if the burden she carried had dissolved. "Very well, I will send in my application, such as it is. If it turns out that he wishes to marry me . . . well, I'll tell him just as soon as is possible. You'll stand reference for me?"

"Of course." Cordelia smiled again, and Plum felt her own lips curving in answer. "I will give you such a glowing recommendation, he would have to be mad to turn you down."

A little giggle slipped out of Plum as she rose, brushing off her gown and collecting her bonnet and reticule. "Mad I could deal with, just so long as he's kind and amiable, and willing to give me a child. Oh, drat, I forgot the new smithy!"

Cordelia walked beside her friend as they strolled toward the large, red-brick vicarage. "What new smithy? Oh, Mr. Snaffle. He is very virile looking, isn't he, what with those huge arms and all that curly hair, and his very, very tight breeches."

"Cordelia!" Plum said, trying to look shocked but afraid the laughter in her eyes was giving her away. "Such a vulgar and unseemly innuendo shocks my maiden's ears."

Cordelia laughed aloud as she paused at the gate. "A less maidenly woman I have never met."

Plum paused as she clicked the gate closed, enjoying the warmth of the sun on her back, the air filled with the scent of honeysuckle. A faint frown tugged her straight eyebrows together. "About that . . . are you sure I shouldn't tell—"

"Absolutely certain."

"But what if I meet someone who knows me? Someone who tells him about my past before I can?"

"As the wife of a simple country gentleman—for a gentleman he must be since his advertisement is very well worded—you are unlikely to come into contact with any members of the ton. No one will know who you are, so you will be able to tell your husband in your own time, when you feel the moment is right. Say six or seven years from now."

Plum looked down the dusty road to the green at the center of the village. Ram's Bottom had been a haven for her, but it had also been a prison. She had hidden herself and Thom away from the prying eyes of gossips, but the years were slipping by, and

Thom deserved to have a better life than the poverty Plum could offer. "Very well. I will call later for the recommendation."

"It will be waiting for you," Cordelia said, waving as Plum turned and resolutely started toward the green, her mind full of the letter she would send to Mr. T. Harris. Along the way she noticed that several women were clustered together on the green in small clumps talking intensely, but she thought nothing of that. The ladies of Ram's Bottom were notorious gossips, happy to spend hours in the analysis and dissection of each others' character, antecedents, and offspring.

"No doubt they're tearing some poor lady's reputation to shreds," she said to herself as she skirted the green and headed for the smithy.

A few minutes later Plum regretted her complacent attitude.

"I want ye," Mr. Snaffle said, leaning in and spraying Plum with the odor of unwashed body, onions, and horse sweat. It was, she found, not a scent conducive to romance. Large arms and thick curly hair he might have, but Mr. Snaffle was definitely *not* going to suit her. "I want ye bad. Feel how bad my cods want ye."

Before she knew what he was doing, a massive hand descended on hers and slapped it over the bulge in his tight breeches.

"Mr. Snaffle!" she gasped, and snatched her hand away as she tried to sidle out from under the brawny arm holding her pinned to the rough planking of the blacksmith's shed. "You forget yourself! I have no interest in you or your cods, so please allow me to pass."

The fetid smell increased as the blacksmith laughed in her face. Plum turned her head, wishing she'd sent Thom to have the pot mended—the convenient ploy she used to meet and consider the blacksmith as husband material—then immediately regretted such a cowardly thought.

"Ye play coy with me, Missus, but I know how much ye want me too. Give us a kiss."

Plum tightened her fingers around the handle of the pot and gritted her teeth. Her life, one moment only mildly horrible, had turned into full-fledged, raging nightmare. "Mr. Snaffle, if you do not let me pass this instant, I shall be forced to take action against you."

He leaned up against her, flattening her against the wall with his broad, sweaty chest. She shifted the pot, relieved he was just leaning his upper parts against her.

"No one cares iff'n ye scream, Missus. They all know ye for the trollop ye are, pretendin' yer all high and mighty by marryin' a man what was already married. Miss Stone says that yer own family won't have nothin' to do with ye. Give us a kiss," he demanded again, spittle collecting in the corners of his fleshy lips.

"I am not a trollop," Plum said softly, moving the pot slightly, so as to give her a longer backswing. "I have no idea how this Miss Stone—whoever she might be—found out about my marriage, but I can assure you that I am innocent of her charges. Now please release me, or I shall do you a bodily injury."

27

He rubbed his chest against hers, his hands on her upper arms, holding her in place. "Everyone knows that ye'll spread yer legs for any man what gives ye a taste of his manflesh." He slid one hand up, grabbing a handful of her hair, jerking her head back. "I told ye to give us a kiss. I'm not of a mind to tell ye again!"

"Mr. Snaffle?" Plum swung the pot as far back as she could.

"Aye?" His repulsive lips were descending on hers.

"This is for your cods." She brought the pot forward as hard as she could, striking him right at the junction of his legs. He screamed and fell backward, clutching at himself, spitting curses and profanities as he rolled over into a ball. Plum took a deep breath of relatively clean air, and stepped forward to stand over the writhing man.

"Henceforth I shall take my smithy business elsewhere," she said, and gave him a swift kick in the kidneys just because she felt like it. "You're lucky I'm a lady and not given to spite!"

With her head held high she left the smithy, a stubborn, brittle smile on her face, the eyes of what felt like the entire village scoring her flesh as she hurried home, clinging to the hope that perhaps it wasn't as bad as Mr. Snaffle made out, but knowing it was much, much worse. She would have to move again, leave Ram's Bottom, and how was she to accomplish that with only five shillings and no friends but Cordelia?

"Blessed St. Genevieve," Plum all but sobbed as she stumbled into the tiny cottage she shared with Thom. "I'm going to have to marry Mr. T. Harris, no matter what sort of man he is. With luck, no one in Raving will know about me until I can marry him."

"Marry who?" a low, disinterested voice asked.

Plum clutched the wall and fought to regain her breath as well as swallow her tears of self-pity. "Oh, Thom, I didn't see you. What are you doing down there by the coal scuttle?"

Thom's golden brown eyes considered her aunt for a moment before her head dipped below the rough-planked table in front of her, returning a moment later when she stood up, a tiny kitten cupped in her hand. "Maple has had her litter. Only three, but one was born dead. I was just making sure the two kittens were all right. Who do you have to marry?"

"Whom," Plum corrected absently, her heart still pounding from the scene in the blacksmith's. "I am going to marry—hope to marry—a Mr. T. Harris. If he'll have me, that is."

"Oh," Thom said, and bent down to return the kitten to the nest she had made for Maple and her babies.

"*Oh?* Is that it? You're not going to ask me who Mr. T. Harris is, nor why I am going to marry him?"

Thom rose and dusted her sooty hands off on her lavender gown, Plum noted with a mental sigh. It wasn't the soiling of the gown she regretted, it was the tomboy nature of her niece. Thom was twenty years old, a young woman of intelligence and high spirits, of a good, if impoverished, family, and if she wasn't the loveliest woman on the face of the earth, she was very pretty, with cropped chestnut curls, large dark gray eyes, and a very sweet smile. *When* she smiled, which Plum had to admit wasn't often,

Thom being a serious, takes-everything-literally sort who would rather spend time with the various animals she had collected than with the two-legged variety most young women preferred.

"Although how you are to catch a husband with no dowry, and a notorious aunt, is beyond me." Plum sighed again, this time aloud.

Thom cocked her head and watched as Plum plucked her bonnet off and sank down into the rickety chair next to the fire. "I thought it was you who were planning to marry? I've told you before that I have no desire to marry. Men are so"—she wrinkled her nose as if she smelled cabbage cooking—"silly. Stupid. Mindless. I have yet to meet one who makes any sort of sense. To tell you the truth, I don't think there are any. I will do quite well without one of my own, thank you."

"Oh, Thom," Plum said, on the verge of tears, but unable to keep from smiling at her niece's dismissal of men as a whole. "What would I do without you?"

"Well, I imagine just what you are doing now," Thom replied. "You do seem to have the habit of talking to yourself, Aunt Plum, so if I weren't here, you'd probably be right where you are, telling the room that you're going to marry Mr. Harris. Who is Mr. Harris?"

Plum blessed the day Thom came to her. If anyone could make her laugh at herself, it was her niece. "Mr. T. Harris is a man in search of a wife, and as I am a woman in search of a husband, I am hoping that we will suit one another. You wouldn't mind me marrying, would you Thom? You know I wouldn't marry a man who couldn't keep you, as well."

Thom shrugged and filled a small cracked saucer with the last of the milk, setting it down next to the new mother. "If it will make you happy, I don't mind in the least, as long as Mr. Harris won't mind me bringing my animals. I couldn't leave them behind."

"No, of course not," Plum said, trying to envision just how she was going to tell her prospective husband that not only was he gaining a wife and a niece but three cats, six dogs, two goats, four tame mice, and a pheasant that thought it was a rooster. Her mind boggled at that thought. She shook her head, clearing it of the morose thought that she was doomed, and rose to find a relatively clean scrap of paper before settling down at the table to write a letter so dazzling, it would be sure to capture Mr. Harris's attention. "I pray he is an honest, likeable man with no secrets that will come back to haunt me. I just don't think I could stand another husband with secrets."

Chapter Three

"How many applicants remain, Temple?" Harry asked, wearily pushing up his spectacles as he leaned back in the private room bespoken at the local inn for the purpose of conducting interviews.

Temple consulted his list. "Let me see, applicant number fourteen was reported too ill to travel. . . ."

"Strike her from the list. If she is of frail health, she won't be able to stand up to the strain of the children. It takes a strong woman, in full possession of her faculties—both mental and physical—to deal with my brood."

". . . and number twenty-three changed her mind at the door . . ."

"Shy. Shy won't do either. My wife has to have a firm sense of purpose. Determination, too. Grit wouldn't hurt, either."

". . . and numbers thirty and thirty-one appear to have run off together . . ."

Harry raised both eyebrows and forbore to comment.

". . . and number thirty-three, the last applicant, appears to have decided not to meet with you." Temple looked up. "There are no more, sir."

Harry stood and stretched, rubbing the back of his neck and collecting his hat. "Well, that was six hours wasted. I hope to God I never have to meet so many women again."

Temple trotted alongside Harry as he strode out of the inn, pausing to pass a few coins to the innkeeper before heading for the small stable block. "Were there none that meet with your specifications, my lord?"

"Shhh!" Harry waved Temple's words away as he waited for Thor to be brought out. "No *my lording*, Temple. The fewer people who know my true identity, the better. At least until I find a wife."

"My apologies, sir. Were there no women—"

"No, there weren't," Harry said, slapping his leg with his riding crop as he looked around the quiet inn yard. "Not a single blessed one of them would do. Most of them were too young, a few were of the right age, but lacked the mental capacity I seek in a wife. I don't expect her to be a genius, but I must have a woman I can converse with, one who has an interest in books and current events and such." Harry noted a very pretty woman hurrying into the inn, the bottom six inches of her dark red gown covered in mud and filth as if she'd been tramping through the woods. "The remaining two qualified applicants were, to put it finely, a little on the homely side."

"You said that you weren't requiring your wife to

be toothsome, sir." Although the words were sub-servient, the tone was most definitely chastising.

"Toothsome, no, but I'd like to be able to look at her without thinking of bulldogs. One of the women today had a great hairy wart right in the middle of her forehead. I couldn't stop staring at it. No matter where I looked, my gaze ended up back on her forehead. I couldn't possibly have a wife whose forehead held such an unwholesome fascination for me. That woman who scampered into the inn just now—she's the sort I'm looking for. Not beautiful, but pleasing, soft on the eyes, with a delicate oval face and lots of"—Harry made a gesture with both hands that was universally understood by all men over the age of fourteen—"curves. Why couldn't one of my women have been like her? I don't think that's asking for too much."

Thor charged out of the stable, snorting like a steam engine, his ears back as he hauled a young stable boy behind him. Harry grabbed the reins with the ease of long practice, thumped the horse on the shoulder in an affectionate greeting, and flipped the boy a coin before mounting the fiery bay. "Hurry up, Temple, I've a desire to get home before the children bring the house down about their ears."

"Just coming, sir," Temple said, looking warily at the new mare Harry had purchased to replace his old mount. The mare bared her teeth and narrowed her eyes at him. Just as he was about to take his life into his hands and climb into the saddle, a feminine cry reached his ears.

"Mr. Harris? Sir?"

Harry turned to watch as the curvaceous woman in the well-used red gown hurried out of the inn, her skirts held up with one hand as she dashed across the muddy yard. He admired the flash of ankle for as long as was gentlemanly (far too short a time since the woman dropped her skirts as she reached them).

"Mr. Harris?"

Temple turned his back on the mare as he faced the woman, an error Harry was about to rectify when it occurred to him that the woman must be the missing last applicant. He eyed her again, closer this time, appreciating not just her pretty face with cheeks bright with exercise but the raven-black hair that was visible beneath her bonnet, the slash of black eyebrows across her brow, and two dark eyes that had an appealing, almost exotic tilt to them. To Harry's great mortification, he became instantly and fully aroused. Clamping the reins under his knee, he pulled his jacket off and laid it across his lap in what he hoped was a suitably nonchalant it's-a-bit-hot-out-today manner.

"Mr. T. Harris? I'm Frederica Pelham. I apologize for being so late, but I lost my way a few times and had to ask for directions."

The woman was speaking to Temple, having given him a glance that took in more of his horse than him. Harry wished he could dismount and speak to her, but his reaction to the sight of her had left him in the unenviable position of having to remain astride Thor. The thought of her noticing his bulging breeches had the unexpected (and lamentable) effect of making him even harder.

"I'm not too late, am I? You haven't . . . er . . . filled the position?"

She caught her lower lip between her teeth,

clearly worried and anxious. Harry wondered why such an attractive woman should be so desperate for a husband. She had no warts, no physical imperfections that he could see, and her voice was educated and well-spoken.

Temple cleared his throat and glanced toward him. Harry shook his head, then remembered he couldn't stand before the woman with his breeches nigh to bursting, and nodded. Temple looked confused. "Er—"

"No, you're not too late," Harry said, fully enjoying receiving the attention of those dark, velvety eyes as they turned upon him. "Mr. Harris is my man of affairs. I am the one who is looking for a wife."

"Oh, I see." the woman said, and eyed him just as curiously as he had been examining her. She didn't appear to find anything objectionable about him, although she must have wondered why he was so ill bred as to remain on horseback, sitting in his shirtsleeves while speaking with her. He damned his own lack of control, and decided that the interview would have to be conducted quickly.

"We were about to return home, but if you don't mind answering a few questions here, I'm sure we can have this business over with quickly. You said your name was Pelham?"

She made an odd sort of flinching movement, but lifted her chin and stared him straight in the eyes while answering. "Yes, sir. Frederica Pelham, although my friends call me Plum."

His eyebrows rose. "Plum?"

"For Pelham. It's a pet name, you see. My father used to call me Plum. He was Sir Frederick Pelham, of Nottingham."

Daughter of an impoverished baronet, no doubt. She had a niceness about her that did not allow her to look on him with scorn despite the fact that he was insulting her by remaining on his horse.

"Do you read, Miss Pelham?"

She looked startled by that question, but recovered quickly enough, although her high color remained. "When I have the opportunity to, yes."

"Ah. Good. I have a large library." Harry considered her, trying to separate the lustful urgings of his body from the less earthy desires of his mind.

"Do you?" Plum asked politely, reaching out to pat Thor's long face. Harry grabbed the reins from under his knee, about to pull Thor back lest the stallion snap at her, but was surprised when his high-strung horse not only allowed her to caress his ears but bumped his nose into her, searching her person for treats. Plum laughed, a low throaty laugh that Harry found utterly sensual and erotic, a sound that seemed to stroke his skin, leaving him harder than ever, unable to keep from visualizing her lying in his bed, surrounded by all that glossy black hair, laughing that sultry laugh.

"He likes you," Harry said as he dragged his mind back to the present.

"He probably knows how fond I am of horses. He's very handsome. What's his name?"

"Thor. Do you ride?"

A wistful look flickered through her eyes as she gave Thor one last pat, then gently pushed his head away. "I love to ride, but haven't had the chance to in a long time."

A *very* impoverished baronet's daughter, Harry amended. Still, possession of a fortune was not one of the qualifications for his wife. Thus far, Plum had exceeded every expectation he had—there was just the one remaining. "Er . . . how do you feel about children?"

"Oh, I love them," she said, her eyes lighting up, their midnight depths soft and compelling.

Harry could not help but believe her, as the truth shone like sunlight on a still pond within her dark eyes. He allowed himself a silent sigh of relief as he moved uncomfortably in the saddle, then waved toward Temple. "Just so. I see no reason that you will not suit. I must . . . er . . . return home. Temple will take down your particulars. Have you an objection to marrying the day following tomorrow?"

Plum didn't even bat an eyelash. Harry wanted to smile, but knew in his present uncomfortable state, it would be likely to come out a pained grimace. There are few things that became a bridegroom less than grimacing at his bride-to-be.

"None, except I have not interviewed you, sir."

He blinked in surprise. She wanted to interview him? None of the other women had. How delightfully refreshing of her! He had the sudden warm satisfaction of knowing that he would not easily be able to second-guess Plum. "Ah. Yes. Of course. You wish to know about me."

"Yes, sir, I do," she answered, and lifted her chin a little higher.

He liked that chin a great deal. He applauded her high spirits, and began to think with pleasure upon his future with her as he quickly rattled off the important particulars about himself. "My name is Harry . . . Haversham. I live here in Raving, out toward the north spit. Do you know it?"

She shook her head.

"Good. That is . . . er . . . it's of no account. I'm forty-five years of age . . ." He paused, narrowing his eyes as he looked carefully at her face. "If you will not be offended by me asking, how old are you?"

"I . . . I . . ." Plum looked nonplussed for a moment, then that adorable chin rose again. "I'm forty, sir."

He did smile then, a pleased smile, a happy smile. Really, she was perfect for the position. Intelligent, liked children, wasn't too young and silly, and heaven knew he desired her in a more fundamental manner. Every time she lifted her chin, he wanted to kiss her. "Excellent. As I said, I'm forty-five and in reasonably good health, possess means that leave me comfortable, and don't have any excessive vices that I'm aware of. Do you have any questions? No? Very well. I shall leave Temple to take down your information, and will obtain a special license tomorrow so that we may be married the following day." He touched his riding crop to his hat in salute, and was about to ride away when it suddenly occurred to him to ask a final question. "Er . . . what village are you from?"

Plum looked a bit stunned around the eyes, but other than a momentary pause, gave him no indication that he had just rushed her through a proposal. "Ram's Bottom, sir."

Harry's eyes widened as he glanced down at her muddy hem. "You walked eight miles?"

The chin rose again, just as he knew it would. He smiled to himself, more than satisfied with his choice. This woman would not leave him bored after a few days, as all the others threatened to do.

"Yes, I did. I find walking quite beneficial to the constitution."

"And so it is, however, sixteen miles in one day is a bit more benefit than anyone could need, even someone who is in your"—he allowed his gaze to caress her curves for just a moment, not long enough to be offensive, but enough to let the lady know he found her attractive—"fit condition. Temple?"

"Yes, sir. I will arrange for Miss Pelham to be taken home."

Harry beamed at her, bid her a good day, and put his heels to Thor, riding home with a whistle on his lips, satisfaction in his heart, and a throb in his breeches that predicted a very happy future.

Plum entered the dark cottage as the hired carriage rattled down the lane, more than a little dazed by the happenings of the day. She was betrothed! To a gentleman she had known for all of five minutes, a very handsome man, a man who had laugh lines around his eyes, and an unruly lock of sandy hair that hung over his forehead. A man who either had some infirmity of the lower limbs that prohibited him from dismounting, or . . . Plum giggled as she lit the candles around the small room. Once when she and Charles were having tea at her old nurse's cottage, he had been unwilling to leave at the end of the visit. He told her later that he had been musing upon the pleasure of their most recent connubial calisthenics, and had to remain seated until several minutes later when he had himself in control. The way Harry had draped his coat over his lap was reminiscent of Charles playing with her shawl in such a manner as to conceal his groin.

"If he was in a similar situation because of me," she told the cat Maple as she lit the fire and prepared to warm up the potato soup remaining from the day before, "I shall be very pleased, very pleased indeed, for it indicates that he is interested in bedchamber sports. Heaven knows I am."

"I am as well, despite the fact that you won't let me read your book," a voice said behind her.

Plum shrieked and dropped the soup ladle, clutching her heart as she spun around.

Thom was seated on the floor in a dark corner, a bowl of milk and several pieces of straw beside her. "Which is silly, when you think about it, for how am I ever to learn the joys of such activities if you won't let me read about them?"

"You swear you won't ever marry, so such knowledge is of no use to you. What are you doing there sitting in the corner in the dark?" Plum, having reassured herself that her heart was not going to leap out of her chest, returned to warming the soup.

"Feeding mice. Their mother was taken by one of the cats that live in the shed. I've found that they'll drink milk easily enough if I use a piece of straw." Plum gave a resigned sigh at the newest inhabitants of their little cottage, and hunted for the stale heel of bread she remembered seeing. "As for the other, I do not intend ever to marry—at least none of the gentlemen you think are so suitable. They're nothing but idle fribbles, bent on wenching their way through their lives. But I should like to see your book nonetheless. After all, one does not have to be married to perform calisthenics, connubial or otherwise."

Plum's cheeks heated as she turned to glare at her

niece. "No, one doesn't, as I know well, but issues of morality aside, to do otherwise is to put yourself in a position of disadvantage. Women have little enough control over their lives, and even less power against men. Marriage at least offers some protection."

Thom shrugged and bent over the clutch of tiny pink bodies squirming in her lap. Plum found the heel of bread, tapped it on the counter, winced at the solid *thunk*, then sighed and tossed it into the goat's bucket.

"Is that why you went to meet with Mr. Harris? For protection?"

"No," Plum answered, and bent down to look in the one small cupboard that served as their pantry. Surely there were a few greens left from last week? A bit of suet their neighbor had given them? A handful of dried beans? "I met with the gentleman—his name is Haversham, and have accepted his offer of marriage—because I wished to be married again and have a family, and he seemed a pleasant man. Wasn't there a rind of cheese?"

Thom ducked her head, and carefully allowed milk from the tip of the straw to drip into the little pink mouth of the baby mouse.

Plum straightened up, dusting off her hands. "I see. I don't suppose you ate it?"

Thom's shoulder twitched.

"No, I can see you didn't." Plum sat on the rickety chair, thought seriously about crying, but decided that laughter was probably the only thing that would save her sanity. She allowed the—only slightly hysterical—giggles to build up inside her, her lips twitching as she asked, "Did you give the cheese to a mouse? A rat? An orphaned vole?"

Thom peeked at her from under her lashes, an affecting look Plum had never been able to master since her eyelashes, like her brows, were thick and seemed to have a mind of their own. "There was this adorable little monkey—"

"Thomasine Laurel Fraser!" Plum gasped in between unladylike snorts of laughter. "To give away your meager luncheon is bad enough, but to make up a falsehood of such magnitude is going too far."

"It's not a falsehood, there really was a monkey. He was with a very old man, so bent and frail he looked as if he would be blown over by a strong wind. He was very charming, however, and told me his name was Palmerston, and his monkey was named Manny. They both looked in such a poor way, I gave him a bit of cheese, and a few other things that I thought you wouldn't mind. . . ."

"At least you have the grace to look ashamed at such a bald-faced lie," Plum said, her lips still twitching as she gave in and had a good long laugh. By the time she was finished and mopping up her eyes, Thom had tucked the baby mice away on an old worn cloth, and was standing next to her, watching her warily. "It's a good thing Mr. Haversham wishes to marry quickly, else I think you'd give the cottage away."

"I'm sorry, Aunt Plum, I know it was wrong of me, but Mr. Palmerston and Manny looked in such need of a little kindness, and he did give me something in return."

"Oh?" Plum allowed one last giggle to express itself, then schooled her lips into a more seemly position. "What did he give you? Certainly not any coin?"

"No, he gave me some advice."

A ripple of amusement shook her for a moment, but she kept it under control. She had a suspicion that if she gave in to it, she'd end up witless and giddy. Or rather, *more* witless and giddy, since she was fast approaching that state. Perhaps it was hunger that was unhinging her mind. Perhaps if she had eaten something earlier, she wouldn't now be giggling at the thought of her niece giving away the last of their stores to a beggar who offered advice in return. "How very gracious of him. What advice did he give you?"

"Oh, it wasn't advice for me, it was for you."

Plum raised both brows as Thom served up two bowls of soup. "For me? Why would he offer advice for me? How did he know who I was?"

"Evidently he stopped in town."

Thom kept her gaze on her soup, a small mercy since Plum still felt sick to her stomach whenever she thought of the townspeople cackling over her past. That the news had spread like wildfire was not surprising, but what made her furious was the way Thom was made to suffer for her ignorance and Charles's cruelty. She didn't mind—much—them ostracizing her, but the drubbing Thom had taken the last few days was untenable. Her conscience rubbing her raw, she fought the desire to immediately pen a note to her intended, informing him of her history and breaking their betrothal. "What's done is done. I will tell him the truth after we're married. It's a matter of self-preservation, not selfishness. I simply have no other choice, and it's not as if he will be losing out—I will be a devoted wife and mother."

44

"Of course you will," Thom said, just as if Plum were making sense, which she sadly acknowledged to herself as not necessarily true. "You'll be a wonderful wife and mother, and I completely agree with you that you're not being selfish."

"Mmm." Plum firmly told her conscience to take a holiday for the next two days, and picked up her spoon. "What was the advice the beggar had for me?"

"He wasn't a beggar, he seemed quite well spoken, although he was rather dusty." Plum glanced up and caught the look of curiosity her niece was bending upon her.

"He said that sometimes that which you've thought is lost, is found, and what you think you have, has vanished."

Plum blinked for a moment, wondering if it was the lack of food that made Thom's words seem incomprehensible, or if the old man's advice was supposed to have some meaning for her. "Well, that was very nice of him, although it doesn't make the slightest bit of sense, but I do appreciate the fact that he didn't say something in reference to his . . . er . . . cods."

They ate in companionable silence for a few minutes, the heavy drone of bees on the wisteria that hung next to the window the only noise. Plum wrestled with a variety of emotions—anger, fear, and a general all-purpose worry—as she spooned up the last of the soup.

"Aunt Plum?"

Plum dragged her mind from the painful contemplation of just how she was going to explain to Harry about her past. "Hmm?"

Thom stood with their soup bowls before the wash bucket, twisting a threadbare linen between her hands, her brow wrinkled in a frown. "You're not marrying this Mr. Haversham on my behalf are you? Because if you are, I wish you wouldn't. I know I'm not of much use to you, but I—"

Plum gave in to the need to hug the younger woman. "No," she said, patting Thom's cheek. "I'm not martyring myself for you, if that's what you think. Mr. Haversham is a very nice man, I could tell that at once. He is a gentleman. He has a library. He wants children. And even if he isn't wonderfully handsome, I like his face. His eyes are particularly nice, an attractive hazel that seems to change color. And the rest of him is"—a warmth tingled pleasantly within her at she remembered his large, strong hands with their long fingers. She had always had a fondness for a man's hands, seeing in them a mixture of strength and gentleness that never failed to intrigue her—"just as pleasant. Does that put your mind at rest that I'm not marrying solely to put food in our bellies?"

Thom smiled, then leaned forward to kiss Plum's cheek. "I hope you will be very happy, Aunt. You deserve a good life. When do you marry?"

"In two days, if Mr. Haversham is able to obtain a special license." Plum turned and surveyed the small room with its two cots, two chairs, one table, and a collection of broken baskets that Thom fixed up as beds for her animals. "What do you say, Thom, are you willing to give up all this in order to live in a home that doesn't leak whenever it rains, or allow the cold in during the winter?"

Thom smiled and divided up the last of her soup

between the cats' bowls and the goat's bucket. "It will be a strain, but I will suffer in silence as best I can."

Plum laughed again, and in a moment of pure whimsy, threw out her arms and spun around in a circle. "A family, Thom! At last, at very long last, I'm going to have a husband and children of my own! Life just cannot get any better!"

Chapter Four

Plum sat stunned to the point of silence as a maid-servant combed out her long black hair. That thought rattled around in her mind like a pea in an empty bowl. She had a maidservant, someone who would comb her hair whenever she so desired. Her husband had provided her the maidservant. She had a husband and a maidservant. And a room of her own. Her eyes looked away from the up-and-down motion of the comb as it slid through her hair, and gazed again with wonder at the reflection of the room behind her, a lovely soft rose-colored room that smelled faintly of fresh paint, with a huge fireplace, a fainting couch, and a bed with rose and dark red bed curtains.

The maid's hand flashed white in the mirror.

"No one has combed my hair for me since I was twenty."

"Is that so, my lady?"

That was another thing, she was a lady. Not that she had behaved in any other manner, for no matter how poor she had been, Plum had ever acted as a lady should—with the regrettable, if extremely satisfying, exception of the pot and Mr. Snaffle's cods—but now her husband of five hours informed her earlier, she was also a lady in title. Lady Rosse, to be exact. Harry turned out to be a marquis in disguise, therefore, she was a marchioness.

A *fraudulent* marchioness, her guilty conscience whispered.

"No. It is too much. I just cannot take it all in," Plum protested to her reflection. "The husband and the maid and the rose-colored room, yes, that I am willing to accept, nay embrace whole-heartedly with a great deal of happiness and pleasure if not outright ecstasy, but the rest of it, I just cannot absorb. It will have to wait for another time, a time when I can think about it without wanting to scream."

Edna the maid carefully set down the silver comb and stepped slowly away from Plum. "Why would you be wanting to scream, my lady?"

There they were again, those two words. *My lady.* She had deceived a marquis, led him to believe she was a poor but honest woman. Well, truly, she was poor but honest, honest with the exception of neglecting to tell him about one minor little fact. . . . Plum moaned softly and leaned forward until her forehead rested in her hands. "Edna, would you happen to know if it's a hanging offense to deceive a marquis?"

"Erm . . ." Edna backed toward the door. "Will you be needing anything else, my lady?"

Plum tilted her chin up and spread her fingers so

she could see the maid in the mirror. "Yes, please. Would you mind terribly not calling me *my lady*? It makes me a bit uncomfortable, not as uncomfortable as I deserve, to be sure, but uncomfortable enough that I flinch, and one can only do so much flinching before one starts to twitch, and it's a short path from twitching to utter and complete madness. Do you understand?"

"Eep," said Edna, and with eyes as big as saucers, she slipped out the door, closing it softly behind her.

"Well, now you've done it," Plum told her reflection, "you've frightened your maid. She probably thinks you are already mad. She's probably right. Stupid, stupid Plum. What am I going to do? How am I ever going to tell Harry—a marquis, for heaven's sake, he's almost royalty—the truth about me?" Plum looked away to the door connecting her bedchamber to her husband's, giving it a righteous glare. "Although I don't know why I should feel guilty about this. After all, it's his fault, it's all his fault. If he had *told* me before we were married who he really was, then I would have told him who I . . . who I . . . oh, pooh. I don't know what I would have told him."

Plum rose from the small gilt dressing table and fidgeted with the ribbon on her night rail. It was an old night rail, patched and mended and somewhat frayed on the bottom, not at all the sort of night rail a real marchioness would wear, especially on her wedding night, but it was all she owned, and she was pathetically grateful that Edna had found a rose-colored ribbon to replace the bit of braided cloth that had previously graced the neckline. "You are a coward, Frederica Pelham. You are nothing but a base coward, and you have no right to whine about anything because this is what you wanted."

The scent of jasmine carried on a warm evening breeze hung heavy on the air as she gazed out the window at the blackness beyond. Because they had arrived after dark, she hadn't had much more than a glimpse of Ashleigh Court as Harry had brought her home, but what she had seen stunned her almost as much as the carelessly tossed out fact that he, Harry, her lord and master, was truly a lord if not her master. True the house and grounds were horribly ill-kept, but Harry had reassured Thom (Plum being at the time too stunned by the marquis's revelation to do much but sputter, "But, but . . .") that he had plans to renovate and rejuvenate the once-proud estate, and he looked forward to the help and advice of his new wife.

"A wife who doesn't deserve to offer any advice or help," Plum said sadly to herself.

"You think not? I'm of another mind. I've always felt that a home needed a woman's touch to keep it from being too utilitarian." Harry strolled into the room through the connecting door, clad in a heavy gold brocade dressing gown that reached to his feet. He stopped next to her and looked out the window, sighing as he did. "There's so much to do here, I would appreciate your help, but if you'd prefer not to take the house in hand—"

"Oh, no, I'd be happy to . . . my lord."

Harry smiled as he turned to face her, a smile that would seem to be made up of mundane things like lips and eyes and adorable little crinkle laugh lines, but the sum result of it was so astoundingly wondrous, it melted all of Plum's internal organs.

Or that's what it felt like happened. She couldn't believe that simply by standing beside her he had whipped her traitorous, not-in-the-least-bit-sorry-she-had-married-him-despite-the-fact-that-she-hadn't-told-him-the-truth-about-her-past body into a frenzy of want, need, and unbridled anticipation.

She had been far, far too long without a man in her bed.

"Are you still having difficulty with the marchioness idea? I am very sorry I didn't tell you before we married, Plum. It wasn't well done of me at all, but you see, I thought it might scare you off, and"—he took her hand, his thumb stroking over the backs of her fingers in a way that set alight all of the previously melted internal bits—"I wanted very much to have you legally mine before I bared my breast of all my secrets."

A warm puddle of happiness did much to soothe her guilt. If he wanted her so much, perhaps the incident in her past would mean nothing to him? She hoped so. She prayed so. She also prayed she would survive the look of mingled desire and admiration that glowed from behind his spectacles. Plum had seen just such a look in the eyes of her first husband, and although it pleased her then, now she found herself responding to it with so great an enthusiasm, she thought her legs were going to give out. "It was a bit of a surprise, my lord—"

"Harry, please."

"—Harry, but I can assure you it wouldn't have sent me screaming into the night had you told me before we were wed. Indeed, the fact that you were baring your secrets to me might have induced me to bare a few of my own."

"Would it?" Harry said, his gaze dropping to the thin lawn of her night rail where it covered her breasts, breasts that were brazenly pushing themselves forward and clamoring for her to walk them into his hands. "And what secrets could a woman such as you have to bare?"

It was the word *bare* in combination with the avid way he eyed her breasts that sent the few wits remaining her flying straight out of her head. "Oh . . . I'm sure I have some. . . ."

"Yes, yes you do have some. You have lovely some." Harry's eyes glittered brightly as he looked at her breasts.

Plum frowned down at them, unsure whether she should affect maidenly mortification about the fact that her nipples were hard little pebbles against the soft linen, clearly outlined, right there for anyone to see, or to indulge in the wanton thrill of knowing Harry could stir such a reaction in her as to set her ablaze with the need to rub herself all over him. She decided that although the maidenly route was probably for the best, wanton was closer to her true nature. At least she could be an honest wanton. She took a step closer to him. "I assure you I have secrets, Harry. In particular, I have one secret. I was married—"

The words dried up on her lips as he—still staring at her breasts much in the manner of a starving man deposited at a feast—spread the fingers of his left hand and gently cupped her right breast.

"Yes, you told me you were married, and if you will recall, I told you that your past was of no concern to me."

A tremor of heat rippled through Plum starting at

her breast and ending at her womanly parts, which were now tingling for all they were worth. She closed her eyes and shuddered with pleasure, her back arching of its own accord, pressing her breast hard against his hand.

"Are you cold?" Harry asked hoarsely.

She opened her eyes as he rubbed his thumb across her aching nipple. "No. Not cold. Hot. Very hot."

"Hot, yes, so hot, I can feel your heat. I wonder if your other—" Plum moaned as he placed his right hand on her other breast. "You are very hot. Feverish, almost. I believe the best thing for you would to be freed of the restriction of clothing."

"Do you think so? Do you think that might help my . . . fever?" Plum ignored the fact that she was babbling like an idiot, too overwhelmed with desire and lust and a variety of other emotions all related somehow to the wonderful tingling going on in her breasts and nether parts.

"I do, I do indeed believe it will help. As your husband, it is my duty to see to your welfare, thus I must demand that for the purpose of your continued good health, you remove your night rail."

What a wonderful man! How thoughtful he was! How concerned he was for her health. "Oh," she breathed, thoroughly enjoying how her breasts moved against the palms of his hands.

Harry's eyes widened behind his spectacles. "NOW!"

"Oh!"

His hands still warm on her breasts, he leaned forward, his hair brushing her jaw as he kissed a hot trail along her collarbone, down to the top of the night rail where the pretty rose ribbon held the garment up. She breathed in the scent of him, part lemon shaving soap, part something earthy and arousing, and entirely male that was solely Harry.

"I will be happy to assist you if you are unable to disrobe by yourself."

Plum looked down to where Harry was pulling away from her, one end of the ribbon clenched firmly in his teeth. "This is wicked, you know, utterly and wholly wicked. We have only known each other for two days, and we're about to . . . you want to . . . and I would dearly love to . . . in bed. Together. With all our bare skin showing!"

The ribbon fell from his mouth as he looked up, a grin so endearing on his face, she wanted to grab his ears and kiss him until his spectacles fogged up. "Yes, I know, it is wicked, isn't it? Delightfully so." The bright glint in his eye slowly darkened with a shadow of doubt as he took a step backward. "You do want to do this, don't you? I'm not rushing you? I meant to tell you that I wanted a wife who desired a physical relationship, but at the time . . . er . . . I . . . eh . . . and today, when you said you had been married, I assumed that you'd want to . . . uh . . ."

Plum smiled a wry little smile as her breasts, heavy and hard and greatly missing his touch, pushed themselves with eagerness back into his hands. "Yes, I very much want to be a wife to you in all ways. It's just that I have only been with my first husband, you see, and we were together only for six weeks—"

Harry gently kissed the words from her lips. "You don't have much experience, I understand completely. You need not be worried on that account— we will discover this new territory together."

Plum was about to object to the ridiculous idea he had about her sexual naivety when his mouth closed upon hers, driving all thoughts but those of a carnal nature from her mind. His mouth was sweet and hot and filled her with the need to taste him. Without waiting for an invitation or even permission, she slid her tongue into his mouth, capturing his delighted moan, pressing herself against him in an attempt to get closer. His hands slid from her breasts to her back, one tangling itself in her hair, the other grasping her behind, pulling her hips tight against him. Even through the heavy brocade of his dressing gown she could feel how aroused he was. His tongue twined around hers in a motion remarkably similar to the sinuous grind of his hips. She slipped both hands around his neck, pressing herself tighter against him, clutching his hair as she mapped out the terrain of his mouth, wanting to burn up with the heat he generated deep within her, needing to burn bright, unable to stop until she had merged with him, joined with him, his heat feeding her flames—

"Papa, Ratty is asleep and won't wake up."

Plum thought she was hallucinating for a moment, but the way Harry stiffened against her alerted her to the fact that she hadn't imagined the childish voice behind her. With much regret, she separated from him, turning to face the small child who stood in the doorway to Harry's room, a limp brown object held carefully in his hands. He eyed her with bright curiosity. "Who's she? Is she going to be my new mama?"

Mama? As in . . . *mama*? Plum blinked in surprise.

"Er . . . yes. My dear, this is McTavish, my son."

He had a son? And he hadn't told her? Plum shook the cobwebs of astonishment from her mind, and smiled at the tow-headed boy. "Hello, McTavish, I'm very pleased to meet you. Yes, I am going to be your mama. What's that you have?"

The boy pushed the brown object into her hands. "It's Ratty. He's asleep. He won't wake up."

Plum, no stranger to rodents after having lived with an animal-obsessed Thom for the past few years, did not shriek or object to the obviously dead rat she found herself holding. In fact, she was rather proud of how quickly she had assimilated the information that Harry had a child he had forgotten to mention during his secret baring. She moved quickly to step into the role of mama to his sweet, motherless child. "I'm afraid Ratty has been called to heaven by the angels, McTavish. Do you see how his chest isn't moving? That means he's not breathing. I'm very sorry. Ratty looks like he was a good companion."

McTavish's lower lip emerged, and his eyes clouded for a moment, then just as quickly the tears were gone and the lip was retracted. "Can I have a kitten now, Papa? You said I couldn't have one because it would eat Ratty, but now Ratty's gone to heaven, so can I have a kitten? Can I? You said I could! Can I?"

Harry sent Plum an apologetic look that begged her forgiveness for his lapse in not mentioning he already had a child. She returned it with one that said although she would have preferred being told earlier, she understood, and was more than happy to be mother to his adorable son. His responding look offered fervent and profound thanks for her complete acceptance of his hitherto unmentioned son, along with general admiration for her maternal nature, and the promise that he would give her many other children of her own. At least that's what she thought he was trying to convey; truthfully, he looked more concerned than anything else, but she was sure she had read the emotions so plainly visible in his lovely, changeable eyes. What man didn't want his new wife to love and adore his child?

"We'll talk about it later, son. Here, you take Ratty and put him in a box. We'll have a funeral for him in the morning. Give it to Gertie on your way back to bed." Harry pushed the small child toward the door, giving Plum another apologetic look over his shoulder.

"I want a kitten! You said I could have a kitten, and I want one. I want one now!"

"Later," Harry hissed, and tried to shove the boy through the opened door.

McTavish grabbed the door frame with the hand that was not holding the rat. His hazel eyes, so very much like his father's that it tugged on Plum's heartstrings, pleaded with her from across the room as Harry tried to pry the five pudgy little fingers off the door. "Mama, I want a kitten. Papa said I could have one."

He called her Mama! She melted into a big puddle of maternal goo. "And so you shall have one, my sweet little lamby-cake. The first thing in the morning I will take you to find a kitten all your very own. It will be our special time together."

"Later," Harry snarled, prying the last finger off the door frame.

He yelped as McTavish kicked him smartly on the shin before spinning around to run through the doorway, yelling to someone named Gertie that his new mama was going to get him a kitten.

Harry shook his fist after the boy. "You little bas"—he glanced back at Plum—"blighter! I'll remember that, see if I don't!"

Plum smiled a shy little smile that went straight to Harry's groin as he closed the door and turned to face her. She was a wonder! Not only was she the most delectable morsel of womanhood he had seen in a very long while; she had lovely breasts; an amiable temper; seductive hips; an intelligent wit; long, lush legs; various other good nonphysical qualities that couldn't at that exact moment be called to mind; nipples that cried out for his touch; a mouth that begged to be kissed; a body that felt like heaven against his. . . . Unable to bear the distance between them, Harry lunged forward, intent on possessing himself of that warm, wonderful woman he had had the extremely good sense to marry.

Plum stopped him with one hand on his chest. He almost whimpered, but he recalled that he was a gentleman, and gentlemen do not whimper, or grovel, or plead, or even get down on their knees and beg when their wives wish to talk rather than make love. No, gentlemen like him drag their minds from the contemplation of just what they'd like to do to the temptresses who stand before them in almost completely transparent bits of cloth, cloth so thin the shadows of her lovely nipples were visible, nipples that called to him, nipples that pleaded with him to take them into his mouth and suckle them with every ounce of desire he possessed, and he possessed an ocean's worth of desire.

"Harry, dear Harry, how silly you are." Silly? She thought he was silly? Was that good? She was smiling at him, it must be good. Hurrah! "How could you possibly think I wouldn't want to know about your son?"

It was on the tip of his tongue to ask which son she meant, but he remembered in time the grand scheme he had concocted just that morning for easing Plum into the knowledge that she was now stepmother to five hellions, a plan necessitated by the fact that said children had set the vicar's carriage alight while the vicar was examining the special license Harry had presented him. She seemed to be pleased with McTavish—then again, it wasn't her shin the little monster had assaulted—which boded well for the future. If he spread out introductions to the children over the next few weeks, relying upon Gertie and George and the rest of the staff to keep the children out of sight, perhaps she wouldn't be too upset with them. And him. He particularly wanted her to be happy with him, because a happy wife was a wife who allowed her husband to do all sorts of wonderful things to her delicious, desirable person.

"He's adorable, he really is. How old is he?"

Harry looked down at the hand that was now softly caressing the middle of his chest, and was struck with a sudden desire to take each dainty fingertip into his mouth. "How old is who?"

She giggled. It was such a delightful, joyous sound, Harry wanted to giggle with her. He probably would have, except he'd never giggled before, and wasn't sure if he knew how.

"McTavish. How old is he?"

"He'll be six in December."

"He's sweet, and he looks just like you. You must be very proud of him."

Proud? Of McTavish? Harry dragged his mind back from the vision of what else Plum possessed that he'd like to taste, and thought about what she said. He owed her that much. Gentlemen did not feel lust for their wives. A gentleman might desire his lady, but he also appreciated her keen intellect. Lust was for lesser people, men who thought solely of their own base needs, and never those of the enticing woman before them. "The lad likes animals. Doesn't care if they're alive or dead, he likes them all. I suppose that's an admirable trait. Yes, I'm proud of him. Underneath the surface clay, there's good soil in him." Harry gave her a curious look. "You're not angry that I didn't tell you about him?"

"Angry?" She smiled again, one of those lovely, charming smiles that captured his heart and filled him with utter and complete lust . . . *desire*. And joy. There was lots and lots of joy, too. Much more joy than base physical desire. "No, I'm not angry. After all, you didn't know that Thom came with me when you offered to wed me."

"But I knew about her before we were married. Temple told me what you'd told him about your niece. You had the decency to tell me everything about you, whereas I—"

A sudden frown diminished the lust . . . *joy* running amok inside him. She nibbled her strawberry-ripe lower lip. "About that—"

He couldn't resist. He had to taste her lips just one more time. Her breath caught and held as he plunged into her sweet mouth, feeling himself harden even more as she moved against him, sliding her fingers into his hair, tasting him as he tasted her. She was heaven, she was bliss, she was—

"There you are. What are you doing in here? Gertie says I can't wear my hair up until I'm fifteen, but I think—oh."

Harry could have cried, he could have sat right down on the floor and cried. He tore his lips from Plum's, smugly satisfied by the misted passion in her eyes, then released her so he could glare at his daughter. She wasn't supposed to be here. He had her down for an introduction to Plum tomorrow at tea.

India was examining his new wife, her brows drawn together, her hands on her hips in a pose that was very much like Beatrice's whenever she had been displeased with him. "Is that her, then?"

He frowned. McTavish might not know better, but India certainly did. "Plum, this young woman who has apparently lost her manners is India, my daughter."

"A daughter." Plum blinked a couple of times, but didn't demand an immediate annulment, something Harry was profoundly thankful for. "You have a daughter. Named India. What an unusual name. Good evening, India. It is a pleasure to make your acquaintance."

He could have kissed Plum, he was so grateful. She didn't rail at him, she didn't accuse him of not being truthful about the children, she just cast him a curious glance, and went forward to give India one of those polite little hugs that women who don't know one another well give each other. Yes, she deserved to be kissed, and he was just the man to see the job done.

"You're Plum?" India asked, her eyes meeting Harry's in surprised horror as Plum hugged her.

Kissing his wife was his duty, after all.

Plum stepped back and divided a bright, sunny smile between India and him. "Yes, I'm Plum. Your father didn't . . . er . . . that is, I hadn't expected to meet you tonight, but I'm so glad you came in to say hello."

Kissing her would tell her just how much he approved of and appreciated her.

"We must have a good long chat in the morning. I know some very fetching hairstyles that I'm sure will make you even prettier than you already are."

Oftentimes, kissing led to other, more full-bodied experiences.

"My niece Thom will want to meet you, as well. Thom has curly hair, like yours. I'm sure she'll have some advice as to the best way to wear it."

Plum liked kissing him, therefore, he would be selfish to keep such a pleasure from her. Cruel, even. Harry was not a cruel man. He might not be madly in love with Plum, but he liked her, and he wanted her happy and sated. Particularly sated. Although happy was good, too.

"Papa?" India said, her eyes huge as Plum lifted her braid and wrapped it in a coronet on the top of her head, prattling all the while about hair-related subjects that were so dear to the female heart.

"Yes," Harry said, agreeing to whatever it would take to get India out of the room and Plum into his bed.

"Yes?" India dipped away from Plum, unwinding her braid and giving his wife an outraged look.

"Yes." He glanced at Plum. Both of her deliciously straight brows were raised in mute surprise. Evidently yes wasn't the answer she expected him to give. "No," he corrected himself. Plum's eyebrows lowered to their normal straight line. He smiled at her, pleased he got the answer right.

"Papa!" India gasped as Harry grabbed her arm. He opened the door to the hallway, and still smiling at Plum, tugged his daughter out. "Papa, you didn't even hear—"

"We had an agreement, didn't we?" Harry whispered, leaning close to India's ear. "You agreed not to disturb me tonight for anything short of death, dismemberment, or the apocalypse, and in return I will buy you the Hamilton's gray mare with white stockings. That was our agreement. I have your signed statement, which I do not hesitate to point out is binding in any court of law."

"Yes, but—"

Harry gave her his best annoyed father look, the one he kept in reserve for emergencies. India, an intelligent little whelp, knew that she hadn't a leg to stand on, and after uttering a word he would take up with her another time, and stomping her foot perilously close to his bare toes, she huffed off. Harry lost no time in zipping back into the bedchamber, and resuming the activities that had twice been so grievously interrupted. He didn't even give Plum time to say anything other than a startled, "Harry!" before he was engaged in a tactile exploration of her wonderfully warm, wet mouth.

"India says you're getting the gray mare for her.

You said you'd get me a horse as soon as we were settled! I'm an earl, she's just a lady. *I* should have the next horse."

Harry pulled back until his lips just brushed Plum's as he spoke. "That's my oldest son, Digger, Lord Marston. Ignore him and he'll go away."

He tried to possess her lips again, but she slipped out of his arms. "Digger?"

"It's short for Diggory. You're Plum. India said you were scrawny and you touched her hair. She doesn't like to be touched. She's a girl," Digger said, as if that explained it all.

Harry fought back the desire to throttle his son and heir—he had other sons, as he had pointed out to Digger on many occasions—and prepared to explain the situation to his wife.

She was looking at Digger with pursed lips, a look she transferred to him. "Another son. Exactly how many children do you have, my lord?"

He winced at the "my lord." Her tone had gone from warm and arousing, to cold and suspicious in the matter of a few seconds.

"Er . . . at last count I had—"

The door to the hallway was slammed open, Anne and Andrew rolling through the doorway in an angry assortment of elbows, knees, and feet.

"It's mine! It has the blue top, that's mine! Yours is the one with the yellow top!" Andrew jerked a small wooden boat out of Anne's hands.

She got to her knees and punched her twin in his belly. "Stupid! Mine is the blue one, yours is yellow!"

"—five children."

"Five?"

"MINE!" Andrew kicked out with both of his

legs, one of which clipped Anne on the jaw. She yelped and dived onto him, her fists and feet flying.

"That's Anne and Andrew. They're twins," Digger said helpfully.

"Yes, that's correct, just the five children," Harry said with a weak smile at Plum.

The twins barreled into the dressing table, knocking over various bottles and pots of feminine unguents and scents that Temple had purchased upon Harry's order. A box of powder exploded as the table went flying, filling the air with a rose-scented cloud while twin sapphire blue bottles holding extremely expensive scents crashed onto the floor, spilling their contents onto the rose and damask rug. Various small pots scattered, disgorging their contents as well. Anne and Andrew began to cough, having gulped in rose powder–laden air. Andrew pulled Anne's hair. She bit his hand. Digger sauntered over to Plum and told her he didn't think she was scrawny at all, she just needed a bit of fattening up.

Harry closed his eyes for a second, praying that when he opened them again, he would be alone with his wife. That failing, he prayed he'd come up with a good enough explanation to keep her from walking out on him.

The sound of glass breaking stirred him into action. "Out!" he bellowed, grabbing the back of Andrew's nightgown in one hand, the back of Anne's with another, pulling them apart and sending them with none too gentle pushes toward the door.

"Out!" he roared again, pointing at the door as he glared at Digger. "And take the twins with you."

"I still want a horse," Digger said, but at least he

managed to get the twins, still fighting, out the door so Harry could slam it shut. He also locked it. Without glancing at Plum he hauled the fainting couch over to the door, just to be sure they couldn't get in.

"Five," Plum said when he finally turned to face her.

All his words of explanation, all his entreaties for her understanding melted before the one cocked eyebrow and the arms crossed over her delicious chest. His hopes of a wondrous, erotic night spent exploring the ways of marital harmony withered into dust, and blew out the window on a faint waft of rose powder.

He rallied a feeble smile, and tried very hard not to cry. "Yes, well, five always has been my lucky number."

Chapter Five

Plum awoke to the uncomfortable feeling that she was being watched. She opened her eyes. She was being watched. Circled around the bottom of her bed, five pairs of eyes stared steadily at her as she pushed her heavy hair out of her eyes, and propped herself up on her elbow. The youngest of Harry's sons, the boy oddly named McTavish, squirmed out from under India's restraining hand and jumped onto the bed next to Plum.

"You're awake now, aren't you? India said I wasn't to wake you up, but your eyes are open now so you're awake. I want a kitten. I have a dead rat. Would you like to see it?"

"No, thank you, McTavish. I try to maintain a strict policy of entertaining no dead rats before breakfast. It's not easy, but life is nothing if not a challenge. What are you all doing in here?"

"Waiting for you to wake up," Digger said.

"Why aren't you sleeping with Papa?" India asked, her lips tight with suspicion. "Gertie said the reason Papa wanted to get married was so he wouldn't get lonely in bed. You're supposed to keep him from being lonely. Gertie said so. Why aren't you?"

Plum closed her eyes for a few seconds before sitting up and facing the bright faces watching her so carefully. "To be honest, I don't feel up to a detailed explanation of my intimate relationship with your father, but as you are obviously concerned about his happiness, I can reassure you that although the situation last night was not one conducive to . . . er . . . keeping him from being lonely, I have every intention of seeing to that task tonight. Will that suffice?"

"I want a kitten. You said I could have one this morning."

"Our *real* mother slept in the same bed as Papa," India said accusingly.

"I don't *want* a new mama," Anne said, then disappeared as she dropped to the floor. Peering over the side of the bed, Plum could see Anne's legs where they stuck out from under the bed.

"I want a mama, I want a mama," McTavish chanted, bouncing up and down on the bed in time with his words. "I want a kitten, I want a kitten."

"That's mine!" Andrew said, and immediately jumped his twin as she emerged with a pretty blue and pink chamber pot. "I saw it first!"

"Our *real* mother took care of Papa. She wouldn't let him be lonely."

"A kitten, a kitten! I want a kitten!"

"It is not, I saw it first! It's mine. You have to find your own."

"Our *real* mother made sure Papa was dressed warmly when he went out in the cold, and took a draught whenever he was sick."

"Mine, Annie!"

"Papa never *was* sick," Digger told his sister. She glared at him, her arms tight across her chest, her nostrils flaring in that particularly effective way young women of three and ten had of expressing their contempt.

"He would have taken a draught if he was sick. Mama would have made him."

Digger gave way before such reasoning. He nodded. "Yes, he would have."

"Kitten, kitten, kitten, kitten."

Plum, starting to get a headache from all of McTavish's bouncing, clutched him to her chest. "I appreciate the fact that none of you wish to have a new mother—"

"I want a new mama," McTavish told her shoulder, squirming to get free. Plum loosened her grip just enough so he could sit next to her and play with the long, inky tendrils of hair that curled around him.

"Thank you, McTavish, I appreciate that."

"I want one, too," Digger said unexpectedly. "And so do the twins, don't you?"

Andrew, in the process of wresting the chamber pot—thankfully unused—from his sister's grip, didn't look up as he nodded. "Yes."

"No, you don't, *I* want one," Anne snarled as she stomped on her brother's foot, crowing in triumph when he yelped and released the chamber pot.

"I thought she said otherwise," Plum asked as

Anne raced out of the room, her prize hugged to her chest. Andrew was directly on her heels, yelling at her that she was a thief to take his pretty pot.

"Oh, that's just the twins. They never agree on anything," Digger said, then started for the door. "Come on, Tavvy, George said she heard that one of the bulls' tails fell off during the night. If we're fast, maybe we can find it before the stable boys do."

"I want a bull tail!" McTavish said as he scrambled across the top of Plum to follow after his brother. "I want a kitten and a bull tail."

Plum blinked at India, who was still frowning at her. "Is it like this every morning, or are you all being unusually bizarre on my behalf?"

India unfolded her arms and marched toward the door. "My *real* mother didn't have black hair. My *real* mother was pretty, and blonde like me, and she didn't touch me when I didn't want to be touched."

Plum sat back against the headboard as the door slammed behind India, blowing out a breath she hadn't realize she had been holding. "You wanted children, well now you have them. Only, what am I do to with five grown children? Babies I could handle, but *children* children . . . hoo!"

The room held no answer for her. Since she didn't want to frighten her maid by asking her any more rhetorical questions, she washed in the water that had been left for her, and with the practice of one who has long tended to herself, slipped into the nicest gown she owned. She was just braiding her hair when there was a knock at her door.

"India said you were awake. I thought I would see

71

how you enjoyed your first night of marital bliss."
Thom entered the room, her arched eyebrow (Plum
had gnashed her teeth many times at the lovely natural arch in Thom's eyebrows) and coy smile an in-
dicator of what sort of an answer she expected.

"I slept quite well, thank you, although not due to
any activities that you are perilously close to smirk-
ing about. And while we're on that subject, I will remind you again that unmarried young ladies of good
family do not allude to matters that are unsuitable."

Thom blew her a kiss and opened the door.
"You're so adorable when you're prudish. Since you
are obviously hale and hearty, I will see you later.
I'm going to investigate Harry's stables. He appears
to have excellent taste in horses. . . ."

Before Plum could do anything more than sputter,
"Prudish! I've never been prudish a day in my life!"
Thom was gone. Plum gave her hair a final pat,
spent three minutes wishing she had a nice gown in
which to greet her new husband, and set off to begin her life as wife and mother.

"Good morning, er . . ." Plum hesitated in the
great hall, unable to recall the butler's name. Her introductions to the staff the previous night had been
so quickly conducted, she had nothing more than an
impression of a heavy Spanish accent, sultry, flashing black eyes, and extremely white teeth against
dark skin.

"I am Juan Immanuel Savage Tortugula Diaz de
Arasanto, and you are my oh, so very, very lady."

"Very, very lady?" Plum extracted her hand from
where the handsome Spaniard was bending over it.

"Yes, you are so very." Juan the butler waggled his

eyebrows at her in what she assumed was meant to be a seductive manner.

She fought back the desire to giggle at him, and instead asked, "Yes, well, Arasanto, have you seen his lordship this morning?"

"One."

"You saw him at one this morning?"

He gave her a very polished leer. "No, Juan. It is my name. You may call me Juan rather than Arasanto. It is preferred, yes?"

Plum took a deep breath and reminded herself that no matter how much she might like to either burst into hysterical laughter, or scream, neither were actions suitable to a new marchioness. "I see. Very well, Juan, do you know where my husband is?"

He shrugged and pointed his thumb over his shoulder toward a narrow, dark passage. "Harry is probably hiding in his office."

"Harry?" Plum asked, a little surprised by a servant addressing his master by his first name.

"He asks me to call him that because he calls me Juan, eh?"

"Oh. I see. Yes, well . . . um . . . thank you." Plum started toward the passage, but found her way blocked by the amorous Spaniard.

"You would like for me to show you around the house first, eh? I have many things of interest to show you." His eyebrows waggled at her again.

Plum knew she should be offended or angry with such blatant flirting by a servant, but she found herself oddly amused by Juan. He was so sure of his charm, so obvious about his innuendoes, she couldn't help but smile. "Thank you, but I will have my husband—your employer—show me around the house. I'm sure he, too, has many interesting things to show me."

"He is old, that one. I am young and how it's said, virile."

"He's not that old," Plum laughed. "And considering he has five children, I would hazard that his virility is not in doubt."

Juan shuddered and crossed himself. "Santa Maria, those ones are spawned by the devil himself."

"Oh, come now, they're a bit high spirited, but they aren't really that bad." Plum sidled around Juan while he was busy rolling his eyes. "A little untamed, perhaps, but that is no doubt due to having been without a mother for the last few years. I quite like them."

Juan grabbed her hand as she moved past him, bowing over it again, brushing his lips against her knuckles before Plum yanked her hand back. "It is because you have not been here with them that you think they are the angels. They are not. And now, most very lady, I will return to my duties. You are mistress here now, you will want to speak to me later about my duties, yes? I will await your pleasure in the pantry of butlers." His black, liquid eyes sent her a message that was unmistakable. Plum's lips twitched as she struggled to keep from giggling. She hurried down the dark passage, wondering how on earth Harry had come to employ such a bold butler, when his words sank in.

"What can Harry be hiding from, I wonder?" she mused as she approached a door. She entered a small, extremely tidy room and smiled at the man

sitting behind a desk piled high with books and papers. "Good morning, Mr. Harris. Can you tell me
where I might find Lord . . . merciful St. Genevieve,
what was that?"

The loud crash that came from the hallway made
Plum jump. She turned back to the secretary, expecting him to leap up and investigate.

"His lordship is through the door to your right. If
you could possibly convince him to allow his room
to be cleaned, I would be eternally grateful."

Plum stared at him as if he had horns growing
from his head. "Didn't . . . didn't you hear the
crash? From the hall? Shouldn't you investigate?"

Temple tipped his head to the side as he considered her. "No. I've found it's much safer not to be
too curious about those sorts of things."

"Safer?" Plum gaped at him, positively gaped,
and she was not a woman who took gaping lightly.
"But . . . but . . . the children could be injured!"

Temple pursed his lips and listened for a moment,
then shook his head and went over to the door leading to Harry's room. "No, no one is hurt. We'd hear
screaming by now if one of his lordship's little darlings were injured. They're very vocal."

"Well, surely *someone* should inquire as to what
happened? Surely *someone* would like to ascertain
just what caused such a horrifying sound?"

Temple eyed her curiously. "I wouldn't advise it,
ma'am. His lordship has found that a strict policy of
unenlightenment is the best for all concerned."

Plum snorted. She hated to do so in front of Temple after so short an acquaintance, but she felt such
an extreme action was called for. "You cannot make

me believe that a man as fond of his children as Harry is would not wish to investigate the noise we just heard."

"As you say, ma'am."

Plum thinned her lips at him. "You're patronizing me, Mr. Harris. I dislike being patronized."

"That thought was the farthest from my mind, you can be assured. I simply wish to inform you that about this, I am well familiar with his lordship's habits."

"Prove it."

His eyebrows rose in surprise. "I beg your pardon?"

"Prove to me that Harry won't want to know what's going on out in the hall. Ask him."

Temple opened the door for her and waved her into the room. A second, less loud crash echoed from the hall. She cocked an eyebrow at Temple and marched into a dimly lit chamber so dusty her nose tickled. At the far end of the long room, with his back to a pair of filthy windows, her husband sat reading a letter.

"Sir," Temple said from the doorway when Harry didn't acknowledge them.

"Mmm?" He didn't raise his eyes from the letter.

Plum looked him over carefully, this man she had married and more or less thrown out of her bedchamber the evening before. His sandy hair was mussed and disordered, as if he had combed it with his fingers, the one rogue lock of hair having fallen over his brow. The planes of his long face were thrown into interesting shadows, the bright gold of his spectacles glinting in the sunlight that bullied its way through the grimy fly-specked windows. This was the man she had bound herself to for the rest of her life. The man who had neglected to tell her about his five children. The man about whom she had built up so many dreams and hopes—or as many dreams and hopes as one could arouse in just two days. This was the man with whom she wished to indulge in many, many connubial calisthenics, the man who would twine his heart and soul (not to mention legs and arms) around hers, the man who would complete her, make her whole, give her what she wanted more than anything in the world. . . .

"Your wife, sir."

"What about her?" Harry asked, still reading his letter, one long finger tapping on his lower lip as he read. At the sight of that finger stroking the curve of his lip, Plum remembered, with an unmaidenly flash of heat to her womanly parts, just how wonderful his mouth felt on hers.

"She would like to know if you are curious about the specifics concerning the two"—another crash, this one followed by a hoarse shout and peals of childish laughter, interrupted Temple—"three indicators of an accident from the hall."

"Why would I be foolish enough to want to know that?" Harry asked, his gaze on the letter as he took a pen from the holder and flipped open the top to an inkwell.

Temple glanced apologetically at her. "I believe your lady feels that you might wish to make sure that one of the children hasn't injured himself or herself."

Plum nodded, wondering greatly whether or not returning to bed and starting the day over would help. She reckoned it wouldn't.

"Don't be ridiculous, Temple," Harry said absently, making a notation on the letter. "If one of them was hurt, there would be screaming and blood and such."

Then again, it couldn't hurt.

"Harry."

He looked up, the adorable lock of hair hanging over his equally adorable brow, his eyes dark and shadowed behind the glass lenses. "Plum! You're . . . er . . . up."

Temple quietly left the room, closing the door behind him as Plum walked toward the desk, glancing at the variety of objects lining the tables and bookcases. "Yes, I've found that if I really put my mind to it, I often manage to arise before the sun has set for the day. Good morning, Harry."

"Oh, er . . ." Harry stood up, more than a little bit flustered, Plum was delighted to see. He pushed back his spectacles, leaving a smear of blue ink on the bridge of his nose. Her fingers itched to push the lock of hair back from his brow as he tugged on his neckcloth (leaving blue smudges on it, too), greeting her with a hesitant (but needless to say, adorable) smile. "Good morning. How did you . . . er . . . sleep?"

Plum sighed to herself. There was no avoiding the fact, Harry was just all-around adorable. "Quite well, the bed is very comfortable. I did, however, have a complaint concerning my bedchamber."

"Oh?" Harry came around the edge of the desk and pulled back a chair for her. Two apples, a number of crumpled neckcloths, and a small brown-and-black salamander tumbled from the mass of papers that sat on the chair. "What—just ignore the salamander, it's one of McTavish's pets, it's harmless, I'm quite sure. Temple's story about it biting off one of the footmen's fingertips is nothing but the grossest sort of fiction—what did you find lacking?"

Plum took a deep breath, and reminded herself that she was neither a shy virgin nor a woman inexperienced with men and the intimate acts they did with their wives. She knew thirteen different standing positions alone for said intimate acts, and women who knew such things did not blush when they were mentioned in casual conversation. She was a mature, rational woman. Harry was her husband. She very much looked forward to investigating his person in a thorough and lengthy manner. She might even take notes about things he particularly enjoyed. She would not, under any circumstances, act maidenish.

Harry's eyes narrowed as he peered into her face. "Are you well? You look flushed, as if you have a fever."

"I'm quite fine," she answered, ignoring the fact that her cheeks were so hot she could probably fry an egg or two on them. "What I found lacking in my bedchamber last night was your presence."

Harry looked confused. "You threw me out of the room."

Drat the man, he would have to remember that point. "Yes, I did, but I didn't mean it."

One dark brown eyebrow rose over the top of the spectacles. "Ah. That would be why you said, and I believe I'm quoting you accurately, 'You deceiving mongrel of a man! You have five children and you never told me? Five? F-I-V-E, five?'"

Plum's blush, to her everlasting mortification, deepened even more. She avoided looking into his lovely, changeable eyes and glared at the dirty window, instead. "I might have said that, but I was a bit upset at the time—"

"Following which, you marched over to the door leading to my room, threw it open, and with a dramatic gesture that would have done Sarah Siddon proud, informed me that I might go to my own room, or to the devil, whichever I preferred so long as I removed myself from your presence."

She made a moue of irritation. "I have often found people with exceptionally good memories to be the worst sort of annoying—"

"I might have been left in some doubt as to what, exactly, your thoughts were on the subject of our marriage, but the fact that you almost brained me with your hairbrushes—"

"They were very small hairbrushes! They couldn't possibly have done any damage more than perhaps a slight bruise or two, although I do concede that if you were not wearing your spectacles, and if the handle was to have lodged in your eye, it might have put it out."

"—as you swore to the Lord Almighty that you never, ever wanted to see me again."

She closed her eyes for a second. How could she have been so stupid? Why had she flown off the hook at him like that? She of all people had no right to be angry at him for having concealed from her something about his past. " 'Never, ever' might have been a slight exaggeration—"

"Plum."

Her gaze dropped to her hands clasped before her as she refused to look at him, too embarrassed to bear seeing the condemnation in his eyes. She truly was a coward. "I'm sorry, Harry. I thought I could do this, but I'm obviously too—"

"Plum, look at me."

Slowly, with reluctance her gaze rose to meet his. Her throat tightened and several odd, butterfly-like things set up fluttering in her stomach. He was smiling at her, smiling a wonderful smile, not with just his lips, but with his eyes too. He took her hands, then bent to kiss the backs of each. Her hands glowed warm under the touch.

"You had every right to be angry with me. I don't blame you at all for ejecting me from your room. I just hope that now that you know the worst, you'll consent to remain my wife. I admit that it's not a particularly good deal on your part, but I would like you to stay. Lord knows the servants could use a mistress—they never seem to know how to do their jobs, or even what their jobs are. And the children are wild, not bad-tempered, just wild. They need you as well."

Plum smiled at the earnest, hopeful look in his eyes and tightened her fingers around his. "And you, my lord? What do you need?"

"A friend," he said, his voice suddenly husky as he drew her closer to him. "A companion. A lover." She was against his chest, her hands sliding up the fine green cloth of his jacket, his muscles bunching as he pulled her tight against him. His lips teased hers, nipping at her lower lip, tasting the corners of her mouth, pressing little butterfly kisses along the length of her lips until her head swam. Harry's voice was rough, thick with desire as he said, just before he accepted the invitation offered by her parted lips, "A wife."

Plum, thinking wicked thoughts about using Harry's desk in a manner she did not doubt would surprise him, prepared to surrender to his worshipful mouth when another, closer crash shook the windows behind Harry.

"Damnation," he snarled as he pulled his lips from hers. "Temple!"

Reminding herself that she was now the children's mother, and thus the likely person to investigate household accidents, she reluctantly pulled herself from Harry's arms. "I should probably see what's amiss."

"No, you stay. Temple, what's going on out there? Why can't I have a single moment of solitude? Is it too much to ask for a man to read his letters in peace and quiet?"

"No, sir," Temple replied, casting a quick glance over his shoulder. "It would appear that a bull, sadly lacking in the tail department, has made its way into the hall. I will see to it that it is removed immediately."

"Don't bother, I'll do it," Plum said, giving him a smile. "After all, I'm mistress here now. If anyone is responsible for removing livestock from the house, I suppose it is me." She turned back to Harry, suddenly shy despite the fact that a few moments before she was entertaining his tongue in a most intimate manner. "Will I see you later?"

He gave her a heated look that left no confusion over just how much she'd see of him later, then kissed her hands again. "You're an angel, Plum, the answer to my prayers. I leave the children in your capable hands, confident that you will restore peace and sanity to my house. You are exactly what we need. I will see you at luncheon . . . no, blast, I won't either. I had a letter this morning that I must attend to . . . er . . . business. You will forgive me?"

He cupped her jaw, pulling her closer. Plum knew if she got within kissing distance of him, she would wrestle him to the floor and have her way with him, so she slipped backward and gave him what she hoped was a dazzling smile (but feared was more a lustful leer). "Yes, certainly. Dinner, then. I will see you for dinner . . . and after."

His eyes blazed hot, hot enough to leave her whole body flushed and aching for him. He swallowed twice and nodded. She blew him a little kiss, then scampered from the room when he looked like he was going to lunge toward her. Temple, who had been politely gazing at a picture on the wall, held the door open for her. She whisked through his room, filled with hope and desire and happiness.

"Temple—you don't mind if I call you that? Thank you—Temple, I have a very good feeling." Plum opened the door to the passage. A medium-sized bull thundered past the door, followed by two large dogs, a pheasant, and the twins. "Today marks the beginning of a new life for all of us."

McTavish raced by, dragging the carcass of a rat tied to a string.

"I will deal with everything life throws my way, and I will conquer it."

"God help you, my lady," Temple said. "I believe you're going to need all the help you can get."

The salamander scampered over her foot, and ran out the door.

Plum sighed. "I fear you're right."

Chapter Six

Harry fought a short battle with his body, which desperately wanted to scoop Plum up in his arms and carry her off to his bedroom, where he would apply himself to keeping her in a state of absolute pleasure for as long as his strength held out, but he reminded himself—particularly those errant parts of his body that were at that moment straining against his clothing—that he was not an animal, he was a gentleman, and gentlemen did not act as if they were stallions around a mare in heat.

It was touch-and-go there for a few minutes as to whether he would throw his honor to the wind and go straight to stallionhood, but in the end, his better nature won out. He willed his arousal to think of something unpleasant like stagnant cesspools and bloated corpses, then sat back down to consider the letter he'd received an hour before.

"Temple!"

His secretary came before the echoes had died down.

"You bellowed, sir?"

"Yes, I did. I want your advice."

Temple allowed a surprised expression to dance across his face. "You want *my* advice?"

"Yes. Sit down, this is going to take some explaining. Some time just before I married Beatrice I was brought up on charges of treason. I believe I mentioned it to you?"

"Yes, sir, you did." Temple's lips thinned. "The charges were false, and you were released."

Harry leaned back in his chair, propping his feet up on the corner of his desk. "Of course they were false, I was working for the Home Office at the time, under direct command of the prime minister. I was the bait used to catch whoever was using the Home Office to stir up insurrection and anarchy."

Temple said nothing, but his eyes glowed with the light of admiration and excitement. "I assume that you found the person?"

"Yes, I did. I was almost hung in the process, but all that got sorted out once I determined that the mastermind behind the plot to overthrow the government was none other than the head of the HO, Sir William Stanford."

"But . . . he was your employer, was he not?" Temple asked.

Harry nodded. "He was. I worked for him for years, never guessing that he was using his own position to feed information to anarchists."

"Good Lord!" Temple's face was a picture of captivation. "What happened to Sir William? Were the anarchists captured? And how did you end up in prison for treason?"

Harry opened a small cedar box situated at the far edge of his desk and extracted a thin brown cigar. He waved his hand toward the box in invitation as he lit the cheroot, settling back with the air of one who has a riveting tale to tell. "Sir William took his own life as soon as I discovered his perfidy. The anarchists were caught, and the leaders hung. I was jailed for treason because Sir William had set me up as a scapegoat, manufacturing a convincing case against me with the help of the anarchists. He knew I was getting too close to the truth, you see, and it had come to his ears that the PM was aware that there was someone high up in the Home Office who was betraying the government, so Stanford decided I would be offered up as a sacrifice."

"Fascinating," Temple said, carefully tapping his ash into the receptacle provided. "I take it the letter you received today has some bearing on that incident?"

"Exactly." Harry dropped his feet to the ground and leaned forward to frown at the letter. "This is from the Lord Briceland, the new head of the HO. He says some information has come to light recently to hint that Stanford might not have been working alone, and he'd like me to go over my documents and papers with an eye to finding proof of a second person's involvement."

"That sounds as if it will involve quite a bit of work."

"It will." Harry sighed, then picked up his pen. "I'll want you to write to Crabtoes and have him dig out my records at Rosehill. Have him send them to me here, as fast as possible. Then I'll need you to help me sort through the papers I have here. I don't have much that is pertinent to that time, but I recall seeing a box of my notes somewhere when we moved. Oh, and don't forget to send in that announcement to the *Times*."

Temple put out his cigar, carried it over to the fireplace, and disposed of both ashes and cigar, wiping out the glass bowl with his handkerchief before returning it to Harry's desk. "Your marriage announcement?"

"Yes. It will save me from having to write to all my friends, and Plum will probably want her friends and family to know about it. Blast! Just when I wanted to spend some time reveling in my wife's charms, I must spend my days pouring over fifteen-year-old notes. . . ."

"I should very much like to know exactly how the bull found itself in the house. Would one of you like to tell me?"

Erk, erk, chirruped the pheasant. Plum gave it a look to let it know she didn't appreciate its opinion, and honed her look to a glare. She sent it down the line of servants and children who stood before her.

"Well? Doesn't someone have something to say?"

The ten pairs of eyes regarding her displayed nothing but innocence, innocence so great, it would make the cherubim themselves feel in the need of a good purging.

Plum sighed. "Very well, if you wish to be difficult about this. Gertie?"

An older woman with brown hair flecked with gray nodded her head.

"You're in charge of the children, are you not?"

"Aye . . . well, I was until 'is lordship married ye, and now yer in charge o' the little buggers."

Plum fought down a feeling of panic at that thought. They were only children, and she had lots of experience with Cordelia's children over the years—experience playing with them, that is, in situations which she knew full well Cordelia would never allow her to suggest romps that might prove to be unsuitable or dangerous. Now, however, she was in Cordelia's position, and she felt sadly at a loss as to what she should and shouldn't do with the children. After a morning's concerted and uncomfortable thought on the subject, she had decided that she would be their friend, helping them, guiding them, mentoring them without being too strict or having to dole out punishment.

That was, after all, what a father was for.

"Just so. However, you have more experience with them than I do, therefore you must have some idea how a bull was let into the house."

The woman named George—a misnomer if ever there was one, since a lovelier, more curvaceous woman Plum had never seen, not even her dull gray gown and stained apron could dim her charms—raised her hand. "Through the door?"

Digger snickered. India rolled her eyes and looked bored as only a thirteen-year-old girl can look bored. Plum narrowed her glare onto them both.

"You wouldn't have something to tell me, would you, Digger?"

"Sure I do, I have lots of things to tell you. Joshua is a friendly sort, kind of like Nash."

Nash, she knew, was the pheasant. She had made its introduction earlier, when she and Juan rounded up the nursery staff, footmen, and children. "Joshua?"

"Joshua is the bull," Digger said. "He's friendly, see? He likes McTavish, so when we came in from hunting for Joshua's tail—"

"I found a bull tail!" McTavish said happily, holding up a withered black object that looked more like a dehydrated snake than a tail. "Can I have a kitten now? You said I could."

Plum raised an eyebrow at Digger and tipped her head slightly toward McTavish. Digger shook his head. She sent a silent prayer of gratitude that she would not be called on to admire the replacement bull's tail, and continued with her morning guidance to the children. "That explains how Joshua might have come into the hall, but how is it that he broke three very expensive looking urns, and put his horns through the door to the necessary?"

Anne and Andrew giggled, realized they were both laughing at the same thing, and changed their giggles to glares.

"The urns weren't expensive, ma'am," George said. The other servants nodded. "His lordship wouldn't put anything expensive in the hall."

Plum frowned. "He wouldn't?"

"No, ma'am. He knows, you see."

"He does."

"Yes'm. About the children."

"Ah." Plum added an extra point or two to her

opinion of Harry's intelligence, and moved on. "About the door—"

"Tavvy was in the necessary," Digger—evidently spokesman for the children—said. India sat at the end of the blue sofa across from Plum ignoring them all, obviously pretending she was a thousand miles away.

"Nash had to use the pot," McTavish said, teasing the pheasant with his dried snake cum bull tail.

Plum successfully removed the image from her mind of a pheasant using a chamber pot, and bravely forged onward. "Since we are all friends here, we'll let this morning's incident go without further comment."

Several of the members of staff sighed with relief, and slouched back against the wall. Plum eyed them all. "I realize that I am a new member of the family, but I really must put my foot down about the entertaining of livestock inside the house. Henceforth, all animals that are not pets will remain outside. Animals other than cats and dogs are not allowed to follow you inside. Do you all understand?"

"Yes," Andrew said, nodding.

"No," Anne said, shaking her head.

Digger shrugged.

Gertie and George exchanged glances.

Juan threw himself to his knees before Plum, one hand on his chest, the other outstretched toward her. "The Holy Mother pours blessings on your head, Lady Plump. The bull, he causes much mess in the hall that the boys and I must clean. Last week it was peacocks. Before that, pigeons." He shuddered and sent her a look of sultry invitation from under half-closed eyes, a look so blatant it would have shocked a harem girl.

Plum ignored him. "Thom, dear, do you have my memorandum pad? Thank you. Oh, have you all met my niece, Miss Fraser?"

Several heads nodded.

"Excellent. Gertie, you and George may return to the nursery. Juan—yes, thank you, I appreciate your gratitude, but I really don't think that kissing my boots is presenting quite the appearance of dignity that the butler of a marquis should strive for—you and the footman may return to cleaning up the damage from the bull." Plum waited until the servants filed from the room, Juan bringing up the rear, his handsome face arranged in a seductive little pout that would have melted the heart of a lesser woman.

"Now, children, as I've always felt it's best to begin as you mean to go, I have made some notes this morning about what constitutes acceptable behavior, and how I expect each of you to—"

There was a mad rush for the door, the children fleeing from the room in a flurry of pheasant feathers, petticoats, and flashing black boots.

"—behave. . . . Well, drat it all!" Plum stared in mingled dismay and annoyance as the door slammed shut behind McTavish. Before she had a chance to say anything else, the door opened again and the youngest of her new brood stuck his head back into the room.

"Kitten," he reminded her.

Plum sighed, then felt her lips twitch as Thom's giggle turned to full-fledged whoops of laughter.

"Come along, Aunt. I'll walk with you and Mc-

Tavish to the stables. One of the stable cats has a litter that she's about ready to part with."

Plum thought about sighing again, but decided that too much sighing was the sign of a weak intellect, and she was only now coming to realize that she couldn't afford to show even the slightest sign of weakness before the children. Harry had left them in her hands, so she would just have to find the proper way to deal with them and make them behave. "I am their friend, I am their friend," she repeated to herself as she set her memorandum book on the table at the end of the couch and shook out her skirts.

McTavish stood watching her with hope, one pudgy little lip prepared to commence pouting if his objective of a kitten was thwarted. She smiled at him and held out her hand. "Shall we go find you a kitten, then?"

McTavish suffered her holding his hand, and led the way out of the house and down to the stables. On the way Plum made a mental note to send a letter to Cordelia asking her for tips and tricks for dealing successfully with the younger generation, and began to plan ways she would win over the children's hearts.

Harry entered the dining room and looked in surprise at the table set for nine. He was used to dining by himself or with Temple. The room was empty of all but Juan and Ben the first footman, both of whom were laying out a dining service Harry hadn't seen since Beatrice passed away. "Are we having a dinner party?"

Juan sent him a look filled with sympathy, and adjusted a lead crystal goblet infinitesimally to the left. Say what you will about Juan—and Harry had heard many things from every female he employed—the man knew how to set a table. "The Lady Plump, she says you are to have the *diablitos* to dinner."

"Little . . . oh, the little devils." Harry gave a wry smile of acknowledgment, glancing quickly at the dark red, water-stained wallpaper of the dining room. "Well, it might be for the best, Plum will want to redecorate anyway. The children dining in here will no doubt hasten her along that task."

Juan snorted something that Harry interpreted as disagreement. He pushed his spectacles up and tried to look like a supportive, confident husband. "We just have to trust that she knows best about these things. Where is she, do you know?"

Juan shrugged. "That is what I do not know. She was here an hour ago, telling us that we must set places for the *diablitos*, and then she left."

Harry tugged at his lower lip as he thought, then left the dining room. Perhaps Plum was having a rest before dinner. Perhaps she was spending a quiet hour in the room he had given over as her sitting room. Perhaps she was with Thom or India and Anne. Perhaps she was lying naked in his bed, waves of ebony hair surrounding her, waiting to entrap him in their silken strands. . . . He shook that last image out of his head and went to search for his wife.

He found her locked in one of the gardening sheds, filthy, hungry, and absolutely furious.

"Harry!" she shrieked when he opened the door to the shed, and fell into his arms in a most gratifying manner, trembling and shaking with what he assumed was horror and shock.

Once again his wife showed her unexpected depths.

"Where are they?" she growled, pushing himself back from his chest. "Where are those little . . . little . . ."

"Devils?"

"Yes! Exactly! Devils! What a very good word that is. Apt, too. Very apt."

She was magnificent in her fury, inky hair tumbling down from its once tidy braid, her eyes flashing with promised retribution, her cheeks pink with emotion. And she was all his, every last delectable morsel of her.

Morsels he was perilously close to losing unless he calmed her down and made her believe the children did not routinely lock people into garden sheds as pranks.

"They have been sent to the nursery without their suppers."

"Good," Plum snarled, and pushed past him to freedom, trying to tidy herself as they walked through the overgrown garden back to the house. "They don't deserve the nice dinner I planned. They locked me in there, Harry, trapped me with all the spiders and beetles and slithery things."

Harry tutted, and murmured sympathetic noises as he slid his hand around her waist, ostensibly to help her walk, but really because he just liked touching her.

"McTavish, the very same McTavish that I had just given a kitten to, lured me into the shed, then escaped out through the narrow space in the corner as the others locked me in."

"Ungrateful little monster."

"They're all ungrateful. They spurned my overtures of friendship, positively spurned them!"

"They don't deserve you, they really don't," Harry said soothingly, then could have bitten his tongue. The last thought he wanted to put in her mind was leaving him.

Plum froze for a moment at his words, then resumed her way to the house at a slower pace, one given more to deep thought. "Perhaps I was overhasty in my judgment. They're not bad children, not really."

Harry thought it best not to comment on that since he was a fairly honest man, one who disliked having to lie unless it was absolutely necessary.

"Truly, I believe they are more spirited than anything else," Plum said thoughtfully, the fire in her lovely dark eyes dying down to a mere smolder. "Spirit in children is something to be hoped for."

"As it is in a wife."

Plum turned her big velvety eyes upon him. "Yeeees," she said slowly, a faint frown between those glorious straight brows. She bit her lower lip, sending a flash of heat to Harry's groin as her small white teeth toyed with that delightful little pink lip. "I wouldn't want you to think I wasn't up to the task of mothering such high-spirited children. I am, I was just taken by surprise by their—"

"Nefarious plot to frighten you?" he suggested, having no false impression of just what were the children's true intentions.

"—cunning ability to create a detailed plot and see it through to its logical end," Plum finished with a small smile of triumph as they approached the house.

Harry held open the one working French door that led from the terrace to the room he had turned over to his wife. "Cunning . . . well, yes, I suppose that's one way of describing them. Plum"—he grabbed her hand as she was about to sweep through the room. Her fingers tightened on his as he stroked his thumb over the back of her hand, musing idly that it had been a very long time indeed when he had been aroused simply by holding a woman's hand—"you need not protect them, you know. I have already informed them that they will wait supperless until you have named their punishment for this afternoon's activities."

"Punishment?" Plum's frown increased as she worried her lip.

He nodded. "You can be assured that whatever discipline you desire for them will be carried out without regard to their entreaties for leniency or compassion."

"Discipline? You wish for me to discipline them?" she asked, her voice a little on the squeaky side.

"Of course. You were the one they injured, thus you must mete out justice. I've found if you don't look them in the eye when you pronounce their punishment, it helps. None of them seem to have difficulty summoning up tears, and they can be quite effective when combined with quivering lips."

"Tears," Plum repeated, a throb in her voice.

Harry wanted more than ever to kiss her at the sound. Could there be a woman more perfect for him? He allowed himself to kiss the back of her hand twice before opening the door to the hall, escorting her to the bottom of the curved oak staircase. "Just don't allow yourself to be swayed when they throw themselves at your feet and beg for mercy." Plum made an inarticulate noise in the back of her throat as he released her hand and started toward the dining room. "I will tell Juan to remove the children's places—"

"No!"

Harry stopped, startled by the vehemence in her objection. "No? Surely you do not wish to reward the little bu . . . devils by allowing them the honor of dining with us?"

Plum took a deep breath (an act he much appreciated considering the tight nature of her bodice) and clutched her hands together in mute appeal. "Please, Harry. I do so very much want us to be a family, and I thought when it was convenient, when no one is dining with us, the children could join us for dinner. My parents often let my sister and me have dinner with them, and I have many fond memories of those times. Please, please let the children join us."

Harry frowned, about to tell her that she was mistress of the house, and as such she did not need his approval regarding who she wanted at dinner, but stopped when she came forward and took his hands in hers.

"I promise you they will be well-behaved and no trouble. I'm sure they are very sorry for their little joke on me, and I hate to see them castigated over something so silly. Please let them join us. They won't be any bother, you'll see."

Harry disengaged a hand and ran his thumb over Plum's abused lower lip, every muscle in his body, every sinew, every iota of his being urging him to sweep her up in his arms and carry her off to his bed. He closed his eyes for a moment against the temptation she presented, fighting for control, one part of his mind amazed at how strongly he was reacting to her. It must be due to the accumulated loneliness (not to mention celibacy) of the past five years. There was no other reason he could be so violently attracted to a woman he'd met just a few days before.

Evidently Plum interpreted his silence not as a struggle of his mind against his body but as a disbelief in her abilities as a mother, for she clutched his hand between hers, squeezing it as she whispered, "Please."

He smiled, and kissed the worry right off her lips, just a short kiss, to be true, since he didn't trust himself with anything other than the most glancing contact with those delightful, seductive berry-kissed lips, but still, it was a kiss, and his body (already aroused by the wonderfully wicked fantasies he was having about her) reacted as if he had given the signal to charge. Without further ado he marched his traitorous body to the dining room, saying over his shoulder, "As you like, Plum. If you want the children to dine with us—and I'm under no misapprehension that they will be the least bit repentant for their act, not to mention ill-behaved—then they will dine with us. I will await you in the dining room." Seated, his bulging lap would be hidden by the lace tablecloth until such time as he regained control of himself, a time which, he mused as he paused long enough to watch her lift her skirt slightly and race up the stairs, would not probably not occur for at least six years. Possibly eighteen. With luck, never.

"Thank you, Harry," Plum called down to him as she reached the top. "It will be wonderful, you'll see!"

It would be a nightmare and he knew it, but he was willing to suffer anything to put that smile of joy on her face. Plum, he decided as he lunged painfully into the dining room, was the best thing that could possibly happen to his band of hellions. He just hoped they appreciated her before they drove her stark, staring mad.

Chapter Seven

"Is it wrong to think about torturing one's stepchildren?"

Edna the maid *eeeped*, and dumped the entire can of hot water on Plum's head, rather than dribbling it in a slow stream that would allow Plum to rinse the soap out of her hair. The maid stammered and backed away from the brass tub as Plum sputtered and frantically wiped soap from her eyes. Thom, quick thinking and not the least bit surprised by Plum's question, handed her a linen towel.

Plum thanked her and dabbed at her eyes, blinking away the sting of soap.

"I believe torture is frowned on these days, Aunt."

Edna made her escape while Plum rinsed her hair in the water that Thom poured over her head. "I'm not actually contemplating torturing them, as you well know. I just want to know if it's wrong to *think* about it. With much relish and enjoyment. Is it wrong to dwell lovingly over the various torments one wishes to inflict on the children who are trying—with no little success, I might add—to ruin one's marriage and life, or is it a natural sequence of events given the evening just spent? Thank you, dear, I think it's rinsed now. Did Edna leave?"

"Yes, a few moments ago. I think you're going to have to look for a new maid—she doesn't seem to be up to serving you."

Plum heard the smirk in Thom's voice rather than saw it. "Mmm."

"As for your thoughts of torture, I think perhaps you're overreacting a bit. It wasn't really that bad." Thom sat next to the small writing table, idly poking through Plum's journals and papers.

Plum turned in the tub to look back at her niece. "Overreacting? Not that bad? Have you lost your wits?"

"I don't believe so," Thom answered, extracting a small red leather-bound volume from the depths of the writing desk. She looked up to smile at Plum. "Yes, the piglet was a bit much, but as there was a bull in the hall earlier in the day, you shouldn't be surprised to find a piglet in the dining room."

"The only piglet I wish to see in the house is one that has been roasted with an apple in its mouth," Plum said tartly, and quickly finished her bath. She dried herself off before the cold fireplace, the heat of the day prohibiting a fire even for a bath. "The fact that they deliberately introduced a piglet into the house after I told them not to—" Plum paused long enough to bite back the harsh words she wanted to say. Ranting to Thom wasn't the answer to the problem. Plum slipped into her worn night rail, and sat by the opened window to dry her hair. "I just wish I knew what the answer was."

"The answer to what?" Thom asked absently, absorbed in her book.

"To the question of how I am to reach the children. They don't mind me in the least, and Harry has made it quite clear that he expects me to take charge of them and turn them from the wild, heedless imps they are into polite ladies and gentlemen, a task that is seeming more and more monumental with each passing hour."

"Oh, that." Thom turned a page and hummed softly to herself.

"It's no insignificant situation, Thom. Dinner this evening was a perfect example of just how unsuited I am for the role of mother to Harry's children, and if he thinks I can't control the children he has now, he'll never give me children of my own."

"Mmm," Thom said, her eyebrows rising as she glanced at the next page.

Plum finished toweling her hair, and began to comb the tangles out of the long black strands. Her hair was so thick, it was always a tedious job to comb it out after washing, but it was easier done damp than dry and full of snarls. "If the piglet in the room with all the children screaming and racing after it wasn't enough to convince him I am a poor mother, the situation later certainly was."

"Yes, but Harry did say the wallpaper needed replacement."

Plum thought back to the scene during dinner, giving a mental sigh. It was the mashed potatoes that had proved to be the children's undoing. After having ordered the removal of the piglet that had ("It just followed me in, honest!") trotted in on Andrew's heels, Plum had managed to get everyone seated without too much ado. She saved the lecture she was aching to read them for later, when Harry's hazel eyes weren't watching her. She extracted the dead snake from McTavish's grip and seated him next to her on a chair with several pillows, allowing the other children to select their own seats. Thom sat on Harry's left hand, while Temple sat across from McTavish, on her right.

"Well, isn't this lovely?" Plum asked, smiling at them all, pleased to see that the children had some sort of training in table manners. It never once entered her head that having dined exclusively on nursery fare, they were stupefied into silence by the vast array of food she'd ordered for their first dinner as a family. "Here we are, all together, just one very large happy family."

Harry, who had been giving his children gimlet glances, nodded without saying anything. Plum's heart fell a little at that wordless nod. Clearly his faith in her was still shaken by the garden shed incident. The dinner would show him how wrong he was to doubt her abilities as a mother. She kept her smile firmly in place as Juan and his footmen glided around the table in an efficient dance, offering dishes to her before moving down the table, assisting the children where needed.

"Digger, don't be a pig. Leave some for others," India said as he scooped an entire quartered capon off the serving tray, and deposited it onto his plate.

Plum, alert to possible signs of malcontent (and its more worrisome brother, outright trouble), saw

Harry turn a frown to his son and quickly stepped in before he could say anything. "Such a healthy appetite, Digger!" she said as she waved on Ben, the capon-bearing footman. "I'm sure Cook will be gratified to know that you find dinner so appealing."

"Huh," India sniffed, and took a dainty wing with a pointed look at Digger.

"Huh yourself," Digger replied, and stuffed a whole roll into his mouth. Harry, turned in the opposite direction to help himself to a portion of the remaining capon, missed the—somewhat amazing—event of Digger shoving a large dinner roll into his mouth, but the boy's bulging cheeks, not to mention the crumbs that sprayed the table before him as he chewed, could not be overlooked. Plum, racking her brain to think of something to distract Harry from the sight of Digger swallowing python-style large chunks of bread, helped herself to a spoon of mashed potatoes, and said—without thinking of possible repercussions of such a foolish statement— "Mashed potatoes! When I was a girl, my sister used to amuse me by making little sculptures out of her mashed potatoes. I can still remember the time she rendered Michelangelo's *David* into potato form."

Eight pairs of eyes stared at her as she ladled gravy over her capon and potatoes. Five pairs of those eyes, alight with sudden speculation, turned to the footman offering the potatoes. There was a brief tussle over who would be served first, resolved when Harry barked, "Sit down, all of you!"

"Children, please," Plum begged, worriedly noting the frown on Harry's face had settled in and looked like it was going to be there for a while. She hurried to correct their behavior before he had an opportunity to comment on the fact that they were out of control. "Andrew, dear, a gentleman does not punch a lady in the arm, no matter if she does poke you with a fork. Anne, do not poke people with silverware, even if they are closer to the potatoes than you. Digger, why don't you wait until your father says grace before . . . oh, never mind. William, would you please bring more beets? It seems Lord Marston has a fondness for them."

Harry cast a disbelieving glance at the huge mound of food on his son's plate. Beets topped the mountain of potatoes that dotted the landscape around the quartered capon set atop a field of French beans.

"Growing boys need lots of sustenance," Plum told him with a weak smile, mentally thanking her stars that she had arranged for three more courses.

"So do pigs," India muttered under her breath.

"I am not a pig!" Digger growled, shooting his sister a mean look. "You take that back."

"Of course you're not a pig," Plum soothed. "Young ladies do not eat as much as young men—"

"Are so! Piggy, piggy, piggy!" India said, narrowing her eyes at Digger.

Plum, one eye on Harry's deepening frown, cleared her throat. "Children, since this is our first night together—"

"Piggy, piggy, piggy," the younger children started chanting. Digger, his face flushed and hot with anger, snarled an imprecation at his siblings that had Plum blinking in surprise.

"*What* did you say?" Harry asked, setting his napkin on the table and looking as if he was about to escort his son out to the woodshed to introduce him to his razor strop.

Plum, desperate now to just get through the meal without anyone being punished, pleaded with Harry. "I'm sure he didn't say what you thought he said. He probably said something similar, but not quite, if you know what I mean."

"He said *merde*," India said smugly as she formed her dollop of mashed potatoes into something that to Plum's eye vaguely resembled a church spire. "Only not in French. Mademoiselle said it was much worse to say it in English than in French, so you see, Digger really is a pig, because only a pig would have such a privy mouth."

"ARGH!" responded Digger. With one deft flip of his wrist, he sent a forkful of mashed potatoes flying at his sister. India, with long practice, ducked the missile, which hit the wall behind her.

"Oh! You piggy, piggy, pig-pig!" She scooped up a spoonful of potatoes, and before Plum could stop her, fired it at her brother. The other children squealed their delight as Digger, intent on reloading his own weapon, was struck dead in the face. He roared a battle cry, and suddenly the air was full of flying potatoes. They seemed to come from everywhere, striking everyone and everything—the footmen, the walls, the children, even Thom was plastered before Harry, bellowing a warning so loud it made the windows rattle, stopped the starchy artillery attack.

"YOU WILL STOP THIS RIGHT NOW!" he yelled, and when the combatants, panting with the exertions of their recent warfare, stood in various positions of attack around the table, he looked at each one of them, snarling, "You are excused from the table until such time as you can eat like civilized human beings, not animals."

"Piggy," India muttered at Digger, a blob of potatoes clinging to the side of her head.

"Am not!" he hissed, wiping the potatoes from his chest.

"Not . . . one . . . more . . . word," Harry roared. "Out! All of you! And I don't want to see any of you again tonight, do I make myself clear?"

Five subdued, potato-coated children nodded, and trickled out of the room. Plum watched them leave with a heavy heart. Her initial reaction was to ask Harry just how his children had been raised to have such terrible manners, but she quickly provided herself with an answer—the little dears had no mother to guide them. She just prayed Harry wasn't so disappointed in her lack of parenting skills that he could not see how much better she could make all of their lives.

Harry sat back down, pulling his spectacles off to remove the blob of potatoes smeared across one lens. Plum stared at her plate as a sobbing Juan was led from the room by Ben, a variety of potent epithets and curses regarding devil-spawned children clearly audible in-between the sobs.

Temple looked around the room, his distaste evident. Thom's face was placid, but Plum could see the merriment dancing in her eyes. Thom picked up her plate, and with a little bob to Harry, excused herself. "I think I'll have my dinner in the nursery this once, if you don't mind. I'm sure the children could do with someone keeping an eye on them."

Harry flinched at her words. Plum, torn between

the nearly overwhelming desire to cry and the urge to reassure Harry that he would not be subjected to another such scene (although she was at a loss as to how she was to guarantee any such thing), nodded at Thom and waved one of the footmen away from wiping potatoes from the window. "William, would you please ask Cook to send supper up to the nursery?"

"They don't deserve supper," Harry said, still obviously a bit snappish about the children, which, considering he was wearing a boutonniere of mashed potatoes garnished with French beans, was understandable.

Plum waved her hand at the footman to do as she ordered, and turned back to apologize to Harry. "I'm sorry," she said at the exact instance he looked up, and said the same words to her.

"I believe I will finish my dinner in the servant's hall," Temple said quietly, and removed himself from the dining room.

The remaining footman followed Temple after receiving Harry's scowl. Plum's spirits sank as her husband threw his potato-riddled napkin down, and rose to stalk down the length of the long table.

"Truly, Harry, the children were just—"

"Abominable, yes, I'm well aware of your assessment of their behavior. It is in complete harmony with mine. Um . . . you have a bit of potato in your hair. If you would allow me . . ."

Plum sat still while he dabbed at her head with her napkin. She was a mass of indecision, wanting to tell him the children's behavior at dinner was her fault, and yet admitting to herself that his label was more or less correct. The key, she decided after they spent the remainder of dinner in silence, was to show him not how badly behaved the children were, but how much she could do for them.

"Which brings me back to the problem at hand," Plum said, shaking off the memories of the disastrous dinner as she combed her now potato-free hair before the soft, fragrant breeze of the open window. As thick as her hair was, it took forever to dry. She particularly wanted it dry soon, since the look Harry had given her after dinner boded very well for her plans to engage in many, many connubial calisthenics before the week was out, and everyone knew that damp hair had no place in the marriage bed.

"How to make the children mind you?" Thom asked, still pouring over the book sitting before her. Plum craned her neck to see what it was that Thom found so fascinating, then jumped up and gasped, "Thomasine! What are you doing with *that*?"

Thom put a finger on a page to mark her spot, and looked up. "Reading. It's very informative. How did you come up with the idea of *Hunter Loosing an Arrow into a Mossy Crevice*? I would think that something like that would hurt, should the gentleman's aim be off."

Plum marched over to her niece and snatched the book from her hands, stuffing it into the back of the writing bureau and slamming the lid shut. "Charles was very inventive and his aim was never off. That is all I am going to say on the subject."

Thom grinned. Plum shook a finger at that grin. "I've told you before that you're not to read the *Guide* until you are married!"

"I have no plans to ever marry. I shall be a doting aunt to your children. And Harry's, too, if he'll let me. I rather like them."

"So do I, but that's neither here nor there. And you're changing the subject—that book is not suitable reading for you, and that's that."

Thom tipped her head and looked Plum over as she returned to her chair before the window and resumed drying her hair. "Are you ashamed that you wrote it?"

"Of course I'm not ashamed . . . not in the sense you mean, I'm not. There is nothing in there that is coarse or distasteful, it's simply instruction of an intimate nature, a celebration if you will of the physical union between a husband and wife."

"Then why did you hide the book away in the bureau? Why don't you set it out so people can see it and know you are the author?"

A look of horror crawled across Plum's face. Her stomach balled up into a tiny little lead weight with the thought of just how their lives would be ruined should the identity of Vyvyan La Blue be made public. "Dear God in heaven, that would be the end."

"Oh, surely you exaggerate," Thom said.

Plum shook her head, horrific visions dancing in her head of ostracization a million times worse than what she'd experienced. "The last scandal took the life of your beloved mother, Thom. This one would . . . oh, it would destroy us all! You, Harry, the children . . . everyone would be tainted, everyone would be shunned."

"Pooh. People wouldn't be so cruel over such a silly thing."

"Silly?" Plum stared at her niece, desperate to make her understand lest the girl inadvertently give away her secret. Before there was just Thom and herself to worry about, but now she had six more souls to protect. "Silly? Thom, I was silly once, when I was your age. Silly and naive to believe Charles was being truthful and honest when he married me. I suffered for that silliness, as did my family, most particularly your mother. Because of that silliness, I will have to spend the rest of my life in the country, which I don't mind, I prefer country life, and thankfully Harry seems disinclined to go into town or polite society, but the fact remains that I cannot go anywhere people know me, or know of my past."

Thom made an annoyed sound. "I don't believe any of your acquaintances would still remember that old farrago. Yes, the people in Ram's Bottom were rude to you about it, but they aren't society, and that's who you're worried about. You told me yourself that the *ton* isn't happy unless it has a new scandal to chew over each week."

"They might need a new scandal each week, but they also have exceptionally long memories. Truthfully, Thom, that scandal would pale in comparison to the one that would be generated should the *ton* become aware that the author of the most infamous book yet published was none other than the Marchioness Rosse. Society might titter and gossip behind their hands about a woman who was foolish enough to marry Charles, but they would cut dead everyone who was related—by birth or circumstance—to the author of the *Guide*."

Thom shrugged. "I know Mama felt differently, but I don't mind being shunned."

"I know you don't, a fact I am profoundly grateful for, one which has me begging for forgiveness every night in my prayers, but your feet trod a different path than most people's. You are not a well-respected and well-liked man who has committed no sin but marrying a woman with a secret; you are not an innocent child with your life spread before you, a life that will be cruelly ruined, with no hope of ever taking your rightful place in the society to which you were born."

Thom held up her hands, and gave a little laugh. "I surrender. I bow to your superior knowledge of society. But surely you have no need to hide the *Guide* from Harry? Oh, don't get your hackles up, I'm not suggesting that you tell him you wrote it—not that I think he would mind, he seems a very fair-minded man—but there's no reason you couldn't show him the book and try out one or two of the more interesting exercises. I was thinking that *Heron Alighting Upon a Still Pond* looked rather fascinating."

"*Heron Alighting*—" A slow smile curved Plum's lips as she recalled just what was involved in that particular calisthenic. "Oh, yes, that would be . . . ahem. Thank you, Thom. I will take your advice under consideration. Now, you'd best be off to your own bed. Will you be available tomorrow to take the children on a nature walk with me?"

"A nature walk?" Thom strolled toward the door, pausing when she reached it to cock an eyebrow at her aunt. "Why would you want to take the children on a nature walk?"

"They have a surfeit of energy. I thought a long walk where they will be free to run and romp to their heart's content will benefit them, and serve to show them that good behavior will be rewarded."

"Clever puss," Thom said with a grin, then shook

her head with rue. "I hate to miss that, but Puck told me the farrier is to come tomorrow, and I wish to watch him. You don't mind if I miss your nature walk, do you?"

"Puck?"

"One of Harry's stable boys. The one with the red hair and freckles."

"Ah. No, I don't mind." Plum had a moment of misgiving thinking of herself alone with the children, but that was quickly squelched. She had triumphed over much worse things, how hard could it be to take five children on a walk through the countryside?

Thom bid her a goodnight. Plum stood by the open window, slowly combing her hair, thinking about the many challenges that faced her, not the least of which was the upcoming evening. Harry believed her to be a shy bride, not a virgin, but virginal, unlearned, and inexperienced. While it was true she had only six weeks of Charles's attention before the marriage was discovered and he was sent abroad by his family, they were very instructive weeks. Thus it would be necessary for her to not take the initiative, nor to attempt anything beyond *Leda and the Swan*. "Which is a shame, because Thom is absolutely right, *Heron Alighting Upon a Still Pond* is extremely fascinating, particularly when the heron in question has legs as long as Harry's."

Plum didn't have long to muse upon her sorrows before her husband burst into her room with a hurried knock at her door. He stopped just beyond the doorway and gazed at Plum, curled up in a chair reading a book (not the *Guide*). His eyes were dark behind his spectacles, but the heat within them was visible to her even across the room. Plum was filled with a responding warmth, her body reacting to that gaze by preparing itself for him. Beneath the soft linen of her night rail, her nipples hardened, her breasts waking themselves up out of a dormant sleep, becoming immediately both extremely sensitive and heavy, as if they needed hands—Harry's hands—holding them up. Her stomach was filled with the same tumbling butterflies that made their appearance the night before, her thighs ached to wrap themselves around him, and her womanly parts were holding a celebration and offered an invitation to Harry to attend the festivities.

"Erm . . . Plum? You're not going to throw me out again, are you? You've forgiven me?" Harry looked so adorable, so hesitant, so . . . *manly* what with his bare feet and ankles, and that little bit of chest that showed at the top of his gold dressing gown, not to mention the enticing bulge in the region of his groin that practically had Plum licking her lips.

I must be innocent, I must be innocent, she told herself, and fought a short-lived battle to keep from leaping up and ripping the dressing gown from his body. Her hands tightened on the arms of the chair with the effort. She cleared her throat and tried to speak, but her words came out hoarse. She cleared her throat again, then offered Harry what she prayed looked like a shy, innocent, maidenly smile, and not the smile of a woman who was anticipating the close examination and practical application of his body against hers. "Of course I'm not angry with you, and no, I will not ask you to leave my bedchamber again. That was very ill done of me, Harry, and I apologize again for my actions. In fact—" She paused and chewed her lip. Should she take the chance of angering him and tell him about Charles? With each day of acquaintance with him she was becoming more and more confident of him, just as her burden weighed more heavily on her soul, but with that confidence came reluctance to harm their budding relationship. Perhaps if she waited until later, after they had a chance to know one another, after he knew just how much of a help she could be in his life, perhaps then would be the time to bare her own secrets.

"In fact what?" he asked, moving closer now, holding out his hands for her to take. He pulled her to her feet, straight into his arms, his body moving seductively against hers as a smile played around his rugged, manly lips—lips that drove all thoughts out of Plum's mind but what pleasure they brought her.

"In fact I should like very much for you to make love to me," she whispered, forgetting to be shy and innocent in her desire for him. A flicker of surprise flashed across Harry's face before he bent and scooped her up in his arms, turning to carry her into his room. Plum had little time to admire the dark blue colors of his curtains and matching chairs before he deposited her on the middle of his bed, stripping off her night rail before she even had a chance to gasp.

She lay exposed to his gaze, every last blessed inch of her, and although she knew she should be embarrassed by her nudity, the way his eyes were eating her, she wasn't. All the tingling and pools of heat within her were stirred to a new level of intensity by the pleasure she saw reflected in his eyes.

She rolled onto her side into a more artful position, and gave Harry a blatant come-hither smile.

"You look uncomfortably hot in that dressing gown, husband. Don't you think you should shed it and come to bed?"

"What?" Harry's voice was just as hoarse as Plum's had been, something that made her smile to herself as she patted the bed beside her.

"Take it off, Harry. I wish to see you, too."

Harry's eyes went practically black as he struggled to relieve himself of the hold his dressing gown had on him. His fingers seemed to have difficulty with the buttons. After fighting them for a few seconds, he snarled and ripped the garment off, throwing himself down beside her, his hands reaching for her.

"No," Plum said, pushing his hands away.

"No?" Harry choked. "No? What do you mean, no?"

"I mean no, I wish to look at you first." Plum sat on her heels and looked at the vast array of Harry before her. He was gorgeous, absolutely gorgeous, better than she imagined. His legs were long and well muscled, not at all scrawny, as Charles's had been. His belly had just the slightest hint of a softness to it, a sign of his age, no doubt, but a sign that pleased Plum immensely. Charles had been thin and boney, and she had always been partial to large men—not fat, but comfortable to touch. Harry's little hint of a belly was the perfect balance to the rest of his hard, muscled self. Her eyes skittered up his lightly haired chest—a chest that was heaving, she was pleased to note—across the broad width of his shoulders.

"What is it about a man's chest?" she mused

116

aloud as she took in the last uncovered bits of him, two strong arms with long, blunt-tipped fingers, a strong neck, and oh yes, the part she had been trying to ignore, the part of him that stood up and saluted her with a cheery wave.

"I was wondering just the exact same thing about your chest," Harry said, his hands twitching on the blue and gold counterpane. "Am I allowed to touch you yet?"

"Not yet. Soon. But not yet."

Harry groaned, and started to protest when Plum took him into her hands. His hips arched upward, the groan strangling in his throat.

"You're very aroused. I like that about you. You're also a bit longer than I expected, but I trust that won't be the cause of any difficulty."

Harry gasped in great quantities of air, and clutched the counterpane with both hands. "I trust not."

She explored the hard, hot length of velvety soft flesh that moved like silk over steel, enjoying the way his eyes rolled up in his head. Sweat broke out on his brow as his chest heaved, desperately attempting to bring enough air into his lungs. Plum allowed her hands to roam, to touch and tease the surrounding skin, then leaned over and nipped at his adorable little belly.

His stomach tightened as he yelped her name. Plum just grinned at him and kissed a path upward even as her hand slid lower. He smelled so good, like lemon soap and aroused male and something else, something a little spicy, something uniquely Harry.

"You have a very nice chest," she whispered as his

light dusting of chest hair tickled her nose. She wanted more than anything to take his adorable little nipples into her mouth, teasing them with teeth and tongue until he pleaded for mercy, but she remembered in time that she was supposed to be innocent of such knowledge, and contented herself with pressing a kiss to each nipple before nibbling a path up his neck and around to his ear.

Harry shuddered and groaned again, his body quivering nonstop, sweat bedewing his chest as Plum nibbled his earlobe. She paused and frowned at the gold wire tucked behind his ear. "Do you need your spectacles?"

"Only to see."

"Oh." She plucked them gently from his face, setting them on the table next to the bed before returning to his ear, laving the outer edge of it with her tongue as she said softly, "Your turn."

She was on her back before the second word left her mouth, Harry braced above her, squinting ever so slightly in order to bring her into focus. Her legs moved restlessly against his, the pressure inside of her increased until it was spiked with pain, a pleasurable pain of emptiness that need to be filled, a pain that only he could ease. His mouth hovered over her breasts, his hot breath steaming her flesh, her back arching of its own accord as his mouth— so hot, it would surely scorch her skin—burned a brand down her breastbone. Her hands slid up the muscles of his arms, her fingers catching in his hair as he kissed a trail of fire over to one heavy, aching breast, a breast that hungered for him, a breast that cried out for him, a breast that demanded that he take it into his mouth right at that very moment or else it would die. "Harry!" she shrieked as his mouth suddenly veered south, burning kisses pressed below her breast.

"What?" he mumbled into her soft flesh, his tongue flickering out to taste her. Plum's back arched even more as she tried to pull his head up to where her breast clamored for it.

"If you don't stop teasing me right this very second, my breast is going to explode, and then I'll have only one, and that will make me lopsided!"

His hair brushed against her sensitive nipple, sending streaks of pain and pleasure through Plum. He grinned at her, then nibbled a feather light circle around her nipple. "What do you want me to do, Plum? Perhaps this?"

He rubbed his cheek, slightly abrasive from his evening's growth of whiskers, against the side of her breast. Her legs moved against him as she twisted, trying to position her breast against his mouth. He pulled back, frustrating her attempt.

"Harry!"

"Or perhaps," he licked with long, sweeping strokes of his tongue around the perimeter of her breast, tracing along the point where her chest ended, and her breast began. "You want this?"

"HARRY!" she demanded, past being able to form her need into words. She tugged at his head again, not hard enough to hurt him, but enough to make him pay attention.

"Ah, I begin to see. You want me to do this . . ." His mouth closed over the aching tip, his mouth hot and wet as he suckled her. Plum bucked beneath him as his teeth scraped gently over her flesh, the fires within her now a roaring inferno that swept her from toes to crown.

"I'm burning up," she cried, reveling in her fiery death. "You're going to kill me!"

"Sweetheart, I haven't even begun to make you burn," Harry swore against her breast, and just as Plum was sending heartfelt prayers to her maker to allow her to survive her husband's attention, her world fell apart.

"Harry?" Plum blinked, wondering why he had left her, why his warm, delicious, hard body had pulled away from hers, then she realized that the pounding of her heart, so loud in her ears as to deafen her to everything but its frantic beat, was really a pounding on the door. "Harry?"

He snatched up his dressing gown, pulling the bed curtains closed to shield her from view. Plum, still trying to gather her wits, finally realized that someone was at the door. She slid over and peeked through the bed curtains.

"—and Mama tried barley water, but he won't keep that down as well. 'Tis the truth, it's coming out of both ends. Mama thought you'd want to know."

"Now?" Harry asked, his voice tight and rough about the edges. Plum understood completely—she felt like a bowstring pulled tight, trembling on the edge of release. "He had to be sick now? It couldn't have waited until later, it has to be *now*?"

"I'm sorry, sir. I don't think he planned this, not as sick as the poor little lamb is."

Harry banged his forehead on the doorframe a

couple of times. Plum winced in sympathy. It had to have hurt. "Now?"

Plum reached through the curtains and snared her night rail, pulling it on before leaving the bed. "Who is ill?" she asked him.

He stopped abusing his forehead and set the candle he'd snatched up onto a tall bureau. "McTavish has some sort of a stomach complaint."

"Mama thinks it's more than that, ma'am," George said, the golden hair tumbling down from under an old-fashioned nightcap tangled in the ties of her night rail as she wrung her hands in worry.

"Mama?" Plum asked, confused.

"Gertie is George's mother," Harry said as he slid his feet into a pair of blue velvet slippers. "Go back to bed, love. I'll see to McTavish. I'm sure it's just the usual complaint. Too many green apples, most likely."

Plum toyed for a second with the thought of doing what Harry suggested, but only for a second. "I'll come with you." When Harry paused in the doorway to cast her a questioning glance, she added, "I'm his mother now. He needs me."

"Yes," Harry agreed, much to her surprise . . . and delight. "He does need you."

She brushed past him, following George up the dark stairs to the nursery, not at all aware that Harry finished his sentence with a soft, "And so do I."

Chapter Eight

"How is he this morning?" Temple asked.

Harry staggered a few feet before the words sank into his sleep-deprived brain. "Better. Kept some broth down. Sleeping now. Thom's with him. Sent Plum to bed."

Temple took the liberty of guiding his employer to the nearest chair, onto which Harry collapsed with a grateful sigh. "You should get some rest too, sir. It's been three days, and I doubt if you've had more than an hour or two of sleep at night."

Harry made an attempt to push his spectacles up, noticed his hand was trembling with fatigue, and lowered it again. "Couldn't leave the poor little lad. Doctor said he almost bought it. Said we came damn close to losing him. Plum was beside herself."

Temple signaled to a footman to bring a decanter and glass to the hall table next to where Harry was sitting. "Surely she didn't blame herself for the incident? I thought the Doctor Trewitt said McTavish had ingested something poisonous, like toxic berries or a bit of plant?"

Harry leaned his head back against the oak paneling, and closed his eyes. There was so much for him to do, so much he needed to see to, but the last few days had drained him of all energy or desire to do anything but sleep for a week. "Plum had some foolish idea that it was the upset at dinner the other night that made him ill."

"That is foolish. McTavish is made of sterner stuff."

"Mmm." Harry tried to focus his mind on the things he needed to do, but they kept slipping from his mental grasp, as if they were made of quicksilver. "Now that McTavish is out of danger, I must attend to those tasks that are awaiting my attention, tasks like unearthing the information Lord Briceland requested. And then there is putting the estate to rights—Plum can't do it all herself."

Harry was so still that Temple thought for a moment that he had fallen asleep, but the groan Harry uttered informed him otherwise. His words, however, were noticeably slurred, spoken slowly as if the mere act of speaking was almost beyond him. "I've been blessed, Temple, twice in my life. The first was when I wed Beatrice, the second was when I found Plum. I'd have lost Tavvy without her ceaseless care. She wouldn't let him go, she just wouldn't let him . . ."

"Go," finished Temple. He set down the glass he was about to offer his employer, and went to fetch a footman to help carry the sleeping marquis upstairs. They laid him down next to Plum, who was sound asleep on her bed, fully dressed, her boots still on. Temple removed Plum's boots, and Harry's shoes and spectacles, loosened the latter's rumpled neck-cloth, and spread a blanket over them both, quietly leaving them to their much needed rest.

Ten hours later Harry awoke with a desperate need to use the pot, a raging thirst, and a vague, nagging sense of something important that he needed to do.

"McTavish!" he roared two minutes later, and having achieved one goal, slammed down the lid to the close stool, tucked himself back into his breeches, and raced out of the bedroom for the upper floor.

He burst into the nursery prepared to find his youngest child gravely ill—or worse—but what he found was an exuberant McTavish crawling around on his bed, giggling and laughing as he played with a gray-and-white striped kitten, just as if he had not been near death a few hours before.

"Good evening, Harry. Did you sleep well?" Plum, sitting in the same chair next to the bed where she'd spent the last three days while they tended McTavish, looked as fresh as a spring daffodil—a somewhat faded and worn daffodil, he thought to himself, taking in her soft yellow gown. He made a mental note to have Temple bring a modiste to Ashleigh Court to fit Plum out with a new wardrobe. "I looked in on you twice, but both times you were sleeping so soundly, I didn't want to wake you. You look well rested."

"I am," Harry answered, then strolled forward to ruffle his son's hair. "How are you feeling, old man?"

McTavish looked up from where the kitten was pouncing on a piece of string he was trailing across the bed. "I'm hungry. Mama says I can't have anything but broth and toast until tomorrow. I don't like toast and broth. I want mashed potatoes!"

Plum's velvety brown eyes were soft and warm as she smiled at him. "I melt every time he calls me that."

"What, Mama?" She nodded. Harry glanced around the empty nursery, a wry twist to his lips. "I have a suspicion it won't be very long before you're taking to hiding from them as they bellow 'Mama!' down the hallways in search of you. And as for you, young man, you do as your mother tells you."

McTavish made a face, and turned his attention back to playing with the kitten. Plum rose and spoke to one of the nursery maids, turning back to him to smile as she brushed a lock of hair off his brow.

"I've ordered you a bath, husband. You look as if you could use a little freshening after the last four days. I'll have dinner held back an hour."

"Ever the dutiful wife?"

Her smiled turned cheeky. "Something like that."

"Plum—" Harry caught her to him, mindless of the fact that McTavish was behind them playing on the bed. The warm glow of happiness her touch brought him was spreading, changing to something more elemental, more earthy. He kissed the tip of her delightful nose. "I didn't have a chance to thank you before, but I want to now."

"Thank me?" Her brow scrunched up, pulling those two straight brows together. "What do you have to thank me for?"

"For helping with McTavish. For saving his life."

Plum stared at him for a moment in open-mouthed astonishment, then struggled from his hold, her eyes all but spitting indignation at him. "Thank me? You want to thank me? As if I was a servant or a doctor?"

It was Harry's turn to stare in astonishment. What had he said that she took so badly? "Not as a servant, no, but you didn't have to attend McTavish. I told you I would do it."

"You would do it because he's *your* child," Plum snarled, her hands fisted at her side.

Harry was at a loss why she was so angry. "Yes, because he's my child."

"Whereas he isn't mine."

"No, he isn't. Since you didn't know about the children until after we were married, I realized that it might be expecting too much for you to tend one of them when he was ill."

Plum's cheeks flared red. Harry was about to ask her what he had said to make her so angry when she slapped him, hard, then spun on her heel and stormed out of the room. He stood for a minute in confusion, rubbing his face as he wondered if lack of sleep had unhinged her mind.

Gertie stood in the doorway to the girls' room. "Ye've insulted yer lady."

He raised his eyebrows at her.

"Ye've insulted her by tellin' her she's not Tavvy's rightful Mama."

"She's not."

"She's his stepmama, and to her that's the same."

Harry shook his head, pinching the bridge of his nose to forestall the headache he felt blossom in the back of his head. "She didn't even know about the children until after we were married. I didn't expect her to plunge into motherhood so quickly. I wanted to ease her into it, so the children wouldn't overwhelm her."

Gertie waved away his explanations. "Ye daft man, can't ye see she's achin' to mother them? She needs them as much as they need her. By treatin' her like she was doin' ye a favor in takin' care of Tavvy, yer tellin' her she's not part of the family. No mother would leave her sick child's care to someone else. Ye insulted her in the worst way ye could by thankin' her."

Harry groaned and rubbed his neck. The headache was getting worse. "I didn't mean to insult her. I just wanted to show her my appreciation for all the assistance—"

Gertie tsked, and shooed him toward the door. "Go and take yer bath. Ye look half dead. And when yer alone with yer lady, don't thank her—tell her how lucky the children are to have her as their mama."

Harry allowed himself to be pushed from the nursery without defending himself further, despite the urge to shout from the highest mountain his recognition of just how lucky they all were to have Plum. Instead he bathed, shaved, and donned fresh clothing, ignoring both the dull rumble in his belly and the thick throb at the back of his head as he went downstairs to make amends with his wife.

"—and I don't see why I shouldn't have them, they will make riding so much nicer, and it's not as if anyone will see—oh, good, Harry's here. Can we eat now? I'm practically faint with hunger."

Plum, Thom, and Temple were all sitting on the verandah, enjoying the cool evening air. Raised voices, shrieks of laughter, and loud accusations of cheating hinted that the children were engaged in a game in the overgrown garden.

"Yes, of course we can eat now." Plum's voice was cool and impersonal as she rose and prepared to follow Thom into the house.

Harry, who had much experience being a husband, knew better than to let another moment pass without correcting the slight he had inadvertently made against his wife. He put a restraining hand on her arm and gestured Temple on. "We'll be along in a moment."

Plum kept her gaze on the wall beyond Harry's shoulder, her face expressionless. He tried to form the words of an apology, but everything sounded too stilted and insincere. In the end, he did the only thing he could do. He pulled her into his arms and kissed the breath from her lungs.

"You've married an idiot, Plum," he murmured against her lips when his mouth finally parted from hers. "A fool, a simpleton, a bona fide half-wit."

Plum, who had been stiff as a board through the entire kiss, relaxed against him, her lips curving under his. "I wouldn't go so far as to say you were a half-wit, but a fool . . . well, we all have our foolish moments."

"Some of us more than others," he agreed, and pressed kisses along her jaw to her hair. "I'm very sorry for what I said earlier. I realize how insulting that must have sounded, and I can assure you that was the last thing I meant. It's been a while since I had a wife, so you'll have to forgive me if I forget to go down on my knees every morning and bless you for taking us all in hand."

Plum giggled and wrapped her arms around his waist. "You've never once gone down on your knees to me."

He smiled into her hair, pressed a last kiss to her temple, and with a sigh of regret, released her, grinning at her disgruntled look. "It's not that I don't want to kiss you, wife, but once I start, I don't think I'll be able to stop."

Plum's eyes went all liquid at him. He sucked in his breath and thought for a moment about just taking her right there, and damning everyone else, but his body—willing as it was to fulfill that plan—was at war with itself over what it needed most.

His stomach won out. It growled in a most vociferous manner.

Plum laughed, and pushed him into the house. "I'd better feed you if I want you to make good on that promise in your eyes."

"I hunger for many things," he teased as he held the door to the dining room open.

"So do I," she said with a provocative glance that went straight to his groin.

Dinner was a trial. Oh, the food was good, and the company—just him, Plum, Thom, and Temple—was convivial enough, but his eyes kept returning to the woman seated down the length of the table. Every time he looked at her, erotic, sensual images arose in his mind.

With the soup, he thought about how smooth her flesh was against his mouth. With the game course, he mused over the flowing silk of her hair. With the fish, his nostrils were filled with the remembered scent of her skin, a scent that was faintly jasmine with overtones of warm, arousing woman. He ate whatever was set before him, his eyes on Plum as she chatted with both Thom and Temple, his mind filled with all the things he wanted to do to her, and quite a few he wanted her to do to him. This evening the house could come down around their ears for all he cared—he was going to consummate his marriage, or die trying.

"What do you say, Harry?"

He blinked away the mental image of Plum writhing with pleasure and looked at Thom. "What?"

"Haven't you been listening?" Thom's gray eyes laughed at him.

"Leave him be, Thom, he's hungry," Plum said, her little pink tongue flicking out to lick her lips. The very sight of it had him hard and aching with desire.

"Hungry. Yes, hungry," he said, his gaze never leaving her mouth.

Plum's eyes lit with sudden recognition, a slow, knowing smile curved her lips in answer to the plea he knew to be in his eyes.

He almost swallowed his tongue.

"You've eaten enough that you can converse civilly. This is important, Harry. Plum is being too old-fashioned for words."

It was an effort, but he dragged his mind away from his wife and tried his best to pay attention to what Thom was saying. "What is?"

She gave a martyred sigh and said, "My breeches."

"Your what?"

"Breeches! I want breeches to ride in, and Plum says it would shock anyone who saw me and ruin all my chances of making a good marriage, but as I've told her time and time again, I don't want to be married. I don't see why I shouldn't have a pair of breeches to ride when we're in the country. It's not as if we *know* anyone here. You wouldn't mind if I were to ride in breeches, would you?"

Harry, no fool he, slid a glance toward Plum before deciding how to answer his niece-by-marriage's plea. Plum's straight brows told him nothing, but the thin line of her lips spoke volumes. "I'm sure that Plum knows what's best for you, Thom."

She made an annoyed sound and glared at Plum. "It's all your fault, he's besotted with you and wouldn't dare do anything against your wishes. Now I'll never get a pair of breeches."

He grinned at Plum. "I'm a bridegroom, I'm supposed to be besotted with my bride."

Plum grinned back at him as Temple made a witticism about husbands being led by the nose. He relaxed, warmed by both the avid look in his wife's eye, and the knowledge that all in his world was well. McTavish was on the road to recovery, he had corrected his first misstep with Plum without too much difficulty, and she was evidently looking forward to the evening's activities as much as he was. If there was one complaint he had to make against his late wife, it was that she seldom enjoyed their bed sport. She tolerated his advances, but no matter how much he tried to bring her pleasure, it was only rarely that he was left with the impression that she enjoyed herself. Plum was different. Harry was conscious of a pleasant tension that filled the air between Plum and him, a slight feel of static electricity in the air, as if a storm was approaching.

Temple turned to him near the end of the meal. "While you were sleeping, I had the footmen scour the estate for poisonous berries. They found several, but none in the area Digger said the children were playing before McTavish became so ill."

Harry nodded, selecting a ripe peach from the bowl before him, his mind automatically traveling the paths of soft, ripe fruit to softer, riper woman. "Send what you found to Doctor Trewitt. He might be able to tell us if that's what the boy ate."

"I wonder if he could have eaten a leaf," Thom asked, slicing a bit of cheese from a large hunk of white cheddar. "My uncle used to tell me he thought I was part goat because I was forever eating leaves. You must be used to this sort of thing, Harry."

He stopped stroking the peach's round, full softness and looked a question at Thom.

"Your other children—you must be used to them having stomach upsets and such."

"Oh, yes. Somewhat used to it, none of them have ever been as ill as McTavish. Thankfully, Plum was here to take care of him."

Plum beamed at him.

"She's very good at that sort of thing," Thom agreed. "She's especially good with babies. They all seem to love her."

"I have no doubt of that," Harry answered, giving Plum a little waggled of his eyebrows, just to let her know he was thinking about her. Her eyes flashed in response.

"You'll see how good she is with your babies."

He turned his head to look at Thom, puzzled by her comment. "What babies?"

"Your babies. The babies you and Plum will have."

If he could have throttled Thom without Plum noticing, he would have. Dear God, what devil prodded her to say such a thing in front of her aunt? A few more comments of that ilk and Plum would leave him for certain. "We're not going to have any babies."

Thom glanced from him to Plum. "You're not?"

"No!" He watched Plum carefully, noting the sudden pallor of her cheek, and the stillness with which she held herself. Damn it! She probably thought the only reason he married her was to be a broodmare, popping out children of her own in between taking care of his five hellions. He prayed she could read the sincerity in his eyes. "I wouldn't put Plum through that hell for anything in the world."

"You wouldn't?"

Plum's face was pale, her eyes black, her lovely chest not moving as if she wasn't even breathing. He mentally cursed Thom, then set about making things right with his wife. "Women die in childbirth. My wife—my first wife—died of a fever shortly after McTavish was born."

"Oh." The word was soft, filled with relief, with understanding. Color rushed back to Plum's face as she spoke. "Not every woman dies in childbirth, Harry. It's tragic that the late Lady Rosse did so, but I can assure you that should you wish to have more children, I would be willing—"

He quartered his peach with a savagery that belied his inner feelings. He would not lose Plum as he had lost Beatrice. He would take whatever steps were necessary to see that she did not become pregnant. "I believe the children we already have are sufficiently challenging to keep you busy for many years yet."

"But"—Thom looked from Plum to him—"but Plum . . ."

"Never mind, Thom," she interrupted, her cheeks pink with a blush. He glanced at his secretary, who kept his gaze on the grapes before him. No doubt Plum was embarrassed by such frank talk in front of Temple.

In order to spare her any more discomfort, he turned the conversation to a general discussion of his plans for bringing life back to the estate. Temple and Thom argued long and hard over the subject of which was the better crop to plant—wheat or corn—and although Harry participated, he noticed that Plum had little to offer on the subject. Once her gaze met his, and her adorable little chin rose as if he had challenged her. He couldn't help but smile at that. She was so utterly perfect, from the tips of her pink little toes, to the gentle curve of that obstinate chin.

The ladies withdrew arguing over whether or not a riding habit with breeches underneath was a substitute for breeches alone. Harry sipped at a bit of port as Temple expounded on his recommendation for rebuilding cottages and charging the tenants a higher rate. He answered mechanically, his eyes frequently straying to the clock that sat on the sideboard. A half hour had passed—surely that was long enough for Plum to have chatted with Thom?

Yes, yes it was. They couldn't possibly have anything else to say.

Smothering a yawn he had to force, Harry stood up, made a pretense of stretching, and said, "Good, good, it all sounds wonderful, Temple. Write it up and I'll look at it in the morning. I'm off to bed."

Temple pursed his lips. "I suppose it would be impolitic to point out that just a few hours ago you awoke from a ten-hour sleep?"

Harry shared an entirely male grin with Temple. "That would be extremely impolitic."

"Then I won't do so. May I bid you a pleasant evening, sir?"

Harry laughed, and threw pretense to the wind as he hurried upstairs to his bedroom. He undressed quickly, dismissed his valet, and waiting only long enough to draw on his dressing gown, went in search of his wife.

He found her in the nursery, sitting on the edge of McTavish's bed, all five children clustered around her in their nightgowns as she read to them from a familiar-looking volume. "*'September 30, 1659. I poor miserable Robinson Crusoe, being shipwreck'd, during a dreadful Storm. . . .'* Oh, Harry, have you come to say good night to the children?"

"Yes, yes, I have. Good night children," he said. He plucked the book from Plum's hands, and handed it to a startled India, scooping Plum up in his arms. "Finish the chapter."

"Harry! I was reading to them—"

"India can read, taught her myself. Good for her." He hoisted Plum high on his chest, and quickly opened the door before she could slide down.

"But . . . but . . . the children—"

135

"Will be just fine without you." He paused just before closing the door and leaned his head back into the nursery. "McTavish? How are you, lad?"

"Hungry!" the boy shouted, jumping up and down on the bed.

Harry nodded, said good night again, and stalked off down the stairs, ignoring Plum's protests.

"You needn't have made such a scene, you know. I would have finished the chapter and tucked them all in, and no one would know that you and I . . . that we . . ."

She really did blush in a most delightful manner. He grinned at her, warmed to the toes by the shy little glances she was giving him. "Sweetheart, not even the archbishop of Canterbury could stop me from bedding you tonight."

"Harry!" Plum gasped in a delighted sort of way.

"Plum!" he gasped back to her as he kicked open the door to his room, just as delighted, if not more so.

She giggled.

He strode over to his bed, his lovely bed, his lovely big bed that would soon be all that much lovelier because it would hold Plum, and said in his best gothic villain voice, "You are in my power, alone with me, my seductive little wife. Now I shall ravish you as you have never been ravished."

"Really?" Plum asked, her eyes aglow with excitement. Her eyelids dropped for a moment, then she peeked up at him in a most fetching manner. "Perhaps I have been ravished many ways before, my lord. What sort of ravishment did you have in mind?"

He set her on her feet, and without waiting for

her to offer assistance, quickly stripped her of gown and stays, leaving her standing in her chemise and stockings. Since he was a gentleman and not an animal, he gave her a moment to recover her breath while he admired the scenery. He nodded his head. Twice. "Yes, yes, you're lovely in your underthings. You do appreciate the fact that I think you're lovely with your clothing on, don't you? I'm not an animal who just wants you naked and writhing with pleasure beneath me while I thrust into you again and again, burying myself in you, losing myself in your heat, wanting to pound my flesh into yours until I pour every single last drop of life I have into your body? You know that, yes?"

Plum looked a bit dazed. "I . . . well . . . I suppose . . ."

"Good!" Without further ado, he grabbed the neckline of her chemise and tore it from top to bottom, gently pushing her on the bed at the same time he yanked off his dressing gown, tossing his spectacles onto the table.

"Harry!" Plum shrieked as he threw himself onto top of her, bracing his weight with his arms so he didn't crush her into a woman-shaped bit of pulp.

"Yes, it's me, how clever of you to recognize me without my spectacles. Now, what have we here? I don't see too well without my spectacles, so you'll have to excuse me if I need to examine very closely the various parts of you. He leaned back to look at her, to allow his gaze to sweep her from crown to toes. "Mine," he said in a voice laden with possession.

"Yes, I am yours, but Harry!"

He dragged his eyes up to hers.

"I still have my stockings on."

He looked to where she gestured, admiring the lovely length of her legs. They weren't too long, or too thin, just right, with the exact amount of curve and softness he required in his wife's legs. "Yes, you do. It's a bit shocking, isn't it? I shall remove them. Later." He leaned closer, his breath brushing her mouth. "With my tongue."

"Oh," she breathed, her eyes huge and filled with hope and desire and a good dollop of anticipation.

Harry gave her a heated look promising a reward for all that anticipation before focusing his attention on the twin mounds that heaved before him. "What's this?" he asked, squinting slightly at one perfect breast. "Breasts?"

"Yes, I have two of them. They're a set," Plum said.

"Matched, too. I loved matched pairs." His mouth closed over the taut little peak crowning her silky white breast. Plum bucked beneath him, her eyes alight with passion as he nibbled and kissed his way around her breasts. He was suddenly filled with the overpowering desire to taste her, all of her, to lick the satin skin that glowed with a pearly luminescence that seemed to fill his soul. He kissed the twin of the first breast just so it wouldn't feel slighted, then licked a path down her ribs to the little mound of her belly. Plum moaned and writhed beneath the onslaught of his mouth, but Harry would not be stirred from his course. He held her down with a hand on either hip, and after kissing each hipbone, nipped his way across her belly, pleased by her reaction to his touch. Her breath shuddered within her, making her flesh quiver and contract wherever he licked. He dipped lower, breathing in the perfume that was the very essence of Plum, reveling in the thought that it was he who stirred her, that she was reacting to him and no other. He kissed a line across the top of her pubic mound, and then paused. "Give yourself to me, Plum. Open for me."

Her legs tensed. "Harry, I'm not sure—"

"But I am," he said, sliding a hand up the soft length of her thigh. He gently insinuated his fingers between the tightly clenched legs. "You'll enjoy this. Trust me, Plum."

He could almost hear her thinking it out, reasoning with that delicious mind of hers, weighing his words against her natural modesty and hesitancy. He willed her to yield, to give herself to him in an absolute show of trust, and thought his heart would be ripped from his chest if she didn't. Just as her legs relaxed, allowing him to spread them and breathe in her scent, the knowledge struck him with blinding force.

His heart was already hers.

He shook the thought away, unwilling to acknowledge it, unwilling to admit that she had such power over him, and concentrated on giving his wife pleasure. He rubbed his cheeks gently along the sensitive flesh of her inner thighs, enjoying the hitch in her breathing his actions caused as he kissed a hot trail to the core of her womanhood.

"You are all pink and rose-hued," he murmured, kissing the juncture between her legs. "You are soft like the finest silk, and these sweet petals hold your heat for me."

Plum arched her back and thrust her hips up

when he parted her woman's flesh, his fingers dancing around her heat, stroking, teasing, rubbing her until she was moaning soft, endless moans, her head thrashing from side to side as she clutched handfuls of the bed linens.

"You'll like this," Harry promised, and leaned forward to lick at the tiny focus of her pleasure.

"Blessed St. Genevieve!" Plum yelled, and grabbing Harry's head, pulled him tighter to her. He held her firmly by the hips, dancing his tongue around her silken folds, suckling and nibbling her until she arched her back again and screamed his name.

"I told you that you would like it," Harry said smugly, pleased with himself, pleased with her response to him, and a bit surprised that the pleasure he had given her was thrumming so strongly in his blood, leaving him hungry and aching with the need to plunge himself deep within her depths. Plum lay panting, quivering slightly with the aftereffects of her pleasure, but when he moved up to cover her, she suddenly twisted out from underneath him, and pushed him down into the soft mattress.

"No," she said, leaning forward to nip at his lower lip. "You've had your turn. Now it's mine."

Harry knew he'd never last through Plum's exploration of him. He was nigh unto bursting now, and just the look in her dark, liquid eyes almost made him spill his seed.

She stroked her hand along his chest. "You have such a lovely chest, Harry. It has just the right amount of hair, not too much, not too little, and your flesh is very firm."

His muscles flinched beneath her fingers as she stroked down the length of his breastbone to his belly, leaving a fiery path in their wake. She leaned forward and gently kissed his collarbone, her hands on either side of his ribs, stroking and petting him.

"Your skin is so warm, so very warm. I like to touch you. I like to feel your muscles ripple beneath my fingers. You make me feel wild inside. You make me want to do things I didn't know were possible. You make me want to—"

A thousand places he never knew existed suddenly kindled into flame as she stopped speaking and bent her head to kiss the breadth of his chest, her hair trailing little streaks of fire and ice as it brushed his skin. She paused for a moment over one of his nipples. He held his breath. Previous to Plum, he had never been a nipple man, had never really enjoyed women fondling him there. A nipple was a nipple was his motto. They were well and fine on women, enjoyable to tease and a sure way to arouse a woman, but his own set were nothing more than decoration as far as he was concerned. All that changed the night Plum pressed hot kisses to his chest. Now she was doing more than kissing, she was tormenting him just as he had tormented her. Her little white teeth closed gently over one brown nub of a nipple, converting Harry on the spot.

"St. Peter's cods!" he bellowed, tears coming to his eyes with the burst of pleasure that burned through his chest. "Is this what you feel? Dear God, woman, do the other one before I expire!"

Plum chuckled a throaty chuckle that vibrated down to Harry's toes. She leaned over to tickle his other nipple with the tip of her tongue. "I like the way you taste, Harry. You taste just like I thought you would—hot and masculine and very, very pleasing."

Harry gulped air as Plum's sweet little mouth closed over his nipple, sucking it and tugging it gently until he thought he would burst into flame.

"Enough," he said hoarsely, trying to twist around so he could plunge himself into her depths.

"No, not yet," Plum said, pushing him down into the bed. "I haven't finished. I haven't looked at the rest of you. You're made so finely, every part of you in perfect accord with the rest. I want to touch you. I want to feel you. I want to kiss you as you kissed me. I want to take you into my mouth and taste you, husband. Will you like that?"

Harry's brain ceased functioning at her question. He couldn't speak, couldn't think, only stare at her with wide, hopeful eyes and nod his head vigorously. Plum smiled a smile that made his legs stiffen with the effort to keep from spilling his seed right then and there, and then she lowered her head and kissed his belly. He groaned his pleasure at her touch.

"You're so hard, Harry, everywhere but your belly. Have I told you how much I love your belly?" She kissed the thin line of hair where it led down his stomach to his manhood. "I love your legs, too. You have horseman's thighs, all long muscles and beautiful contours."

He gritted his teeth as she trailed kisses across one thigh, her hand closing around the two globes of softness between his legs. They contracted instantly, anticipating her touch elsewhere, enjoying the light scraping of her nails against the soft flesh.

"God in heaven," he moaned, every muscle straining, waiting for her touch. Her breath steamed over the length of him as he stood hard and ready and near to bursting. It was his turn to grasp big handfuls of the bedding to keep from grabbing her, thrusting brutally into her, claiming her for his own.

She touched the very tip of him with her finger, spreading the moisture that had gathered there, gently pushing the outer layer of skin back. "It doesn't look comfortable to be so very hard, husband. And you're hot, I can feel the heat radiating from this part of you. I never thought it possible to be so hot, but you are, hot and very hard and yet your skin is like velvet here. You match the fire inside of me, you make me burn hotter for you."

Her hand closed around the base of his shaft, squeezing slightly as her mouth descended upon him, her tongue rasping his length.

"St. Genevieve's cods, Plum, you're going to unman me!" Harry gasped, senseless to all but the euphoria she generated in him.

"You are so very different from what I remembered," Plum murmured, sliding her hand along his hardness, stroking him as his hips thrust his length through her fingers. "Touching you like this makes me feel quivery inside. Do you feel quivery as well? You are enjoying this, are you not?"

Harry's head snapped back as he thrust in time to her strokes, unable to keep himself still, oblivious to all but the ecstasy she was giving him. A gargled moan came from his throat as she bent over him again, her hair spilling like ink around his hips as her tongue teased the underside of his most sensitive spot. He moved twice, three times, and roared a wordless roar of elation as he reached his climax.

"Oh, my!" Plum said a scant few seconds later. Harry lay twitching slightly on the bed, too exhausted to open his eyes. He knew what he'd see when he did, and a faint flush rose over his cheeks at the thought of it. She had done what no other woman had: she unmanned him.

"How interesting. I've never actually seen that happen before. This has been very enlightening."

Harry felt the bed shift slightly and cracked one eye open to see his wife pad over to the washstand, her long hair sweeping just above her adorable behind. She wetted a cloth and brought it back to the bed, cleaning him with a tenderness that almost undid him. His cheeks reddened even more under her ministrations, and he was heartily glad when she finished and went to replace the cloth. He knew what he had to do, but every instinct within him cried against it. It wasn't fair, it wasn't right that he should have to apologize for a natural reaction, since it was entirely her fault he had succumbed to the lure of her hands and mouth. He wanted to proceed upon proper lines, but she had insisted, and he being a gentleman, naturally let her have her way. And now just look what he had to show for it! He had to apologize to his wife for his selfishness when it was really all her fault for making him lose control!

"You have my apology, madam," Harry ground out, rolling to his side and giving her his back.

"Apology? For what?"

Good God, did she have to make it more difficult? "You have my apology for my thoughtless act just now."

"What thoughtless act?" Plum queried. She placed a hand on his hip and tugged, but he would not be moved. He wouldn't look at her, couldn't look at her, probably would never be able to look at her again in his whole, entire—now miserable—life. "Harry? Are you angry about something? Did I hurt you? You seemed to be enjoying yourself—have I done something wrong? Would you like me to touch you again?"

Harry groaned in a breath, and lurched as his wife's hand closed around him. He was still partially aroused, still wanted to bury himself in her heat, to feel her silken folds closing around him as he thrust into her. He wanted to watch her eyes mist with passion as she found her own release, wanted to feel her buck and arch beneath him as he filled her. He shuddered with the effort to remain in control as her hand explored him, caressing and stroking him to full arousal.

"Harry?" Her breath was hot on his ear. "I'm glad I gave you pleasure. I felt how much you enjoyed it, and it made me happy, too. Perhaps we can share that joy again?"

Harry's muscles quivered for one indecisive moment, then the choice was made. He whipped around, pulling her underneath him even as he was spreading her legs and settling himself at the entrance to her center.

"Look at me, Plum," he demanded, the tip of him pressing against her heat. She arched her hips in invitation as her eyelids fluttered open. "I want to watch you as I take you. I want to watch the passion fill your eyes as I slide deep within you. I want to watch you lose your control when I pound into you, thrusting myself deep within your body. I want to watch you gasp when your pleasure overtakes you. I want to watch you as I make you my wife."

He stroked slowly into her, his soul singing with

joy as her body yielded in welcome, a thousand little muscles gripping and holding him tight, parting with him reluctantly when he pulled back. He moved in time to the rhythm she set, her hips thrusting against his, her mouth welcoming when he bent his head to sip her sweetness. The bite of her nails stung his shoulders as she gripped him, crying soft little moans of delight, urging him wordlessly to move faster, deeper, stronger against her. Her hands slipped down the slickness of his back to his behind, clutching him and pulling him tighter to her. He grunted with the effort of holding back his own climax until he had brought her to satisfaction, denying himself and taking his pleasure in her cries of joy. His head dropped to her neck as he gasped for air, fighting the need to pour himself out into her, wanting her fire to fuel his own to a height he had not known before. As her hand slipped down over his behind, she wrapped her legs around his waist and bit his neck.

"Sweet St. Peter!" she cried, taking him deeper into her heat until it seemed as if he was touching her womb. "I love you, Harry. You are my life, my being, my everything. Dear God, how I love you!"

As her slickened muscles tightened around his length, he took her ecstasy into himself and with an effort that had to be nigh onto miraculous, pulled out of her body just before he spilled his seed. Her words echoed in his ears, fulfilling him, making him whole, joining him with her in a way he had not known possible. He shouted her name as he poured his life onto her thighs, and knew in that moment that he could not live without her. She was his homecoming, his safe harbor, and he knew with a knowledge inborn of man that his soul was inexorably bound to hers, that they were twined together, and nothing could ever part the two of them into separate people again.

She was his own true love.

Chapter Nine

Plum was not happy.

Oh, she knew she had no right to be unhappy—everything she'd ever wanted had been handed to her: she had a husband, a kind man with whom she suspected she had fallen in love; five children who, if they weren't exactly what she'd imagined when she thought of her ideal family, were at heart good children ... *relatively* good children; she had a home and security and was free from want or need; but despite all of the many blessings she counted as she lay snuggled up against her husband's chest, the soft rumble of his snore ruffling her hair, she was not happy.

She felt particularly ungrateful when she thought about the reason she was so unhappy—Harry was not impressed with her mothering skills. She dismissed his explanation about not wishing her to die in childbirth as simply Harry being kind and not wanting to embarrass her in front of Thom and Temple by admitting that he thought she was a poor mother.

"I am ungrateful," she whispered as she traced a finger along Harry's bicep. "What does it matter if he doesn't think I'm as good a mother as his first wife? Del is right, mothering isn't everything. I have other qualities, other talents. My whole life does not revolve around being a mother. I am a person unto myself, and do not need to be judged either by my ability to bear children, or my ability to raise them. I am me, Plum. That should be good enough for anyone."

Brave words, her inner Plum said in an annoyingly mocking tone. *The truth is, being a mother is what you want, it's what you've always wanted, all you've wanted. A family—that's what you've craved your whole adult life, and now you have one and you're not happy.*

Plum told her inner voice to go take a long walk along a short cliff, and turned her attention from self-pity to proving her excellence as mother to both Harry's existing children, and the ones she hoped to bear.

One thought leading to another, Plum's fingers found themselves stroking a path from Harry's arm, down his side, over his hip, to that part of him that lay nestled in quiescence along her thigh. She knew full well why he had spilled his seed outside of her body the previous night, but she had been too caught up in the moment of passion, in the knowledge of her love for him to beg him to give her a child. Instead she said nothing while he gently cleaned her off, reluctant to ruin the warm feeling that came when he settled back into bed, pulling her up against him, their arms and legs entangled as if their bodies could not be separated.

Plum tipped her head and glared down at the part of him that was the cause of all her woes. "You're not even handsome like the rest of Harry. To be truthful, you're a bit funny looking."

He stirred (all of him), his arousal stiffening and growing before her eyes.

"Funny looking?" Harry sounded annoyed. Plum smiled at his cute little belly. "What sort of comment is that for a wife to make the morning after a wedding night?"

She kissed his chest, then tipped her head up to smile into his disgruntled face. "I didn't mean it as an insult, husband, but you have to admit that part of the male anatomy is rather . . . comical."

His eyes widened. His nostrils flared. His arousal hardened. "My rod is not comical! It's an extremely fine specimen of its kind."

"Harry, I'm sorry if you're offended by my opinion, but I can't help it—it looks . . . funny. Look at it!" They both looked. It waved at them. "You see? It's all red and purple, and has that silly little bit of skin that slides back and forth like a purple visor on a helmet."

"Plum," Harry said, breathing loudly through his mouth, "you will cease deriding my rod. It is not comical or funny looking. It is manly. It all but throbs with virility. Vigor is its byword. I'll have you know that women the world over have been known to swoon before it. I have had nothing but praise and gratitude from all of the women it has pleasured."

Plum's giggle died a cruel death as she narrowed

her eyes at him. "Oh, really? Women the world over?"

"There are legions of women out there who would be happy to write up affidavits attesting to the completely *un*-funny nature of my rod," Harry continued, waving his hand at his crotch. "It is a majestic thing, a masculine testament to the act of love, a warrior, if you will—"

"A purple-helmeted warrior of love," Plum snorted as she wished all of those women who had shared Harry's body to the devil. "You sound like the very worst sort of prose, husband. I didn't say it was not a thing of great enjoyment—"

"You mocked it! You derided it!"

"I did not mock—"

"It's a wonder you haven't shredded my confidence in my use of it," Harry said as he rolled her over onto her back. "In fact, I believe you owe proof to my rod and me that you still believe in it. Me. Us."

"Women the world over?" Plum asked, her body melting wherever Harry touched. "*Affidavits*, Harry?"

He nipped her nose. "Perhaps that was an exaggeration."

"I fervently hope so," she answered, wrapping her legs around his hips, moaning softly as he claimed her mouth. His breath was hot and quick on her lips, but not nearly as rapid as the wild beating of her heart. He sucked her lower lip into his mouth, and Plum thought she was going to cry with the pleasure of it. He nipped the corners of her mouth, wordlessly demanding she part her lips to him, and she thought she would faint. His tongue plunged into her mouth, sweeping all objections before it, tasting her, teasing her, stroking her own tongue, and she thought she would die. But when he began to suckle her tongue, when he coaxed her tongue into exploring his mouth, when she tasted his groan of sheer delight, she knew she was in heaven. She pulled him down onto her body, pulled his head closer, trying to taste him, feel him, join with him all at the same time. Her senses swam with the contact, too much too quickly, too much stimulation, too little control, but none of that mattered as she arched up against him when he plunged his tongue into her mouth, little whimpers of pleasure gathering at the back of her throat.

Harry heard those whimpers and lost the thin shred of control that had kept him from plunging himself into her body. "St. Peter's cods, woman! I'm just a man! I can't stand such temptation."

She blinked at him, her eyes misty with desire, her skin heated with passion. She knew he was speaking, but she didn't understand the words. "Why are you talking? Now is not the time for talk, Harry. Now is the time for making love."

"Stop that," he ordered as her legs moved restlessly beneath him, rubbing against him in a provocative movement. "Don't move, don't kiss me, don't breathe. Just lay there, and perhaps I'll be able to get through this without shaming myself a second time." He bent to caress her breast with his lips. She slid one leg out from beneath him and wrapped it around his calf.

Harry reared backward like he had been shot in the behind, his eyes positively feasting on her flesh, his look so heated she swore she could feel its touch. "So soft," he said hoarsely as he looked at her. "Everywhere I look, creamy white skin, glistening, a veritable playing ground of delectable flesh, and it's mine, all mine."

Plum couldn't stop the laughter from burbling out. Harry looked like he was about to rub his hands with glee. "Yes, I'm yours, all yours. The question is, what are you going to do about it?"

"I want to touch you everywhere, I want to taste you, I want to plunge deep into your silken folds and lose myself in your heat."

She ran both hands up his arms. "And what's stopping you?"

He made a noise deep in his chest. "I'm a gentleman. You must have the choice of what you want first. Touching, tasting, or plunging?" His voice was rough, gravel-edged, and it thrummed deep within Plum.

Harry kissed her again, a deep kiss, a demanding kiss, a kiss that gave no quarter. "Make up your mind. Quickly. I don't have much time before I . . . er . . . I don't have much time."

"Mmm. Perhaps I can do something to help." Plum squirmed out from beneath him, pushing him over onto his back. "What a perfect opportunity for the *Steeplechase.*"

Harry stared at her in delighted surprise as she straddled his thighs.

She smiled. "You're absolutely right, Harry."

"Yes, of course I am. Er. About what?"

She put out a hand to touch him, and he groaned deep in his throat. "You're hot and hard and velvety smooth, but not funny looking. Not any more."

He grabbed her wrist and stopped her exploration. "For the love of God, woman, not now. Not unless you want it all to be over." His voice sounded like it was made up of gravel, all hard corners and grit. Plum smiled, and slid herself forward on his lap until the tip of him teased her heated core.

"In the *Steeplechase,* the jockey—me—has absolute control over the stallion. That's you," she added, just in case he missed that point. "The jockey's responsibility is to make sure her stallion doesn't run himself out before the end of the race."

His eyes opened even wider as she slid herself a little more forward.

"Timing is everything in the *Steeplechase.* Slow and steady wins the race."

Harry stared at her, speechless, a pulse pounding furiously in his neck as she slid along the length of his arousal where it pressed stiffly against his leg.

"I've found that by delaying our gratification, by prolonging the sweet torment, the final moment of ecstasy can be heightened tenfold."

She slid down his thigh, her body tightening in anticipation. "A hundredfold."

Harry whimpered hopefully as she moved upward toward his groin.

"A . . . a . . ." Their combined moisture provided a delightful friction, a friction that coiled tighter and tighter inside her until Plum opened her eyes very wide, positioning him against the center of desire. She looked deep into his hazel eyes, eyes that spoke louder than any words, eyes that told her how much he wanted and desired her, and with a sob of happiness that at last she had found him, the ideal man to share her life, she took his lower lip into her mouth, nipping it as she suddenly plunged downward. ". . . a thousandfold!"

"St. Peter and all the saints," Harry gasped as she sank onto him, holding his shoulders and panting slightly as her woman's flesh quivered around him.

Plum closed her eyes for a moment to enjoy the sensation of having him buried so deep inside her, but opened them again when her husband uttered a garbled, strangled choke. His fingers flexed into her hips, holding her tightly down against him, prohibiting her from moving the way she wanted to move. She felt muscles she didn't remember she had twitching around him, gripping him tightly, wringing harsh moans of pure masculine pleasure from Harry's throat. His head had lolled back against the pillow, his eyes were fixed on her face but she could swear they were unseeing.

He had also stopped breathing.

"Harry? *Husband?*" She shifted forward to administer a rousing slap, but the sensation of sliding along his hard length made her pause. Harry's chest heaved once, then again. Plum sat back, her eyes narrowed with pleasure as he slid back into her. She gripped his shoulders hard, her fingers digging into his muscles as he shuddered beneath her. She rose up, pressed her forehead against his, and eased back down, inch by slow inch.

"Stallions in the *Steeplechase*," she said as she experimentally flexed a set of inner muscles, smiling a slow, knowing smile when Harry growled in response, "can be run for a very great length of time if the correct pace is set."

Harry seemed to have other ideas. By the time she

had found a rhythm that made him moan nonstop deep-throated moans, he suddenly flipped them both sideways until she was on her back again, her legs hooked around his hips, as he plunged into her so deep she thought he had pierced her heart.

"You're mine!" Harry snarled possessively as he pounded into her heat. Plum didn't care that he was acting like a primitive, possessive, dominant male. All she cared about was that he was hers! All hers!

"Mine!" he said again, and seemed to want some sort of response from her, but she wasn't capable of words. That delicious tension, that coil wound up inside of her was tightening and twisting and spiraling her out of control again. She lifted her hips to him, pulling her knees high on his back, taking him in deeper than before, nipping his neck with joy. The coil was starting to unwind and she had no idea when it was going to stop.

"My wife," Harry groaned, plunging into her again and again. Plum began to sob a litany of nonsense, words that had no meaning, only emotion as she felt her being come loose from its moorings and merge with Harry's. Their two souls together lit up like a bonfire behind her eyes, and she cried out his name, sobbed it against him as he suddenly withdrew from her body, shouting his own declaration of fulfillment into her neck as he thrust himself against her belly.

"I . . . believe . . . you . . . won . . . that . . . race . . ." she gasped against his shoulder, holding him tight against herself.

"Bloody right, I did." Harry responded into her neck, his voice as shaky as she felt. "You helped a little, though."

Plum didn't have the strength to smile. Truly, she had no strength for anything, not even to protest his withdrawal from her body. She knew his reasoning for such a ridiculous act had nothing to do with his own pleasure, but she also knew that she would have to redouble her efforts to prove her worthiness as the mother of his yet unborn children. She didn't have much time left to her, biologically speaking. It was now or never. "And I choose now," she said softly, mustering enough strength to turn her head and look at her husband.

Harry's chest rose and fell quickly as he struggled to catch his breath, his skin slick with perspiration, his eyes closed. He raised a hand as if to protest her words, but it fell back to the bed, lifeless. "Now is completely out of the question, wife. You killed me. I am dead. I am deceased. I am a former Harry. Later, perhaps in a year or two, after I've recovered from this insidious method of murder you chose to destroy my poor man's body, we'll discuss my resurrection, but not now. Now is not possible. Now does not even exist for me. See? I am no more."

Plum used the cloth at the side of the bed to wipe off her belly, then rolled over onto her side and propped her head up on one hand. "You can speak." She sighed a mock forlorn sigh. "I must not have done it right if you can still speak. I shall simply have to try better the next time. I will make it my life's goal to improve, Harry. No doubt with practice, I will."

His eyes rolled back in his head. "If you do, you really will kill me."

"Flatterer," Plum said, and snuggled up against his damp chest.

"How did you know about the *Steeplechase*?" he asked a few minutes later.

Plum had been prepared for that. While she wasn't willing to admit she was the author of the *Guide*, she had decided that Thom was right in judging Harry open to such instruction, and that hinting she had read it would not be a bad idea. The key was to tell him the truth without telling him too much truth. "The *Steeplechase* is one of the activities described in the *Guide to Connubial Calisthenics*."

Harry cracked open one eye. "You've read it?"

"Yes. I've read it." Frequently over the past few years, if for no other reason than to remind herself exactly what sort of things went on in a marriage bed. It had been so long since she had any experience in that matter. . . .

"Ah. I was hoping to get you to read it a bit later, after we've had some . . . uh . . . experience with one another, but it's just as well if you're familiar with the book. I assume your first husband gave it to you?"

Plum picked her words carefully. "He was responsible for me reading the *Guide*, yes."

Harry made a noncommittal hum and closed his eye again, his arm tightening around her as she relaxed against him. That was one hurdle past. Things were going to work out. They had to. It was simply a matter of her putting her mind to the task.

"My life is going to rack and ruin, you know that, don't you?" Plum asked four weeks later.

Unfortunately she asked it of Edna, her timid maid. Edna had improved over the past few weeks to the point where she now no longer crossed herself whenever her mistress spoke, but she was still a bit twitchy whenever Plum gave free rein to whatever unconventional thought floated around in her mind.

"But ma'am, that's ever such a pretty gown," Edna said, her eyes puzzled as she watched Plum frown at herself in the looking glass. "The color suits you perfectly. I don't see that it will ruin your life."

"That's not what I meant, although Harry does have a very good eye for color, much better than mine." Plum stopped frowning at her thoughts and took a good long look at herself in the glass. The rich wine of the watered silk set off her dark hair well, and the cut of the gown, although a bit higher in the bodice than she was accustomed to, was flattering. "He really is very good to us, bringing in Madame Sinclair to make new wardrobes for Thom and me, and yes, Edna, the gown is very pretty, but the fact remains that despite being the possessor of ten new day gowns, four dinner gowns, six chemises, three ball gowns, two riding habits, and more stockings and gloves than I can count, my life is still going to rack and ruin."

Edna made an inarticulate, near-*eep* sound that had Plum closing her lips over the rest of her complaint. Edna was looking wary enough; the last thing Plum wanted was for the maid to be run off before her hair was done.

Fifteen minutes later Plum dismissed Edna and went in search of her husband. Today was the day of reckoning. Her reckoning. "Good morning, Thom. Have you seen Harry?"

Thom paused at the top of the staircase, the two

footmen who were trailing her halting obediently behind. "I believe he went down to work on his project."

Plum nibbled her lower lip. "Oh."

"He was whistling, and he looked like he wanted to smile," Thom said helpfully.

"Was he?" Plum blushed a little, just a tiny bit, just a wee little pinkening to her cheeks. She had to admit that although there were definitely parts of her life that could be improved, her physical relationship with Harry had been absolutely perfect. Harry had been most enthusiastic about working through the exercises presented in the *Guide*, and even had a few calisthenics of his own to show her. In addition to their nightly engagement, Harry had awoken her each morning with another testament to his stamina and creativity. Plum didn't wonder that he was smiling. He often left her grinning her head off.

"Yes, he was," Thom answered, eyeing her with far too knowing a look. Plum made an effort to not look smug. "Temple told me he hasn't seen Harry so happy in years, since before the first Lady Rosse died. He says it's because you're keeping Harry content."

"Temple is impertinent." Plum's blush turned a bit hotter. "Where are you off to with that large net and the ladder?"

"Bats," Thom said succinctly, and after giving Plum a cheery smile, turned to march up the next flight of stairs. Plum stood back to let the footmen pass, trying to decide whether to go beard Harry in his den, or to check on the children first. It was really a matter of the lesser of two evils—the children were always up to something, usually something guaranteed to make her look bad in front of their father, while going to speak to Harry . . . she took a deep breath and turned her feet toward the stairs leading down to the hall. She loved Harry. She loved him a great deal, more than she had ever loved a man, and after the incident last night, the time had finally come for her to tell him the truth. Or part of it—the part concerning Charles. She owed him that much.

"Good morning, Lady Rosse. You look as charming as one of the tea roses you uncovered in the garden."

Normally Plum would have enjoyed Temple's compliments, although she knew his approval had more to do with the fact that she had persuaded Harry to allow his study to be cleaned rather than anything else she'd done since she married him, but this morning she had an ugly secret to bare. Trading compliments would have to wait. She bit her lip. "Is Harry working on his project?"

"Yes. Another two crates arrived from Rosehill early this morning. He's sorting through them."

Drat it all. Boxes of papers had been arriving for him at a steady rate for the past two weeks, the arrival of each heralding a period when Harry was incommunicado until he staggered out for the evening meal. Plum was dying to know what the project was about, but all Harry had told her was that he was looking into an episode in his past for someone in the government. She hadn't wanted to pry, although the fact that he didn't trust her with the details about his project rankled. The irony of her situation—that she hadn't trusted him with her own secrets—did not escape her; they just made the rankle that much more uncomfortable. Only the fact that she had been busy trying to bring some order to the house, the staff, and the children, not to mention attend daily fittings from the modiste Harry had brought in, choose wallpapers and paint colors, select furniture to be thrown out or refurbished, prowl the attics in search of hidden treasures to scatter throughout the house, and a hundred other everyday tasks kept her from pressuring Harry into telling her more about his project.

"Temple . . ." Plum eyed the door to Harry's room for a moment, then turned her attention to the secretary standing before her. "Just what exactly is this project Harry is engaged upon?"

Temple's glance slid from her to a spot on the wall just beyond her shoulder. "I couldn't say, ma'am."

"Of course you could, Harry tells you everything. You mean you *won't* tell me."

Temple inclined his head to allow that was so.

"I dislike secrets, Temple," Plum said, pushing back the knowledge that she had no right to adopt such a self-righteous tone, justifying her annoyance with the memory of just what sorts of secrets men kept. They could be very harmful, indeed. "Harry said his work has something to do with an event in his past. What event?"

"You'd have to ask his lordship that, ma'am."

Plum allowed herself to have one of her three daily sighs, and turned toward the door to Harry's inner sanctum. "I'm disappointed in you, Temple, I truly am."

"I am indeed grieved to hear that."

"I had expected better of you."

Temple bowed his head as if he was overwhelmed with grief.

"I had thought we were friends. Friends, as you must know, tell each other things, particularly when those things concern a much loved individual."

He didn't look the least bit contrite. "Do they, indeed, ma'am? I will remember that for the future."

It was no use. She couldn't shame him into telling her Harry's secret, and in a way she admired him for standing firm; she knew what the repercussions could be of someone spreading details that were not meant for common knowledge. Taking a deep breath, she rapped briefly on Harry's door, then entered the room. It was still dark and murky, but at least it was clean, and the windows shown brightly, allowing in more than just a mote or two of sunlight. Today they stood open, the fragrant smell of baked earth and newly scythed grass wafting in, the distant low of cattle and the chatter of birds reminding her of just how wonderful summer could be. If only she could get Harry outside to enjoy some of that lovely weather.

"Harry, do you have a moment?"

He looked up from a mountain of papers, his eyes brightening. "For you, however many moments you desire."

She gave him a weak smile, nervous and feeling a bit clammy about her mid-section now that the moment had come to unburden herself. She walked toward his outstretched hand, allowing him to pull her onto his lap.

"I don't suppose you came in here to work your womanly wiles on me?" he asked, nibbling along her neck. "Dare I hope that you've come to seduce me and save me from the mind-numbingly tedious work of sorting through these papers?"

Plum squirmed on his lap, trying to slow her beating heart, trying desperately to hang onto her good intentions. Harry always managed to drive even the simplest of thoughts from her mind whenever he touched her. Delaying her moment of truth, she seized the opening he offered. "Is your work so unpleasant, then? Is there something I can help you with?"

He kissed her ear. "Thank you for such a selfless offer, but no. I wish you could, but it's something I must see through myself."

She squirmed again, and he caught her hips, holding her still. "What is it you're looking for?"

"Just some boring old notes. Nothing to concern yourself with."

"I'm very good with notes. I would be happy to be of assistance."

The wonderful laugh lines around his eyes crinkled delightfully as he grinned at her. "Sweetheart, I wouldn't be able to get a single thing done were you to try to help me. I'd be too busy planning what calisthenic I wanted to try with you."

"But—"

"No, thank you, Plum. I should be done with this in a week; then I promise I'll be a better husband."

Guilt washed over her in a wave that had her heart contracting painfully. He was so wonderful to her now, how could he think he was anything less

164

YES! ☐

Sign me up for the **Historical Romance Book Club** and send my TWO FREE BOOKS! If I choose to stay in the club, I will pay only $8.50* each month, a savings of $5.48!

YES! ☐

Sign me up for the **Love Spell Book Club** and send my TWO FREE BOOKS! If I choose to stay in the club, I will pay only $8.50* each month, a savings of $5.48!

NAME: _____

ADDRESS: _____

_____

TELEPHONE: _____

E-MAIL: _____

☐ **I WANT TO PAY BY CREDIT CARD.**

☐ VISA   ☐ MasterCard   ☐ DISCOVER

ACCOUNT #: _____

EXPIRATION DATE: _____

SIGNATURE: _____

Send this card along with $2.00 shipping & handling for each club you wish to join, to:

Romance Book Clubs
20 Academy Street
Norwalk, CT 06850-4032

Or fax (must include credit card information!) to: 610.995.9274. You can also sign up online at www.dorchesterpub.com.

*Plus $2.00 for shipping. Offer open to residents of the U.S. and Canada only. Canadian residents please call 1.800.481.9191 for pricing information.

If under 18, a parent or guardian must sign. Terms, prices and conditions subject to change. Subscription subject to acceptance. Dorchester Publishing reserves the right to reject any order or cancel any subscription.

JOIN NOW!

than perfect? Shame made her words sound pettish and ungrateful. "Very well. If you don't wish to share your burden with me, I won't pry."

Harry laughed and kissed her chin. "As if I haven't burdened you with enough?" Plum's heart sank. His words and tone were playful, but his meaning was clear. She hadn't done very well with the responsibilities he had given her, it was no wonder he didn't trust her with anything more. Before she could protest, he continued. "Before I forget myself and investigate the charming breasts I know are hiding beneath your bodice, what was it you wanted to see me about?"

Plum couldn't meet his eyes. She bit her lip, told herself to stop being such a coward, and blurted out, "It's something . . . unpleasant."

Harry groaned. "All right. Out with it. Who did what now?"

A month's experience of rescuing animals, objects, and sometimes people from the almost always disastrous attention of her stepchildren gave her an understanding of just what he was asking. "The children haven't done anything."

"No? There hasn't been another accident, has there?"

Plum frowned. "No, you know I'd tell you if anything else happened, but as you bring that up . . . Harry, don't you think it rather odd that so many things have gone wrong during the last few weeks? First McTavish got sick eating something that we've still to identify—"

Her husband cocked a brow. "I thought we decided he ate a poisonous berry by mistake?"

165

Plum shook her head. "I'm not convinced of that. He says he didn't eat any berries, but he's hiding something. Then the girls and Thom were accosted by that gypsy while they were out walking in the fields—"

"That was likely just a vagrant looking for a handout."

"—and then Digger had that fall from his horse. You said yourself that you found two burrs under the saddle, so poor Frozen Dawn had no choice but to buck when Digger mounted him."

Harry's hand slid up her thigh in a most distracting manner. "Yes, but I also said that the boys had been playing with the saddle blankets, and they could have inadvertently picked up a burr or two while they were being dragged God knows where."

"That's unlikely," Plum argued, ignoring the heat his touch generated.

"But not impossible."

"Then there's—"

Harry sighed—he did not have to ration his sighs. "Plum, are you going to recount every incident that's happened during the last month? Because if you are, I'd prefer you be naked so I can at least enjoy the scenery."

She slapped his hand away from where it was creeping, annoyed that even after a month of her trying to control the children, they still behaved like maniacs. "Harry, I'm serious."

"I know you are, sweetheart, and I appreciate that you're so concerned for the children, but close acquaintance with them forces me to be blunt—disaster follows them like shadows. What they don't cause by their own actions, seems to be drawn to them. Once you learn to accept that, you'll be much easier in your mind."

"Hrmph." Plum didn't agree with that, but realized the moment to fight that battle was not now.

"Was that all you wanted?"

"No, what I have to say to you concerns me."

Both of his eyebrows raised. "You? What could you have to tell me about yourself that was unpleasant? You haven't changed your mind about me and now want to run off with Juan?"

"No, it's not that," she answered, unable to keep from responding to his teasing grin. She kissed the tip of his nose. "There's no other man who could possibly compare with you, Harry."

He had the smug look of a man with a well-pleasured wife, but as she was the wife in question, she didn't mind.

"It's . . . uh . . . about last night."

"Last night?" His eyebrows rose again. "What about it?"

Plum's cheeks turned pink under his gaze. Stupid cheeks. She had worked through a great many of the calisthenics with Harry, had seen, touched, and tasted almost every part of his person, and still she blushed whenever she mentioned their activities. "Last night, when you performed *Matador Facing a Wild Bull*, you . . . you"—her gaze dropped to his shoulder—"finished inside me rather than out, as you have done in the past."

"Ah. Yes. That." Harry's voice sounded a bit strained. Plum peeked up at him, unsure of what she would see, but surprised to find his eyes filled with remorse. His jaw tightened, a muscle flexing in his cheek before he spoke. "I apologize, Plum. I had not meant to do that, but the matador move had me a bit closer to the edge than I anticipated. I assure you it won't happen again."

Her hopes plummeted. "It won't?"

"No. I made a promise, and I will hold by it."

Well, hell. She should have known it was a mistake, and not a sign he was softening toward her. Still, she had promised herself weeks ago that when Harry finally trusted her with his seed, she would trust him with at least one of her secrets. "I see."

"Plum?" He lifted her chin and peered into her eyes, worry evident in his. "I didn't hurt you when I did the matador, did I?"

"No, you didn't. It's always been one of my favorite calisthenics, but Charles was never very good at it."

Harry relaxed, a slight smile playing around his lips. "I suppose it's not right to wish the dead ill, but I have to admit I'm happy to know that I can outperform your first husband on at least one front."

Plum bit her lip again, damned her weak spirit, took a deep breath, and steeled herself for Harry's reaction. "Charles wasn't really my first husband, you are. That is, he *was* my first husband, except he was already married when he married me, although I didn't know that until six weeks later, when he admitted that our marriage was bigamous, and he had done it simply because he knew I'd never become his mistress, which was true, I would have never agreed to anything so shocking, only what I did turned out to be more shocking, because everyone thought I had simply jumped into his bed, when I truly thought we were wed, and they cut me, cut my entire family until I was disowned, and sent my poor sister into a fatal decline as a result of the scandal."

She ran out of breath before she could finish the explanation. Harry sat still as a stone throughout all of it, his eyes steady on hers, not a word passing his lips. Her gaze dropped before his, unable to bear looking at him any longer. She had known telling him the truth would be awful, but this was unbearable. "I should have told you before we were married. I was too afraid you wouldn't marry me if I did. I am a coward at heart, Harry, and for my deception I am very sorry. You deserve better. If you'd like me to . . . to leave, I will."

His finger curled around her chin, lifting it, forcing her to meet his gaze. His eyes were dark and unreadable. "Leave this room, or leave me?"

Tears pricked behind her eyes. She swallowed, her throat tight and aching. "Whichever you prefer."

His kiss took her completely by surprise. His mouth was warm, so warm and loving as he feasted on her lips, then slid his tongue inside to take full possession. Hope, blighted into dust, began to gather itself again. "Silly wife. As if I could survive without you."

"You couldn't survive without me?" Plum asked, her voice quavering as the tears filled her eyes. He wasn't upset? He wasn't angry? He wasn't hurt and disappointed and shocked by her past?

He kissed her again, gently this time, his thumb wiping away the tears that spilled over her eyes. "You should know by now that I can't live without you, none of us can. I'm sorry you were treated so poorly, both by the man to whom you'd given your trust, and by your family, but you can't imagine that it has any effect on us now."

"But . . . but . . . the scandal!"

Harry chuckled, he actually chuckled. Plum's spirits, which had been residing in the bottom of her new boots, rose and soared. He wasn't angry! He could laugh! He wanted her still! "I think I like you silly as you are now. It's such a refreshing change from the competent, unflappable Plum. It gives hope to those of us who are made of much coarser earth."

"It was a very bad scandal," Plum said, ignoring his teasing compliment, feeling that as long as he knew the worst, he should be told the full extent of its ramifications. "My father said I would never be received in polite company again, and that no one nice would know me."

"Your father didn't reckon with me," Harry said, his slow smile making Plum's eyes fill with tears again, tears of love this time. How could any man be so wonderful? "You're my wife now, Plum. The fact that you were taken in by the worst sort of rogue twenty years ago will not be an issue."

"But, Papa said—"

"Your father was wrong. I know the *ton*, and although there is nothing they like more than scandals, this one will not be fodder for their picking."

"How do you know that? They were very cruel to me and my sister. Thom has been made to suffer, too, by not being brought out when she should, by not having the advantages she should, or being taken in by my family when her uncle died. I wouldn't want my sin to hurt the children as she has been hurt."

170

"Thom looks anything but hurt," Harry laughed. "She's blossomed here, in case you haven't noticed. The only blight on her horizon is those blasted breeches you refuse to allow her."

"Yes, but the children—"

"Are fine and this cannot hurt them. You might not think much of my title, but I assure you being a marquis has a few benefits, one of which is the ability to blot up any spills in your copybook. What my title can't induce people to forget, my reputation will."

"I happen to be a very messy writer," Plum said, thinking that not even Harry could wield enough power to make the *ton* to accept the notorious Vyvyan La Blue as his wife. That secret, at least, was safe. No one but her, Thom, and her man of affairs knew the truth, and none of them would speak.

Harry laughed again, hugged her, and kissed her very quickly before gently pushing her off his lap. "If you don't leave now, I'm going to throw everything on the floor, set you on the edge of my desk, spread your lovely white thighs, and—"

"Harry!" Plum stared pointedly at the open window. A newly employed gardener stood just beyond, staring in with his mouth hanging open.

Harry gave her another of his infectious grins. "You see? You're a bad influence on me. Now go, before I really give him something to gape at."

"But, I'm not finished speaking with you about the scandal—"

"There's nothing more to be said." He made shooing motions with a handful of papers. "Take your lovely, tempting self off and do something frivolous.

But not too strenuous, you'll need your strength later. I've thought up a variation on *Hummingbird Supping Nectar* that I think you'll like."

Plum clung to the door frame, her knees weak at the thought, but she made one more attempt to reason with him. "The scandal—"

Harry set down the papers and walked over to the door, gently pushing her through it. "The scandal is no more. I swear that to you."

"But—"

"But nothing. There is nothing to but. I defy you to but me again." He pried both of her hands off the door frame, kissed each finger, then started to close the door. "Thank you for warning me, but now I must get back to work, else I won't have time to demonstrate my improved hummingbird technique."

"Harry—"

"Leave. Begone. Avaunt. Off wit' ye. Bye-bye."

The door clicked quietly as it was closed in her face. Plum stared at the door for a moment, thought about using the second of her three daily allowed sighs, and decided the moment wasn't sigh-worthy enough. "Pooh," she said, instead.

"Just so," Temple agreed as he rose and handed her a salver full of letters.

"What's this?"

"His lordship asked me to give them to you."

"Oh." A sudden thought brightened her. "Is it something to do with his project?"

"I'm afraid not. They are invitations and letters of congratulations from the local gentry."

Plum blanched and backed away from the salver as if it contained a poisonous asp seated atop a large pile of offal. "I don't want them. Take them away.

172

Tear them up. Burn them. Bury them deep in the compost heap."

Temple watched her back up toward the door, pursing his lips as she fumbled for the doorknob. "I sense you have a reticence with regards to correspondence of a social nature. I do not wish to pry, but would I be permitted to ask for the reason you wish me to destroy invitations issued to his lordship and you from polite persons of an upstanding nature and general good reputation?"

"No, you may not," Plum said, then made her escape through the door, closing it quickly behind her and standing with her back to it as she tried to calm her wildly beating heart. Harry might be convinced that his name alone could keep people from gossiping about her, but she had no such conviction. Until she was sure that he really did have that sort of power, she'd spurn all invitations that might bring her face-to-face with someone who knew of her past.

Coward, the mocking voice in her head whispered.

"About this I'm simply being cautious," she said aloud, and went off to see what sort of deviltry the children had gotten into.

Chapter Ten

It was the sheerest fluke that Plum happened to be strolling through the lowest levels of the garden when she heard the scream. She was supposed to be receiving the local vicar, but she left Thom to do those honors, and went out with Burt the head gardener to look at reclaiming the last bit of wilderness in what was once a grand tiered garden.

"I believe this was an herbaceous border at one time," she said to Burt. "If you were to clean it up and plant some—good heavens, what are the children doing now?"

Plum and Burt turned to look at the crescent of willow trees that lined a small pond filled with stagnant, odiferous water. She frowned and started toward the pond, her chin set. Burt trotted behind her. "Drat those children, I told them just two days ago they weren't allowed to hunt frogs on that pond anymore. The last time they did, Anne pushed Andrew out of the boat, and came in reeking to high heaven."

"Pond gets the runoff from the compost heap, it does," Burt said.

"That would explain the stench. If I find that they're out in that boat again, I'm going to—"

Plum never had time to complete her threat. As she and Burt cleared the trees, a sight to chill any mother's blood met her eyes. The boat had capsized, its bow pointing upward, the stern submerged. Digger had one child—Anne or Andrew, she couldn't tell which—under his arm, and was swimming through the algae and slime to the shore. Another child—McTavish—clung to the side of the sinking rowboat, shrieking like a banshee. The water beyond McTavish rippled, and the top of a tow-head emerged for a moment before it sank again.

Plum didn't waste any breath on exclamations— she kicked off her slippers and ran for the edge of the pond, instinctively taking a deep breath before diving into the foul water. Dimly she heard Burt beside her, and set off for whichever child was drowning beyond the boat.

She gasped as her head cleared the water—the pond was so foul, it tainted the air sucked into her lungs, searing them as if she was breathing in smoke fumes, making her choke and gasp. Digger yelled from shore that he had Anne, which meant it was Andrew who had gone under. Plum took a deep breath, and dived. The water stung her eyes, and was so murky and filled with matter churned up by Andrew's flailing body that she could not see. It was only by luck that her outstretched hands felt the whisper of fabric. She lunged forward, both hands trying to follow the elusive material until an arm came into her grasp, an arm that snaked itself around her in an iron grip. She grabbed a handful of jacket, and kicked upward, her lungs burning, her eyes an agony.

"I've got him," she yelled as soon as she surfaced. Andrew coughed and sputtered with her, his arms and legs thrashing as she tried to keep his face out of the water. "Stop fighting me, Andrew, or you'll drown us both."

"Can't swim," he gasped, and wrapped both arms around her neck, cutting off her air.

"Just . . . ow! Stop choking me, we're only a few yards from shore . . . relax. You're safe now."

Slowly, hindered by Andrew attempting to climb her as if she was a ladder, Plum got them to shore. Digger was bent over a retching McTavish, Anne lying in a moaning heap next to him. Burt waded back into the pond to pry Andrew off her body.

"All right," Plum said just as soon as she spat up some of the foul water she'd swallowed. She wiped her green slime-covered hair out of her eyes and glared at the four children lying on the grass before her. "You are all in so much trouble, you cannot possibly begin to fathom the depth of it. Did I not just tell you two days ago that you were not to go out on the pond?"

Digger groaned and picked gelatinous ropes of algae off his front. "Lord, she's going to lecture us now."

Plum gasped. "Digger! Language!"

He rolled his eyes, an act that had Plum seeing red—despite being covered in stinking green. "Don't you roll your eyes at me, young man!"

"I'm an earl," Digger said, pulling himself up to his full height. "I can do whatever I like."

"You're a young man perilously close to having his breeches down to receive a thrashing," Plum snarled. Burt, sensing that all was well—at least health-wise—slunk off to change his clothes. Anne and Andrew snickered.

Plum glared them into silence before turning back to her oldest stepson. "Of all the stupid, inconsiderate acts—you could have drowned yourself and your brothers and sister with your foolishness! Do you have any idea how annoyed your father would have been if I had to tell him you all drowned?"

Digger shrugged. Plum, stinking to high heaven and scared more than half out of her wits by the near-drowning of four children who had become—despite their tendencies to drive her insane—very dear to her, shoved him toward the house, turning to help Anne to her feet as the other children slowly got to theirs.

"Digger's going to get a whipping," McTavish said with great complacency as he took Plum's hand in his. "Papa will be mad at Digger, won't he Mama?"

Digger's shoulders twitched.

"Don't you 'Mama' me in that endearing, adorable tone, you little rapscallion," Plum said, shaking with the aftereffects of terror as the blissful numbness of anger wore off. "Your father is going to be very angry with all of you. I wouldn't be surprised if he takes each of you out to meet his razor strop."

Anne's eyes opened wide. "He wouldn't whip me, I'm a girl!"

Plum, who knew full well that Harry had never

lifted a hand in punishment toward his children, wholeheartedly supported his policy of instilling in them the belief that they were just a heartbeat away from a well-deserved beating. "You think not? *I'm* not so sure of that."

Anne's brow puckered worriedly. Plum, who wanted to clutch the children to her with one hand, while shaking them with another, decided that it wouldn't hurt to let them stew over their punishment. When she thought of how near they had been to real tragedy . . . "I wouldn't like to be in your shoes now, I certainly wouldn't."

McTavish's hand tightened around hers. He looked down at his feet. "You wouldn't?"

"No, I wouldn't. Wasn't it just yesterday your father lined you all up in the library and lectured you for twenty minutes about disregarding orders he and I give you?"

Digger snorted. Anne looked more worried. Andrew scowled. McTavish released Plum's hand and tried to run off after a pretty butterfly. She grabbed the back of his shirt and marched him toward the house. "Yes, indeed, I would be very, very worried had *I* been one to disregard your father's strictures."

"What's a stricture?" McTavish asked as Plum gently pushed him up the steps to the verandah.

"Order."

"Papa won't whip me, he says I'm too young," he replied, and scampered up the last of the steps. "Race you to the kitchen!"

"Nursery!" Plum bellowed as the children turned left at the top of the stairs and ran off down the length of the verandah. "Change your clothes before you do anything else, and don't you think you've escaped so lightly! I have not finished talking to you about ignoring—don't you give me that look, you are in enough trouble already, you do *not* want to be pushing me any further!"

Plum sighed her third sigh of the day as the children raced away, wondering for the hundredth time how she was to prove her excellent mothering skills to Harry when his children defied her attempts to mold them into well-behaved examples of manners and decorum rather than the wild heathens they were. She sniffed back a tear of self-pity, and immediately wrinkled her nose. The sun warming her wet shoulders heightened the horrible stench to the point where it could drop a horse at fifty paces. "Bath first, then Edna can burn this gown," she said to herself as she squelched wetly through the French doors into her sitting room. She would just run upstairs before anyone saw her. . . .

That thought died as she realized the sitting room was already in use.

Plum blinked in surprise as Harry rose from the rose damask settee, a cup of tea in one hand, a small plate of biscuits in the other. "Ah, there she is. Plum, my dear, may I introduce mister . . . mister . . . Good Lord, woman! What *have* you done to yourself?"

The vicar! She'd forgotten about the vicar paying a call! Plum's eyes closed in horror for a moment as she tried to blot from her mind the sight of the vicar's and his wife's appalled faces turned to gape open-mouthed at her. A third woman clutched a handkerchief to her nose as she surveyed Plum from slimy head to weed-encrusted foot.

Thom, seated beyond Harry and playing mother

as she poured tea, stared at her in equal surprise. "Been swimming, Aunt Plum?"

Harry took a step near her, then quickly retreated once he got a whiff of the eau du pond. "What the devil . . . sorry Vicar . . . what's going on?"

"I . . . er . . ." Plum glanced to the side. The vicar, a pleasant-looking, mild little man gazed at her with real concern. His wife fanned herself vigorously while discretely extracting a small vial of perfume from her reticule. The other woman, dressed in puce with a bonnet that resembled a warped saddle, wore a look of pure, malicious delight. Plum dragged her gaze from her to Harry. "There was a little accident at the pond. No one was harmed, but I . . . er . . . fell in. If you will excuse me, I will change into something a little more suitable."

"Suitable?" the woman with the saddle on her head snorted. Plum paused at the door, unsure if she should apologize for her untoward appearance, or just gracefully sail out of the room and act as if she was above such petty concerns as smelling like a bog. "Anyone *less* suitable to be the Marchioness Rosse than Charles de Spenser's whore you would have a long way to find."

The vicar's wife gasped and dropped her vial. Harry turned slowly to look at the woman. Thom, with calm deliberation, removed the cup and plate clenched in Harry's hands, then rose and stood by her aunt.

Plum lifted her chin and gazed as coolly as possible—not an easy feat when one was dripping with pond slime—at the woman. "You must be Miss Stone."

"I am," the woman said in a loud aggressive tone. "I know who you are, as well."

"Yes, of course you do, you would be a fool not to know," Harry said suavely, but Plum could see the tiny muscle in his jaw twitch. He was angry, very angry, and although she knew he wasn't angry at her, it was her fault he should be exposed to the scorn of such a vile woman. She felt sick, nauseated that what she had dreaded would happen, had. "She is my wife, the stepmother of my children. She is my marchioness."

"She is also the mistress of Charles de Spenser, youngest son of Viscount Morley," Miss Stone crowed.

The vicar's wife swooned backward, drooping in the approved manner on her husband. The vicar's eyes were wide with astonishment as he waved his wife's vial under her nose.

"*Was* the mistress of Charles de Spenser," Harry said calmly, the tension in his hands belying his placid tone.

Miss Stone's vicious smirk of triumph dimmed a bit in the face of Harry's complacency. "You know of her shame?"

"I know of her marriage to Charles de Spenser, yes. And although I don't believe my wife's past is the concern of anyone present but her and myself, I will this once make an exception to my natural distaste in discussing such a private subject with persons not related to us."

Plum blinked back a few tears of adoration for Harry. She'd never heard him speak in such an aristocratic, cold voice, but she knew he did it for her sake. She was torn between a desire to kiss her darling avenging angel, and the need to shield him from the contempt she knew he would face.

"A bigamous marriage," Miss Stone spat. "He was married already when she went to his bed."

"I had no idea Charles was already married—" Plum started to say, but ceased when Harry took her hand in his, stroking his thumb over the pulse in her wrist.

"You don't have to defend yourself to these good people," he said, never once taking his eyes off the evil Miss Stone. "Although obviously they have heard only the basest lies, no doubt being good Christians they will be delighted to learn the truth, not to mention being filled with joy to learn that you were innocent of any wrongdoing other than having a too loving heart. They will be shocked when they are told of the cruelty practiced upon you by a disgusting cur of a man who thought nothing of using and abandoning you, and I'm sure they will do their utmost to remedy any false impression created by the slanders that other foolish and stupid people have spread in the misguided belief they were speaking the truth. Surely, everyone here knows how I worship the very ground you walk on, and that I would never, under any circumstances, allow anyone to say ill of you without exacting the most heinous and exhaustive of retributions."

Plum held her breath, her eyes on Harry's as they glittered meaningfully behind his spectacles. Miss Stone was no match for him. Before his threatening gaze, her eyes wavered, then fell as she slumped back into the chair, deflated of the spite and venom that had puffed her up like a balloon.

Harry turned to the vicar and his wife, both of

whom immediately swore their whole-hearted devotion to clearing any misconception regarding Plum's past.

Plum herself stood in silent misery-laden bemusement, watching Harry carefully. He turned to her, pulling her hands to his mouth as he winked before kissing her fingers. "My dear, I'm sure you wish to change into something a little less reminiscent of a cesspool."

"Yes." Plum blinked at him, her mind more than a little numb. Had he just winked at her? Had he taken the wind so effectively out of Miss Stone's sails? Had he with just a few words, erased the shame of her past?

"Now, perhaps, would be a good time?" His eyes twinkled at her. She goggled at that. He could twinkle after what just happened? *Twinkle?*

"I'm sure you will all excuse my wife. Thom?"

"I'm right here. Come along, Aunt Plum. What you need is a bath to wash all that pond off you."

Thom's arm was warm on her damp sleeve, but Plum couldn't stop staring at Harry. He winked and twinkled? Was he *mad?*

"It was a pleasure meeting you, Lady Rosse," the vicar said, standing and giving her a little bow.

Was *she* mad?

His wife hurried to add her niceties. "Oh, yes, it was, it was very nice, and I hope we see you on Sunday."

Mayhap they were all mad, and none of them knew it?

"A pleasure," Miss Stone said in a begrudging, surly tone. Her face was dull red with anger, but Plum found little sympathy for her.

"Plum?"

Her name was soft on Harry's lips. She turned to him. "Hmm?"

Harry made shooing motions with his hand.

She blinked, then suddenly reason, blessed reason was returned to her, and she realized that he had done the impossible just as he said he would. She wanted to kiss him, but felt she'd shocked the vicar enough for the day, so contented herself with allowing her love to shine in her eyes. Harry mouthed, "I told you so," at her as she let Thom escort her from the room.

"What a nasty, vile old cat that Miss Stone is," Thom said as they walked up the stairs.

"And what a wonderful, adorable, marvelous man Harry is," Plum replied, her mind full of her husband. She sighed happily. "Could any man be more perfect?"

She was married to a raving lunatic.

"We're *what*?" Plum cried ten days later.

"Leaving for London in three days." Harry stuffed another handful of papers into a leather satchel. "Gertie assures me the children's things can be packed by then—you won't have any difficulty, will you?"

"No, of course not—that is, yes! Yes, I will! I couldn't possibly pack everything by then. London? All of us? *Why*?" Plum was well aware that last word was pronounced desperately close to a wail, but she was too distraught to worry over such trivialities. He wanted to go to London? Now? Wasn't the shameful scene they'd recently survived—admittedly due to his ability to forcibly erase her past—enough for him? He had to be scorned and ridiculed in London as well? Why now, when she was just starting to feel comfortable with her role as his wife? Why couldn't he wait, oh say, ten or twelve years, just until she felt like she really had a firm grasp on the job of being his wife?

Harry stopped satchel-stuffing long enough to make a face. "I have to go to London to meet with the head of the Home Office. It's nothing I want to do, Plum, but it is my duty to go when it concerns a past investigation of mine."

"Investigation? What sort of an investigation?"

He set down the satchel. "I told you that I did some work for the government, didn't I?"

"Yes, although you didn't say what sort of work, exactly." And at that moment, Plum didn't care what he had done in his past, except in terms of it necessitating his return to London.

"The nature of the work is neither here nor there, the fact is that I have to present the results of my findings to the new head of the HO, and discuss with him the possible repercussions. As it is my preference not to leave my new wife alone for who knows how long, and since I know you won't wish to leave the children, I have decided that we will all go to London. Granted the city may never be the same after the children get through with it, but we'll just have to take that chance."

Plum wrung her hands and tried to convince her husband to leave the children and her at home, but he would have none of it. "Plum, I don't want to leave the children behind because . . . well, I left them earlier this year to check out this property when it had been left to me, and during my absence there was a fire. An entire wing burned down, the wing housing the nursery. It was only by the quick thinking of Gertie and George that the children were saved. You know that the girls' governess died?"

"Yes, but—"

"She died in that fire. The children were upset about it for months." His thumb stroked a line down her jaw. "I know it's silly of me, but I don't want to leave them again. I almost lost them once— I don't wish to tempt fate again."

Her heart melted under the look in his eyes. "Harry . . . the scandal—"

"What scandal?" he asked, nuzzling her neck.

She gave up. She knew there was no way she could stand against neck nuzzling, so she didn't even try. Instead she gave the (reluctant, and with much misgiving) orders for their things to be packed, and three days later they set out in numerous carriages.

"You're making too much of it," Thom told her two days after they had started their journey, as they were about to leave the inn at which they'd spent the night. "Probably no one will recognize you—it's been twenty years, Aunt! And how long has it been since that man you married died? A year?"

"Six months. Even if no one remembers the scandal itself, *I* will be recognized, and then everything will come out," Plum said glumly, one eye on the younger children as they romped around the inn yard chasing geese. "The whole dreadful thing will be aired once again, and everyone will mock me, shame Harry, ruin the children's and your lives, and then he will regret marrying me, probably going so far as to hate me, no doubt ending with him going to the Lords asking for a divorce, at which point I shall die homeless and friendless living in a ditch with an earthworm named Fred as my sole companion. I just hope Harry will be happy then."

Thom laughed and patted her on the arm. "Don't be such a pessimist. I'm sure you'll have a perfectly lovely time in town, and no one will know who you are if you don't want them to. Twenty years is a long time."

"Not nearly long enough, but at least I can do right by you," Plum said thoughtfully, noting how well a new gown suited Thom. Her dark curls were glossy with health, her cheeks bright, her eyes sparkling with good humor and happiness. "I can see my duty through with regard to *your* future. You will make your debut. You will go to balls and routs and breakfasts, and possibly the opera, if I can arrange all of that before I'm recognized and our lives are completely and utterly destroyed."

"No!" Thom said, her face turning pale. "I don't want to go to balls and routs and breakfasts, and I especially do not want to go to the opera! I can't think of anything I'd like less! I'll be miserable! I'll hate it! I'll be wretched!"

"Welcome to my world," Plum said, then hurried off to rescue a goose that had been cornered by the twins and McTavish.

Two nights later Plum stood with a trembling hand on her husband's arm as they paused at the top of a long curved flight of stairs. She wondered briefly if she threw herself down the stairs whether or not she'd break her neck outright, dying instantly, or if she'd just bounce down the steps, embarrassing Harry by displaying to everyone not only her sad lack of ability to navigate stairs, but also showing too much limb and perhaps even petticoat. Since she suspected it would be the latter, she allowed him to pull her unwilling self down the stairs, a grim smile curving her lips.

"Plum."

"What?" she asked, transferring her grim smile to her husband.

"You look like you've been asked to roast a small child over an open fire."

"I do not."

"You do. You have a horrible expression on your face."

"It's called a smile, Harry."

"Yes, but it's a I've-been-asked-to-roast-a-small-child-over-an-open-fire sort of smile, one that is going to frighten the elderly and make everyone else stay away from you."

"Good," Plum said, her voice rich with satisfaction, the first morsel of satisfaction he'd heard her express since he had informed her that morning that they would be venturing into society by way of Lady Callendar's ball. "Perhaps that way no one will discover who I am and I might just possibly survive this evening."

Harry stopped at the bottom of the stairs and drew his wife aside, out of the way so he could speak to her without being overheard. He stopped her next to a large man-sized potted palm. "Why do you think I would lie to you?"

"Lie to me?" Plum looked startled, her lovely brown eyes wide with surprise. At least that wiped the child-roasting smile off her face. "I've never thought you'd lie to me, Harry. Never!"

"Then why do you assume that what I've told you before—that your past will not be an issue—is untrue?"

"I . . . I—"

Harry kissed her hands, damning the need for him to prove to her that she had nothing to worry about with regards to her past. He'd much rather be home with her now, trying out yet another of the inventive *Connubial Calisthenics,* but he couldn't just think of his own needs, he had to re-assure his wife once and for all that she was worried needlessly over something so trivial only she and a few countrified tabbies remembered it. "I will say this just one more time, and then if you continue to disbelieve me, I shall be forced to pun-ish you—no one will care what happened to you twenty years ago. You are my marchioness, and that is all."

Plum stopped worrying her lower lip and pursed it, instead. Harry resisted the urge to kiss the wits right out of her. "Punish me? What sort of punish-ment are you talking about? Because frankly, hus-band, forcing me to come to this ball should count as the worst sort of punishment."

"Look at it this way," he answered, tucking her hand into his arm. "At least you're not alone in your desire to be elsewhere. Thom is miserable, too."

"Yes, there is that," she said, looking to the right. Thom was marching down the stairs with a mar-tyred look on her face that almost identically matched Plum's grim smile. Harry couldn't help but smile at the two of them—two of the loveliest women he had ever seen, and both looked like they were being sent to their own executions.

Harry had no qualms about the evening's outcome—he had done a little investigating on his own regarding Plum's first husband (as he then thought of the bastard) when Plum and he were first married, and had found that the man had drowned in a boating accident off the coast of a small Greek island where he had been living the past ten years. Harry had enough experience with the collective mind of the *ton* to know that without the stimulus of de Spenser, no one would recognize Plum, let alone remember the scandal. He also knew, however, that despite assurances to the otherwise, Plum believed with every morsel of her being that she would be the tool of his destruction.

Harry did his duty. He strolled around the crowded, overheated rooms, introducing his wife to every person he knew, and quite a few he hadn't met, not even flinching when her grip on his arm turned painful. He dragged her around to every single person he could find, and only when they had met and had a few polite words with everyone present did she begin to relax. He coaxed her into a waltz, a dance that normally Harry loathed, but one that afforded him the possibility of holding his wife in his arms. He pulled her tighter than was polite, grinning at her mock-scandalized look in response. "You no longer look as if hot pokers are being inserted under your fingernails, so I assume that means you are beginning to enjoy yourself?"

The smile that had been teasing her lips faded as

guilt flashed in her lovely eyes. "Oh, Harry, how selfish I have been! I'm sorry, I'm so sorry for ruining your evening."

"My evening hasn't been ruined. Well, it will be if you don't accompany me out into a dark corner of the garden where I can kiss you silly, but assuming you have no objections to that plan, I will survive an evening in society."

The delicate blush he was delighted to see touch her cheeks grew darker as her eyes flashed a challenge he felt obliged to meet. "You can certainly *try*, my lord. As for the other—you were right, no one remembers who I am, not one person! Harry, truly you have my humblest apology for not believing in you. You've performed a miracle!"

Harry held her for a few seconds after the dance ended, wishing more than ever he was at home where he could receive her—unnecessary—gratitude in a much more tangible form. He took her hand in his as he led her to the next room, his eyes alighting on a familiar—and very welcome—figure. "Much as I would like to be worthy of such an appealing look in your luscious eyes, I can't claim the responsibility for a miracle. The *ton* is notoriously fickle, and voracious where gossip and scandal are concerned. They no sooner consume one, then they're on the prowl for their next source of entertainment. Now, if you can stand one more introduction, I've just seen a man whom I'd very much like you and Thom to meet."

Plum looked around as Harry led her through the throng toward a group of men near the card room. "Where has Thom gone to?"

"No doubt she's made her escape while we were distracted. My dear, may I present to you Lord Wessex? Noble, this is my wife, Plum."

The tall, dark-haired man spun around at his voice. "Harry! What the devil are you doing here?"

Harry allowed himself to be enveloped in a hug of such enthusiasm that his wife's eyebrows raised in surprise. He grinned and thumped his old friend on the back. "We had a little business in town. I thought you were in the north?"

"Came back for Parliament. It is a pleasure, madam. I had no idea you'd married again until I saw the notice in *The Times*."

Plum's hand twitched. He patted it. That announcement had been a sore point with her, but he'd be damned if he hid the existence of his wife as if he were ashamed of her. "Is Gillian here? I'd like her to meet Plum."

Noble's brows pulled together in a scowl. "She's home with the children. The two youngest are down with chicken pox—you must come for a visit if you've had 'em. Nick's due to meet me here in a bit. He'll be delighted to see you as well—it's been how long? A year? Too long."

Harry agreed, and spent an enjoyable ten minutes catching up with all of his friend's doings, aware the whole while that Plum was distracted, nervously looking around herself. He took the opportunity of an acquaintance drawing Noble's attention away to ask her what was wrong. "You're not still worried, are you?"

Plum's gaze swept the room. "Not about myself, but where do you think Thom has disappeared to?"

"Probably dancing. She's a good girl, Plum. She won't do anything to shame you."

"Shame me?" Plum gave him a disgruntled look. "I'm not worried about her shaming me, I'm concerned that she was so bored she left without telling me. I think I'll go look for her. . . ."

Plum hurried off. Harry mingled with the gentlemen lounging inside the card room, pulling Noble aside when he was free.

"I like your wife," Noble said to him as they strolled to the far end of the room. "And you look happy with her. I'm glad you remarried, Harry. It was time."

"It was beyond time, but that's not what I want to talk to you about."

"Aha!" Noble said, his grey eyes alight with humor. "I knew it. You didn't just come to town to introduce your lady, did you?"

"Hardly. You know I have no love for society. I'm here because the new head of the HO wants my advice concerning the Stanford situation."

"Stanford?" Noble frowned, shaking his head when Harry offered him a cigar. "Wasn't he responsible for bringing you up on charges of treason?"

"That's the man. Lord Briceland had heard some disturbing rumors that Stanford wasn't acting alone. He asked me to look into it. I've spent the last six weeks combing my records looking for a clue to the identity of the man who might be involved."

"And now you're here to report in?"

"I'm here to find proof." Harry lit a spill and waved it under the end of his cigar until it glowed red. "It shouldn't be too difficult."

"Who is it you suspect?" Noble asked, his voice dropped so no one would overhear.

Harry smiled a wry smile. "The last person you'd imagine. I believe it's—"

"Harry!" Plum pushed her way through the room, oblivious to the curious glances she was receiving. She grabbed his arm and started tugging him toward the door. "Forgive me for interrupting you, Lord Wessex, but this is a grave emergency. Harry, you have to help me find Thom. She's disappeared! No one has seen her for the longest time. You don't think something's happened to her, do you? She's never been to London before. I'll never forgive myself if someone said something cruel to her, and she ran away. . . ."

Harry threw his cigar into the fireplace, casting an apologetic glance at his friend as Plum dragged him out in search of his errant niece-by-marriage.

Chapter Eleven

Thom was bored. She was more than bored, she was nigh on moronic with the insipidness of the *ton*. She had heard much of them from her aunt, and although Plum seemed to recall her pre-Charles days of dancing and flirting with much fondness, Thom had no desire to waste her life in such frivolousness. It wasn't that she was serious, per se, nor a bluestocking, it's just that she felt there was more to be had out of life than talking about nothing but gowns, babies, the latest rake to hit town, and the hundreds of other meaningless things that caught the attention of the upper class.

She wandered around the big house, exploring those rooms that had been opened in honor of the ball (and a few rooms she suspected had not), smiling at people, but initiating no conversation. She finally settled on the dark, quiet library as the best place to pass time uninterrupted by the demands of her aunt that she dance with one foolish man after another. She'd suffered through dances with three such men, men so similar in their banalities and appearance, she couldn't distinguish one from another, let alone remember who they were.

"No one will notice if I spend a bit of time in the library," she said to herself as she slipped into the room she had noted earlier in her wandering. "No one will bother me, and I won't be a bother to—oh! You there! Stop! What do you think you're doing?"

Thom closed the door behind herself and marched into the room, not the least bit intimidated by the fact that a young man with filthy hands and face had turned to scowl at her. She grasped a poker from the fireplace and pointed it at him, taking in his shabby, dirty clothing, a small cloth bag at his feet, and the window he was in the process of opening. It was obvious what was happening—the young man's hand was on the sill as if he was preparing to escape with his bag of no doubt ill-gotten goods.

"You're a thief!" Thom said, a secret thrill running through her. At last, something of interest to save her from the mundanity of the evening. A thief, a real thief. How *very* fascinating. What was the correct way to deal with one, she wondered as she eyed him. Polite but firm, that should do it. "I've never met a thief before. Especially not one so—" She stopped. There was no need to tell the villain that despite the dirt and grime, she thought he was a very handsome man.

"Especially not one so what?" he asked, his hands rising in surrender as she prodded his dirty waistcoat with the poker to make sure he wasn't armed.

"Bold. Only a bold person would think of burglarizing a house while a ball is going on. That or a very stupid one, and to be truthful, you don't look particularly stupid. Oh. I probably shouldn't have said that, should I? I should be convincing you as to the folly of your current path. It is foolish, you know. Sooner or later you're bound to be caught, especially if you insist on burglarizing houses where the occupants are holding entertainments such as a ball."

The man smiled, and Thom found herself unable to keep from smiling in response before she realized what she was doing—smiling at a burglar! What was next, laughing with an arsonist? Swapping charades with a strangler?

"'Bold,'" the burglar said, looking oddly pleased by her words. "I rather like the sound of that. What would you say if I told you I wasn't a burglar?"

She snorted. What did he take her for, one of those simpering, idiotic young ladies in the other room who knew nothing but how to look pretty and flirt and embroider nicely? She walked around him, keeping her poker handy in case he got any ideas. "Let me see, why would I think you were a burglar? Well, for one, there is the matter of your clothing. It is ill-kept and just the sort of thing that I imagine thugs and ruffians and men of bad repute wear when they engage in acts of a nefarious and illegal nature. It fairly reeks of burglary."

The man looked down at his clothes, rubbing a bit of dirt off a grimy waistcoat so tattered, she wouldn't bed down one of her cats on it. "Ah. That. I can explain—"

"And then there is the fact that you have in your possession a bag of such dimensions as might be used to hide your swag."

"Swag?" The man's lips twitched.

Thom felt a corresponding twitch in her own lips, but quickly regained control of them, schooling them into what she hoped was a stern, forbidding line. "That is, I believe, the correct slang? I read it in the *Flash Dictionary*. It does mean stolen booty, does it not?"

"It does," the young man said, giving in and grinning at her again. "I'm just surprised you should be familiar with such a word, let alone the *Flash Dictionary*."

"I have a very eclectic reading taste," Thom told him, momentarily charmed by the amused light in his handsome gray eyes. Really, he was very agreeable for a burglar. He seemed well-spoken despite the obvious wicked nature of his employment. "In addition to the other items, there is the fact that you were attempting to escape via the window."

He looked behind him to the window, his head tipped on the side as he studied it. "It seems to me that unless you actually caught me in the act, you can't be sure of whether or not I was opening or closing the window when you arrived."

"Don't be ridiculous, your bag is positively bulging with swag and such. It's quite clear to me that you've allowed your lower nature to run amok, and now you are escaping with the fruits of this labor. Can you deny that the bag holds your swag?"

"I could," the man said, leaning back against the wall, looking just as comfortable as if he had been born there. "But that would take all the enjoyment out of you attempting to sway me from my sinful path. You were going to try to sway me, weren't you?"

"Oh, yes," Thom said guiltily, dragging her mind away from the pleasing contemplation of his eyes. "Of course I am. It is my duty. Er . . . I'm not quite sure how to begin. I've never had to sway a burglar before. How would you advise me to proceed?"

He looked thoughtful for a moment. "You might get further if you told me your name. It's the personal touch, you know."

"It is? Very well, if you insist. I am Thom."

"Tom?" He looked a little surprised.

"Thom. It has an *H* in it."

"Ah." He nodded wisely. "That makes a difference."

"Yes, it does. What is your name?"

"Nick. No *H*s in it whatsoever. And your surname?"

"Is none of your concern. We can be personal without it. Now, Nick, it is my duty to lecture you about the sins of your chosen path."

"You may proceed," Nick said, his lips curving slightly as if he found something she said amusing. Thom had no idea what that could be, but admitted to herself that she found the young man in front of her a hundred times more pleasing than the dandified fops she had just left. At least this man was real. He had a goal in life, even if that goal was to steal items belonging to others. "Don't spare me. I am ready and willing to hear your thoughts on the despicable life I have chosen to lead."

She pursed her lips and tried to think of something to say to him. "The problem is," she said with a sigh a few moments later, "I don't really see what's wrong with your despicable life. Oh, the stealing part isn't good. You shouldn't steal something that doesn't belong to you, you really shouldn't, but as for the rest of your life, I can't imagine it's too despicable. You are free to do whatever you want with your life, are you not?"

"Within reason, yes."

"And if you don't want to do something—"

"Then generally I don't do it."

"Exactly. That seems to me to be the ideal life, really. Freedom and your own choice to guide you— the burglary aside, of course."

"Of course," he said, his eyes laughing.

"Are you a very good thief?" It didn't seem to be quite a correct thing to ask, but Thom was not so naive as to be blind to the fact that her entire conversation was not quite appropriate, so it didn't seem to her to matter if she compounded that by asking something she wanted to know.

"Not really, no. I haven't had much experience at it."

He looked a bit distressed by that thought, and Thom hurried to reassure him. "You needn't worry that I will tell anyone that I saw you here. You will, of course, have to replace those items you took, but I can see that you aren't a terrible person."

"Thank you," he said gravely.

Thom gestured to the bag. "May I?"

He handed it to her. She set it on a nearby desk, opening it, extracting from within it a set of gentleman's evening wear, and a pair of highly glossed shoes. She stared at the clothing for a moment, sympathy for him welling up inside her as she moved her gaze to his laughing gray eyes. "I have ten guineas."

The laughter within them died as he watched her. "You do?"

"I do." She nodded and put the clothing back into the bag, handing it to him. "My aunt's husband gave me a quarterly allowance of twenty guineas. I can only give you ten, though, because I promised the children to treat them to Astley's and the toy shop."

"You did." He still looked a bit surprised.

"Yes, I did, and I would hate to disappoint them. They get very inventive with their revenge if you disappoint them. When it rained two weeks ago and we couldn't go on a picnic, they filled my bed with slugs. If you give me your direction, you may have the ten guineas."

Nick considered her for a long moment before replying. "Do you offer money to every burglar you meet?"

"No," she said, smiling. She couldn't help herself, he was a very charming burglar, one who seemed to deserve smiles. "Only those who need it. Your direction?"

He looked confused as he slowly said, "A message to The Tart and Seaman will reach me."

"The Tart and Seaman?"

"It's an inn near the docks, but Thom, don't send me your money. I can't—" Nick's head snapped up at the sound of voices outside the hallway.

"Go," she hissed, shoving the bag into his arms and pushing him toward the half-opened window. "I won't say anything about seeing you. Go now!"

Nick squawked something as she shoved him out the window, but she didn't wait to hear what it was before slamming the window shut, closing the curtains and spinning around just as the door to the library opened and her aunt peeked in.

"There you are! We've been looking everywhere for you. Oh, Thom, you don't know how worried I was—never mind, it doesn't matter now, I've found you. Harry, I found her!"

Thom allowed herself to be bustled out of the library, casting a quick glance over her shoulder toward the window. What a very interesting evening it turned out to be. She couldn't help but wonder if she'd ever see the handsome, disreputable burglar again.

She rather hoped she would.

". . . and please, in the future, Thom, if you have to disappear, would you have the goodness to tell me first, so I won't worry?"

"Yes, Aunt Plum." Thom's head was bowed. Plum felt a momentary pang of remorse for having to lecture her in this manner, but no one knew better than she just what sort of rakes and rogues lurked in the background, ready to pounce on an innocent young woman.

"You have no idea the pitfalls and traps that lie waiting for an unwary young woman to stumble into them."

"Yes, Aunt Plum."

"I don't wish to seem unreasonable, Thom, but truly, your disappearance worried me half to death."

"Yes, Aunt Plum. I mean, no Aunt Plum."

"Even Harry was worried, were you not, my lord?"

"Not in the least. Thom seems a sensible sort,"

Harry said. Thom flashed him a grateful smile. Plum could have throttled them both. "Ah. A country dance. Shall we, Plum?"

"I'm sorry, but I have a good seven or eight minutes left of a lecture for Thom—"

"She'll have to hear it later," Harry said with one of those persuasive twinkles in his eyes. Plum never could hold out against his twinkles. He added a devilish grin to his twinkling eyes, and she knew she was doomed.

"My spleen will become enlarged if I do not unburden myself of the entire lecture," she protested, but gently for she knew that her spleen could never win against both the grin and the eyes.

"I will personally guarantee that your spleen will not suffer," Harry said, bowing low to her as the first figure of the dance began. Plum curtseyed, casting a warning glance over her shoulder to her niece. Thom waved and sat down next to a large matron in a voluminous puce gown. Praying she would stay there out of trouble, Plum relaxed enough to enjoy the lively dance, something she hadn't done in twenty years.

"I'm surprised I remember the steps," she told Harry as the dance brought them together. "It's been so very long."

"You never looked lovelier," Harry answered before they were separated to dance with their adjacent neighbors.

Plum glowed at his compliment, knowing that he was deliberately attempting to bolster her spirits in what he realized must be a trying night for her, but still pleased that he took the time to tell her how well she looked. The truth was that she was beginning to enjoy herself. Probably a good part of that had to do with the fact that there were so few people present whom she remembered from her two seasons.

A short, red-haired gentleman with a receding chin was her partner for this turn. As she danced forward to him, she realized with a start that she knew him—he had been one of her first beaus. What was his name? Sir Alan? Alec? Sir something-starting-with-an-*A* didn't seem to recognize her in the least. He smiled at her as she danced around him, returning to stand as he danced a circle around her.

"This is a very charming ball, is it not?" she asked as they came together.

"It is indeed. Very charming."

"Are you here with your family?"

"Yes, my eldest daughter is coming out. That's her near the duchess—Mariah, her name is."

"She's very pretty," Plum answered, noting the resemblance between the short, red-haired girl and her partner. "Is your wife here as well?"

"Yes indeed, Lady Davell is just beyond Mariah."

Davell—he was Sir Ben Davell, the first man to ever send her a bouquet following her coming-out. And here he was, a middle-aged balding man with a daughter almost as old as she had been when they first met.

And he didn't recognize her.

"I am Lady Rosse," she said as they clasped hands and made a bridge for others to pass under.

"Yes, I know, you were pointed out to me."

"Really?" Plum stiffened, wondering why anyone would point her out unless it was to pinpoint her for rumor mongering.

"My wife pointed you out to me. She said you are newly wed to Lord Rosse."

"Oh, yes, we are." He was polite, respectful—everything a gentleman should be. There wasn't even the faintest whiff of anything condescending or smug about him. Plum relaxed again and danced the rest of the figure in a thoughtful mood, returning to Harry even more grateful than before that she'd found him.

"Happy?" he asked at one point in the dance.

"Ecstatic," she answered a few minutes later, when they were again brought together.

And she was. Everything Harry had promised had come true—she had met nearly everyone present, from the duchess who was a cousin to the hostess to the Feehan sisters, two very old wrinkled ladies who were said to have been the late George II's mistresses. The Feehan sisters of Plum's memory had sharp eyes for scandal, and sharper tongues, and yet when she was introduced to them, they cackled over her newlywed status by making a rather questionable remark comparing Harry to a stallion and her to a mare, but not one eyelash did they bat over her. It was as if the last twenty years were nothing but an unpleasant dream, lingering in the back of her mind, but groundless, with no substance.

The fiddles drew out the long last notes of the dance, and she sank into a deep curtsey, smiling at Harry as he took her hand to guide her off the floor. "Thank you."

"For the dance?"

"For making my life wonderful. No one else could do it but you. No one else could give me such happi—"

The words froze on her lips as the people before her parted, baring to her view the sight of a man bending over their hostess's hand in greeting. The man straightened up, his eyes meeting hers, recognition dawning as she froze into a giant lump of solid horror.

"Gack," she gasped, her blood turning to ice.

"What?" Harry asked, his voice concerned.

In a panic, Plum's first thought was to run. Since that was impossible, nor would it do any good, her second was to get rid of Harry. "Water. I need . . . water. Or punch. Could you please get me a cup, Harry?"

"Yes, of course." Harry guided her over to an empty chair. "I'll be right back."

Plum cast a quick glance around the room, but no one seemed to have seen anything out of the norm. Thom was chatting with a pretty young woman, and didn't in the least bit notice when Plum got to her feet to greet the man of middle height and nondescript brown hair who approached her.

"Plum?" the man said, his nostrils flaring for a second, his mud-colored gaze sliding over her bodice. The boldness with which his gaze rested on her left her feeling dirty, as if she needed to bathe in order to remove the taint of his attention. "It is you, is it not? My dearest Plum, what a pleasure to see you again."

Plum closed her eyes for a moment, swaying a little as the room dipped beneath her feet. "Yes, it is me, Charles. What a horribly unpleasant surprise. They told me you were dead."

"They were wrong. I was insensible for several months, having received a blow to my head in a boating accident, but as you can see, my health is quite well." He took her hand and made a show of kissing the back of it.

Plum snatched it back. "Go away."

"My dear, wild horses could not drag me from your side. Can it be you hold some animosity toward me regarding that regrettable experience so many years past?"

"Regrettable experience? You ruined me, deliberately and willfully." Plum's hand itched to strike the smug smile off his face.

He shrugged, still wearing the abominable smile. "A young man's folly. My family told me you had gone into seclusion, and yet here I return to my native shores to find you as delightful as ever—and quite in the thick of society. You have done very well for yourself, Plum, very well indeed. Might I ask who your protector is?"

"Protector?" Plum's eyes widened as she realized just what he implied. "Harry is not my protector, he is my husband."

"Really?" Charles drawled, looking about himself with his quizzing glass. "You managed to marry? How very droll. I had assumed no man would wish to burden himself with another man's leavings, but then, I have been away for many years. Evidently not all is as I remembered."

"Not every man has as crass and disgustingly low a nature as you possess, Charles," Plum said, noting that Harry had returned to the room, and was starting around the dancers with a cup of punch in his hands. She had to get rid of Charles, and fast, and at the same time squelch any notions he had of discussing her past. If she could just get through the

207

evening, then she could think how best to deal with him. "Some men have honor. My husband is well aware of the sad trial I have lived through, and doesn't give a fig for it. As you can see I am received by all, so nothing you can possibly say about the past will have any effect."

"No?" Charles said, raising his hand in acknowledgment when an acquaintance beckoned to him. "Indeed, you have done well for yourself, Plum. My congratulations on your success . . . both in your happy marriage and your literary endeavors."

Plum froze again, this time into a glacier of fear and horror and every last one of her worst nightmares.

Charles leaned close, his breath hissing in her ear as he whispered, "How very satisfying it is to be the man who taught the infamous Vyvyan La Blue everything she knows."

For an awful moment, Plum was sure she was going to vomit, but as the seconds passed and Charles took himself off, she managed to push the bile that rose within her down enough to give Harry a feeble smile when he made it to her side.

"Your punch, my lady . . . Plum? Are you unwell?"

Harry's voice was warm with concern, breaking through the wall of ice that had enclosed Plum. She turned to him, desperately needing his strength, needing him to comfort her, but the look of concern in his eyes was her undoing. How could she repay him with cruelty for all the kindnesses he had shown her?

She couldn't. She wouldn't. Harry had done everything he said he would do—he had effectively

208

erased her past. It was up to her to deal with Charles . . . somehow.

"I'm not feeling terribly well, no. Would you mind if we left now? I'm sure Thom won't care, and if you're done speaking with your friend—"

"We will leave at once," he said soothingly, and went to collect Thom. Plum used the few minutes to say good-bye to her hostess, keeping a wary eye out for Charles. She wouldn't put it past him to confront Harry, although she suspected he would not be happy with a mere scene in public. She had experience with Charles—he was a coward at heart, and would not wish to risk giving Harry the opportunity to call him out.

"If only I knew what he wanted of me," Plum said softly, then dismissed that thought as Harry and Thom came up to her. She was certain Charles would make her desires known to her by one means or another. He was never one to disregard his desires.

"Plum?"

"Hmm?" Plum absently checked the leather cuff that bound Harry's left hand to the massive ebony headboard. What would Charles want from her?

"You seem to be distracted."

"Am I?" How was she to keep Harry from finding out about Charles until she could take care of the situation?

"Yes, you are. Distinctly distracted. In fact, I sense that you are disturbed about something. Are you?"

"Am I what?" She slid across his body to secure his other wrist. How Charles knew she was Vyvyan La Blue was no surprise—they had made it a game to name all of their connubial calisthenics; no doubt he remembered that, but what would he do with that knowledge?

"Disturbed."

"No, not particularly. Why do you ask?" Perhaps he just wanted to gloat over his knowledge? Perhaps he just wanted to revel in the power he must feel in knowing her secret?

"Well, for one, we were supposed to be doing *Gladiator and the Shy Dove* tonight, and yet you seem to be bent upon *Gallant Knight at a Blind Maiden's Mercy.*"

No, that wasn't like Charles; he didn't enjoy hoarding secrets, he enjoyed profiting from such knowledge. No doubt he thought to profit from hers. A toe nudged her calf. She looked down, somewhat startled to find her husband spread out naked before her, tied to his bed with the fur-lined leather cuffs he had given her just two weeks before. "I thought you were going to be the gladiator tonight? Why are you bound?"

He frowned. "You *are* distressed about something. What is it, Plum? Did someone say something to you at the ball?"

She couldn't look at his eyes while she lied to him. Her gaze dropped to his chest, then stayed there awhile as she enjoyed the scenery. "No, no one said anything. I just feel a bit . . ."

"Neglected," Harry said, nodding his head. "I understand completely. It's my fault, but I was thinking of you, Plum. I knew you were tired from the travel, and since we had little privacy in the inns, I felt our nightly exercises would be best curtailed until we arrived. Therefore, as the fault is mine, so must the solution be. Climb on."

"I beg your pardon?"

"Climb onto me. Onto my . . . er . . . you'll feel better afterward, I promise."

Plum thought of pointing out that *that* would never be in dispute, but decided instead to humor him. Clearly he was worried about her—as a dutiful and loving wife, it was her responsibility to ease his worries as best she could. "Well, as long as we're doing *Blind Maiden and Knight,* we might as well do it properly."

She blew out the candles so they were in the dark, the faintest sliver of moonlight showing silvery blue through a gap in the curtains. Enjoying the experience of relying solely on touch, Plum slid her fingers up Harry's chest, reveling in the way his breathing hitched as she stroked a path up the warm hills and valleys of his chest. Her hands slid higher until both palms framed the long planes of his face. Her fingers teased his short little side-whiskers, then traced downward along the strength of his jaw until they met together on his gently squared chin. She bent her head and lightly brushed her lips against him, a fleeting kiss that promised much, and which was so sweet she had to repeat the action. Harry's mouth opened in invitation beneath hers, allowing her to tease the entrance to his mouth with her tongue. She captured his bottom lip between hers and bit gently, his resulting moan coursing through her, igniting fires deep in her center.

Of their own volition, her fingers slid up his head, plucking off his spectacles before returning to comb through his close-cropped hair, her head dipping again to his, this time allowing her tongue to enter the warmth within. He lay strangely passive, allowing her to stroke his tongue, to tease his mouth into reacting, but when he did it was as if he had set her afire. A groan of pure pleasure rose in her throat as his tongue swept into her mouth, demanding that she match his passion, firing her to greater heights.

The leather straps creaked as Harry tried to reach for her, but could not. Plum pulled her mouth from his, having forgotten for a moment that she was supposed to be comforting him.

"Do you want me to unbind you?"

"Yes."

She nuzzled his neck, sliding away from him as she said. "I'm sorry, but I'm not feeling terribly merciful at the moment. Perhaps later?"

"Plum! Come back here!"

"Yes, my lord?" Blindly, Plum slipped out of her dressing gown, smiling in the dark. She knew Harry was hot and hard—he always was whenever they were in bed together, bless him—but he really should know better than to think she'd leave him in that unpleasant state.

"Come back here. I . . . er . . . you intend to finish what you've started?"

"I do?" With one hand on the bottom of the bed, she padded softly around to the other side.

"Yes, you do," Harry said sternly. She smiled again. How adorable he was. "You are suffering from the trauma of attending a ball after a prolonged absence. If I do not affect a cure for your condition, it will return and leave you helpless come other such engagements. Therefore, you will straddle yourself across my thighs, and seat yourself upon me. *Now!"*

"Such a thoughtful husband you are," Plum said as she climbed into the bed. Linens rustled provocatively beneath him as she stretched out a hand, finding the hard muscle of his thigh. "Thinking only of me."

"I am the very best of husbands. There are none better than me," Harry answered, sounding oddly as if the words were coming from between grinding teeth.

"That goes without saying, Harry."

"Plum?"

"Yes, my dearest?"

"If you do not wrap your long, luscious thighs around my hips in the next ten seconds, I will die. Do you understand?"

"I think so." Plum stroked a path up his thigh to where the texture of the light down covering his legs changed to a denser hair. She closed her fingers over him, tracing the long, velvety length of his arousal.

"St. Peter's cods," Harry groaned, thrusting his hips upward in her gently stroking fingers. "This is for your own good, wife: GET ON ME NOW!"

Harry's voice was coming out raspy and hoarse, his breath fast and rough. Plum chuckled a little to herself over the fact that her breath was just as ragged as his.

"I am ever the dutiful wife," she said as she swung her leg over his, positioning herself so the silky tip of him bumped against the skin of her inner thighs. Then she adjusted herself and felt his heat at her entrance, pulling from her an answering heat that started deep inside her and spread through her soul. "And as you seem to think this will help me . . ."

Their groans of pleasure were spontaneously given as Plum sank slowly down on him, but her husband's pleasure fed hers, spiraling her on that delicious journey she had learned could take her to heaven and·back. She felt a brief moment of power when she remembered that one of the joys of the *Blind Maiden* was that she could set her own pace; no insistent hands would grip her hips and hurry her into a tempo that would send them heedlessly toward paradise. Instead she rose and fell upon him slowly, ignoring her husband's throaty pleas to cease tormenting him and ease his torture.

"You said this was for my benefit," she pointed out as she tried a little swivel to the side. Harry bucked beneath her, his hips rising as a harsh moan was torn from him. "I'm simply trying to maximize the cure."

"You're trying to kill me," Harry accused, panting, his entire body shaking beneath her. Plum tried an interesting little circular motion as she sank down on the hardness that pierced her to her core, her eyes closed despite the darkness, feeling every nuance of him sliding deep within her.

"I can feel your heart beating," she said dreamily, leaning forward to kiss him. "You're so hot within me, Harry, we must be burning up. I love the feel of you, I love the feeling of you entering me, piercing me, and joining with me. It makes me feel as if I'm part of you."

"You are part of me," Harry answered, his tongue and lips teasing her mouth until she opened and let him in. "You're the best part of me. I could never be whole without you. You are my wife, my lover, mother to my children, my heart. I couldn't exist without you."

Plum squeezed her eyes tight against the tears that threatened to spill out at his words, and kissed him with every ounce of passion she possessed. Their souls were joined, entwined as they were both lifted toward the pinnacle of pleasure, her mouth plundering his as he plundered hers, both straining to incite the other to greater heights of passion. Plum moved urgently against Harry, kissing him frantically as the wonderful power within her uncoiled and filled her with joy and love that overflowed her being and spread to him, bonding her to him, merging the two beings into one, blinding her to all but the strength of his love.

She sobbed out her love as he shifted beneath her, spilling his seed against her thigh as he shouted her name, the two of them caught in a maelstrom that receded slowly, leaving Plum drained and boneless, resting on her husband as she attempted to catch her breath, trying to understand the power of the experience she had been given, wanting but unable to put into words what it meant to her, what *he* meant to her, how very much he had enriched her life, giving her something more valuable than all the riches in the world.

Instead she tipped her head back and kissed him on his jaw, whispering, "I love you, husband."

"There, you see?" Harry gasped, his chest heaving beneath her. "I told you that you would feel better afterward."

Plum bit his chin.

Chapter Twelve

Harry set off for the Home Office the next morning with a song in his heart and slight leather burns on his wrists. All was right in his world—the sun was shining, the children hadn't done anything worse than soap up the banisters in order to conduct banister races down the main stairs, and he had left Plum lying exhausted in his bed, her raven hair tangled and spread out around her, a smile on her face as she slept. He whistled a jaunty little tune as his carriage bowled along the streets of London, making a mental note to remind Plum that the choice of tonight's activities was his, and *Gladiator's Revenge* was most definitely in the cards. He much looked forward to wielding his sword in a manner that was sure to keep her captivated.

"Lord Rosse?" A slight young man with suitably deprecatory tones bowed and murmured Harry's name as he handed over his hat and gloves to a

Home Office flunky. "Lord Briceland is waiting for you. If you will come this way."

Harry was escorted into a small office at the back of Whitehall. The tall, thin man with a wispy blond mustache who was seated behind an immaculate desk rose as he entered, holding out a pale hand. "Lord Rosse, what a pleasure it is to meet you at last. I've heard so much about you from the PM and others, I feel as if I know you."

Harry greeted the new head of the Home Office, and took the offered seat. "I take it you've read my report?"

"With great interest, yes," Briceland said, leaning back in his chair. "I must tell you, I find it difficult to believe that you willingly allowed yourself to be used to prove Sir William's guilt. What the PM must have been thinking . . . but it's not my place to question either his or your actions. The plan proved fruitful and you did acquire the proof needed to charge Sir William with treason."

"Just so. About your information—as you will have read in my report, I can find no proof that Sir William was working with anyone but the anarchists who were later hanged. I checked and double-checked my notes with the various informants and runners employed by me at the time, and no word of another individual was ever breathed. As far as I can find, Sir William was alone in his perfidy—at least as far as individuals in the Home Office went."

Lord Briceland offered Harry a cigar. He shook his head, desirous of ending the interview as soon as could be managed. He had a wife to smother with attention, not to mention five hellion children who were at that moment quite probably up to some nefarious plan or another.

"I understand your reticence to believe that there was another individual involved, but I believe that not to be the case. I called you to London because the PM assures me that there is no one better to sniff out the truth than you." Briceland pulled open a drawer, extracting a limp, stained, much-battered piece of parchment. He handed it to Harry. "What you see is a letter that was sent to us anonymously. As you might notice, it is dated some fifteen years ago."

Harry glanced at the letter, his eyebrows rising at the date. "It was written the day before Sir William took his own life."

"Yes," Briceland said, leaning back in his chair. "Please read it. I assure you it concerns you enough to justify calling you to town when you must be wishing to be with your new wife and family."

The letter was not addressed to anyone, although it was signed "Bill." *This will find you after I am dead*, the letter read. *Do not despair of my death; I always knew the price of freedom would be a high one. All I ask is that you avenge my death, seek my murderer and strike at him as surely as he has struck me. I do not lightly ask this of you, for I am certain Rosse has a friend in Addington, and the PM is stalwart where his friends are concerned, but I have faith that in this you will not fail me.* Harry looked up. "Interesting. Your informant gave you no clue as to who it was addressed to, or how he gained possession of it?"

"No information whatsoever. It was sent as you see it with no accompanying note. You can see my reason for concern; the letter contains an obvious threat to your life."

Harry handed the letter back with a slight smile. He liked the new head to the Home Office, but never again would he put himself in a position where his life could be destroyed by treachery—not now, when there were so many other people dear to him. Until he had proof of the identity of the man believed to be behind the attacks he would disregard Briceland's concern about the threats against him. "One that is fifteen years old, yes. I believe it's safe to assume that whomever the letter was sent to decided not to act on Sir William's urging."

Briceland leaned forward to take it, a frown between his brows. "Regardless, the fact that the letter should come to light now indicates that the grudge against you by this unknown person might well still pose a threat to you."

"I hardly think so," Harry said as he got to his feet. "But if it will make you easier, I will do a little investigating as to who Sir William's friends were. I doubt if many of them are left, but it can't hurt to check."

The two men shook hands, Briceland accompanying Harry to the door. "Rosse, a word of caution, if I may. Do not take this threat lightly because it is of long standing. I understand that you lost a governess to a house fire recently."

Harry smiled. "A tragic event, I agree, but one due to a faulty flue and not the hand of Sir William reaching fifteen years beyond the grave."

"Have caution," Briceland repeated. "You might be surprised to learn just how far-reaching Sir William's influence was."

* * *

Plum rose from where she had been clutching the closestool, shakily wiping her face with a damp cloth. This was the fourth morning she'd woken feeling extremely ill, and although the other days could be excused by the less-than-wholesome food they'd eaten at inns on the way to London, she was no fool. She had been carefully keeping track, and although her monthlies were never of the terribly reliable variety, the fact that she'd missed two, plus the morning indispositions confirmed her hopes and desires and dreams . . . only sweet St. Genevieve, how was she to tell Harry? Not only had the man insisted that he would not give her a child—only spilling his seed in her twice in the two months of their marriage—but just the night before, when they arrived in town after four days of travel with the children, he was growling very detailed threats about locking them up in a garret until it was time to return home.

Perhaps now was not the time to inform him there was another child on the way. She only hoped she would be able to keep her extreme joy and happiness at finding herself with child dimmed to a level he would not find suspicious.

Another wave of nausea overtook her. She lunged for the closestool, just barely making it before her stomach relieved itself.

"I'm joyous and extremely happy," she told herself between retches. "I just can't let anyone know that yet."

Somehow, she thought as she heaved over the porcelain bowl, she doubted if that would be too difficult. Besides, she had other things to occupy her mind, one item in particular—Charles. What his intentions were, and how she was to keep him from telling everyone what he knew were uppermost in her mind, but selected secondary considerations such as how to shield Harry so he wouldn't hear of Charles's return from the watery grave also filled her thoughts.

"Are we ready for our morning excursion?" she asked as she—joyously, and with much happiness—clutched the banister while descending to the main hall. Particular care was needed around stairs, as one never knew when the children might decide to arrange for a concealed trap. Harry was becoming very adept at avoiding the traps as he clattered down the stairs, leaping gracefully over steps made slippery with grease, but with the precious burden she knew herself to be carrying, she would have to be particularly careful.

All the children were present—India was reading a book, the twins were rolling on the floor arguing over a wooden figure meant to go in their sailing boats, Thom was chatting with a one of the London footmen whose name she couldn't remember, and Digger was standing at the bottom of the stairs, glaring up at her. Behind him, Juan was dressed for the outdoors, holding her parasol and gloves.

"You're late," Digger said with a scornful curl of his lip. "You said ten o'clock. It's three minutes after!"

"I beg your pardon," she said humbly, eyeing Juan as she took the parasol and gloves. "We can get started now if everyone is . . . Juan, are you accompanying us?"

Evidently he was waiting for just such an opening, for he flung himself at her feet and scattered wet kisses over the back of her hand. "It will be the greatest joy in my heart to be of the many services to my most very lady."

Gently Plum disengaged her hand. "Is it the norm for fashionable butlers to attend their mistresses? I had rather thought that was in the line of a maid or a footman."

He got to his feet, giving her a sidelong glance that would have simmered stew. "It depends on the mistress, does it not, delicious one?"

Plum opened her mouth to dispute the innuendo he was making, then decided it wasn't worth the trouble. To be truthful, she liked Juan despite—or rather because—of his flirtatious nature. "Well, we shall just have to make it a fashion, shall we not? Are we all ready? Excellent. Off we go."

Fortunately for her nerves, she did not have long to wait before her questions regarding Charles and what he wanted were answered. She and Thom were strolling across the park while the children shrieked and ran circles around them when she noticed Charles bowing to her from the back of a bay gelding.

"I see an acquaintance I must speak to," she told Thom. "Could you please take the children on to see the Serpentine? Don't let them go into the water, and don't let the girls climb any trees, or they'll tear their gowns, and don't let the boys pretend they're beggars and solicit people for money like they did yesterday, and don't let them—"

Thom laughed and held up her hand. "I won't let them do anything but sail their boats."

"Thank you," Plum said with a grateful smile. "I'll

be with you shortly. Juan, and you and . . . er . . . the footman may attend to Miss Fraser."

Juan shook his head, simultaneously waggling his eyebrows. "Harry would not be liking that."

"He wouldn't?" Plum asked, one eye on the approaching Charles.

"It would not be making him happy, no. He would want me, your Juan of the most devoted nature, to be always at your side, protecting you against the rousing rabble."

"Traditionally there are very few rabble-rousers to be found in Hyde Park," Plum pointed out, shooing him toward Thom. "I will be fine by myself."

"I will tear my heart out with my own hands and stomp on it heartily before I abandon the most beloved of all my mistresses," Juan said with a dramatic flare to his nostrils that warned of the strength of his intentions.

Plum gave up trying to shoo him away. "Very well, but stay well back. I have no need of your protection now. Go on, Thom. I will meet you later."

Thom cast a curious glance to where Charles was dismounting, handing his reins to a groom before strolling toward Plum, but made no further comment as she hurried off after the children. Juan loitered around in the background; she hoped far enough away that he couldn't overhear her conversation.

"Charles," Plum said as he stopped before her, making her an elaborate bow. "I rather suspected I might run into you. I just had no idea it would be so soon."

"As effervescent a wit as ever, my dear," he said,

holding out his arm for her. "I find myself unable to pass by the opportunity to have a cozy little chat with you. Shall we stroll in this direction?"

She scorned the offer of his arm, but began walking in the direction he indicated, thankfully in the opposite direction to the artificial lake the children had been headed to. "About what do you wish to chat? Surely there can be little you wish to say to me, and I have nothing pleasant to say to you."

"My dear, my dear," Charles protested in so patently false a tone of dismay that Plum wanted to kick him in the shins. "I am wounded that your thoughts have not softened toward me over the years."

"Softened?" Plum asked in mingled horror and fury. "You ruined me, cast me aside without any protest to your family, without any regard or interest as to my well-being or future. For all you knew I might have been pregnant, and yet you allowed your family to bundle your wife and you off to the continent without so much as a second thought about me. How is your wife, by the by?"

"Dead these last seven years, poor soul. I remarried, the daughter of a Greek nobleman, a rather rough girl, but pleasing enough." Charles tried to chuck her under her chin. She smacked at his hand. "Helena is much more biddable than you were, my dear, but alas, that has its drawbacks. She has not the fire you had in bed—"

Plum slapped him, as hard as she could with her gloved hand, which unfortunately did not allow her much of a slap. Still, it was better than nothing. "I tolerate your presence here simply because I must know what you want of me, but I will not allow you to abuse me any further, not even verbally—Juan, no, release him, he is not a rabble-rouser."

"You struck him the blow," Juan said, his eyes filled with Basque vengeance as he grabbed Charles by the neckcloth. "Now I must strangle him. Harry would not like it if I did not avenge the dishonor this one has done you."

"It's all right, he simply spoke without thinking. Please release him, Juan," Plum soothed, pulling the distraught butler from a red-faced Charles.

Juan allowed himself to be stopped from throttling Charles, but he spat something out to the latter that sounded like it was a curse before walking a few feet away to seethe in a menacing manner.

Charles sputtered over the incident until Plum snapped at him. "Stop acting like such an infant, you brought that upon yourself. Now, please do me the kindness of stating your goal without harassing me further—"

"I can assure you that I have no intention of harassing you," Charles said, his muddy brown eyes alight with anger. He rubbed his cheek, his lips thinned. "Indeed my thoughts of you have been quite of the opposite variety, especially upon my arrival in Paris last month, when a very interesting tome was placed into my hands, a tome concerning acts of great intimacy that seemed oddly familiar."

Ah, now they were arriving to the meat of the discussion. Plum said nothing but raised her brow in imitation of Harry's best quizzical look.

"I find myself—naturally, it is embarrassing to have to admit this—in a particularly unpleasant situation of having my funds tied up."

Plum almost laughed aloud, a sigh of relief on her

lips. Money—that's all Charles wanted, just money. Both the laughter and sigh dried up as she realized that she had no money whatsoever.

"As it would appear that the book you so cleverly penned using our experiences together as man and wife—"

"Illegally man and wife, although you hadn't bothered to tell me that until it was too late," Plum couldn't help but add.

"—as the sole basis of this, I'm told, very popular book, I cannot help but think that you might be willing to show gratitude and appreciation in a pecuniary sense to one who made the book possible, as it were."

"Gratitude," Plum sputtered, outraged almost to speechlessness. "Appreciation? For ruining me?"

"Appreciation for me giving you the means to raise yourself from such an ignoble end to the lofty heights of a marchioness."

"*The Guide* had nothing to do with Harry marrying me—"

Charles bowed to an acquaintance, lifting his hat politely before turning back to Plum. "If you do not lower your voice, my dear Plum, you will find that the silence I suspect you so desperately seek will be of no use."

Plum took a deep breath, reminding herself that she had Harry and the children to think of. She couldn't punch Charles in the nose as he so rightly deserved. "I owe you nothing, Charles, no appreciation, no gratitude."

"Alas," he answered, giving her an odious smile. "I had feared you might adopt such a regrettable attitude. Might I take a moment to remind you of the peculiar situation you find yourself in? From what I gleaned last night at the ball, you have been married to Rosse but a very short time, and no one—other than myself—seems to be aware of the fact that the Marchioness Rosse and the bawdy Vyvyan La Blue are one in the same. I doubt if even your honorable husband is aware of that fact."

Plum wanted to deny it, but knew he would see through her lies. She did the best she could to salvage the situation. "Harry knows about you. I told him everything."

"Which is why I am taking great pains to avoid that gentleman. From what I hear, he would not be above calling me out, and as you are no doubt aware, my dear, I am a lover, not a fighter."

Plum's stomach roiled at the slimy tone in his voice, but she clenched her hands together in fists to keep from striking out at him. "How much do you want?"

Charles smiled. "I think the sum of five thousand will suit me. For now."

"Five thousand!" Plum gaped at him, her mind boggling at such an amount. "I don't have five thousand pounds!"

"No? I would have thought that the proceeds of *The Guide to Connubial Calisthenics* were ample enough to allow you to share a small portion with the man to whom you owe all."

"I haven't had money from that for years, and I most certainly don't owe you any of it. As for the figure you named, it is ridiculous. I simply do not have that sort of money."

"Ah, but your husband does." Charles leaned toward her. She recoiled. "I checked on that last night, too. Rosse is one of the richer marquises gracing our fair isle. I am sure that if you put your mind to it, you will come up with some excuse to acquire the money. I understand many ladies have gambling debts for much more."

Plum all but spat fury at him, grinding her teeth together and digging her nails into her palms to keep from flying at him. "I am not a gambler," she finally said, admittedly in a strangled voice.

Charles shrugged. "I will leave the inventive excuses to you, my dear. I have every confidence that you will not wish to ruin both your recent marriage and your husband's reputation should word of your literary pursuits be made public."

"You're despicable," Plum couldn't help but saying. "I thought you were odious twenty years ago, but you're a vile, disgusting creature now. You make me sick."

Charles laughed and captured her hand, pressing his lips to the back of her hand as he made a show of bowing over it despite a growl of objection from Juan. "Do you know, I had not wished to return to England, but now I'm quite looking forward to the future. I anticipate much reward for my past efforts. And speaking of that, do let me know if you are planning a future book." His gaze raked her in a brazen manner. "I would be very pleased to guide you to further knowledge of connubial exercises."

He stepped back before Plum could slap him again (although what she had in mind was more of a fist punched into his stomach), walking back toward his horse as if he hadn't a care in the world.

Juan was at her side in an instant, his jaw set at in an aggressive manner as he glared after Charles.

"That one is the stink most foul. He did not bother you again, beauteous lady?"

"Not in the way you mean, no."

"Are we to go after the *diablitos*?" he asked, nodding in the direction Thom and the children had disappeared.

Plum hesitated between following them and returning home to be sick into the nearest receptacle—a result of her discussion with Charles, not of the babe she carried beneath her heart.

"No, I think not," she said slowly. "Thom will have no difficulty managing the children—heaven knows they seem to mind her better than me. I think instead I will go home. . . ."

An idea flared to life within her brain. "No," she corrected as Juan turned toward home. She pointed to the right, toward Piccadilly Street. "I've changed my mind—I wish to go to Old Bond Street. Would you see if a hack is available for hire? It's a bit of a walk, and I want to visit Hookham's Library and be home before the children return. I have a great deal of thinking to do, a very great deal, and most of it is unpleasant."

Juan said nothing, but set off to find her a hired carriage.

Charles was going to have to be disposed of, that's all there was to it. She shied away from the actual word *murder* but that was the path her thoughts were leading. If she had just herself to think of, she wouldn't even contemplate such a thing, but there was Harry and the children now. Charles would have to be eliminated.

"I just hope Hookham's has a book on how to murder someone without being caught," she sighed as she walked after Juan.

"Good Lord, they're drowning! Save them! SAVE THEM!"

Nicholas Britton, the eldest son—albeit illegitimately—of the Earl of Wessex, paused in the act of handing a prostitute two shiny new guineas, glancing over toward the artificial lake known as the Serpentine. The prostitute, worried that she wouldn't get her money, snatched the coins from his hand before scurrying off. Nick paid her no attention as he started toward the lake, his gray eyes narrowing as he watched a familiar young woman with short, curly dark hair rip her shoes from her feet and prepare to dive into the water. Beyond her, floundering around a few feet from shore were a handful of children, shrieking and thrashing in the water. Without a thought to anything but the need to save the children, Nick raced toward the water, throwing himself into it without even pausing to remove his boots.

"Save them!" Thom yelled, pointing at the children. Hampered by her skirts, she was having a hard time reaching where the children, surrounded by a variety of toy boats, were obviously floundering.

"Stay calm," he yelled, long powerful strokes bringing him to the children. "I have you, don't worry. Just stay calm, and I'll get you out." He grasped the nearest child around the waist, only to have the child—a boy of some eight or nine years— kick him in the shin and bite his hand.

"Save them, they're drowning!" Thom yelled again.

"I'm trying," Nick snarled, wrestling with the boy as he reached out to a girl who splashed by him. "Stop struggling, I have you! You're safe!"

"Not the children," Thom yelled, swooping down on one of the boats that floated toward her. "They can swim. The mice, save the mice! They're drowning!"

"Mice?" Nick asked, looking at a blue-and-green painted boat that bobbed up and down near him. Sure enough, clinging desperately to the mast was a little white mouse. The child in his arms kicked him in the kidneys, squirming out of his grasp. It was at that point that Nick realized two important things— first, the water was only waist deep; second, that he had risked life and limb to save a mouse.

Well, to be truthful, the life and limb part was an exaggeration, but it was an exaggeration that Nick felt allowed given the circumstances.

"Mice?" he bellowed to Thom, who had corralled a second boat and was rescuing its rodent inhabitant. "I jumped into the water fully clothed to rescue *mice*?"

"No one asked you to," Thom said indignantly. Nick tried very hard not to notice the effect of water on light gauze, but it would have taken a saint not to appreciate the lovely lines of Thom's body, and Nick was no saint.

"I distinctly heard you say, 'Save them, they're drowning.' If that isn't asking me to save them—"

"Them being the mice," Thom interrupted, reaching for a third boat. The children, having had their dip, scrambled to shore where they called out advice and suggestions for gathering up the remaining boats.

Nick fished a sodden mouse out of the nearest boat, tossing the boat to shore where it was pounced on by two wet children who argued over its ownership. "I didn't know you were screaming about the mice, I thought you meant the children were drowning. It was a logical mistake, considering the evidence."

"Well?" Thom asked, three drenched mice sitting on her shoulder. She pointed to one last boat, which had floated well out into the middle of the lake.

"Well what?" he asked, knowing exactly what she wanted.

"Aren't you going to get it? The boat could sink at any time."

"I am not a mouse rescuer," Nick said with great dignity, or as great a dignity as one could have when one was wet to the neck while clutching a squirming white mouse.

"No, you're a burglar, but even burglars can have high morals—at least about some things. You're not going to be responsible for that poor innocent mouse's death, are you?"

"Why not? I don't see it doing anything to save my life."

Thom gave him a look that would have blistered a lesser man.

Nick splashed his way over to her, admiring against his will how delightfully the damp gown clung to the curve of her hip and the high roundness of her breasts. He thrust the mouse at her, gave her a look that he hoped was stern and unyielding and didn't in the least show the fact that he was fast becoming utterly besotted by her, and swam out to return the remaining boat and its passenger safely to shore.

"There, you see? You do have some good in you after all," Thom greeted him as he sloshed his way to the grassy banks, taking the mouse and boat from him. "I knew you couldn't be all bad. Digger! Just look at Rupert! He almost drowned!"

"*He* almost drowned," Nick muttered, shaking the water from his boots.

"Rupert can't swim," Thom said, kissing the mouse on its little wet head. "I assumed since you jumped into the lake that you could. I think, however, they have suffered as much as anyone could expect from mice. I shall have to let them go."

"That would probably be best for all concerned," Nick said, somewhat sourly as he attempted to wring the water from his jacket.

She released the mice to the freedom of a nearby shrub, then looked up and gave him a smile so dazzling, he promptly forgot his grievances against her. "That was very brave of you jumping into the lake. Quite dashing, in fact. I was very impressed."

"You were?" he beamed at her.

"Very much so. Burglars, after all, usually operate on dry land. You did splendidly in the water. I'm sorry you got wet," she said, eying his chest, "but I doubt if it will do anything but benefit your clothing."

Nick looked down at his grubby outfit he wore when he was incognito, and thought briefly of telling her just who he was and why he had been sneaking into the house the previous evening, but decided that silence on the subject was probably the wisest course. He bowed and plucked a weed from his shoulder, offering it as if it was the rarest hot-house rose. "I endeavor always to be of service."

She accepted the weed with a giggle, quickly rounding up the children and dismissing the foot-man after a glance at Nick.

"Your brothers and sisters are a little . . . lively, aren't they?" Nick asked, falling in beside Thom as she herded the chattering children away from the lake. The oldest boy looked familiar, but Nick couldn't quite place his freckled face.

"Oh, they're not my brothers and sisters. I don't have any. These are my aunt's new children. They belong to her husband."

"Ah," Nick said. "And who would that be?"

Thom pursed her lips as she thought about his question. He had the worst desire to kiss her, an urge he knew that he had no right to act on, cer-tainly not while she thought him a burglar. "I shouldn't tell you, but if I don't, you might burgle Harry's house by mistake, so I suppose it would be smarter to tell you."

"Harry?"

"Harry, my aunt's new husband. Lord Rosse. He's a marquis, and I don't think he'd take kindly at all to being robbed, so I would appreciate it if you'd strike his house from your list of possible sources of revenue."

Nick almost choked, pushing his wet hair back from his head to glance at the children running ahead of them. These unrecognizable monsters were Harry's children? True he'd been away at Ox-ford having an education pounded into him the last few years, but had it really been so long since he had seen them? He counted and found it had been almost five years since he had accompanied his father and stepmother to Rosehill.

Thom was looking at him with a worried frown. He hastened to reassure her. "I think I can swear without any difficulty to never robbing Lord Rosse."

"Oh, good," she said with obvious relief, pausing before they crossed a busy street. "I was hoping you'd see reason. Harry isn't as big as you are, but my aunt says he's fought duels. Of course, he wouldn't challenge you to a duel since you aren't a gentleman, but still, I imagine he'd thrash you soundly if you were to rob him."

"Undoubtedly so," Nick answered, about to explain to her that he might not be a nobleman, but he was a gentleman. When they stepped into a narrow alley between two houses, down which the children had run, he assumed it was a shortcut to Harry's town house. But before he could say anything, Thom gasped and darted forward.

Ahead of them, about twenty yards away, the children were yelling in horror as they ran toward them, looking over their shoulders at a carriage that bore down on them, the coachman slumped sideways in the seat as if he had fainted, the horses foaming as they thundered unchecked down the confined passage.

Nick took in the children, horses, and distance to safety in one quick glance as he raced after Thom. There was no way he could get the children out of the alley, and not enough room to hope the carriage would pass cleanly by. The horses were wild and obviously heavily panicked, and there was no guarantee they wouldn't plow down anyone who stood in their path. The only solution was the miniscule rubbish area for the house on the left. If he could get the children into that area, they would be safe.

He passed Thom, who had evidently had the same thought since she was waving her hand to the left and yelling at the children to run to the rubbish area. He ran past an oncoming India and Ann, snatching the youngest boy out of Digger's arms.

"Run," he yelled at Digger, lunging awkwardly after him. Thom had reached the girls and was shoving them into the area, Andrew following. The horses screamed behind him, the clatter of their hooves deafening in the confined space, drowning out even the pounding of blood in his ears. The horses were almost on him, flecks of equine saliva splattering his back. With one last desperate burst of strength, Nick threw himself out of harm's way, curling himself to protect McTavish from slamming up against the wall. The horses charged past just as he hit the brick wall, the carriage ripping by them with such force that the boxes of rubbish were knocked to the ground behind it.

"Stay here," Nick shouted, getting to his feet and running after the carriage.

"Nick!" Thom yelled after him, but he didn't stop. If those horses continued down the street, someone else would be in danger. He ran out the end of the alleyway, skidding to a stop at the street. The coachman was sitting up, the reins firmly in his hands as he shot a look over his shoulder toward the alley. At the sight of Nick he whipped up the horses, barreling down the street without regard for anyone else.

Chapter Thirteen

"Oh, this is ridiculous," Plum said to herself, standing behind a bust of Shakespeare, a ribbon draped around its neck. She consulted an open book. *"Slip the noose over the forefinger of the right hand . . .* yes, I've done that. *Pick up the remainder of your garroting cord with the left hand while silently approaching your victim.* Silently, that is the key, isn't it? Where was I? . . . *Use your left hand to throw the noose over the head of your victim . . .* mmm . . . *twist it tightly . . . victim at arm's length,* yes, yes, I've done that . . . *strangling should be instantaneous . . .* well, pooh."

Plum frowned at Shakespeare. She couldn't imagine that it would be easier to throttle Charles, and yet here she was unable to successfully manipulate a ribbon around a statue. She held little hope that she would do better with a sturdier cord and a live person.

"I'm just not applying myself," she said, taking her ribbon from the statue. "It can't be that difficult. The book says the element of surprise is the most important part. Very well, I will practice until I am sure of myself."

Plum made a loop with her right hand, and whistling a sprightly air, casually strolled toward the bust of Shakespeare as if she was taking an innocent walk in a garden, the thought of garroting a man to death the farthest thing from her mind. As she approached the bust, she threw the ribbon over Shakespeare's head, jerking back quickly as the book said, only she had forgotten that the bust was not fixed to anything.

"Eek!" she shrieked as the bust flew backward past her directly toward the door, which opened at that moment to admit Thom.

The bust crashed into the wall beyond, fracturing into a dozen plaster pieces as it struck the hardwood floor.

"What on earth are you doing, Aunt Plum?"

Plum allowed herself a heartfelt sigh as she fluttered the ribbon toward the broken bust. "Trying to garrote Shakespeare, but it's no use, I am simply no good at all at strangulation. It will have to be something else, and I just don't think I'm up to shooting him."

"Shooting who?" Thom asked as she stepped over the remains of Shakespeare, closing the door behind her.

"Charles," Plum answered, then noticed her niece's gown was sopping wet. She put her hands on her hips, and gave Thom her best scowl. "Didn't I tell you not to let the children swim in the lake?"

Thom waved that away, her cheeks bright with excitement. "It was the mice, the little devils smuggled the mice onboard the boats and didn't tell me until it was too late. You'll never guess what happened on our way home!"

"You received a good number of indecent proposals from gentlemen who thought you were practicing the dubious art of dampening your muslin?"

"No, the children were almost run over by runaway horses! It was very exciting, and I'm sure we would have all been killed if it had not been for Nick. Why are you trying to kill Shakespeare?"

Plum's knees gave out. She sank bonelessly to the chair, her heart beating widely. "It's not good for me to be excited or startled. I must be calm, for the babe's sake, I must be calm."

"Are you carrying?" Thom asked, kneeling beside her aunt. "You must be thrilled. Have you told Harry?"

Visions of little coffins danced before her eyes. "The children—they're all right? All of them?"

"Oh, yes, didn't I say that? Nick saved them. He's very brave, even if he is a burglar. He walked us home, as a matter of fact. He wanted to see Harry, no doubt for a reward, but Harry's not home yet so I told him to come back later. Aunt Plum? Are you all right? You look a bit pale."

"A burglar saved you?" Plum asked in a weak voice. Her head was spinning in such a way that she was sure she was going to swoon, but she was not the swooning type, and made an effort to get a hold of her tumultuous emotions.

"Yes, he was walking us home. He really does have nice manners, especially for a ruffian."

Then again, there was something to be said for a good swoon. "Thom?"

"Yes?"

"Why were you allowing a burglar to escort you home?"

"He's a very *nice* burglar," Thom said, twisting her damp skirt between her fingers. "I'm sure if you were to meet him, you'd see that right away."

Plum tried to think of something to say to that, but she was having a little difficulty putting her thoughts into words. "The children are all right?" she asked again, not being able to think of much else.

Thom nodded, smiling as she patted Plum's hands. "Yes, they're fine, a little wet, but no harm done. I sent them up to Gertie and George to change into dry clothing. Who is the Charles you want to kill?"

"Charles, my Charles, or the Charles who used to be mine, not that he really ever was, a fact I find myself profoundly grateful for now that I have Harry." Plum's mind, a bit dazed, was beginning to return to her normal state of lucidity. She would have to tell Harry about the latest accident concerning the children. Perhaps if he thought they were too headstrong in town, he would send them all home, and then Charles wouldn't have the opportunity . . . oh, but that wouldn't work. Even if Harry did send them home, he would stay, and Charles would simply avoid him while spreading the news about Plum far and wide. No, she'd have to stay where she was and deal with him.

Thom sucked in her breath. "I thought he was dead."

"So did I. He isn't. He's very much alive, and blackmailing me."

Thom's jaw sagged. Knowing her secrets were safe with Thom, Plum filled her in on the morning's conversation with Charles, ending with her solution to the problem.

"You're going to kill him?" Thom asked, her eyes wide.

"I don't see any other way around it, do you?"

"Hmm." Thom thought for a moment, then shook her head. "No, I think you're right, the only way you'll ever truly be free of him is if you silence him forever. How are you going to do it?"

"I have no idea," Plum answered, somewhat pettishly she knew, but if anyone had a right to be pettish, surely she had. "The book I borrowed from Hookham's is about methods of execution, not how to eliminate a blackmailer. I don't suppose Charles would willingly put his head in a noose or allow himself to be drawn and quartered. There's shooting, but I don't own a pistol, let alone know how to shoot one."

Thom rose to her feet, and paced the length of the room. "How about setting his house on fire?"

Plum waved that offering away. "No, that would harm others, and no one else should suffer for Charles's sins."

"Mmm. Well, there's drowning."

"Difficult to arrange."

"Bow and arrow?"

"My aim is very poor."

Thom stopped in front of her. "What about poison?"

"I wouldn't know what to give him. Oh, this is

ridiculous," Plum said, getting to her feet to pace with Thom. "We are two intelligent, well-educated women. You would think we would be able to think of something so simple as the way to kill a man."

"You're the one with literary skills," Thom pointed out. "What would you do if you were writing this in a book?"

"Arrange for a convenient accident to eliminate him from the plot," Plum snapped, then sat down and burst into tears. It was useless! As hard as she tried to justify to herself the act of killing Charles, she just couldn't condone the taking of his life. And now because she was so weak, Charles would tell everyone who she was, and Harry would leave her, and she would ruin the children's lives, and Thom's, and her poor babe's, and life would be horrible, and she would end up in the ditch with the earthworm, and why oh why didn't Charles drown when everyone said he did?

"I'm so sorry, Aunt Plum. Is there anything I can do?"

"No. It's hopeless. No one can help me now." Despite her gloomy words, Plum gave herself a mental shake. She had to think her way out of this horrible situation. She would not allow Charles to ruin more lives. If she couldn't kill him, what would stop him from blackmailing her? A threat? Bribery? Or what about a scandal so horrible the threat of it being made public guaranteed his silence?

Thom wrung her hands and paced nervously, periodically stopping to pat Plum on the shoulder, murmuring little things about it being all right, but Plum was oblivious to it all as she turned over several ideas of manufactured scandals that might do the job of silencing Charles on the subject of her own past. "I think, perhaps, that is my only option," she said softly, renewed determination flaring within her. "Yes, it is. But I will need help with the plan . . . someone to carry out my instructions. Someone unsavory who won't mind getting his hands dirty, so to speak."

"Help? Instructions?" Thom's air of distressed quickly dissipated. "With your plan for Charles, you mean?"

"Yes," Plum answered, distracted by the sudden fertile fields of imagination that opened before her as she contemplated the many options of coercing Charles into holding his tongue. She was more than a little bit relieved that she wouldn't have to use threats, or try to find the money to bribe him. Her way was much simpler. She would pay someone to create a potential scandal so hideous in its nature, Charles would be forced to give up his blackmail in order to stop her from enacting the plan.

"I know just the man to help you!" Thom clutched Plum's hands in hers, pulling her to her feet. "He will do anything you desire. He's bright, and intelligent, and if you tell him what you want done, he'll do it!"

"What? Who?" Plum asked, wondering if a brainstorm could strike someone as young as Thom.

"Nick!"

"Who? Oh, your burglar?"

"Yes, him!" Thom hugged herself and spun around again. "Nick is very unsavory, in a savory polite sort of way. He wouldn't mind doing anything you asked of him, even . . . er . . . you know."

Plum blinked at her niece in confusion.

"What you mentioned," Thom said in an under-tone. "You know, the unsavory things."

"Ah." She was referring to the scandal. Plum thought on that for a moment. Thom's burglar might just fit the role of scandalmonger very well. A man in his line of business certainly couldn't object to helping her with her righteous cause. "It has merit. I wouldn't have to effect the act myself, which I will admit has been causing me some worry. Very well, I will speak with this burglar of yours, but I make no promises! It behooves me to keep all avenues open. I will continue to investigate possible men I can employ until I know whether or not your burglar can do the job, or find someone to do it for me. Thank you, Thom! You might just have saved all our lives."

Harry, returning home from a quick meeting with a couple of handpicked Bow Street Runners, was surprised to learn that there was a person of obviously low repute awaiting him in his study. He was even more surprised when that unsavory person turned out to be his godson.

"Nick! What the devil are you doing soaked to the skin, and in such repulsive clothes?" Objection-able garments notwithstanding, Harry hugged his godson, noting to himself that Nick—who had always resembled his father—was now the spitting image of Noble. They shared the same black hair, gray eyes, and big frame. "You've grown since I last saw you," he added. "You've got one or two inches on me now."

Nick didn't respond to the banter, although he did give Harry a bone-crushing hug. "Papa said you'd hung up your spy hat years ago. You're not doing another job, are you?"

Harry, mildly surprised by the serious look in Nick's eyes, shook his head and waved toward one of two calf-skin chairs. Although he hadn't seen Nick for a few years, it wasn't hard to see that the young man had done a bit of growing up since last they'd met. He did a bit of arithmetic and was surprised to find that Nick was now twenty-three years of age. Had it really been so long? "No, not really. I'm doing a bit of looking into something that happened years ago, but not a job, not a real job. Why do you ask?"

"Someone tried to kill your children this afternoon."

Harry shot up out of the chair and was halfway to the door before Nick's voice stopped him. "They're all right, Harry. Thom was there, as was I. No one was hurt. I escorted them home, just to be sure another attempt wasn't made." Nick frowned and pulled at his lower lip. "I'm fairly certain it was an attempt on their lives, but I suppose it could have been just an accident. . . ."

The word *accident* resonated in Harry's mind. Plum had been concerned about the numbers of accidents the children were having of late . . . but that was foolish. They had been random accidents caused by the children's heedless determination to do whatever fool thought entered their collective heads.

Or were they?

"Tell me what happened," Harry said slowly as he returned to his chair, leaning forward with his arms on his knees. "Tell me everything that happened."

Nick narrated a story that sounded all too familiar—the children sending mice out to sail their wooden boats—but cold chills shivered down his neck at the retelling of the near miss with the runaway carriage.

"You're sure the horses were under control once the carriage was in the street beyond the alley?"

Nick nodded. "The coachman must have been feigning a swoon. He clearly looked over his shoulder at the alley, and when he saw me, whipped the horses up even harder and tore down the street. I asked Thom on the way home whether it was usual for them to take that alleyway to your house. She said you'd only been in town for three days, but that they'd taken it each day as they returned from the park. No, it couldn't have been unintentional." Nick lifted worried eyes to Harry's. "Who'd want to harm your children, Harry?"

"Someone who has a very long memory," Harry said softly, thinking of the letter Briceland had shown him. He was cold with fury, a fury so deep he had the unreasonable urge to strike out at something, anything, in response to the threat against his children. He had always accepted the danger to his own person as part and parcel of the jobs he had chosen to undertake, but the thought that his family could be made to suffer for his actions . . . he closed his eyes for a moment, his hands fisted to keep from tearing the room apart.

"I'll help you all I can," Nick said, aware of the struggle Harry was having to keep his temper leashed. "You can count on me and my men."

Harry opened his eyes, unaware that they were

dark with anger. "Forgive me, I hadn't thought to ask, and I didn't have time to talk at any length with Noble. How is your work progressing?"

Nick shrugged. "As well as can be expected. There's another reform policy up for discussion in the House that I'm sure you've heard about. Yet another feeble attempt to do away with prostitution without addressing the real issues of poverty and class structure. We do what we can to help the women who sincerely want a better life, but it's like throwing pebbles in the ocean."

Harry managed to find a smile. It was a grim smile, to be true, but still it was a smile, and he hung onto it for all he was worth. "Still trying to save the world, are you? First it was foundlings and child labor laws, then war veterans, and now you've taken on Gillian's pet project?"

Nick grinned. "She can be persuasive when she puts her mind to it." He gestured toward his damp, rumpled, filthy clothing. "The last few weeks I've been in the stews trying to locate the madame behind a particularly nasty string of brothels. Four prostitutes have been killed in the last two months. Gillian's worried sick about it, so I've been interviewing the girls to see what they know. It's difficult going, but I think I might have a lead at last. I'm more than happy to set that aside, though, if I or my group can be of any help to you."

Harry's grim smile grew a little less grim. "Thank you. I may take you up on that, but there are a few things I can do myself to see to my family's safety."

Nick's grin broadened. "Speaking of your family, I approve of your choice of nieces. Thom's got her wits about her, and has a cool head in an emergency, even if she does have the deplorable taste to befriend a burglar."

Harry cocked an eyebrow and glanced at Nick's shady garments, thinking to himself how very interesting life had become of late . . . a thought that was stripped of all amusement when an image came to mind of charging horses running down his children.

The two men chatted a bit longer, then Nick left to go about his business. Harry called the male house staff in and gave them strict instructions regarding the admittance of anyone unknown to the house. He pulled Juan aside, and gave him further orders that neither the children nor Plum was to leave unescorted.

"I will not allow the Lady Plump to be so much accosted," Juan replied with a fiery look in his eye. "There was a man today in the grande garden who put his big English face into my very most lady's and made such comments that she had to strike him a blow to the cheeks, but he will not do so again. I have made sure of that."

"A man accosted Plum?" Harry asked, startled into immobility. "When? Where? Who? Is she all right?"

Juan tossed his head as he cracked his knuckles. "It was today, while the lady and the young miss and the *diablitos* were in the grande garden. I don't know who the man was, but Plump, she has the fire in her heart. She struck him on the face, and I told him to begone, and he left. Then we went to a very boring shop with only books and old ladies and no one who paid us any attention, and then we came home."

Harry was mildly relieved to know that Plum wasn't upset enough by the incident to cease her regular calls, but he felt the time was ripe to have a discussion with her. "If you see the man who accosted her again, tell me immediately."

"I will be happy to rip out his heart and spit on it if he should offend my most passionate lady."

"I'm sure you will," Harry said dryly, "but I think a word to me first would be best. Mind you attend to what I've told you."

Juan swore eternal fealty. Harry left him for Plum's sitting room feeling moderately better, but still worried. He made a mental note to set a few of his runners onto the task of watching the children when they were out. He found Plum sitting before her escritoire, brushing her lips with the tip of a quill as she hesitated over a letter. Love roared to life in him at the sight of her. Should one of the children be harmed, he would be devastated, but if anything happened to Plum, he would be destroyed.

He paused for a moment, watching her as she smiled and rose to greet him, wondering how it had happened that he had fallen so completely in love with his wife that his very vitals were gripped with pain at the thought of losing her.

"Harry! You're back earlier than I thought. I'm so pleased you're home. I was going to send for you, but I didn't now where you'd gone. You're not going to believe what happened—the children are fine, all of them, no one is hurt in the least, but they almost suffered a most grievous accident."

Plum told him what had happened to the children, viewing it as a neatly avoided accident rather than anything with more sinister overtones. He hesitated about telling her what had happened, nearly overwhelmed with the desire to protect her and keep his family from harm, but he admitted to himself that Plum was a smart woman, and the more she knew, the better she could guard against any danger.

He took her hands and led her over to the blue-and-green settee. "In the future, I will leave word as to my exact destinations, so you will always know where to find me if you should have need of me. As for the accident with the horses, I've heard about it. Plum, do you remember a few weeks back when you were commenting on how odd it was that the children were experiencing so many accidents?"

Plum's gaze dropped to her hands. "Yes. Harry, I know I haven't been the ideal stepmother to them—"

"I don't think they were accidents," he interrupted, dismissing her notion that she wasn't a good stepmother. No one could have more patience or tolerance for the five hellions he'd spawned—five dear hellions for whom he would fight to the death. "I have reason to believe that someone is deliberately trying to hurt them."

"Hurt them?" Her face went pale as she clutched his hands tightly. "Who would want to hurt the children?"

"I don't know for certain yet, but I'm going to find the proof I need in the next day or two. It has something to do with a situation in my past, a job I did." He gave her a brief resume of his past work with the Home Office, along with reassurances that he had long left his spy days behind.

"Someone is trying to hurt the children," Plum repeated, for a few seconds obviously not believing what he said. She stood up, her hands fisted tightly, her cheeks bright with anger. "I will destroy him."

Harry was a bit startled by the vehemence in her voice, but warmed by it as well. Only Plum could love them all so well. She truly was one woman in a million. "That won't be necessary, sweetheart. I've taken steps to see to it that you'll all be protected, but I wanted to warn you so you'll be aware of what's going on, and won't try to get rid of the footmen or Juan when they accompany you. I'll send a man down to Ashleigh Court to look into the accidents there, but I don't hold out hope that he'll find much."

"Ashleigh Court?" Plum blinked and looked at him curiously. "But . . . those accidents were weeks ago."

"Yes," Harry said, his jaw tight at the thought of someone stalking his children, someone invading their home to do them harm. "As I said, the person doing this has an old grudge against me. I have men looking into possible sources of information here in town, as well."

"Oh," Plum said, sitting down, looking oddly relieved. "Then it couldn't be—you must find the man who is doing this, Harry. He must be stopped."

Harry was about to ask Plum to whom she had been referring when she gave him an odd look and bit her lower lip. Immediately his mind was drawn to that lush, sweet lip, how it tasted, how he wanted to nibble on it, and in return, the many things he would enjoy it doing to his body. It was with an effort he wrenched his mind off her moist little cherry lip and focused on what she said.

"If you were a spy, there must have been occasions where you had to . . . kill someone."

She wanted to know about the men he'd killed? Harry wondered for a moment if there was a hidden side to Plum he hadn't seen, then relaxed. Surely she was just concerned that he had the experience to protect them from whoever sought to do the children harm. "Yes, I have, regrettably. I don't like to take a life, Plum, and I've always tried to avoid it whenever I could, but I would not, and will not, ever allow anyone innocent to suffer at the hands of the guilty."

Plum glanced toward her escritoire. "Was it an extreme measure? That is, did you try to resolve the situation by less fatal means first? Did you try to reason with the people first? Bribe them? Or perhaps, give them a taste of their own medicine? Did you try those things first, Harry, before you were forced to kill?"

Harry smiled a reassuring smile. Dear, sweet innocent Plum. He hesitated to have such a gruesome discussion with his delicate wife, but perhaps it would be for the best. She would no doubt understand just what lengths he was prepared to go to in order to see to the children's and her protection. He spent the next half hour detailing the more outstanding of circumstances, allowing her to question him closely about the methods he employed to avoid having to kill his enemies, as well as general information about the surrounding events. If the situation facing him weren't so heinous, he might almost have found her avid interest amusing, but in the end, he rose, gave her what was meant to be a reassuring kiss, but turned into a fiery plundering wherein he tasted the sweet depths of her mouth, then took his leave of her more than a little pleased with the gentle, loving woman he had wed.

Chapter Fourteen

"My very most Lady Plump! You must come quickly!"

"What is it, Juan?" Plum asked absently, brushing the end of the quill against her chin as she thought. Would it be better to have Charles found naked in the monkey cage at the Zoological Gardens, or in flagrante delecto with another man?

Juan threw himself to his knees before her. Plum paid little mind to such a show of histrionics. Juan was always throwing himself to his knees over something. Usually it was of no consequence. "It is a most terrible occurrence! It is the even very catastrophic!"

Plum sipped the cold tea that had been sitting at her side while she labored the last two hours, a slight frown between her brows. "Is anything on fire?"

"No, it is not the fire—"

"Is anyone bleeding?" The monkey cage had a

certain appeal to it, but sadly, the other would involve the shame of another man. She hated to make anyone but Charles suffer. Perhaps if he was shot while trying to escape after the theft of an object from the newly opened British Museum?

"That I am not knowing. You must come now, it is of the most terrible event—"

What of a harlot? Would that be enough to shame Charles? She shook her head even as the idea formed. The Charles of old certainly had no qualms about making it known to other gentlemen that he used the services of harlots. Then again, if it was a harlot like no other, that might do the trick. Plum wrote a note to investigate whether there were any procurers of sheep for gentlemen of unnatural tastes. "Has any property, real or otherwise, been destroyed?"

Juan clutched her knees. "You are not listening to me! I am trying to tell you—"

"Does the situation involve any sort of weaponry? Swords? Axes? Firearms?"

"*Madre Dios*, no—"

"Then I don't want to hear about it. I am very busy at the moment, and as long as no one is in any danger, I will attend to the situation later, when I have time. Is that clear?"

"Of course it is clear, I have not the potatoes growing out of my ears. You must come with me—"

"Is that *clear*, Juan?" Plum said more forcefully, her frown intensifying.

Juan released her knees, got to his feet, and stalked to the door. "You are being stupid, most lovely lady! I try to tell you, but you will not let me.

What am I to do? I do my job. I try to tell you, but you, you would try the saint, you would!"

"Yes, yes, thank you, Juan." Perhaps if word got around that he carried a plague . . . no, that had the possibility of harming his wife and children, who were innocent of his sins. Sadly, a plague was out. "You may leave me now. Tell the children I will attend to them later."

"I will never understand you English," Juan said with a dramatic air of one grievously injured. He marched over to the door. "You make the fuss most big about the children, but when they have been kidnapped, you will not listen. I try no longer! Bah, I wash my hands!"

"Fine," Plum said, waving an airy hand and returning to the problem that greatly concerned her. "Water, now there's an idea. Perhaps it could be put about that he is nigh on insane regarding the subject of water. Bedlam would loom before him, and that, surely, is enough to keep anyone in line. It certainly should stop him . . . *kidnapping*?"

Plum was up from her seat the instant the word penetrated her consciousness. Juan, who knew his employers better than he allowed, stood outside the door counting. He opened it just as she raced through.

"I am the butler extraordinary," he said as she flew past him. "The carriage is waiting for you."

"Find Harry," she yelled as she ran down the stairs and across the hall, leaping down the front steps to the waiting carriage. Two footmen clung to the top of the carriage, one of whom was Sam, sporting a dashing white bandage around his head.

Plum didn't give him a thought as she threw herself into the carriage. "Go!"

The door slammed behind her. Plum fell backward as the horses were sprung. Struggling to sit upright, she opened the trap and yelled for the footman. "Ben, what happened? Where are the children? Who has taken them?"

"I don't rightly know, my lady. Sam, he went out to the park with the two men his lordship hired to watch over Miss Thom and the children, and he came home with his head all bloody, raving about someone who attacked them and stole the children. The two men and Miss Thom went after the kidnappers."

"How are we ever to find them in all of London?" Plum wailed.

Sam leaned over to the trap. "They thought I was dead, Lady Rosse. One of the blighters who was standing over me told the others to meet them at the ruins."

"Ruins? What ruins, London doesn't have any . . . oh! Vauxhall."

Ben's face reappeared in the square. "That's what we thought, milady. It was the only ruins we could think of in London."

"I just pray we get there in time," Plum said, and sat back to commence some really thoughtful worrying.

"What do you mean my wife wants to hire a murderer? Plum would never do any such thing." Harry stormed across the smoking room at Britton House, a small headache pulsing to life at the back of his head. Noble had to be wrong, that's all there was to it. He must have read Thom's note incorrectly. "She just wouldn't do it."

"According to Thom, she's hoping Nick'll be able to provide her with an introduction to someone who won't mind killing a gentleman she assured him no one will miss."

"That's ridiculous. It's a joke. The two of them are having Nick on."

"I don't think so, Harry. Evidently Thom asked Nick first if he'd do it, but seemed to credit the lad with the niceness of not being a murderer by continuing that if he didn't have the stomach for it, could he please refer someone to her aunt who would."

"My lords, my pardon for interrupting, but there's a man by the name of Juan at the door inquiring for Lord Rosse. He says it is most urgent—"

"Just a minute." Harry held up a hand to the short, round butler who stood in the doorway, and turned back to the man before him. "Do you mean to say that *Thom* wrote this letter to Nick? It's a joke, man! That's all it can be. She's testing him. You know how women like to do that to men. It's in their blood. No doubt she fancies him, and she wants to see just how honorable he really is."

"My lord, I sense the matter is of some urgency. The butler Juan claims it is life or death."

"Juan lives his life like a melodrama," Harry told Tremayne the butler. "Everything is life or death to him. Pay him no mind for a few minutes, and he'll calm down."

Noble had been frowning into the empty fireplace. He looked up with a speculative air. "I don't think it was a joke or a test, Harry. Thom was very specific that Plum wanted to hire a thug to kill a Mr.

de Spenser without being caught. Why would she be so adamant about that if it was a joke?"

Harry stared at his friend in disbelief for a moment, then bellowed, "De Spenser? It's de Spenser she wants killed? Are you sure about that?"

"Yes, that's what the letter said. Would you like me to fetch it? I believe Nick left it somewhere. He's gone off to see if your niece is in the park, to try to get more information about this odd request. I take it you know this de Spenser?"

"Bloody hell, why didn't you tell me it was de Spenser in the first place?" Harry roared.

Noble's face took on the expression of the deepest righteous indignation. "You never asked!"

"Gaaaah!" Harry yelled to the heavens, and spinning on his heel, ran for his horse.

"My lord! Harry, you must hear me out!"

"Later," Harry shouted to Juan as he ran down the front steps, leaping into the saddle.

"It concerns the *diablitos*!" Juan bellowed after him.

"I'll settle with Plum later for whatever they've done," Harry yelled back.

Juan swore fluently, then made for his own horse, kicking the animal into a gallop after his quickly disappearing employer. "Harry, it is the most important that you stop and listen to me!"

Harry didn't acknowledge the cry of the man behind him. He had more important things to focus on, such as finding his wife and worming out the reason she felt obliged to hire a man to kill a man who was already dead. Could it be a brother she was targeting?

"My lord—" Harry dodged carriages, gigs, peo-

ple, dogs, horses, children, and all the other assorted obstacles that made up the morning traffic,
pulling up only after the words thrown at him made
sense.

"The *diablitos* were kidnapped!"

"They were *what*?" Harry exploded. He turned
his horse and grabbed at Juan's coat as the butler
pulled up next to him, hauling the unfortunate servant halfway off his horse. *"THEY WERE WHAT?"*

"Stole your children," Juan panted. "They are
gone to Vauxhall, to the ruins, Sam says. You see? If
you had listened to me at first, then you would not
be so very angry now. No one listens to me. It is my
most tragic fate."

Harry snarled an invective into the man's face,
then tossed him back into the saddle and urged At-
las into a gallop oblivious of traffic and pedestrians
alike.

"What do you think, Nick? Those men won't hurt
the children, will they?"

Nick glanced from Thom's worried eyes to the
young woman sitting opposite him. Although he
hadn't witnessed the kidnapping himself—and
sorely wished he had been present, for he would
have given the bastards a good fight—he had come
across Thom and India racing down the street bor-
dering the park afterward. "No, I don't think they'll
hurt the little ones. They have no reason to—kidnappers only kidnap because they want something in return. They know that Harry will demand proof of the
well-being of his children before he pays a ransom."

"I suppose so," Thom said, worrying her lower
lip. "And they'll have Digger, assuming he made it

onto the carriage without the men seeing him. I just don't understand why they took only the youngest three. It doesn't make sense."

Nick shrugged, glancing out the window. He wanted to be questioning the footman who currently clung to the top of the hired hackney about what he had seen, but had held off because of the erroneous assumption that Thom would be too distraught to be left by herself. He had wronged Thom on that score—she was worried, yes, but not hysterical. "Tell me again what happened. Everything."

Thom took a deep breath. "We were strolling through the park, as usual. The children wanted to go to Kensington as a change of scenery, so the younger ones were having a little footrace there. One moment then were running and laughing as we approached Kensington Park, the next minute two carriages pulled up, and several men jumped down and snatched up the children. Sam and the two men Harry hired all ran forward, but the other men were armed and struck them all down. Sam was the only one we could rouse, and he said one of the men mentioned meeting at a ruin. Digger ran off after one of the carriages, and I think he made it onto the back without being seen, but I was paying attention to Sam at the time, and I didn't see for certain. India and I chased after them as well, but they were too fast, and no carriages would stop for us! We must have run for fifteen minutes before you found us. Thank heavens you were able to make one of the hackney drivers stop. It's most vexing that they wouldn't do the same for me! We might have been at the ruins much earlier if they had."

Nick thought of the wild figures India and Thom

had made, racing down the street yelling like ban-
shees, their hair windblown, their skirts covered in
dust, but said nothing.

"What was that? Did you hear something, Malmseynose? Did you hear that slithering noise? I distinctly heard a slithering noise! God's blood, if
you've got a snake on your person, I'll have you
hung by your cods from the highest tree!"

Max Malmseynose, hired ruffian and primary kid-
napper, looked startled at both the thought of carrying a snake around, and the mode of revenge
espoused by the gentleman who hired him. "I didn't
hear nothing, sir."

"Well I heard something, something slitherish. Be
quiet, you little brat! I need to listen, and I can't do
that with you sniveling."

Max put a hand out to the right to push the small
boy back into the corner of the carriage, giving him
a warning look in the process. He felt badly about
his role in the children's nabbing since they were
younger than he expected. The twins were quiet,
holding each other for comfort, while the smaller
boy was sniffling and crying for his mama. It was almost enough to break his heart.

Almost.

"I want Mama."

"Shut up," Max said without any real heat.

"Jackson wants Mama, too."

"Keep that little bastard quiet! How can I listen
for slithering with him babbling!"

"McTavish isn't a bastard," the older boy said. "A
bastard is someone whose mama and papa aren't
married, but ours were."

"QUIET!" the man yelled. He took a deep breath, then suddenly jerked his leg up. "There, do you hear it? Slithering! Stop the coach! Stop, I tell you! I won't go one more foot without the interior checked for snakes!"

Max sighed and resigned himself to searching the carriage for snakes while the gentleman paced outside, ranting against the person who thought to make a cruel joke on him. He set two men to watch the children, then turned back to the carriage. Just as he lifted a cushion to peer underneath it, the twins began attacking the men with fists and feet. He turned back to assist the men, but was knocked backward by the flying body of the small boy.

"Jackson!" the child screamed in his ear, climbing him like he was a tree. "Jackson's loose! Jackson!"

From the corner of his eye Max saw a yellow-and-black striped shape slide under the seat opposite. Evidently the gentleman was right. There was a snake in the carriage.

Max sighed again. It was going to be a long, long day.

The trap in the roof of the carriage lifted, and Ben leaned down to announce, "Vauxhall Gardens, my lady. We will take you as close to the ruins as possible."

"Thank you," Plum said, chewing her lip as she watched out the window. "The ruins, what would they want at the ruins? They're not even real, no more than the faux castle and cannons and cascade are real. What on earth can they want at the ruins?"

The carriage came to a halt before Plum could puzzle out an answer. "Which way are the ruins?"

she asked as she leaped down without waiting for the steps to be lowered.

"That way, through the long lawn, to the left of the iron bridge, beyond the thatched pavilion."

"Ben, you come with me. Sam, you stay here in case Lord Rosse shows up. You can tell him where we've gone. Are you armed, Ben?"

"Aye, my lady."

"Excellent. Try not to kill anyone unless you absolutely have to."

"Right you are," Ben said cheerfully. The two of them set off at a run across the small, delightful groves, charming lawns, serpentine walks, and shady bowers that made up some of the sixteen acres of the famed Vauxhall Pleasure Gardens.

As they approached the ruins, Sam pointed and yelled that they were close. Suddenly the figure of a man burst from behind a partially standing wall, spinning and yelling and waving his arms around like he was a madman. Clinging to his back was the lithe shape of a tall boy.

"Digger!" Plum cried, and picking up her skirts, dashed toward the pair. It wasn't easy going with crumbled bits of stone, rotted wood, and awkward mounds of grassy earth that had been artfully arranged as part of the romantic ruins, but where there was Digger, there was bound to be the rest of the children. The man Digger was beating about the head caught sight of her and bellowed a warning, then turned and lumbered back behind the wall. Behind her a shout included her name. Plum slowed and glanced backward. Thom and India and a tall, handsome young man were running toward them. She waved and spun back around, catching up to

Ben as they rounded the corner of a large piece of ruins. The scene before them was of utter chaos. Plum paused for a brief moment, unable to believe what she was seeing, then with a quick smile and a whoop that rivaled those the children were making, threw herself into the fray.

If the situation had not posed danger to the children, Plum thought as she raised her skirt high enough to kick out at the man who was dragging Digger from his back, it would be amusing. Digger's assailant clutched himself, doubled over, and rolled to the ground screaming something about his unborn children. Digger gave her a cheeky grin and the pair turned to where a ginger-haired man was trying unsuccessfully to tuck Andrew and Ann under his arms. The twins were shrieking and squirming and biting at the man, but Plum didn't stop to lavish praise upon them for their intelligent behavior—she lowered her head and charged across the rocky ground toward the man who had her stepchildren. The cowardly miscreant took one look at her—and the three people following on her heels—and dropped the twins, spinning around to head for the scenic wood that bordered the faux ruins.

"After him," Plum cried to the young man who accompanied Thom, falling to her knees to embrace the twins. "Are you all right? Are you hurt?"

"Mama! Mama help me!" a youthful voice cried. Plum turned from where she was pressing kisses onto the squirming twins, jumping up to look down what was meant to represent a ruined cloistered walk consisting of a few broken archways and fallen columns.

"Digger, take care of the twins," Plum cried as she

dashed off. At the far end of the walk rose a large block of stone topped by wildflowers. The ginger-haired man stood next to the stone, a pistol in one hand and McTavish in the other. Movement behind her indicated that Thom and India had followed her.

"Stand back, all of you, or I'll see to it this little bastard goes to meet his maker! You! You the boy's mama?"

Plum walked forward slowly, gesturing behind her back in an attempt to warn the others off. "Yes, I am his mother. You can't want to harm him, it will do you no good. Why don't you take me, instead?"

"Come closer, and we'll talk about it," the ginger-haired man said.

Plum turned her head slightly to the right, never once taking her eyes from the muzzle of the pistol pressed to her youngest stepson's head as she slowly paced toward him. "Digger?"

"Yes, Plum?" His voice was as soft as hers.

"Take the others to the carriage. Be very quiet and do not attack anyone. Their safety is in your hands."

"I'd rather stay here with you."

Plum risked a glance to the side to where her stepson stood. He looked just like Harry at that moment, a realization that wrung her heart. "I know you would, but you must think of their safety first."

"All right. I won't let you down."

"Tell Sam and the other men to stay back." Plum stepped forward, her hands spread to show she was unarmed. "Let the child go. He's not as valuable as I am, surely?"

"That's as may be, but I was hired to take the youngsters." The man edged nervously around the side of the stone, his grip on the boy's neck tightening as he had to drag McTavish over a small hillock. "No closer now, my lady. I wouldn't want you getting heroic. You, there, in the back. Release my man or I shoot the lad."

Plum prayed that the man who accompanied Thom would do as he was asked. Evidently he did, because a thin, weedy man with two bruised eyes and a bloody nose staggered to the far side of the walk, wiping his nose on his sleeve.

The man with the pistol nodded toward her. "Take the lady, Davey. Hold her in case the gent back there gets any ideas."

"Who is it?" Plum asked in a whisper as the bloodied man limped toward her.

"The gentleman? That's Nick, my burglar," Thom whispered back.

"Tell him to be ready. I will pretend to stumble and fall toward the man with the pistol. You must grab McTavish while the burglar takes care of this one."

Thom stepped away as the hired thug grabbed Plum's arm, snarling an oath under his breath. His fingers bit cruelly into her arm as he jerked her forward.

Plum, mindful of the broken stones and the debris that littered the ground, knew full well that she was endangering herself and her babe, but she would not tolerate the devils having McTavish. She braced herself, spying a likely looking piece of stone over which she would stumble, but just as she was about to throw herself forward, the sound of muffled hoof beats reached her ears.

"If that's another one of your men, tell him to stay back," the ginger-haired man warned, cocking the pistol. "Or I'll blow this little bastard's head from his neck!"

Plum was incapable of speech, so furious was she, but even she paused for a moment when a riderless horse burst into the open space from beyond the ruins. Its reins were hanging loose, and immediately upon sighting the group of men, it shied and veered away. At that moment a dark shape leaped out from behind the far edge of the standing wall, seeming to fly across the empty space before landing on the ginger-haired man. McTavish was knocked forward as the two men fell, a pistol shot breaking the peaceful quiet.

"Harry!" Plum shrieked, and kicked out at her guard before throwing herself protectively over the top of McTavish. He squirmed beneath her, and she eased up enough to let him breathe, but when she saw Harry knock the pistol from the ginger-haired man's hand, she leaped to her feet, hauled McTavish up, shoving him at Thom before running forward to see how badly Harry had been hurt.

"Hurt? Me? Woman, what are you babbling about?" Harry asked, shaking his hand and pushing his spectacles back.

"I heard a shot! The pistol was pointed toward you! When you shoved McTavish out of its path, you were in the way! Where are you bleeding? Are you in pain?"

Plum started checking over her husband's arms and chest, but he put a stop to her stripping him bare in front of everyone only by grasping both of her hands and shaking her slightly.

"Plum, I'm not injured. The pistol discharged without striking anyone. If you look to your right, you can see where it struck what's standing of that wall."

Plum looked, and then sagged against him in relief. "Oh, Harry! I'm so glad you're not hurt."

"Well, as to that, so am I," Harry grinned. "This brute hasn't fared as well, however."

"Oh, he deserves to be unconscious," Plum said indistinctly, her face pressed against her husband's neck. She didn't even spare a glance to the man who lay fallen behind him. Harry and the children were all that mattered.

"He does, but I would have liked to ask him a few questions. We'll just have to hope he didn't scramble his wits when he hit his head on that rock," Harry said, pushing Plum gently from his chest to squat down and examine the man. "Damn. Well, I guess there's only one left. Nick, thought you'd be here. You didn't kill that one, did you?"

"I assumed you'd want him alive," the burglar Nick said. The man who had grabbed her by the arm was lying on the ground, moaning and cradling his head.

"Good. Plum, you and Thom take the children to the carriage. Ben, you go with them."

Plum, shaking a little in the aftermath of the attack, rubbed her arms. "Do you know Thom's burglar?"

Harry grinned. Now was not the time to explain about Nick. "We've met."

"Oh, what will you do now?"

He prodded the man with the toe of his boot. "Hmm? Oh, Nick and I will stay behind and have a little chat with our friend here. And make sure the other ruffian is taken into custody. Is this all there were, two of them?"

"No, there were four all together, but the other two were in a separate carriage. I didn't see them when we arrived," Thom said.

"Must have run off once they realized there was trouble," Harry mused. "Ah well, we have the one. You ladies go on home, now."

"I think we should stay. You may need some help persuading him to talk," Plum said, giving him a look that warmed him to his toes. No other wife but Plum would want to stay and torture the truth out of a roughneck. Was it any wonder he loved her so? Still, such business was not for women.

It took some convincing, but at last Harry managed to get Plum and the children off toward home, but only after he promised both ladies that he would fill them in with all the information he gleaned from the hoodlum.

"And now, my good fellow, let us have a little discussion," Harry said cheerfully as he turned back to the battered man. Nick grinned. The man looked like he was going to be sick.

It didn't take much to make the bloodied man talk—faced with the threat of a couple of fingers broken, and he sang like a nightingale—but unfortunately, he was evidently not in the confidence of the man who had arranged the kidnapping.

"I don't know 'im," the thug Davey whined, nursing his fingers. "Max, 'e was me boss. I worked for 'im. Max is the one what knew 'is nibs."

"His nibs? The man who hired Max was a gentleman?"

"Aye, talked right proper, and dressed fair to make yer eyes water."

"His name," Harry snarled.

"Don't know it, 'onest I don't!" Davey shrieked as Harry raised his fist. "Max never tol' me, 'e just said as we 'ad a job to snaffle some cossets, that's all 'e be tellin' me, so 'elp me God!"

Harry questioned the man for an hour before he passed out, but long before that he realized that what the man claimed was true—he was just an underling, hired as a body to help kidnap the children, nothing more. He damned the situation that left the leader, Max, insensible. He was so close to finding out who was behind the attacks. If only he had arrived earlier. . . .

"Can you take care of them, Nick?"

"I'd be happy to," Nick said as he heaved the unconscious man none too gently onto his shoulder. "I'll take him to the police, shall I?"

"Yes." Harry stood staring down at the ginger-haired Max. "I'd best speak to the magistrate about this, but first I'm going to have a sketch of his face made and take it to the Home Office. Maybe someone will recognize him."

Nick hesitated, worry furrowing his brow. "Are you in some sort of trouble?"

Harry swore under his breath as he turned away from the man. His face was grim and set with determination as he admitted the truth to himself. He was no closer to naming the man behind the plot against his family. He would have to redouble his attempts to dig out the proof that was needed to identify the villain. "It's nothing I can't take care of."

Chapter Fifteen

"Well?" Thom asked two days later as she burst into Plum's sitting room.

"I have an appointment tonight to meet with a man your burglar says will take care of my problem," Plum said triumphantly.

"Oh, thank heavens," Thom said, plopping gracelessly into a nearby chair. "I just knew Nick wouldn't let me down. He's so wonderful, don't you think? He was very brave at Vauxhall."

Plum glanced from her niece to the letter she'd received from the burglar named Nick. "He writes legibly, I'll give him that, but Thom—he's a burglar."

"I know," Thom said, kicking her foot idly as she slouched back. "He's a very good one, too, I'm sure."

"A burglar is not at all a suitable beau for a young woman of your family," Plum said sternly, although she suspected it would do little good. Thom was al-

ways rescuing some needy creature or another—
usually it was cats and dogs, but evidently now
she'd felt this burglar needed saving. "I'm sure he's
not at all nice for you to know. He isn't—"

Thom's face set into a mulish expression as she
sat up. "He isn't what?"

Plum's hands fluttered about expressively. She
hated to sound like a snob, but there were limits to
how far she was willing to bend for Thom, and burglars were that limit. "He's not a gentleman."

"Hrmph. I don't care about that. He's my friend. I
like him. And he saved Harry's children from certain death. Twice!"

Plum bit back her objections. Thom was absolutely right, no matter how unsuitable the young
man was for her, he had saved the children, and for
that she would be eternally grateful to him. Perhaps
once Harry had caught the person responsible for
the horrible attacks, she could do something for the
man. Clean him up, educate him, find him a good
job . . . "As you say, we all owe him a great deal, and
I will be happy to do what I can to show my gratitude. Now, I have been busy writing, and I'd like
your opinion on some of the scenarios I've created."

"Scenarios?" Thom leaned forward to peer at the
sheets of paper on Plum's writing desk. "What scenarios?"

"Scenarios for Charles, of course. Oh, speaking
of him, I've had another letter. That makes the third
in as many days."

Thom made a rude face. Plum, who agreed
wholeheartedly with her niece's unspoken opinion,
said nothing but handed the letter over, watching as
Thom read it with growing indignation.

"He has nerve threatening you like that! How dare he?"

"Evidently he feels that my lack of response to his demands for money are an indication I am not taking care of the matter." A particularly unwholesome—for one Mr. Charles de Spenser—smile curled her lips. "Little does he know that I am, indeed, taking steps to resolve the situation."

Thom smirked, tossing the letter back onto Plum's desk. "The beastly man. I should just like to see him make good his threats. Harry has so many men attending us whenever we go out, a butterfly couldn't get through their defenses."

The smile left Plum's face at the reminder of the cloud that hung over their heads. "Yes. I do hope he finds out soon who is behind the attacks. The stress of it is weighing very heavy on Harry. Last night he only had the strength for one—" Plum stopped, blushing a little as she realized what she was about to impart to her niece.

"Yes?" Thom asked brightly, a wicked glint to her eyes.

"Never mind, it doesn't concern you. Now, let us go over these scenarios I have created."

Thom smiled. "You are the only woman I know who has the strength of mind to create scenarios for the murder of her ex-husband-who-wasn't."

"Murder!" Plum looked up in surprise. "Oh, no, Thom! I gave that idea up days ago. These scenarios are regarding Charles's scandal, not murder!"

"But . . . but . . . you said you wanted him killed! I saw you attempting to garrot Shakespeare's head!"

"That was days ago," Plum said, waving away the idea. "I changed my mind that very day when I real-

273

ized I didn't have the stomach to kill Charles. No, this plan is much better. I will hold the threat of a scandal over his head so that he is forced to keep silent on the subject of me. I have several excellent scandals planned."

"But I told Nick—he thinks you want someone to kill Charles!" Thom's eyes were wide with worry.

"I don't!" Plum objected.

"I know that now, but I didn't when I wrote to Nick!"

Plum's straight brows pulled together as she mulled over what to do with an unwanted murderous henchman, deciding after a few minutes of contemplation that since she was paying him, he would just have to do as she told him. "He will simply have to revise his expectations. If he does not agree to participate in the scandal-creation, I will find someone who will. Now, let me show you what I have come up with."

"I don't understand why you have to create scenarios at all," Thom complained, obligingly pulling up her armchair to sit next to Plum. "After everything I've seen of the *ton*, it seems all you have to do is look sideways at someone and you have a scandal."

"It's not quite that easy. The threat of the scandal is what I will use, not the event itself. For that reason, I have used my literary skills to draw up several convincing scenarios."

"*The Shameful Secret Truth Regarding a Viscount's Youngest Son and His Unnatural Love for a Milk Cow Named Junie,*" Thom read aloud. "Well, I like the title. Very lively and colorful."

"Thank you," Plum said modestly. "I have always felt I had a gift for turning a neat phrase."

"Mmm. What's the next one?"

"I call it simply *Lost His Wits and Believes He's a Large Willow Tree on Hampstead Heath*. As you can see, it is a bit more involved in that Charles has to be first drugged, then taken to Hampstead Heath where several willow fronds will be tied to his arms."

"Very interesting," Thom said. She tapped a finger on the bottom of the paper. "And the loosed tigers?"

"They are there to throw suspicion away from anyone who might have noticed that Charles was drugged. I thought that a particularly clever touch in that it will confuse people. Otherwise, they might just think it was a jest on the part of his livelier friends, and dismiss the idea that he was insane."

Thom frowned. "But wouldn't a tiger be likely to maul innocent passersby?"

"Yes, but if you read the note at the bottom, the tigers' handlers are to be available at all times in order to keep an unwanted tragedy from occurring. The tigers are there just to cause confusion, really. If you were there and tigers were on the loose, would you stop to consider whether or not a man dressed as a tree had been drugged?"

"No, I suppose I wouldn't. That is a good distraction. And the third scenario?"

"The tigers gave me this idea. It's called *Soulless Wretch of a Man Who Enrages and Torments Innocent Bear Cubs*. That is a bit more difficult to enact, since a bear cub must be found and enraged before it can be discovered with Charles, but I am convinced it would work."

"Yes, I see your point."

Plum nodded sagely. "I have two more scenarios,

but I'm not as pleased with them as I am the first three. I will present them to the murderer that your burglar found, and convince him that it's much better to simply arrange for a scandal than to murder Charles."

Thom didn't look convinced, although she said, "If you say so. When do you meet with him? And may I come with you?"

"Tonight." Plum eyed her niece, chewing on her lip as she thought how best to phrase her request. "I don't want Harry to know where I'm going."

"No, of course not," Thom said, supportive to the end.

"So I thought to tell him that you and I had been invited to a recital. Harry dislikes recitals—he says they bore him to tears, so if he thought that we were going to one, he might not insist on accompanying us."

"But he would send Juan and the footmen with us."

"Yes, but here's where it pays to have a devious mind—I have written to Lady Davell, and told her how well I've heard her oldest daughter plays and sings, and as I expected, she invited us to an intimate dinner so we can hear the girl. I've accepted on your and my behalf, and to Sir Ben's we will go . . . only I will make an excuse early on and return home. Or they'll think I will."

"Oh!" Thom said, her eyes full of admiration. "But really you'll go to meet the murderer!"

"Exactly." Plum smiled, pleased that Thom grasped the finer nuances of her plan. "I shall slip out of the house with no one the wiser, returning home after I am done."

"There's just one thing—you won't have anyone to protect you if you slip out unnoticed. What if you are attacked?"

"The accidents have all involved the children, not me. I'm quite certain no one is the least bit interested in me."

"Harry won't like it," Thom said doubtfully.

"Harry won't know, so it won't disturb him. *Will it*?" Plum asked with meaningful emphasis.

"No, I suppose not. I do wish I could come with you to meet the murderer. I've never met one before, and if he's anything like Nick—"

"I'm sure he wouldn't be. You said Nick turned down the opportunity to do the task himself, which I admit shows a niceness I hadn't expected in a burglar, but still, a murderer is a different sort of individual all together. Now, here's what I want you to say in case Harry decides he wishes to accompany us—"

Her worries were for naught. Harry, who had been acting a bit strangely ever since he returned from a visit to his friend Lord Wessex's house—he was prone to subjecting her to odd, unreadable looks—posed no objections when she mentioned casually that she and Thom had been invited to dinner at the unexceptional Sir Ben Davell's.

"I have an engagement myself this evening," he said, giving her yet another of those odd, piercing glances, as if he wanted to speak to her about a subject, but couldn't bring himself to it.

"Oh, do you? Something to do with *the situation*?" Plum asked in a whisper, casting a worried glance over to where the children were playing a game of Goose.

"It has to do with a situation, yes," Harry said, his beautiful changeable eyes filled with enigma.

Plum, who half expected her conscience to object to going behind her husband's back rather than enlisting his aid with a problem, was pleased to find that about this, at least, her conscience was quiet. Charles was her problem, and it was her responsibility to see to it that he was taken care of just as Harry was responsible for seeing to the children's safety.

The similarity of their situations struck her in a manner so profound that Plum was able to kiss the children good night, and wish Harry a pleasant evening without the slightest twinge of guilt. She was doing this for his sake, for all their sakes, and although it was undoubtedly a sin to willingly threaten another person with scandal, Charles was a detestable snake, and no doubt the good Lord would understand her actions.

In fact, Plum reflected a few hours later as she made her escape by a side door of Sir Ben's house, the ease with which her plan was enacted seemed to be proof of a blessing from on high. She hailed a hack loitering around the square, and ordered him to take her to Green Park. Once there the man was agreeable enough to wait for her return.

"I shouldn't be long," she told him as he handed her out of the carriage.

"I'll wait for 'owever long ye need me," the man said.

She smiled and gave him a coin for his trouble. The poor man looked as if he could use it—he actually had a hook in place of his left hand.

Five minutes later the large young man named

Nick stepped out from behind one of the trees lining the walk. He was dressed shabbily, but he met her gaze without wavering, and she renewed her intentions to do something to repay him for his kindness in saving the children.

"Lady Rosse? We haven't been properly introduced. I'm Nick Britton. Do you still wish to go ahead with your plan?"

Plum clutched her reticule nervously. She was not a fool; she knew that ladies who wandered around parks after dark were leaving themselves open to attention from less than desirable individuals, which is why she brought along one of the pistols she had found in the bottom of Harry's desk. It was a very small pistol to be sure, but she had great faith that it would dissuade anyone who bothered her. Although she probably had nothing to fear from a mere burglar, she would take no chances. The pistol was loaded and ready to be pulled out at the first sign of trouble. "Yes, I do wish to go ahead with it, although with one slight change. I don't want the man killed. My niece misunderstood my plan, you see, and she thought I was looking for a murderer, when what I really need is someone who will assist me in arranging for a scandal."

Nick looked startled for a moment, then rubbed a hand across his mouth, mumbling his answer through his fingers. "I see. Yes, that is quite a misunderstanding. I'm sure the . . . er . . . individual you have hired will be most interested to hear the truth."

Plum bit her lip. "You don't think he'll be disappointed, do you? I should hate to have a disappointed murderer on my hands. I imagine they are difficult enough to deal with when they are happy."

Nick bowed his head and looked to the side, where trees threw black shadows so dark that not even the light from the lamps on the street could penetrate it. "I should say that this man will not be in the least bit disappointed, but perhaps I had better let him tell you that in person. Good luck, Lady Rosse."

Plum watched nervously as Nick left. She had assumed he would stay with her while she met with the murderer, receiving an odd sort of comfort from the knowledge that she wasn't alone, but that, she said to herself as she reached into the reticule for the pistol, was just how much she knew about the underworld. Evidently one didn't meet with one's murderer in the presence of a mere burglar.

"Lady Rosse?"

A man stood in shadow against the tree, his voice rough and uncouth.

"Yes, I am Lady Rosse. Might I know your name?"

"No. The boy tells me you want some gentry cove orfed."

"Orfed? I'm not sure—"

"Killed."

"Oh, yes. That is, no, I don't want a gentleman . . . er . . . dispatched. I never did. Well, I did, but I changed my mind almost immediately. I want the gentleman scandalized. I have several scenarios . . . oh, blast! I left them at home! How could I be so stupid?" Plum stamped her foot with frustration. She had forgotten all about the scenarios in her rush to escape without Harry deciding to join them. "Well, I *had* several scenarios regarding several means of causing a scandal that would ensure the gentleman hold his tongue, but I shall have to send them to you later. As for your fee—"

The shadow moved, as if he had shifted his weight, leaning against the tree. "You don't want the man killed?"

"No, of course not! What do you take me for?"

The murderer seemed to be at a loss for a moment, growling a low, "That's what I was told."

"Well you were told incorrectly," Plum answered righteously. "If you are not flexible enough to follow along with this change of plans, I must dismiss you and hire someone a little less obstinate and set in his ways."

The murderer took a deep breath. "Why do you want to make a scandal about this cove?"

Plum frowned at the man's tone of impatience, but decided not to make too much of it. Murderers were not known for their pleasant tempers. "That is a private issue, one I do not intend to discuss with you. Your task is to create the situation that will lead to a heinous scandal unless I step in to prohibit it."

"If it's so private, why're you comin' to me with it? Why don't you go to your husband? Won't he take care of a private issue for you?"

"Yes, of course he would, but that's not the point. My husband is busy at the moment with his own concerns, and I don't want to burden him with mine."

The man's arm moved, as if he was scratching his head. "Seems to me a bloke would want to make that his concern. Don't you trust your husband?"

"Of course I trust him. I trust him with my life!" Plum made an annoyed sound. "We were not discussing my husband, we were discussing the situation—"

"Know what I think? A wife shouldn't have secrets from her husband, that's what I think. Shows a lack of faith in him, it does. Shows she thinks he can't take care of her."

"Perhaps in other wives it does, but in my case, it doesn't. I have the utmost faith and confidence in my husband, but this is something that could harm him and his children, something to do with my past, and I will not have their lives ruined because of me."

"What's the gentry cove done to you? Said a few nasty things about you, no doubt?"

Plum shivered. There was something eerie about talking to a faceless man standing in the shadows of the great trees lining the walk. "It's much, much worse than that. It would bring shame and dishonor to everyone in my family."

"Maybe you just think it would. Maybe it's nothing so very terrible at all."

Plum made a dismissive movement with her hand. "You don't know anything about it, and frankly, I have no desire to discuss it further. If you do not wish to do the job—"

"I didn't say I wouldn't, I just said it seems to me you should have talked to your husband about it. That's what a husband is for, isn't it? To help you out when you need it?"

"Perhaps your wife sees you merely as a solution to her problems, but I most certainly do not view my husband in that light. Oh, I admit I did at first, he seemed like such a godsend when I most needed him, but then I realized just how wonderful he is, and I became determined to do everything I could to protect him."

"That's a man's job," the murderer grumbled.

"Is it? Your wife must not love you very much if she doesn't wish to protect you. That, however, is neither here nor there, nor is my relationship with my husband. The fact is that I need Charles de Spenser quieted, and I cannot do it myself. I do not wish to be known to be involved, and as I am with child, and—"

"You bloody well aren't! I made sure you aren't!"

Plum clutched the pistol tighter as the man stepped out of the shadows. There was something familiar about that bellow. "Harry?"

Her husband stormed out of the shadows toward her, a furious look on his face. It *was* Harry. Here! But why? And how? "Harry what are you doing here? You haven't taken up murdering as a pastime, and you were afraid to tell me?"

"No, you foolish woman," he snarled, grabbing her by her arms and giving her a little shake. "What do you mean you're with child? You can't be, I pulled out almost every single time."

"Yes, *almost* every time," she said, trying to get over the shock of seeing Harry where she expected a hardened criminal. "But there were two times you didn't, and . . . oh! That doesn't matter right now, what does matter is that you've tricked me!"

Harry's eyes glittered dangerously behind his spectacles. "Tricked you? How have I tricked you? You've tricked me! You deliberately impregnated yourself when I wasn't looking!"

Plum poked him in the chest. Hard. "*That* would be a very neat trick indeed! You were not only looking, you were moaning. And thrusting. And . . . and . . . sweating! And doing all those other moaning-thrusting-sweating–type things you do when you spill your seed, so don't you dare tell me you weren't aware of what was going on . . .

argh! You did it again! You distracted me! Well, I won't allow it. You, my Lord Rosse, tricked me into thinking you were a murderer, which is a very cruel thing to do to a wife, very cruel indeed. I shan't forget this evening for a long, long time."

"Neither will I," Harry roared at her.

"Good!" Plum yelled back. "Just what is your connection with Thom's burglar Nick?"

Harry swore and released her arms, stomping off a few steps, running his hand through his hair as he spun around to face her. "He's Noble's son, and my godson, if you insist on knowing. He's not a burglar, he's a social reformer. As for your pregnancy, I will not lose you, do you understand? I will not lose you! I lost one wife to childbirth, but I refuse to lose another. No. I won't have it, I absolutely will not have it! You'll swear to me right here and now that you won't die!"

Plum, who had been teetering between anger that her husband had tricked her, and tears due to his reaction to her wonderful news, swung firmly into the puddly camp, her anger evaporating as she realized what was driving his fury. He was concerned about her health. He wasn't angry because she was such a poor mother, he was worried that she would die. She gave a tiny little sniff and swallowed back a large lump of tears, her voice soft and warm with understanding. "Harry, not every woman dies in childbirth. Your first wife bore five children without problem. Gertie told me she died of a fever. She didn't think it had anything to do with McTavish's birth at all."

"She was weakened by the birth, that's why she caught the fever." Harry placed his hand on her forehead. "There, you see? It's already begun. You feel warm. Too warm. You're obviously gravely ill."

She laughed and pulled the hand down so she could press her lips against it. "I'm not gravely ill, I'm warm because it's a warm evening, and I was flushed with anger, but truly, I feel fine. Well, no, that's not strictly the truth, I'm sick every morning, and my breasts are sore, and I seem to be discomforted in a most unmentionable place, and no matter how much roughage I eat . . . well, that's not important. Other than those unmentionable things, I feel wonderful. I want you to be happy about this baby. I had a midwife look at me, you know. She said I wasn't too old to bear a child, and that everything was as it should be, so really, there is nothing to worry about."

Harry allowed her soft words and warm touch to ease his anger. He really had no choice; the situation was one that he was powerless against. There was another, however. He hugged her closely for a moment, sending a silent prayer that she not be taken from him. Just as she lifted her lips to his, he pushed her gently away. "What the devil do you mean by coming out here alone meeting with a murderer? You could have been killed or worse!"

"I can't imagine what you think is worse than being killed," Plum said with a distinctly annoyed look to her face. "But I assure you that I did take steps to guarantee my protection."

"Oh, really? And just what might those steps be?" No doubt she left a melodramatic letter on his pillow, as ladies in gothic novels always did.

She pointed a very real, very un-melodramatic pistol at him. "It might not kill someone outright, but I imagine it would give anyone intent on harming me pause for thought. Now, would you mind telling me please why you are here in place of the murderer I arranged to meet me?"

Harry fought the urge to shake his wife, yell at her, kiss her, make violent love to her, yell at her some more . . . he took a deep breath, and with great control, took the pistol out of her hand, noting as he did so that it was not only loaded, but primed. He closed his mind to the horrors of what might have happened to her carrying a pistol that could go off at any moment, and with a firm but gentle hand, spun her around and marched her back toward the road. "The question at hand is not why am I here, it's why you would attempt to hire a man to kill someone who drowned six months ago. It *is* Charles de Spenser you wanted killed, isn't it?"

"Yes, but as I told you, I didn't really want him killed. Thom misunderstood me. Why was Nick pretending to be a burglar when he wasn't?"

"He's heavily into reform work that requires him to blend into low-class surroundings. When Thom saw him the other night, he was returning from a raid he instigated on a working man's brothel. He slipped into the Willots' house with the intention of changing into his dress blacks there. Now you answer my question."

"You haven't asked one." Plum stopped and turned toward him, her face pale, her dark eyes huge and filled with dread. "Oh, Harry, Charles isn't dead. It's all so horrible—he said he was insensible after a boating accident and everyone thought he was dead, but he isn't. He's back, and I didn't want to add to your burdens, truly I didn't. I see now why you were asking me those questions when I thought you were the murderer, and even though it will take a long time for me to forgive you tricking me like that, it is the truth that I never once doubted you could take care of Charles if I asked you to, only your way of taking care of him would be challenging him to a duel, and you just can't do that. Not only might you be harmed, but it wouldn't stop Charles from telling what he knew, and then we'd all be ruined."

Harry, who was indeed planning that very action, put a temporary halt to his thoughts of firing a bullet through the man who was torturing Plum just long enough to admit she had a point. "Regardless of the steps I will take to revenge the dishonor he did you, I have sworn to you time and again that nothing about your marriage to de Spenser can hurt us—"

"This isn't about that," Plum wailed, turning and walking toward the carriage.

"It isn't?" Harry stared after her for a moment, then caught her arm, turning her so her face was illuminated by the gas lamp on the street. "Then why the devil do you want the man killed? Did he offend you by some other means? Is he the man who met you in the park, the one Juan said you slapped?"

"Yes, he approached me in the park, and yes, he offends me, but not how you think. I . . . I'm not sure how to put it . . . it's . . . it's difficult to explain."

"Try," Harry said, pushing his spectacles up so he could better see every fleeting expression on her face.

She explained. In great detail. So great a detail, in fact, that Harry wondered once or twice if he was going to be able to stop her long enough to get her home. It seemed that once she started, she was determined that he know everything, right down to the scenarios she had planned, scenarios that were not only frightening in their inventiveness, but so ludicrously ridiculous, Harry had an uneasy feeling that they would succeed brilliantly. Forty minutes later Harry lifted his wife into the carriage. "Take us home, Crouch."

"Aye, my lord. Everythin' turn out all right, then?"

"Yes," Harry said as he climbed in after his wife. "Thank Nick for me. And Noble. And my thanks to you for seeing to my lady's safety."

"Enjoyed it," Noble's pirate butler said with a grin. "Life has been a bit on the dull side of late what with Lady Wessex tied up with the young 'uns 'aving the chicken pox."

It was a relatively short ride home distance-wise, but Harry used every minute to mull over the tale his wife had told him. That she could be the author of the most notoriously sexual book ever published was no surprise to him—he had ample proof of her skill and knowledge of the connubial calisthenics, a skill and knowledge that left him wrung out like a limp rag each night—but that she should believe the only way out of the true identity of Vyvyan La Blue being made public was by blackmailing her former lover was a bit of a shock. His Plum, his gentle, loving Plum who made his life whole, his heart sing, and his body harden with just the thought of her, that Plum was the same woman who cold-bloodedly planned another man's social ruin just to keep his reputation clean.

Harry thought he couldn't love Plum any more than he already did, but he was wrong. He loved her more, bless her vengeful little heart.

That didn't mean he wasn't going to blister her ears with a lecture about not sharing her burdens, but still, he couldn't keep from tasting her, just once before they arrived home.

"You're not still angry with me, are you?" she asked once he released her lips. The scent of her was dizzying, seeping into his skin, going deep into his body and soul, making him burn to claim her. "You couldn't kiss me like that if you were angry."

"Of course I am, you wonderful, adorably silly woman. I'm going to be angry for a very long time. You're going to have to use every morsel of talent you possess to woo me back into a good mood, and I assure you I am going to take a lot of wooing."

"Are you?" Plum asked, a wicked light dawning in her eyes. Harry felt himself responding to that light. He loved it when she got wicked. "Well, then, I shall have to put my mind to some inventive ways to woo you."

"You do that." He leaned forward to possess himself of her lips again. "It might just save you."

"Might save me from what?" Plum asked five minutes later, breathless, her eyes misty with passion and love.

"My retribution," he breathed, and hauled her onto his lap in order to kiss her properly.

Chapter Sixteen

The Honorable Charles de Spenser was not having a very good day. First there was a nasty note from his bank that informed him that his credit was of the quality that sadly did not allow the bank to extend its services to him further, followed quickly by a visit to his family solicitor, who pointed out that under the terms of his late father's will, his quarterly allowance was to be paid only if he remained outside of England. When he returned to the rented rooms he had engaged for himself and his wife, it was to find her surrounded by boxes bearing the names of some of the finest modistes and shops. He didn't mind in the least that she had bought items for which he had neither the means nor the intention of paying; what rankled was the fact that the bank would spread the news of his insolvency, thus he wouldn't be able to visit any of the gentlemen's outfitters and purchase *himself* a new wardrobe. It just wasn't fair.

And now Plum of all creatures, soft, stupid Plum had the nerve to ignore his demands. Well, he would see about that. He had a plan to bring her to heel, and if that plan called for him to use her body as well as her husband's money, that was her own fault. She had had it easy for too long while he suffered as an outcast; now he would have his revenge.

But first he had to get into her house to leave her proof of his intentions. Charles stood in a small garden, pursing his lips as he best considered how to get into the house unseen. The place was locked up tighter than a virgin's thighs, but at long last, he selected a small window in the back of the house to break with a convenient brick.

"Damned nuisance," he muttered to himself as he climbed into the window, cutting his hand on a shard of broken glass. "She'll owe me for this, too."

He sucked at the wound for a moment, then felt in his breast pocket for the letter he would leave on her pillow, a letter containing specific instructions on how the money was to be paid to him, as well as a reminder that a copy of his statement regarding the true identity of Vyvyan La Blue would be sent to *The Times* should she not pay him what he was due. He sucked at the cut once more, wrapping his hand in his handkerchief as he crept through the dark room toward the door.

The house was quiet, no footmen on attendance in the hall. Charles climbed the first set of stairs quickly, nervously glancing around to make sure no servants were about. He looked into one or two rooms, but they were day rooms and not the bed-chambers he sought. He paused at the foot of the stairs, holding his breath as he listened. There was the faintest sound of voices, but they were young and high voices. No doubt it was Rosse's children.

A nasty smile spread across his face. He had a taste for young girls, and had heard that Rosse had a daughter who was about the age he enjoyed. Perhaps he could force Plum into turning her over to him, as well.

His mind was so full of lewd thoughts, he failed to noticed the trip wire set at the top of the stairs, nor the bucket carefully suspended from the ceiling. He did notice, however, when a bucket full of stinking, slimy, muddy water poured down onto his head, as if the skies had opened and rained down on him.

He swore profanely, wiping the muck from his eyes, unaware that the noise of children playing before bedtime had ceased for a pregnant moment before being replaced by various whoops of delight, followed by the thunder of several bare feet upon a wooden floor.

All Charles de Spenser knew was that suddenly two children in nightgowns appeared as if by magic, both of them staring at him as he pulled out a sodden handkerchief to wipe his face.

"Who're you?" a tall boy asked.

Charles was tempted to snarl an answer, but quickly changed his snarl into a hoarse chuckle. He knew well enough that one caught more flies with honey than with vinegar. "Well there, aren't you a fine-looking young lad. You must be Rosse's eldest."

"I'm Lord Marston," the boy said with a smug

look that Charles wanted to smack off his face. "Who are you?"

"Why, I'm a friend of your mother's." Charles smiled as he wiped the slime off his face, vowing revenge on the little bastards as soon as he had Plum in his grip.

"What are you doing here?" the tall girl next to Rosse's whelp asked.

That must be Rosse's daughter. Charles leered at her and thought about taking the girl aside, but time was of the essence. He had to leave his letter in Plum's bed and escape before any adults noticed his presence. The children were of no consequence—he never believed a thing his own children told him; no doubt Rosse and Plum were the same way. Regretfully he swallowed his desire for the girl.

"Which way is your mother's chamber?" he asked, gritting his teeth. "I have a little present I want to leave her."

"Our mother is dead," the girl said, giving him a suspicious glare. "Does Papa know you're here? He said we're not supposed to talk with any strangers. We don't know you. What sort of a present?"

"I'm not a stranger. I know your stepmother," he said, taking a step toward her, unable to keep a leer from his lips as his eyes wandered over the lithe shape concealed by the voluminous nightgown. He pulled the letter from his pocket and showed it to them. "You see? It's just a simple little note for Plum. You look like an intelligent little poppet, why don't you tell me which room is hers, and I'll leave this for her as a surprise. Won't that be nice?"

"Pet Harry!" a small child of about five demanded as he popped up in front of Charles holding up a scrawny grey kitten.

"Er . . . no, thank you. I don't have time for kittens." Much as he'd like to stay and approach the girl, he was growing increasingly more nervous as each second passed. He bared his teeth again. "If you show me which bedchamber is Plum's, I will give you a shiny new penny."

"What's in that, then?" Marston asked, crossing his arms over his chest as he nodded toward the letter.

It was hard going hanging onto his smile, but he did. "Something that will interest Plum. Do you like sweets? I will give you sweets if you show me where Plum's bedchamber is."

"You've ruined Papa's surprise," a young girl said, pushing by the elder one. A boy followed her, a twin by the look of him. How many blasted children did Rosse have?

"Eh . . ." Charles said, trying to think of some way to bribe the little bastards. He was swiftly running out of time—any moment a servant could happen upon them.

"Now, listen, all of you, this is surprise for Plum, so you mustn't say anything about it. I'll just slip it into her chamber and leave, so no one will know I was here—"

"I don't like you," a younger girl interrupted him. His hand itched to slap the complacent look off her face.

Her twin nodded. "And we *like* Plum."

"I wager he's the man Papa's been talking about," Marston said. "You know, the bad one."

"Andy, you and Ann go fetch the rope," the eldest girl said, picking up a vase as she started toward him.

"I'll get the flint and tinderbox," Marston said, his eyes lighting up with unholy glee.

"Now, just one moment," Charles said, slowly backing away. A coward by nature, he never thought mere children could be threatening, but judging by the hell-spawned looks in their eyes, these weren't normal children.

From below he heard approaching voices. Desperately, he grabbed the youngest boy and shook him, hissing into his face, "Show me where Plum's room is *this very minute!*"

Charles's last coherent thought before he fell down the stairs was that he would never again be taken in by childish innocence. In a flash they had gone from innocuous, if annoying, innocent children into five murderous terrors bent on his destruction. The youngest boy threw the kitten at his face, scratching his cheek just as another one of the monsters kicked him. A third bit his hand, while the eldest boy and girl shoved him backward until he lost his balance and tumbled down the stairs.

Snarling, furious, and in no little amount of pain, Charles half-fell, half-limped down the remaining flight of stairs, followed by the shrieks and screams of the children as they ran after him. He shoved aside a startled footman who appeared at the bottom of the stairs, flinging the front door open and throwing himself out it, trailing curses and promises of revenge behind him.

Fortunately for his abused body, neither the children nor the footman pursued him. The children stood on the front steps and hurled taunts at him as he limped across the small green that graced the square, but he ignored them, pausing in the shadow of tree to wipe the blood from his cheek.

"They'll pay, they'll all pay," he swore as he gingerly felt around the bite on his hand. The door to Rosse's house closed with a loud bang. He shook his fist at it. "I'll see them groveling and begging for mercy before the week is out. She thinks she's smarter than me, she thinks she can outwit me, well I'll show her! I'll have her on her knees before I'm through with her. With all of them! They'll *all* feel the weight of my wrath."

"Having a spot of trouble, are you?" A voice emerged from behind him, deep into the shadow of a nearby rhododendron. "It looks as if you had a less than pleasant send-off."

Charles spun around, almost jumping from his skin at the man's voice. His own voice shook as he tried to brazen his way out of the situation. "What? Who . . . who are you, sir? Come forward where I can see you!"

"I am a friend, I assure you," the voice said. A shadow flickered, then resolved itself into the figure of a man of middle height and age. "Someone who thinks we might be of mutual help to one another. I sense you have a grievance against Lady Rosse. Perhaps we might have a little chat, you and I, and you can explain the nature of your grievance."

"Why would I want to do that?" Charles asked, relaxing at the sight of the man's bland, placid face. Although the stranger wasn't a gentleman, as he was, his voice was relatively educated and not that of a thug.

"I thought you might want to bend a sympathetic ear to your tale of woe."

Not likely. Charles wasn't about to share the ripe goose that was sure to be his. Plum owed *him*, and *he* would collect his reward. "I don't know you, do I? What the devil do you mean accosting me in this fashion? Who are you?"

"I told you," the man said, smiling. "I'm a friend."

"You're no friend of mine," Charles said with a haughty sniff, straightening his waistcoat.

"Is it not said that my enemy's enemies must be my friends? I believe we have a shared interest in the Rosse family. Yours, I gather, is to seek revenge on Lady Rosse, while mine . . ."

"Yes?" Charles said, only moderately interested in the man. He had no time to waste in idle gossip. He had to return home so he could best plan out the next step in his revenge.

"Mine is to see them *all* destroyed."

Charles's head snapped up at that. He eyed the mysterious man for a moment, considering whether or not he might make use of the man, then gestured graciously. "I find that you interest me strangely. Shall we take a little stroll?"

"Indeed we shall," the man said, smiling again. "Indeed we shall."

"I'm quite able to walk, Harry."

"No you're not. You're not doing a blessed thing until you're safely delivered of the babe. Not one single thing, do you understand me? Not one. I shall beat you mercilessly if you attempt even the littlest act."

Plum kissed Harry's ear as he carried her up the

steps to their home. "But some exercises are beneficial for ladies in my condition."

"No," Harry said abruptly, kicking the door until Ben the footman opened it. "No walks, no riding, no driving through the park, nothing. You are to remain off your feet at all time. Exercise of any form is entirely out of the question. I might allow you to lay in a chaise and read if you promise not to exert yourself while you do so."

"My lord, if I might have a word with you?"

"Not even calisthenics?" Plum whispered in his ear, ignoring the footman trying to get Harry's attention. Her teeth grazed his earlobe. "Say, perhaps, ones that might be done from the comfort and safety of one's bed?"

"It is a matter of some importance, my lord."

Harry paused at the foot of the stairs. He looked at her with narrowed eyes. She rubbed her nose against his. "Do you honestly believe, madam, that my will, my resolute, inflexible, unbending will is so easily swayed?"

"Yes," she said, all but purring in his arms.

"You know me so well," he said with that wonderful twinkle in his eyes as he started up the stairs.

"My lord, I would not bother you if it was not a matter of some urgency—" Ben was summarily ignored by both Plum and Harry.

"Papa!"

Both Plum and Harry looked up at the shouts that greeted their arrival.

"Papa, you'll never guess!" India said as she appeared at the landing.

"—but you should know, my lord, about the incident that happened here earlier."

"I get to tell it, I'm the one who pushed him down the stairs," Digger said. The other children followed quickly, swarming Harry and Plum, all of them talking at once.

"I pushed him, too, and I'm the eldest."

"You're just a lady, I'm an earl."

Ben gave it another valiant try. "It was just a short while ago, my lord. I was on duty in the hall, as I have been these past three nights—"

"Children—" Harry said, trying to make himself heard above the din.

"Mama, pet Harry!"

"Papa, Andy bit the man, and I kicked his shin, and he ran away!"

"—when a man ran down the stairs, followed by the children."

"An earl is nothing compared to being the eldest," India informed her brother. "The eldest is the most important."

"One at a time! You can't all speak at once." Harry ordered. No one paid him any attention.

Plum giggled, filled to overflowing with love and happiness and hope even in the midst of such a maelstrom. Harry knew the worst about her, and he didn't care.

"He ruined our surprise, too. Tell him, Ann."

"My lord, the man appeared to have met with some accident, which, Lord Marston later informed me, was of his and the other children's doing."

"Pet Harry, Mama!"

"He did, he ruined our surprise. I didn't like him."

"I didn't like him more than you didn't like him, Ann!"

"An earl is a title. Being eldest isn't a title, it's just a thing."

Harry loved her still! How could she have been so foolish as to ever doubt his strength of character?

"I cannot understand when you all talk at the same time. Calm down, all of you. Who are you talking about?" he asked.

Plum kissed the muscle that was jumping in his jaw. He was the most divine creature on the whole planet.

"Being eldest isn't a thing! Plum, tell Digger that being eldest is more important than being an earl."

Perhaps the most divine creature that ever was.

"PET HARRY!"

"Nothing is more important than being an earl except being a marquis or a duke, isn't that right, Papa?"

And he was hers, all hers. They all were hers, every last one of them, right down to Ben the footman who was so desperately trying to get Harry's attention. She loved them all—her family.

"You take that back! I didn't like him the most, not you!"

"Lord Rosse, you must listen. I tried to ascertain the man's business in the house, but he ran off before I could know what was what."

Everything was right in her world. Harry knew all, and he loved her, and she loved him, and everyone loved everyone else, and wasn't life the most fabulous thing that ever was?

"The children later said that the man claimed he knew Lady Rosse, and was attempting to find out the location of her bedchamber."

"That's a lie! I told him I didn't like him, and you

didn't, so I didn't like him most of all. Papa, tell Andy I didn't like him most of all."

"SILENCE!" Harry roared.

"Harry?" Plum asked, her cup of happiness over-flowing.

"What?" he barked, then immediately looked contrite.

"I love you. Shall we try *The Virgin and the Unicorn* toni—" Plum's eyes widened as Harry's lovely hazel eyes went dark.

"Man?" she asked him.

"Bedchamber?" he asked her.

They both turned to Ben.

"What man?" Harry yelled. "What was he doing in Plum's bedchamber? Good God, man, don't stand there gaping like a fish, tell us what happened!"

Plum nudged Harry until he set her on her feet, clinging to him as the incoherent bits and pieces the children and Ben tripped over each other to tell merged into one horrifying narration.

"It must have been Charles," Plum said, her happy world crumbling about her. "The description sounds like him, but how could he dare come into the house—"

"He's a dead man," Harry snarled.

"And you thought *I* was bloodthirsty," Plum said under her breath, then gasped aloud as her husband started for the door, "No, Harry! You can't call him out, remember?"

Harry paused to shoot her an outraged glare.

She put her hands on her hips, ignoring the captive audience of children and servants who were gathering behind her. She might yield to Harry about other things, but over this she would not, and the sooner he learned that, the happier they all would be. "Even if you did kill him, and I wouldn't want that because I like living in England, even if you did, it would be too late. The second Charles thinks you're threatening him, he will tell as many people as he can find the truth about me."

"It's my right, Plum," Harry growled, pacing back and forth before the door. "What the devil am I going to do if I can't call him out?"

"I don't know, but there has to be another way."

Harry paused. "What if I were to thrash him within an inch of his life? He wouldn't know about that until it happened, and afterward he would not be in any condition to tell anyone."

There was a distinct wheedling tone to his voice that made Plum want to smile. Such a dear man he was. She pursed her lips and thought it over. "Alas, my darling, if he survived the thrashing, he would tell someone sooner or later, and if he didn't survive it, you would be hung for murder."

"Bah," Harry said, resuming his pacing.

"You see my dilemma," Plum said, all her attention on her angry spouse. "You see why I had to hire a mur—" She stopped and shooed the children upstairs to bed. They didn't want to go, but Plum was in no mood for argument. She waved the rest of the servants away, pulling Harry into the library to discuss the situation.

"Harry, sit down, you're making me dizzy," she said a few minutes later as he paced a circle around her chair.

"This is ridiculous. I'm to allow—without challenge—the man who dishonored my wife to creep into my house for who knows what reason? I'm supposed to tolerate the scum who dared ruin your name, and let him escape without justice? I'm to turn a blind eye when he threatens you? I won't have it, Plum! I have to call him out. It's the only way."

"Then our lives will be destroyed," Plum said softly, her gaze on her hands. She knew not one word of blame would ever pass Harry's lips, but the truth of the matter was simple—she should never have married him. She knew she wasn't to blame for Charles's lying to her, but Harry . . . he was another matter. She had willfully hid the truth from him, and now he and the children and Thom were going to pay the price for her selfishness.

"You're exaggerating," Harry scoffed. "Our lives will not be destroyed."

"Am I?" she asked miserably. "You know society better than anyone, husband. You said you could hush up the scandal of my marriage to Charles, and you were right. Can you say the same thing about the scandal that will be born should the world know that the marchioness Rosse is the author of a book as notorious as *The Guide to Connubial Calisthenics*?"

Harry paused in his pace, resuming it with a little less vigor, his eyes dark behind the lenses of his spectacles. "I don't see why anyone should care if you wrote the blasted book if I don't. And I don't. Why should such information do us or the children any damage?"

"Now who's exaggerating?" Plum asked, her throat growing tight with unshed tears. "You know that there is no way a scandal to end all scandals could be avoided if the truth were made public. A marchioness simply cannot be the author of such a book without receiving censure. Oh, Harry . . ." Plum's bravado dissolved as her heart crumpled. Her worst nightmare had come true, and it was all of her own making. Self-pity warred with guilt. The guilt won. "I should never have married you, but you were so nice, and I was desperate, but now look what it's come to—"

Harry took Plum's hands and pulled her to her feet, allowing her to sob into his shoulder. He pressed his lips to her forehead, a caress so sweet that it made Plum cry that much harder. She wept for several minutes, aware every second just how much she owed the man who gently stroked her back and murmured soothing words in her ears.

"Tears solve nothing, my love," Harry said softly when she stopped weeping and started sniffling.

"I know, but sometimes they make you feel better. Unfortunately, all I feel now is stuffed up." She hiccupped, wiping her eyes on his cravat before looking up to him. "Harry, one of the things I wanted in a husband was someone who had no secrets from me, and yet I went into this marriage keeping secrets of my own. I'm very sorry about that. You deserve better. I know you don't blame me for this, but I also know that we wouldn't be in this situation now if it wasn't for me, and for that I humbly apologize."

"This isn't your fault, sweetheart. None of it is. You did nothing wrong. To tell you the truth, I'm proud of you."

"Proud?" She goggled at him, a tiny goggle to be true, but still a goggle. He was proud of her? For what? "How can you be proud of me? I've done nothing to be proud of, quite the contrary!"

"I beg to differ, you've done much to be proud of. You survived a bigamous marriage that might have warped lesser women."

Plum sniffled again, her heart still heavy. "I didn't have much choice."

"You wrote a book that has brought pleasure to hundreds of people."

"A book so notorious that no bookstore would admit to carrying it." Plum took the handkerchief Harry offered and delicately blew her nose.

He tipped her chin up, smiling down at her with love shining in his beautiful eyes. "You married me."

"Any woman with a shred of common sense would have done that," Plum replied, warmed by the look despite the knowledge of what she was going to have to do.

He kissed the tip of her nose. "You accepted my five little hellions into your heart despite their best attempts to drive you mad."

"Well," she said with a little smile, "I will admit that might have taken a tiny little morsel of courage, but they are good children. Most of the time. Sometimes. Underneath, where it counts, they're good. Even India has come around, and I thought she'd never warm up to me, although I admit, allowing her to wear her hair up and that pair of pearl earrings I bought for her birthday might have something to do with the thaw in her affections."

"She simply realized her good fortune in having such a wonderful step-mother. Not many women would stop running from the little monsters long enough to see their better qualities," Harry said dryly, then pulled her closer, his hands warm on her backside as he teased her lips with his own. "What amazes me the most is that despite everything, you love me."

She melted completely against him, unable to hold out under the heat of his passion. "I would have to be witless not to, you're eminently lovable."

"I am," Harry agreed, swinging her up in his arms. "I am so lovable, you should worship me in tangible methods that will leave me exhausted, but sated. Would you mind opening the door?"

Plum turned the latch. "Harry? Where are we going? I thought we were going to discuss Charles, and what to do with him?"

"We are. We will. Later. Right now I must address the issue of a wife who keeps secrets from her husband." Harry climbed the two flights of stairs without the least sign of strain.

Plum, for a moment concerned by what Harry said, realized by the heated gaze that seared her that he was truly not angry with her for not telling him everything before they married. "There simply couldn't be a more perfect man than you," she sighed, tugging at his cravat, freeing the tanned column of his neck from its snowy hold.

"No, there couldn't," Harry said shamelessly, the twinkle in his eye warming her almost as much as the stark, burning desire she saw there. He pushed open the door to his bedchamber, kicking the door shut behind him. "Which is why I feel you should worship me. Daily. Hourly, even. I am a god amongst men, wife, and I expect you to treat me as such. Let us discuss the form this worship will take."

"Well," Plum said as he allowed her to slid down

his body until she was standing. His fingers danced along the back of her gown, slipping free button after button. Plum shivered with anticipation as her gown parted. "I thought that first I might make a sacrifice."

"A sacrifice?" Harry cocked an eyebrow at her. She gently took the spectacles off, followed by his jacket, waistcoat, and shirt. "You wouldn't happen to be talking about—"

"Acolyte Worshiping the High Priest," Plum said, her hands dancing along the fastening to his breeches.

Harry sucked in his breath, looked wild for a moment as she reached within his breeches to wrap both hands around the hard length of his arousal. "You said that was the one connubial calisthenic that had not been taught to you. You said that was the one you had thought up all yourself, the one you had never put into practice, the pinnacle of all the calisthenics, the one you were saving for a very, very special occasion."

"This is such an occasion," she said, smiling because he was panting. Her smile deepened when he shuddered, prying her hands off him with a look that warned her he was close to losing control. He jerked her gown off, not even pausing to admire her lovely new frothy shift before he removed it, too. She kicked off her shoes. "My stockings?"

He eyed her, a deliciously wicked glint to his eyes. "We will leave them. You are, after all, a deliciously naughty acolyte. You will have to be punished later."

"Oooh," Plum said, giving up the last of her guilt. She loved him, and knew he loved her. She would do whatever she had to do to make sure that nothing tarnished that love. She took a deep breath, then immediately lost it when Harry's warm mouth closed over her breast. His mouth was hot as it kissed a path around her soft flesh, teasing an already aching nipple with both tongue and teeth. Her fingers bit hard into his shoulders as she tried to keep her legs from giving way under her. "What sort of punishment are you speaking of? Will it involve your hand and my bare . . . um . . . sit-upon?"

"It might. Or it might involve two feathers, and the leather cuffs," Harry said as he pulled her close to him, fitting the soft curves of her flesh exactly against his hard planes as if they were designed specifically for one another.

She breathed in the wonderful scent of his lemon soap, allowing her head to fall to his shoulder as she pressed her lips to the pulse point in his throat. "And what sort of form would you like the ritual purification of spirit to take, oh mighty High Priest?"

"Bathing," Harry said, sliding his hands along the long length of her thighs, his eyes alight with love and passion and desire. "You will need to bathe me. Later. Much later. I plan on being very sweaty."

Plum opened her eyes and tipped her head back to gaze into his face as he slid an arm around her waist, lifting her and carrying her the few steps to the bed. She mused for a moment about the ridiculously wonderful nature of men that made them feel it necessary to carry their women to a bed, then pushed that thought aside to concentrate on more important things. "About Charles—"

One boot thudded to the floor. Harry glanced at Plum for a moment, a glance so full of promise she squirmed on the bed as he used the bootjack to pry off the other boot. "Later, Plum. We'll talk about that bastard later."

"Yes, but I am worried—"

"Later," Harry repeated, quickly stripping off the rest of his clothing, standing before her in all of the glory of his masculinity.

Plum's breath caught in her throat as her gaze greedily consumed him from toes to nose, tossing aside her cares, worries, and unhappiness, giving herself up to the wondrous love that bound her to her husband.

"Harry," she mumbled against his breastbone some time later, her fingers trailing up the side of his rib cage, reveling in the heat of him. "We should talk about Charles."

Harry groaned slightly and shifted beneath her. "You're insatiable, woman. Give me a few minutes to gather the tatters of what strength you've allowed me to retain, and I'll be happy to oblige."

Plum giggled, lifted her head, and gently bit his chin. "It was a particularly successful calisthenic, wasn't it? I very much enjoyed the benediction."

Eyes closed, but with a smile on his face, he answered. "I thought you might like that. A little somethi— ought of one day when I saw a balloon asc—

"It was— y." Plum rested her mouth against Harry's nec— moment, and then raised back up, resting h— n her hands crossed on top of his chest. She —r hips slightly to get his attention, and imm— felt his manhood begin to stiffen against her thighs. Two strong hands settled on her hips and held her still. A little gleam of green shone through slightly opened eyes. She smiled. "Now we'll talk about what to do with Charles. I think if you were to find a murderer, and I modified my scenarios—"

Harry sighed, sliding his hands down to massage her behind in a manner that made her groan in pleasure. "Much as I think the bastard deserves to be killed, there is another way. I will simply threaten to destroy him if he so much as breathes a hint of your literary identity."

Plum raised both eyebrows. "Really? Are you sure you can do it? I thought a scandal might stop him, but after tonight—"

Harry kissed her forehead and slid his hands lower, chuckling a sexy chuckle that set Plum's blood to simmering. "What a violent bit of baggage you are. It's one of the many things I adore about you."

Plum wiggled again in silent protest of this new train of thought.

Harry gripped her behind. "You don't have to kill a man to destroy him, sweetheart. If anything happened to you or the children, it would destroy me."

"Yes, I know it would, but that's because you are a singularly wonderful man. Charles, however, is an absolute rotter. I doubt if he feels anything for anyone but himself, let alone affection for his family."

Harry shook his head slightly and slid his hands along the warmth of her inner thighs, parting them as he said, "I had not intended on striking him through his family. You're quite correct, that wouldn't affect him at all. But there's something that will—money. I will simply pay the man a visit and inform him in no uncertain terms that if he mentions anything about you, I will see to it he is destroyed financially, to such an extent that he will never recover."

Tears of gratitude pricked her eyes. "Can you do that?"

Harry shrugged, not a very easy act considering she was lying on him. "With the help of my friends, yes."

"And you really think it will work?"

"Yes." His fingers stroked ever tightening circles on her thighs.

"He won't tell anyone? We won't face another scandal?"

"No, and no."

Plum was distracted for a moment by the path his fingers were taking, but she had one last shameful secret to bare. She had to say it now, while he was in a forgiving mood. "About the babe—Harry, I used you. Shamefully. I wanted a child of my own so badly, even though I know you don't think I'm a good mother, but truly, I am trying. That incident with the twins and the cow in St. James's Park was truly a fluke—that cowherd was exaggerating when he said the cow was frightened to death. And yesterday, when Digger put the fish down India's back while we were in the glass shop picking out new crystal, I lectured him most sternly about taking responsibility for his actions, and told you would take the cost of the broken decanters out of his quarterly allowance. And later, at the fruiterers, where we had gone because the children had never seen a pineapple—and they were quite taken by the one in the window display—I told them all we would *not* go for ices at Gunters as we planned because they would insist on wreaking havoc with all those lovely pyramids of oranges and apples, not to mention what they did to the figs, but honestly, you can't lay the blame for *that* at my door, because I did tell them before we went in not to touch anything."

Harry, who had been shaking beneath Plum as she recounted event after shameful event, finally gave up and roared with laughter. She slapped her hand down flat upon his chest and gave him a look to let him know she wasn't amused. "Harry, this isn't funny! I'm baring my soul to you!"

"You're baring something," he leered, sliding his fingers into her damp heat. "I never thought you were a bad mother, Plum. Far from it, I doubt if anyone could have done as good a job with the children as you have done. You are patience personified with them."

"Hardly. Oh, my, Harry!" she gasped as he rolled her onto her back, coming into her with a smooth movement that never failed to thrill her. "The *Kingfisher*? Now? Here? But we were talking about . . . about . . . about *something*! Oh, yes, the children, that's it, we were talking about the children and the babe and . . . and . . . mmmmrowr!"

Harry kissed the knees that rested on either shoulder before he stroked deeply into her. "Do you really want to talk about that now?"

Plum arched up beneath her husband, sliding her legs down to his waist as she pulled his head down to her own. "No," she whispered on his lips. "It can wait until later. Much, much later."

Chapter Seventeen

"Well, I guess that settles the question of what to do about him," Noble said, nudging the body with the toe of his boot. "You sure your wife didn't hire someone other than you and Nick to take care of the matter?"

Harry steeled himself for the unpleasant task of examining the bloated corpse, rolling it onto its back, trying not to think too much about the ghastly expression on the face, or the damage normal to a body that has floated in the water for several hours. "Quite sure. That was all a misunderstanding between her and Thom. She wanted simply to blackmail de Spenser. When did your man say he found the body?" Harry glanced up to the two large men who stood beside him in the pale light of dawn.

The younger one answered. "About two hours ago. He found the body caught up in a net on the pier, and since it had obviously been someone of quality—and this is my particular patch—he alerted me before he sent for the watch. I told Papa, and he suggested that since you are in touch with a number of runners, you might ask them if they had heard anything about a gentleman being killed." Nick's gray eyes were just as puzzled as his father's. "I had no idea that *you'd* have a connection with the body."

Harry grunted and conducted a quick search of de Spenser's pockets. He found nothing but a few coins, and a cheap snuffbox painted with a pornographic scene.

"He wasn't robbed. Interesting. I don't suppose you'll leave the investigation up to the proper authorities?" Noble asked.

Harry glanced over to where the representative of the city police force was questioning a couple of drunk sailors. "I doubt if they're up to the sort of challenge that de Spenser's body presents."

"They're not so bad," Nick said with a grin. "Stanford's all right, although he's a bit of a stiff neck when it comes to reform."

"Stanford?" He stood up slowly, rubbing his nose, frowning at the name.

"Sir Paul Stanford. He's the head of the city police force."

"Yes, I know of him." Harry's gaze met Noble's. The latter raised his ebony brows. Harry answered the unasked question. "Sir Paul was Sir William's brother. Been out of the country for a few years. Had some business in Canada that he ran—something to do with trading. One of my men checked up on him. He's been back in England for almost a year."

"Ah," Noble said. "So it's not likely he has anything to do with your other business?"

"Not likely, although I suppose anything is possible. I have a man taking a close look at his affairs." Harry examined the body one more time before covering it up with an oiled cloth, the three men moving slowly to their carriage. "De Spenser was strangled, that much is clear, but by whom? And why? Assuming Plum didn't hire anyone to kill him—and I certainly didn't—who would want de Spenser dead?"

"Sounds like it's another task for your runners," Noble said. "How is your other investigation coming along?"

Harry sighed and climbed into the carriage after his friend. Nick took the seat opposite, his eyes interested and watchful. Harry hesitated speaking about the threat to his children, but in the end he gave a mental shrug. He had told both men about Plum's history with de Spenser after seeing the body because he trusted them; Nick learning about the other situation couldn't hurt. "It's not coming along at all. The few leads we had—men known to be friends with the anarchist group Sir William led— are either dead or in prison. He had few close family members, and fewer friends. No one from the anarchist group is left. We can't find proof that anyone who worked under him at the HO has an ulterior motive. If Briceland didn't have the damned letter, I'd say it was all a mare's nest, built on nothing but a foundation of tissue."

"That's understandable. What will you do next?"

Harry sat back against the soft cushions of the carriage, closing his eyes for a few moments while he tried to order his thoughts. "First I will hire a few more men to look into de Spenser's activities since he arrived in England. Then I will meet with the men looking into the situation with Stanford, and see if anything has turned up. Later I'll talk with Sir Paul Stanford, and ask him myself about his brother, as well as de Spenser. Following that," Harry opened his eyes and grinned at his childhood friend, "I intend on introducing my wife to one or two calisthenics she has not yet tried."

The day passed quickly, much to Harry's surprise. He rallied his men, gave assignments to those who were conducting desultory investigations into a man who died fifteen years before, received a report from the man in charge of his family's safety, met with Lord Briceland to discuss the possibility of one of the junior secretaries who had absconded with some funds as being the person they were searching for, lunched with Noble at his club while both of them sent out feelers as to what the feelings of the *ton* were regarding de Spenser's death (a sort of shocked diffidence was the most common reaction, de Spenser having been out of the country for so long that few people remembered him), sent a note to Plum that he would be home for dinner, and received an answer to his request for an appointment with Sir Paul Stanford.

"I'll see Sir Paul tomorrow," he told Noble later, as the two men were parting for the evening. "By then the runners will have hopefully gleaned a few kernels of information about de Spenser's comings and goings, not that I particularly care who killed the man. Still, Plum will want to know, so it won't hurt to take a closer look at his life."

"Can't hurt at all," Noble agreed, punching Harry in the arm as they parted. "Enjoy your calisthenics. Er . . . you think you could get me a copy of the book? I have a feeling Gillian would like it, not that she's not very inventive on her own, but you looked positively haggard this morning. Anything that can result in the sort of satiated look you've had plastered on your homely face all day is something I want to look into."

Harry punched him back, not hard, but not gently either. Just hard enough to let him know he appreciated the quality of the insult. "Do you think you're up to it, old man? You are five years older than me. Gillian would never forgive me if you found the calisthenics were too strenuous for your aged body."

"Right, that's it, tomorrow. Five Courts. We'll just see who's too old."

Harry cracked his knuckles with delight. "I accept. Been a while since I boxed with you. I still owe you for the time you blackened my eye."

Noble rubbed the bump that marred an otherwise flawless nose. "And I owe you for breaking my nose. Good luck, and Harry?"

Harry paused as he was about to get into his carriage. "Yes?"

Noble gave him a look filled with concern. "Have a care. With all the men you've got guarding the children and your wife, your mysterious assailant may think it's easier to attack you."

"What a singularly charming thought. If only he would be so kind as to do that." Harry shook his head as he waved his friend off. He was still dwelling on the number of tortures he'd like to inflict on the man who had tried to harm his children when the carriage pulled up outside his biscuit-colored stone town house. He frowned. There seemed to be a number of people outside on the street, and was that yelling he heard from inside the house?

Harry pushed his way through the crowd that had gathered at the steps leading to the doors, racing up them with a heart suddenly wrung painfully tight at the thought of trouble.

The sight that met his eyes as he dashed inside was so astounding he came to a halt. It was as if a tornado had set down right there in the hall, a tornado made up of several rings of people and children and a number of cats he recognized as belonging to Thom. The cats were running in a frenzied circle in the ring closest him, around the perimeter of the hall, being chased by a small white-and-black calf that bore a short piece of rope tied around its neck, and a wild look in its eyes. McTavish—who for some reason was nude except for a pair of cut down too-large slippers that Harry recognized as being an old pair that used to belong to him—chased after the animals. Two footmen and George chased after McTavish. Beyond the circling animals, one man lay on the floor, evidently having been knocked unconscious, while another was on his hands and knees, his arms held protectively over his head as he yelled a number of curses at the twins, who were taking turns beating him with two chamber pots. Harry spent a moment in gratitude that the pots had not been in use before the twins decided to beat the stranger with them, then moved his gaze to the next group of people.

Thom was arguing violently with a man in the

dark clothing of a watch officer, waving her hands and yelling above the sound of the children and animals. Beyond Thom a man of middle years was being accosted by Digger and India, both of whom were trying to pull him away from the door to the library. The man was obviously trying not to hurt the children as he pried their hands from his arms, but no sooner had he removed one hand than another latched onto him, the children yelling at the top of their lungs all the while. Plum stood in the doorway to the library, wringing her hands and pleading with Juan to remove himself from where he stood with outstretched arms, as if protecting her from harm.

Harry watched it all for a moment—animals, children, servants, strangers, and Plum—then put his fingers to his lips and blew a piercing whistle that sounded painfully in such a confined space.

Miraculously, it worked. For a moment. Then the animals, children, servants, strangers, and Plum all descended upon him. "Halt!" Harry bellowed, then took immediate charge. He pulled off his jacket and handed it to George. "You children, to the right, over there in the corner. George, put this on McTavish. Ben, Sam: you two and Juan to the left, near the door. You, the one on your knees, help your friend into that chair. I don't know who you are, sir, but I will thank you to stop glaring at my wife, she's in a delicate condition. Please move yourself over there, near the stairs. Plum—" He held open his arms. She ran to him, clinging to his shoulders as she glared back at the man.

"Harry, that man says Charles is dead. Is it true? Is he really dead? Did you—you didn't—you didn't arrange—"

"Yes, yes, and no to all the rest." Harry dropped a little kiss on her head just because he felt like it. He gently removed her hands from his shoulders, turning her so her back was to him, wrapping his arms around her in a protective gesture that he assumed the man standing near the stairs could not mistake. "I gather you are with the police force?"

The man bowed. He was a few inches shorter than Harry, and had black eyes that glittered brightly in the soft glow of the lamps. "I am Sir Paul Stanford, my lord. I have the honor of being in command of the police within the bounds of the city. If I might have a word with you and your lady, I believe we can clear up this situation."

"You will not take my most very lady into custard!" Juan declared, tearing himself from where the footmen held him, throwing himself at Plum's feet, spreading his arms wide to protect her. "I will tear out your heart and eat it before your so black eyes if you try to take her, you worm the most pestilential, you!"

"Don't let them take Plum," India cried, running forward. The remaining children erupted from behind her, swarming him and Plum. "We like her! We want her to stay! She takes us places and doesn't make us do our lessons and she lets me put my hair up. Don't let that man take her!"

"Want Mama!" McTavish said, holding up his arms.

"Oh, you darling children," Plum said, gathering them together in a hug. "You all mean so much to me! I couldn't love you more if I had borne you myself. My sweet, adorable darlings."

Harry had a very, very bad feeling. He looked

over her head to where Sir Paul stood. "Would you care to explain why my family and servants are under the impression you mean to take my wife into custody?"

Sir Paul had the grace to look abashed. "If we might discuss the issue in private?"

Plum released the children and turned to him, her lovely velvety eyes hard with pain. "Sir Paul says he has proof that I killed Charles. He said he has a letter from Charles threatening me, and one of his men—"

"The one we hit on the head until he went to sleep," Anne interrupted with no little amount of satisfaction, pointing to the still unconscious man now slumped into a chair.

"—one of his men found my scenarios when he searched the house. Harry, I didn't kill him."

He took her face in his hands, and before everyone kissed the protestations right off her lips. "I know you didn't, love. Don't worry, we'll get this straightened out."

Plum trembled, but it wasn't with fear, it was with the soul-deep love for Harry that made her feel as if she were invincible. As long as she had him and Thom and the children, she could not be harmed.

She turned to the man who had apologetically informed her that he had reason to believe she was involved with Charles's death. "Would you please go into the library, Sir Paul? Thom, you and George and the footmen take the children to the park for their outing. Juan, I greatly appreciate your brave and very selfless attempt to save me, not to mention your offer to tear out Sir Paul's heart, fry it, and eat it before his eyes while it was still smoking, but do you think you could release my knees? Harry, shall we?"

"Most certainly we shall," Harry said, giving Juan a meaningful look as Plum extricated her knees with some difficulty from Juan's fervent embrace.

With her head held high, Plum led the way into the library, seating herself in one of the two chairs before the large ebony table that Harry used as a desk. "Perhaps you would repeat to my husband what you told me?"

Sir Paul accepted her gesture toward the second chair, composing his face into one that reflected abject apology and no little distaste for the task at hand. Harry, to Plum's surprise, did not take his seat at the desk, but stood behind her, one hand on her shoulder as if to show his support. Joy swelled within her for a few precious seconds before Sir Paul's words deflated it, turning her insides cold and clammy as if they were made up of day-old gruel.

"It is with the greatest reluctance that I inform you I am ordered to take Lady Rosse into charge until such time as the magistrate can review the case against her regarding the mysterious death of the Honorable Charles de Spenser, youngest brother of the earl of St. Mead."

"What case?" Harry asked, his voice even and apparently unconcerned, but Plum knew better. His tight grip on her shoulder belied his placid facade. "What reason, what proof can you possibly have that would make you think my wife, a gentle lady, a marchioness, would dirty her hands with the murder of a man so wholly unconnected to her?"

Plum smiled a sad little smile to herself. Harry was using what she had privately dubbed his marquis voice, the voice he used whenever he wanted to intimidate someone with his title and consequence. Unfortunately, she had no belief it would hold sway with Sir Paul.

"There are three reasons we believe that Lady Rosse is involved with the death of Mr. de Spenser. The first is this letter, recovered from his body."

Harry looked startled for a moment as Sir Paul handed him a somewhat battered and grubby letter. Plum flinched a little at the sight of it. She'd read it earlier when Sir Paul had come to take her into charge. She could not deny the letter was from Charles, addressed to her.

"Hmm . . . vague innuendo, vaguer threat . . ."

"Keep reading," Sir Paul said, his eyes black and impossible to read.

"*If you do not pay me the sum we discussed Monday past, I will be forced to reveal all I know, thereby regrettably causing the ruin of yourself and your noble husband. I have not yet spoken to any-one of our past, but do not fool yourself into think-ing the price for my silence is gratitude. I do not fear bringing my own good name into speculation. Our relationship was of a nature such that censure cannot fall upon me, but you will, I fear, feel it most heavily once the truth is known about your literary accomplishment. Lest you imagine I am not serious in my intention to make all known, I would be happy to forward you a copy of a letter which is but awaiting word from me to be delivered to* The Times. *They will, I have no fear, print it im-mediately upon receipt. I remain, yours . . .* I fail to see how de Spenser's threats of blackmail lead you to believe that my wife—a woman in a delicate condition—would murder the man. It's outrageous! Entirely unlikely! You could just as soon say my children were responsible for his death than Plum."

Plum tried to rally a smile at Harry's outraged attempt to shield her. The truth was much less amusing.

"My lord, you will forgive me, this is no slight upon the characters of your children, but as they did bring down one of my men armed with nothing but two chamber pots, and were quite likely to bring down the second—"

Harry cleared his throat. "Regardless of that, this letter is no proof of Plum's guilt."

"There are also these."

Plum licked her lips nervously. She had no trouble recognizing the sheets of foolscap she had used to write out her scenarios.

Harry glanced at them, not even bothering to take them. "I know about those. My wife has literary ambitions. She was no doubt simply putting to pen a few scenes for a novel."

"A novel featuring a variety of detailed methods of ruining a man named Charles?"

"I have always detested the name Charles," Plum said without the slightest conviction that Sir Paul would believe her. "It just came to me."

His black eyes considered her for a moment. Harry's fingers tightened on her shoulders until the grip hurt.

"My lady, I do not doubt that you have the greatest literary skills—anyone who could write so imaginative and detail-rich book as the *Guide to Connubial Calisthenics* could not help but write creative methods to destroy the man who threatened her future—but I do not for one moment believe you wrote these descriptions as a piece of fiction."

"You mentioned three items," Harry drawled in a bored voice before Plum could dispute Sir Paul's statement—not that she could without lying, and she hated to lie outright, although she would if it meant saving Harry or the children from grief. "What is the third?"

"A description given by a man who saw Mr. de Spenser walking last night with a very agitated woman of Lady Rosse's coloring, a lady who was wearing a blue-and-gold dress remarkably similar to the one we found in Lady Rosse's wardrobe."

"That's ridiculous," Plum snorted, nervously aware that if Sir Paul found out she'd left the Darvell's home early, her goose would really be plucked. "My niece and I were out last evening at a private dinner party at the home of Sir Ben and Lady Darvell. They will tell you we were there."

"I have already spoken to Lady Darvell," the police head answered, his eyes filled with a light of speculation that had all hope within her plummeting to her boots. Her goose wasn't just plucked, it was roasted and carved. "She informs me that you left early, leaving your niece behind. No one seems to have seen you leave. I find that extremely . . . curious."

Plum glanced at Harry, unsure of what to say about their assignation.

"My wife was with me after she left the Darvell home," Harry said quickly. "I can vouch for her whereabouts from nine o'clock on. Your witness is mistaken."

"No doubt you can vouch for her," Sir Paul said

smoothly. "Alas, sometimes gentlemen are mistaken about such matters as time, especially when it concerns their wives."

"Dammit, man, are you accusing me of lying?"

Plum got to her feet, holding Harry back as he lunged forward.

Sir Paul also rose to his feet, slowly, as if he was savoring a pleasure. "I would not be so foolish, my lord. I suggest simply that you might be mistaken. And now, if you will excuse me, I must return to my offices . . . with Lady Rosse. I'm sure you understand that it is with the greatest regret that I must ask her to accompany me, but as you have no explanations for the proofs I have submitted—" He shrugged a delicate shrug.

Plum decided she loathed him, but realized that if she did not agree to be taken into custody, Harry would fight to the death to keep her free. She couldn't allow that; she couldn't bring even more trouble onto his head than she'd already caused. She had to go with the odious Sir Paul even though every fiber of her body protested against leaving Harry.

"Your proofs are nothing but cobwebs, insubstantial and unbelievable. I will not tolerate you slandering my wife in this manner. You will take her from this house over my cold, lifeless body!"

"Harry," she said, turning her back to Sir Paul, facing her husband. She took one of his hands, rubbing his knuckles gently against her cheek, smiling into the fury that darkened his eyes from their normal hazel to almost pure forest green. "It's all right. We both know I'm innocent, and the innocent have nothing to fear. I will go with Sir Paul now, and you will contact your solicitor and see about having me remanded to your custody."

"No. It's unthinkable that my wife should be taken away like a common criminal—"

"I know, my darling. I don't like it any more than you, but I will not have anyone suffer any more for my folly and Charles's cruelty. You have the children to protect. Once the scandal about Vyvyan La Blue is made public, they will need to be reassured and comforted."

"Plum, you can't do this," Harry said softly, pulling her to him, his breath brushing her face, his eyes bleak with pain. "You can't leave me. I need you."

"And I need you," she whispered, annoyed that such an intimate scene be witnessed by Sir Paul. She swallowed back the tears that wanted to form, knowing she must put a good light on the situation to keep Harry from forcibly ejecting the head of police from the house. She smiled, and took his hand, placing it on her still flat belly. "We both need you, but you can't help me if you're arrested for assault or worse. You have to let me go with him. You have to stay here and protect the children from the scandal. I love you. I need you. But right now I need you at home more than with me." She softened her words with a kiss, her lips clinging to his as if they hated parting.

Harry's jaw tightened as he looked over her shoulder. "The least you can do is not say anything to anyone about Plum being Vyvyan La Blue. If that's made public, it will ruin her reputation."

"And no doubt yours, my lord," Sir Paul said with a slight bow of his head that didn't quite hide the slight smile that left Plum with an even greater loathing of him. "I will of course endeavor to do all that I can for Lady Rosse, but the papers have ways of finding out such dirty little secrets."

Harry's fingers tightened around hers. She tugged his hands until he looked at her. "It will be all right, Harry, I promise. We won't be parted for long. You must stay here. I count on you to . . . count on you . . ." She frowned, a sudden thought claiming her attention. She turned to Sir Paul. "How did you know I was Vyvyan La Blue?"

"Eh? Oh, it was mentioned in de Spenser's letter."

Harry's quick intake of breath confirmed her dawning suspicion. "Is it? I don't remember that he specified which book I had written."

"That's because it wasn't there," Harry said, stepping in front of her at the same time he shoved her behind him. Plum made a mental note to take issue with him regarding that action at a later date.

"You're wrong. I distinctly remember de Spenser referring to Lady Rosse as being the author of a book that would cause no little grief should it be made public."

"A fact that appears to give you great enjoyment," Harry growled.

Plum moved to his side, putting a restraining hand on his arm. "Where did Charles mention that? It wasn't in the letter you showed me."

"Nor the one you showed me. Could it be that the letters are a forgery?"

"Your lady herself confirmed that the handwriting was that of Charles de Spenser," Sir Paul said, but

Plum interrupted him before he could go further.

"I said I thought it was Charles's writing, but I couldn't be certain."

"It doesn't matter if de Spenser did write the letter," Harry said softly. Plum was aware that Harry's muscles were tense, as if he was coiled, ready to spring. "He mentioned nothing about Vyvyan La Blue in the letter. Which brings us back to my wife's question—how did you know about it?"

Sir Paul's head came up, his face filled with scorn and condemnation. "Does it matter? The fact is that your wife is a pornographer. That alone would be grounds for her arrest."

"I think not," Harry said smoothly. Plum eyed him warily, worried about the lack of emotion on his face. The sense of an animal about ready to spring was heightened by the way Harry moved toward Sir Paul, every movement filled with masculine grace and strength. "Plum? Who are the only people who know the identity of Vyvyan La Blue?"

"You, Thom, my friend Cordelia who would never reveal it, Mr. Belltoad the publisher, and Charles."

Sir Paul started to protest, but Harry's voice cut across it like a lash. "And of those five people, who do you imagine to be the most likely to tell Sir Paul who you were?"

She looked at the older man, noticing the line of perspiration across his brow. "I would imagine Charles would be the most likely."

"That is ridiculous—"

"SILENCE!" Harry roared. His voice dropped to its normal volume, although he still spoke in that controlled manner that warned Plum he was incredibly angry. If he was suspecting the same thing she was, he had every right to be furious. "I concur with your reasoning, Plum. If we follow that idea to its logical conclusion, we must assume that in order to have heard from de Spenser the truth about Vyvyan La Blue, he must also have met Charles. Perhaps he met him last night. In the evening. As de Spenser left our home, driven out by the children, fleeing into the night like the coward he was."

Sir Paul made an inarticulate choking sound, but said nothing.

"But how would he know Charles came to the house?" Plum asked, keeping one eye on the head of police. "How could he have seen Charles leave unless he was—oh!"

"Yes," Harry nodded, slowly approaching Sir Paul. "He would have seen de Spenser leave only if he was passing at that moment—a coincidence so unlikely I won't even entertain it—or if he was watching the house."

"The children," Plum breathed, her hands fisting as anger rose inside her. "He's the man who kidnapped the children! He's the one who threatened them, who tried to hurt them."

Sir Paul stumbled backward as she lunged toward him, but Harry caught her and pulled her back before she could do more than inflict a few scratches.

"Everything you said has been the merest speculation," Sir Paul said heavily. With a swift move he pulled a pistol from inside his coat, pulling back the hammer as he pointed it at Plum. "You have no proof, and as long as I am in charge of the police, you will not be able to buy justice with your wealth or title. Your wife will be found guilty of murder based on the evidence I supply the magistrate. She will be hanged, and you, my Lord Rosse, will be left to go on, to suffer long after justice has been carried out."

"But why?" Plum asked Harry, her eyes on the man who stood before them. Harry looked completely bored, but she could feel the tension in the arm he slid around her.

"Sir William Stanford was Sir Paul's brother. Why was the letter your brother sent you delayed? Or did it arrive fifteen years ago, but you took the time to make your fortune in Canada before seeking revenge?"

"So that self-righteous bastard of a valet turned it over to you after all? I should have taken care of him when I had the chance. William gave the letter to some damn fool servant who forgot about it. When he died earlier this year, the letter was found in his effects and sent on to me." Sir Paul's lip curled as he hurled curses at Harry. "I swore that I would have vengeance on you and your family for taking my brother's life. You could have kept the manner of his death hidden, given him a hero's burial, but you didn't. You made sure that bit of scandal was on everyone's lips, laughing at him, mocking him, mocking *me* for being brother to a coward. The fire in your house, the accidents I so cunningly arranged for your children—they are all on *your* head. I swore your family would suffer the same as I did when it became known that William took his own life. As for your wife, it was by the merest coincidence that I found out about her secret, but I fully intend to use it to bring about your destruction just as you destroyed my brother."

"And what about me?" Harry asked calmly, as if the pistol weren't pointed at Plum's breast. Plum became aware that Harry's hand against her waist was exerting pressure to pull her backward. No doubt the foolish man believed that if he shoved her behind him when he disarmed Sir Paul, he would not be shot because she was his target. That wasn't true, of course. It was Harry he wanted to destroy. Dear Harry, normally so smart about these things, but this time, so obtuse.

Sir Paul smiled, a nasty, oily smile of pure malice that sent shivers of horror down Plum's back. "If you do not allow me to take your wife into lawful custody, you will regrettably be shot and killed while attempting to keep me from the course of my duty. A tragedy, but alas, an unavoidable one."

Plum knew Harry was going to strike even before he moved. His fingers tightened on her, jerking her backward as he lunged forward. She was ready for that move, however, and knowing that Sir Paul needed her alive in order to torment Harry, she threw herself between the two men shrieking, "No!" just as Harry grabbed her.

The blast from the pistol deafened her ears; the smell of gunpowder burned her eyes. Time froze as she stood in front of Harry, watching as surprise dawned in Sir Paul's eyes. She looked down at herself, amazed to see a bloom of red on her side, quickly soaking her gown in an expanding circle.

"I was wrong," she said somewhat bemusedly as Harry snarled an oath, jumping forward to knock the pistol from Sir Paul before grabbing him and slamming him against the wall of the library repeatedly until he hung limply in Harry's hands. Harry threw the man down, rushing back to where Plum was gently prodding the red stain on her gown.

"I was wrong. He did shoot me. I don't understand. I had it all figured out, but he shot me anyway. He wasn't supposed to. Harry, I've been shot. Do you think I should swoon?"

"Plum, Plum, my beautiful, brave, ridiculously wonderful Plum, you may swoon if you like. I have it on the highest authority that all the best ladies who have been shot do so." Harry swept her up in his arms, cradling her as if she was made of the costliest porcelain. The strain in his voice warmed her, driving out some of the icy pain that started to throb in her side.

"Will it harm the babe, do you think?" she asked, suddenly feeling as if Harry was a very long way from her. His voice was distant and hard to make out, and his face seemed to be dimming.

"No, the babe won't be harmed. And neither will you. You'll be fit as ever in just a day or two, you'll see."

"Oh, good. I think I'll swoon now if you don't mind. If all the ladies do it, I feel I should, too." Now her voice sounded distant and strange, as if it belonged to another. She tried to cling to Harry, but couldn't make her arms work. She relaxed against him, giving up the struggle, sinking silently into the oblivion that claimed her.

Epilogue

"You are solely to blame for being in this situation, Plum."

"Push, madam."

"Oh! I am not! What a thing to say to me!"

"The blame lies completely on your head," Harry said, scowling down at her. "I declaim all responsibility. You insisted, if you recall. I said no, I won't risk your health, but you insisted."

"And another one, madam."

"Ha! I like that! I never insisted, and you *are* responsible. If your seed was so potent that it could impregnate me after just a few incidences of spillage, it's most certainly your fault, not mine."

"Perhaps you might put a bit more effort into the next push?" the gentleman lurking at the end of the bed asked her.

"I'm trying," Plum snarled to the physician. She had a difficult time seeing him because of the bedclothes heaped on her massive belly. She struggled to sit up so she could give the man a really good glare, a quality glare, one that he would remember for the rest of his life. Harry, supporting her from behind, immediately came to her assistance, adjusting himself so that she could lean against his chest and level her glare at the physician. "It's not easy, you know!"

"I am aware of that fact, Lady Rosse. I am also aware that the babe's head is about to crown, and in order for it to do so, you need to push. Now, if you have gathered your strength, I believe another contraction is coming. Please oblige me by pushing at the peak."

"No one ever told me about this," Plum gasped, her gasp turning to a shriek as she bore down. Behind her, Harry murmured soft words of love and encouragement as she struggled to keep from shredding the skin on the arms he wrapped around her in support. She thought she was going to be sick from the pain, or swoon, or start shrieking and never be able to stop, but just as the pain grew so great she knew she was going to die from it, she pushed again, bearing down with every last bit of strength she had to rid her body of the invader, as she had taken to thinking of it. She pushed and pushed and pushed until there was nothing but a red well of all-consuming pain.

"Excellent, madam. A fine job. You may relax for a moment." The physician turned to his assistant and asked for a cloth.

Plum collapsed backwards against Harry, her body aching and still screaming with the echoes of agony. "No one told me about the pain," she gasped, "not the real pain, not what it *really* feels like, not Delia, not Old Mag, none of the ladies ever told me it was going to be so very bad. All they talked about was the joy of holding their baby in their arms, but did anyone think to tell me that there would be so much pain involved? No, they did not. I am going to have a few words with them, on that you can—"

The sound of a baby's squall cut her words off. A tingle swept her body, a wave of joy and love and pride so great it brought tears to her eyes. Harry nuzzled her temple moist with perspiration, his hands warm and comforting beneath her breasts. "I love you, Plum. I love you more than anything I can think of—"

His words dried up too as the physician presented her with a bundle. "My lord, my lady, your daughter."

"A daughter," Plum said, tears of happiness spilling over her lashes as she took the baby, pulling back the cloth to admire the red-faced, pointy headed, splotchy skinned baby who yelled her opinion of the world she'd been pushed into, the volume of her protests indicating she would one day make a very fine opera singer. "She's beautiful. She's the most beautiful baby in the world, isn't she?"

"Yes, she is." Harry kissed her temple again, reaching forward to stroke the baby's clenched fists. "The most beautiful baby there ever was."

"I think so too. Harry, look! She has toes!"

"Ten of them, I'll wager. Shall we count?"

Delightedly, the new parents counted the baby's toes, then feeling giddy with delight, counted her fingers as well.

"Promise me something, Harry," Plum said some time later when she had been cleaned, and the babe tucked in beside her. He leaned across their daughter to kiss her.

"Anything, my darling," he said against her lips.

"It's about the baby."

"Whatever you want, my love. Ponies, toys, the best education, frocks galore—it's all hers."

Plum's eyes were alight with love as she nipped his lower lip, soothing the sting by sucking it into her mouth for a moment before releasing it. "Promise me she'll never have children. It's the most ghastly experience I've ever lived through! No woman should have to go through it. You can't imagine the sort of pain you feel in labor. It's indescribable, it's absolutely indescribable, it's so bad you want to set your hair on fire just to distract yourself from the consuming, absolute horribleness of it all. I will never, ever forget it, it's bound to haunt me to the end of my days, giving me nightmares with the memory of the torturous, never-ending horror of it all. I think I'd rather be stomped on by a herd of elephants than go through another birth. Truly, the elephants would be nothing compared with the searing, burning, ripping, tearing, soul-rending sort of pain felt during the birth—"

"As you wish, my darling."

The couple was silent for a moment, watching the child they'd made together until Plum felt the burden of the things she'd said to her beloved husband.

"Harry?"

"Hmm?"

Plum gave him her most winsome smile, which considering the nightmare she'd just been through, said much of her character. "I didn't mean what I said earlier."

"Ah. So you won't really castrate me with two egg cups and a fish knife if I ever touch you again?" The devilish glint she loved so dearly was back in his eyes.

"A *dull* fish knife, and no, I won't."

"That's reassuring to know."

Her winsome smile faded as she adjusted her position, her body protesting the action. "Mind you, if you impregnate me again, I will take your scrotum, pull it over your head, and—"

"Thank you, my dear, you have made yourself quite clear." Harry laughed and stopped Plum's threats with the simple act of kissing her until she had no more breath, standing back when the door flew open and five children and Thom burst into the room, all chattering at once, all excited to see the new baby. Harry's gaze met Plum's as the children swarmed the baby, his heart filled with all the love and happiness she had brought him.

"What are you going to call the baby?" Thom asked, looking from Plum to him.

"We haven't decided yet," Plum said.

"I have," Harry announced, a slow smile filling his eyes with laughter.

"You have? You said you didn't have any preference. What name would you have the baby called by?" Plum asked him, her brow wrinkling in a puzzled frown.

He kissed her again, unable to keep from tasting the sweetness of her lips. His Plum, his delightful, entrancing, beguiling Plum.

"Vyvyan," he said. "We'll call her Vyvyan."

And so they did.

Improper English
KATIE MACALISTER

Sassy American Alexandra Freemar isn't about to put up with any flak from the uptight—albeit gorgeous—Scotland Yard inspector who accuses her of breaking and entering. She doesn't have time. She has two months in London to write the perfect romance novel—two months to prove that she can succeed as an author.

Luckily, reserved Englishmen are not her cup of tea. Yet one kiss tells her Alexander Block might not be quite as proper as she thought. Unfortunately, the gentleman isn't interested in a summer fling. And while Alix knows every imaginable euphemism for the male member, she soon realizes she has a lot to learn about love.
